I0649908

The Messengers

And the Forgotten Choice

Obadiah J. Dalrymple

Copyright © 2014 Obadiah J. Dalrymple

All rights reserved.

ISBN: 0991286316
ISBN-13: 978-0-9912863-1-7 (Obadiah J. Dalrymple)

IMPORTANT!

How to Read This Book…

This book can be read in the exact same manner as *any* other novel. The endnotes are <u>NOT</u> necessary to understand or enjoy the story. If you are content with reading this book like a normal story, <u>without endnotes</u>, then feel free to <u>jump to the first chapter</u> and begin your adventure. However, if you wish to have a more complete understanding of why this book includes endnotes, then please read the explanation below.

Disclaimer and Endnotes

Endnotes are littered throughout this work of fiction much like one would see in any textbook intent upon validating its claims or theories, but that is not the purpose of the endnotes contained here. This book is not intended to be an argument for any type of deep theology, nor does it claim to introduce any new deep theological ideas. In this story, theological truths are often stretched to the point that one has no right to consider them truths at all. At other times, theological concepts can more accurately be described as complete and utter fantasy. The endnotes, then, serve two purposes. The first is to simply show the origin of the many fantastical ideas in this story. The second purpose for the endnotes is to facilitate the discerning of reality, as taught in Scripture, from the many fictional concepts developed and explored in this book. As such, for a good and interesting story, read the book without the endnotes. For a deeper understanding of the true spiritual world, view the endnote references as you read.

And know this, the mission of this story is to illustrate (not argue) the very simple truth that there is a God, and mankind can choose to follow Him or not. There is good in this world, and there is evil. There are good spirits (angels) and evil fallen spirits (demons). The choices we make daily reflect which side we truly follow.

i

A STORY OF CHOICE

Fallen from grace and sealed with a fate,
A plan of pure evil and a town lay in wait.
The story that shows perseverance through strife,
And teaches the lessons to follow in life.
For whenever you face the deceiver of man,
When damnation is coming and life's out of hand,
It is then that God's gift brings the only real chance,
To see through the clouds and get a new glance.
So, fight the good fight, and hear the heart's voice,
The good or the bad, it's always a choice.

ACKNOWLEDGMENTS

In memory of my best friend, Adam Olin Smith, who went home to glory before me.

Thank you:
To my dad, who made it his life to teach the Good News.
To Ms. Pappenfoht, who taught me to love reading and writing.
And to my mom and my wife, who believe in me far more than I believe in myself and who provided the constant encouragement I needed to finish this work. Without you, this procrastinator would still be dreaming of writing.

CONTENTS

CONTENTS

CHAPTER ONE

THE FIRST TEMPTATION

This story begins with a small dab of greed,
When desire becomes want instead of just need.
A cloud of confusion and a shadow of sin,
The first of three trials is set to begin.
A tug at the heart with strong rationale
Could be a temptation from the fires of hell.
A mistake! And left open is a free trip to wealth,
But succumbing to sin destroys spiritual health.
The battle within just starting to see,
One master you'll serve, one master you'll flee.[1]
It starts with a choice, to give in, or to fight,
It starts with a trial that happens this night.
A part of the plan that was doomed from the start,
But could change with a choice in just one person's heart.
A victory for one, you can't see just yet,
But as for the plan, in motion it's set.

*   *   *   *

MONDAY NIGHT, MAY 20, 1985

A ceiling light flickered above me, momentarily stealing my attention. I shook my head. What was I doing paying attention to a light bulb at a time like this? My eyes turned back toward the gym floor. Not even a breath disturbed the silent anticipation of the crowd. Sheer disbelief held our eyes captive to the spectacle playing out before us. None of us had ever seen anything like it.

With unwavering passion, Tom Reynolds refused to quit. Dribbling the basketball and flanked by three defenders, he sped down the court with only one thing on his mind . . . it was

CHAPTER ONE

a race against the clock and he was determined to make the final shot.

The timer counted down . . .

FIVE . . .

Tom cross-over dribbled, leaving one defender in his wake . . .

FOUR . . .

A spin move left another one behind . . .

THREE . . .

He was at half court . . .

TWO . . .

The final defender was no match for Tom's acceleration . . .

ONE . . .

Tom released the ball into the air just as the final buzzer sounded. The basket would count if it went in. Every unbelieving eye was locked onto the flight path of the ball as it sailed toward its destination with perfect arc, precise distance and direction . . .

THE FIRST TEMPTATION

SWISH!

Disbelief filled the gymnasium. Tom had made it! Yet there was no applause, no celebration. Shock seemed to be the only emotion anyone was capable of showing. The light above me flickered again, but everyone's eyes were locked onto Tom.

"Nice job, Tom. You loser!" rang out a man's harsh voice from the otherwise speechless crowd. "That was a great shot . . . now you only lost by 45 points," said the man. Tom hung his head as the crowd turned toward the man in disgust. The light flickered yet again.

Tom's father had never been accused of being a kind man—especially when he drank. However, even he should have had his limits to cruelty. Tom had put everything he had into the game, fighting to the end, even when victory was entirely beyond reach. What had his efforts earned him? Only a humiliating defeat and jeering from his own father.

I had never particularly liked Tom, but I wouldn't wish that type of humiliation on anyone. However, if Tom's father was worried about how his son might be affected by his mockery, he certainly wasn't showing it as he began a solo chorus of "boos" that propagated powerfully throughout the otherwise silent gym and caused everyone to continue to stare at this merciless man.

This disgraceful betrayal was more than Tom could take. He raised his bowed head and charged toward the other team with his fists clenched tightly, ready to lash out his anger on anyone he perceived as an enemy. Several of Tom's teammates reacted as if they had been expecting him to lose control and were able to quickly restrain him before he could reach the other team and cause any more damage to our school's reputation—which was taking quite a beating that night thanks to the brutal defeat and Tom's angry drunken father.

"Let's go man; this is embarrassing," came the quiet, shamed voice of my best friend, Brice, from the seat next to me. He was right. Watching our old high school team get clobbered so badly was downright depressing.

Silently, I nodded my head and began to stand up, but just as I did, the gym went pitch black. My eyes groped the darkness, but everything was gone. I stood frozen, waiting for someone to announce what was happening, but no voice came. In fact, though the gym was filled with people, the noise of the crowd had been completely extinguished.

Suddenly, a bright light flickered on above my head. Looking up, the source of the light was unclear, but it seemed to be getting brighter. Assuming this was the faulty light that had flickered on and off above my head so many times that night, I returned my gaze to the gym, hoping to see what was going on.

Shock coursed through me as my eyes rested on a completely new environment. I was no longer inside the gym. My heart pounded and my stomach sank as I realized that I had somehow travelled outside of the school, and I was all alone. Before I could even wonder how I had gotten there, the light above me intensified, drawing my eyes back toward it.

In continued astonishment, I watched as a bright golden ladder descended onto the dark street. Its unnatural glow stretched down from the heavens, illuminating the night sky, and yet left no reflection on the cars that lined the road. It was a ladder unlike any other ladder on earth. Its very presence terrified me. I suddenly felt as if a terrible storm were approaching.

Silently, a man fell to the earth, gripping the golden ladder as he did so. His feet touched the ground with the softness of a whisper, even though the man was great in size. His white robes and luminescent aura looked as out of place as the majestic ladder, which pulsed with energy as the man lingered where he had descended. With his back to me, he peered off into the distance, as if searching for something.

Finally, the man released the golden ladder, and as he did so, it disappeared like a flood light that had been switched off. The man paid no attention to the sudden absence of the spectacular ladder as he began walking down the dark road in solitude. Behind him, light suddenly flooded into the street as the doors to the gymnasium burst open and people began to pour out. The man appeared to have no time for this either. He marched steadily down the street toward the top of a hill in a determined fashion. It was as if he were heading to war . . .

*   *   *   *

"Micah, did you hear me?" said a familiar voice in my ear. And with the voice, the sound of the crowd suddenly returned as well, causing me to take my eye off the man in the white robes. I looked around and it appeared that the entire contents of the gym had now emptied out into the street. All of the families were walking across the road, heading to their cars, which were parked in the school parking lot. Brice, however, was standing by my side, staring at me with a look of confusion.

"Micah! What's wrong with you?" he asked. "I said, did you hear me?"

I ignored him and turned my eyes toward the end of the street again, searching where the man in the white robes had been. He was gone. He had disappeared over the top of the hill.

"How did we get here?" I asked Brice in a panic.

"We teleported of course," he replied with a slight chuckle and a look of amusement.

"*What?*" I asked, my eyes wide and my heart continuing to pound in my chest.

"Dude, seriously, what's the matter with you?" Brice said, his face now bewildered and concerned.

"How did we get here?" I repeated again, a little frantically.

"We walked, man. How in the world do you think we got here?" he asked rhetorically. I lowered my head in confusion.

Realizing I was not going to respond, Brice continued. "I was asking you about whether or not we could work with the high school basketball team this summer—you know, to help them improve so they don't get beat again like they did tonight—but you wouldn't answer me. And now you're acting all weird, asking how we got here and stuff," he finished, now sounding a little defensive.

"But did you see the guy . . . did you see the guy and that bright ladder . . . did you see them?" I continued to question, now feeling like I was losing my mind.

"Okay man, I can't tell if you are joking or what, but you're starting to weird me out. If you don't want to practice with the team this summer, that's fine, but we had a lot of fun last year and it was a big help to the high school guys," he said in an exasperated tone as he began walking slowly away from the school and toward his car. I followed in silence.

My mind was racing. What in the world was going on? Had Brice really not seen the man in the white robes and his golden ladder? I looked around at the families leaving the school. No one else seemed panicked or dumbfounded at having just experienced a blackout and then watching a man fall from the sky. Had no one else experienced any of it? Had any of it been real?

My eyes wandered back up the street again, but the strange glowing man was probably several blocks away by that time—if he even existed. I knew what I had to do. There was only one way I was going to find out if he was real . . . or if I was crazy. I had to go after him.

"Anyway," Brice said, breaking my train of thought, clearly ready to move back to a topic he found more comfortable, "this is going to be a rough year for them."

"What? . . . Oh, yeah, I know," I agreed, deciding there was no point discussing the topic with Brice any further. I did not need my best friend thinking I was crazy . . . especially if it might be true. "That was painful to watch," I added, mainly to show him I had returned to the conversation.

His eyes lingered on me for a moment, as if deciding whether or not I was still messing with him. "Still, that kid Tom, he wasn't bad . . . and those other two could hold their own . . . but the rest of the team . . . yikes!" Brice continued, getting a little louder as we reached the farthest parking lot of the school and were out of earshot of the players' parents, who might be offended.

"Well, at least we have all summer to work with them," I encouraged, still trying to seem interested.

"True," Brice said as he opened his car door and sank into the driver's seat. I stood there frozen. I had ridden to the game with Brice, but all I really wanted to do was walk down the street and search for the mysterious glowing man. I had to know if he was real.

"What are you doing?" Brice asked, the look of confusion returning to his face. "Aren't you getting in?"

"No thanks, man. It's a nice night; I think I'll walk. Besides, I need to clear my head after watching that game," I answered, trying to think of a reason he might accept.

"Fair enough," he said with a chuckle, though I could tell by his expression that he still suspected something else was going on. "See you later this week, then—to work with the high school team?" he asked as he closed the door to his car and stuck his head out of the open driver's window and into the clear night sky.

"Oh yeah . . . they desperately need our help," I replied.

Brice nodded his head in agreement and started to turn the key to his car, but stopped to say something else.

"Oh, have you thought anymore about what we talked about?" he asked, with the eagerness in his eyes barely hidden. "About coming to the university with me next semester?"

THE FIRST TEMPTATION

"I've been thinking about it, yeah," I answered sheepishly. "I'm still not sure, man. I guess that's another good reason to walk home; a chance to think by myself," I said, hoping he'd leave it there.

"Okay, then . . . I'll see you later." He knew me well enough not to push a topic; I would come to a decision in my own time. With that, he started his car and took off out of the school parking lot, leaving me standing alone as I watched all of the parents and families climbing into their cars on the warm and starry summer night. Hoping to avoid a conversation with anyone else, I began my journey home, in search of the man in the white robes with the golden ladder.

* * * *

As I stepped out onto the street in pursuit, there was no way to know what events had been set into motion. There was no way to know that I was about to be faced with decisions that would shape the course of my life, threaten the lives of the people I loved, and open my eyes to an entirely different world.

My name is Micah Jones, and I was about as ordinary a twenty-year-old kid as you could find. I was from a small, ordinary Missouri town. It was always quiet there; nothing exciting ever happened, and that's just how we liked it. I had an ordinary family, who held ordinary jobs—a teacher and a preacher.

I was just a good kid with no extraordinary abilities. As such, there was no reason to suspect that something extraordinary was about to happen to me. My life had not exactly worked out the way I had planned, but whose does? At twenty years old, I was still plenty young to set my sights on other goals, but honestly, that just didn't interest me much. Witnessing my former high school team get demolished that night had reminded me of all my own struggles with basketball—the game I loved so much.

Just out of high school I had actually made the basketball team at a small private school called Shepherd's College, but they had not offered me a scholarship to play, so the tuition had been far too expensive for me. Since I couldn't attend Shepherd's, I had decided to go to a junior college close by, in hopes of making their team. But my two years had come and gone, and I had never made the team, despite trying out several times.

Now my time was over, and I was no closer to being able to afford the private school than I had been two years ago. Moving on to a different school or to a job meant giving up on the passion and the dream I had been clinging to since I was a little kid—playing basketball.

So yeah, I was frustrated. And sure, you could say I was directionless. But personally, I thought I was just fine. I mean, these were small problems; common even. Lots of people get frustrated with their lives, and tons of people don't know exactly where they're headed, but I was a good person. As far as I was concerned, my life was okay—I was okay. Little did I know, though, I wasn't okay—not even close, actually. Never in my wildest dreams could I have imagined that something was coming for me that would turn my world upside down and change my life forever . . .

THE FIRST TEMPTATION

*　*　*　*

With no thought of my own safety, I took off toward the end of the street, determined to find the magical man. I refused to believe he was only a figment of my imagination. I raced up the small hill toward the last place I had seen him.

My heart pounded as I reached the top of the hill. Even though the man had a head start, I hoped that his glowing white aura would be bright enough to point me in his direction. However, there was nothing to see at the top of the hill except quaint little houses that lined the small street and looked sleepy in the moonlight. There was no golden ladder and there was no trace of the mysterious man.

My eyes scanned the dark, vacant streets in front of me for any sign of where to go, but the man had disappeared as quickly as he and his ladder had come. I knew that any road I chose to explore would be as unlikely to lead me to him as the next. There was nothing I could do to find him—there was nowhere for me to go, now, but home. Disappointed, and slightly wishing I had accepted Brice's offer for a ride, I started the long walk to my house.

Slowly, I wound through the small, dark back roads, watching house after house shut off its lights as people headed to bed. It seemed not a blade of grass was out of place in the tiny, picturesque town. It was the type of carefree, beautiful night one could get only by living in the country.

Having just returned from college for summer break, it was the first time in months I had been able to see so many stars. They were shining bright, and the moon was almost full. I breathed in the night's air, heavy with the Missouri humidity but still so fresh and calm.

My feet continued to trace their own path as though my mind had placed them on auto-pilot, and I was free to enjoy the beautiful solitude of a glorious night—my consolation prize for having not found the glowing man. It was such a peaceful walk that I was only subconsciously aware when I arrived on Main Street and turned left toward my road, Dogwood Lane.

Just as my feet touched the Main Street sidewalk, I was awakened out of my blissful walk by the most unusual of feelings. The town had virtually no crime and there wasn't a soul in sight. Nevertheless, I was suddenly certain that someone was watching me. Immediately, the hairs on the back of my neck stood on end, as if to warn me of danger. As paranoia captured my senses, a rustling of leaves filled the air and a cold gust of wind split through the otherwise warm and still night sky, shaking the trees on every lawn as it did so.

My heart pounded and I quickened my pace as I began to realize how foolish it had been to set out alone in pursuit of a mysterious glowing man who had fallen from the sky, especially one no one else had seen. The unnatural chill from the wind now surrounded me, erasing all traces of the previously humid summer night. I folded my arms across my chest and began to shiver, wishing I had a jacket. *But who needs a jacket in Missouri during the summer?* I thought.

As the cold and the sense of danger urged me forward ever faster, a new and indefinable feeling began to slow me down. Just moments before, my mind had felt sharp and my eyes clear, but now I began to feel as if a drug were invading my system. As it spread, my eyes and my mind began to resist me. Like a sleepy driver trying to keep his eyes open on a windy road, I shook my head and stumbled forward, barely able to continue walking.

The more I resisted, the more I was invaded by what seemed like a dark cloud that sought to conceal the outside world from me. Weight pressed in on my chest. Even the air I breathed was heavier. As if my life depended on it, I fought, but I was failing. *What on earth is happening to me?* I wondered desperately.

In a senseless stupor, I staggered forward for several minutes, knowing I was close to Dogwood Lane, knowing that just a few blocks separated me from my parents' house . . . I was so close to safety, I had to press on.

Nearly blind, I finally reached the intersection of Main Street and Dogwood Lane. Squinting and feeling my way through the darkness with my feet, I took my first step off of Main Street and onto my parents' road. As my sneakers hit the pavement, a flash of light ignited across the street.

Inexplicably, my clouded eyes locked onto the bright light with singular sharpness; all else remained obscured. Strangely, the light was emanating from our town's small bank. While the bank appeared to look the same as ever, the light that shone from it was dazzling and powerful. Even in the midst of coldness, near blindness, and clear danger, the burst of light caused my heart to leap in hope. Fear and discomfort aside, I still wanted to know where the man in the white robes had gone, and I was certain I had found him after all . . . or perhaps he had been waiting for me.

My sluggish eyes glanced around through the dark cloud that still surrounded me as I tried to decide what to do. The normally bright street lights were blurred and drowsy. Even the previously beautiful night with its stars and moon had all but faded away. It was as if a tunnel of darkness had been created around me, and the only thing I was meant to see was the unnatural light in the bank that seemed to penetrate the dark cloud like no other light could. It beckoned me forward.

I knew the smart thing to do would be to turn down Dogwood Lane and stagger my way home through the darkness. It was a straight shot; no turns or hills or other impediments. Even nearly blind I could be home in less than a minute. All that stopped me was my own curiosity. It felt dangerous and reckless, but I was magnetized to the light in the bank. I didn't want to leave. Danger or not, I was drawn to it.

Transfixed, my eyes gazed across the street and easily peered inside the bank windows. It appeared no one was inside and no cars were in the parking lot. A wild compulsion overtook me . . . I *had* to know who the man was, and I *had* to know why I was suddenly experiencing all of these unnatural things. And I was certain the answers were just inside the bank.

With my back to Dogwood Lane, I quickly ran across Main Street and hurled up the few steps at the bank's entrance faster than I had run in a while. Shock and a strange excitement stole through me as I peered through the glass door and stared into the steady bright light. The bank was empty!

Instinct or madness guided me. I reached for the door handle. To my surprise, the door pulled open effortlessly. I squeezed inside before contemplating what I was doing. Finally, self-preservation reignited my mind as a startling thought struck me: *what if I was walking into a robbery in action? Was I about to be a victim?*

I paused to listen before moving any farther. Nothing happened; no noise, no anything. I still had an uneasy feeling, so I remained quiet, but again an uncharacteristically reckless impulse stole through my veins, commanding me forward. In continued madness, I began to advance silently, still not giving thought to what I was doing or what might be waiting for me.

On my right, the counters that were normally occupied by tellers during the day now sat uniform and vacant in the night. On my left, large windows revealed the dark street outside, and directly ahead of me at the back of the room was the reason I had recklessly rushed into the empty bank. An office door was cracked open, and out of it poured intense, white light.

My heart pounded in my chest as worry and fear battled against temptation and adrenaline. Something continued to compel me forward, but I didn't know what. Against all reason, and without hesitation, I dashed straight for the office door, into the potentially dangerous unknown. Perhaps I was about to come face to face with an armed robber, but for reasons I couldn't explain, I rushed ahead with an eagerness and assurance I should not have felt in that moment.

I reached the door, ripped it open unflinchingly, and prepared myself for whatever was waiting for me. Instinctively, I shielded my eyes and squinted as a blinding light erupted from the room. I waited for something to happen, but nothing did.

CHAPTER ONE

Why is no one here? Where is the man in the white robes? My heart continued to pound.

My eyes slowly adjusted as I peered into a bright, empty room I had never seen before. Only bank employees were allowed this far beyond the counters . . . but I had come too far to stop now. Curiosity filled every cell in my body as I stepped through the doorway. My eyes were drawn to the right side of the room and they rested upon the apparent origin of the light.

I was puzzled . . . it was impossible to tell how this one thing could have produced a light powerful enough to catch my attention from all the way across the street . . . especially in a room with only a slightly cracked door. Even as I stared, everything seemed to dim slightly. It was as if the bright light had served its purpose in luring me into the bank, and upon my arrival had been reduced to its normal wattage.

But now the object itself piqued my interest far more than the light ever had. The man and the magnificent light had been intriguing and mystifying, but this object enticed every part of me. It was as if it held the solution to all of my life's frustrations and uncertainties . . . it was the bank vault . . . and just as the previous door had been, it was cracked open!

My stomach dropped in apprehensive excitement as I considered what to do next. I knew I should run. I knew I should call the police, but my mind was ignoring all normal reason.

The room darkened as if the cold, ominous cloud had traveled inside the bank with me. The only light remaining came from inside the vault, taunting me forward. It was too much to resist. Without further hesitation or thought, I headed straight for the vault, almost as though my body were acting completely of its own accord.

It was not a large room by any means, so in a couple of quick steps I was there. I stood in front of the vault door. My mind raced as I analyzed the scene. My eyes pored over my surroundings, searching everything around me.

I remained motionless, in deep thought, alarmed at the whole situation. It had been so stupid to enter the bank alone after hours. *What if I were caught? What would my parents think?* Reason told me to turn and run home and to call our town sheriff, who was nearly always on duty, but something held me in place.

The hairs on my neck had not ceased standing on end. The danger had certainly not passed, and if anything, it had only been heightened by running into the open bank alone. I had watched enough suspenseful movies to know not to approach an odd entrance by myself at night, especially if you expected foul play. And yet, there I was, continuing to stare at the slightly opened door with an increasing desire for what was bound to be inside the vault.

A longing overtook me. Impulse and risk were generally at odds with my personality. But right then, despite my moral upbringing, I had never wanted to do anything more in my life than to peer inside the vault that was just inches from me. *All I have to do is reach my hand out, and it will be mine*, I thought insatiably.

Desire easily overcame the warnings inside of me. An urge for action pulsed through me, numbing any feelings of guilt and blocking all moral sentiment. It felt as if something were leading me in, and my body subconsciously acquiesced as I finally moved, raising my hand toward the door. I advanced absentmindedly, taking the final step toward the vault as though led by a string attached to my mind.

My hand reached out and grabbed the door handle. Slowly and silently the vault door swung open, and I saw . . . nothing. Well, there were papers, drawers that I secretly hoped would contain money, and other office-type stuff, but nothing else. The light on the ceiling was normal—certainly not as bright as the light I had seen from across the street. There were no robbers or criminals, or even bank employees—and most surprising of all, there was no sign of the man in the white robes.

In fact, besides the bank being unlocked after hours and the light left on, there was nothing unusual at all. It was just me, alone with the drawers that were potentially full of cash. Instinctively, I looked around, half expecting to still be attacked or caught, but no one came.

I turned my gaze back into the open vault and the drawers I knew would be full of money, and in an instant, my whole persona changed. All of the frustrations that I had been burying deep inside of me now came to the surface in full force, as if shot into my brain by a fire hose. My chest heaved in great, deep breaths as the air thickened and my heart rate increased.

It was two years too late, but that didn't matter now. I had it at last! Now I could go to the private school, and I wouldn't have to burden my parents or take a loan, I thought hungrily, as I stared at the drawers.

There I stood just a step away from an abundance of the

one thing I needed more than anything else. Anger, despair, resentment, and desire all flooded my mind as it filled with the painful memory of being inches from achieving my goals, only to be kept away from realizing my dream because of one thing: *money*! My heartache of the past and my worries for the future all came down to one thing. I needed *money*, and there it was, sitting right in front of me, almost gift wrapped.

All of it is insured anyway. It wouldn't really hurt anyone, a voice in my mind rationalized, as if any argument could actually justify the action I was considering. I knew it was more absurd than anything I had ever considered in my life. But somehow, in that moment, the idea made perfect sense. I was convinced. A trance had overcome me, eliminating reason and logic; only desire remained.

But then, faintly I felt as if a voice was speaking directly to my heart, *Run, get help, this isn't something you should do . . . it will ruin your life*. I shook my head as if trying to rid myself of this unpleasant thought . . . *of course it is something I should do . . . this is the one thing that could fix my life*.

After all, I just want the money for school—that's a pretty good reason, I thought. Justifying, tempting thoughts poured into my mind, echoing around as I stared into the vault that waited so patiently, begging for me to fulfill my desire.

I began to succumb. I felt myself indulging in the notion of committing this crime. My heart rate continued to quicken. Sweat dripped down my face. Gravity itself seemed to push me forward and the outside world darkened entirely. Only two things existed in that moment: me with my problems and the vault, which carried the answer to everything. Nothing else in the world mattered. The temptation threatened to overtake me. In fact, I was certain it soon would—and I was only too happy to let it.

Sweat ran down my cheeks. Whatever I was going to do needed to be done quickly. I stretched my hand forward . . .

– BANG –

A terrible boom echoed through the night. I screamed and threw my hands over my head as I hit the ground, waiting for whatever had finally come for me. I lay in silence as I heard a vehicle in the distance driving away from the bank. I sighed with relief. The loud boom had just been a backfire from someone's old truck.

As I got to my feet, reality came rushing back to me. I had been staring at the vault in a trance for what seemed like an eternity, but at last, fear surged through my body. It was the fear that should have sent me staggering home long before, but somehow I had all but ignored. Now back under my own power, I didn't hesitate, as I sprinted out of the bank quicker than I had entered.

Worry entered my mind as I considered what could have happened had I been caught. *What came over me? How could I have been so stupid, so reckless, and . . . so tempted?*

A dark shadow loomed in the back of my mind as I rushed onto Dogwood Lane, determined to get away from the situation before I was tempted again.[2] I couldn't trust myself.

I sprinted down the street determined not to stop until I reached my house. When I finally reached the safety of home a few seconds later, I jumped our fence in the front yard and leapt up our porch with one bound. I stopped at the front door, out of breath, my mind racing, as I desperately tried to decide what I should do next. *Do I need to tell someone about the bank?*

With my mind now clear and the money far behind me, the right choice was obvious; I had to let someone know. I exhaled deeply, turned the door handle, and ran into the house yelling for my parents. In hardly any time, I told them about the light in the bank and the unlocked door. I even explained how I had gone inside the bank and saw the open vault, but I decided to leave out the story of the glowing man with the mystical ladder, and I definitely left out what I had been thinking as I had stared into the lucrative possibilities lying in the vault.

My parents were shocked, but they thankfully focused more on the situation than they did on me. My dad immediately called our county sheriff, Sheriff Sentry, and explained everything while my mom listened to his conversation intently, letting me slip away to my room without another word.

Feeling guilty about my recent display of greed, I didn't want to wait to hear what was going to happen; I just wanted to distance myself from the whole situation. I felt emotionally drained, as if I had been through a rough ordeal, even though all I had really done was go for a walk, look into a bank vault, and sprint a short distance home. In fact, it was odd, really, how exhausted I felt, considering the little effort I had actually exerted. But for some reason, the event had taken a lot out of me. I felt stretched thin in a way normal activities don't cause a person to feel.

I took a quick shower and then climbed into bed with a

new worry on my mind. Not only was I afraid of the repercussions that might come in the morning, having entered a bank after hours, but I was even more worried about what was happening to me.

Normal people didn't see mysterious men falling from the sky. Normal people didn't feel like someone was watching them. And normal people certainly did not walk into an unlocked bank at night and seriously consider robbing the place. Yet I had been just one moment away from committing a felony.

I had begun that night disappointed in a humiliating basketball game, but the game had then been instantly wiped from my mind by a series of supernatural encounters that I could not begin to understand or explain. However, more disturbing than anything I had experienced that night was what I had felt inside of myself.

I was more worried than I had ever been in my entire life because for the first time in my life, I didn't trust myself. I didn't trust what I saw or what I thought. It felt as if someone were playing mind games with me, and I knew deep down that whoever or whatever was doing it, was far more than I could handle.

CHAPTER TWO

FACING THE TRUTH

Awake in the morning to face what was done,
A taste of the aftermath from trial number one.
A guardian waits to hear what is true,
And offer a lesson of what goodness would do.
Be strong and cling to all that's held dear,
Do what is right even when no one is near.
For to do what is good when all by yourself,
Is a measure of greatness worth far more than wealth.
When no one can see, and no one can hear,
That is when darkness is waiting to rear.
Avoid the dark clouds that cover the eyes,
By holding to goodness and seeing through lies.
A lesson is learned and will be put to the test,
Because overcoming temptation is the theme of this quest.
Old friends are close by and a new friend is made,
But be wary the road just a moment away.
Now though, it's safe, so enjoy this short time,
When happiness lingers and life is just fine.

* * * *

TUESDAY, MAY 21, 1985

A dark, thunderous cloud was closing in. Ferocious heat and bitter cold waged war against each other, ripping through the air as they battled for dominance. With a **CRACK**, lightning hissed through the sky, but illuminated nothing, for its light was overshadowed by the black fog that was heavy upon me. Fire roared and electricity sizzled down my spine. This was no ordinary storm.

Suddenly I saw red eyes glaring at me from the darkness.

CHAPTER TWO

I could feel them on me. They prodded my very soul as I stood there, vulnerable and alone. The dark cloud pushed in, tighter. The face of my enemy was just behind the cloudy veil, and he was ready to strike . . .

—*CRACK*—

Lightning flashed as the red eyes closed in slowly . . .

—*CRACK*—

Another bright flash of lightning struck as the eyes continued to move steadily toward me . . .

—*CRACK*—

"Micah!" I heard a voice cry in the distance.

—*CRACK—CRACK*—

Two loud bangs sounded, but no lightning struck. Instead, there was a new light that was growing brighter and had begun to shine through the storm around me. The dark cloud was fading away . . .

"Micah! Did you hear me?" said a woman as I slowly opened my eyes.

—*CRACK*—

FACING THE TRUTH

It wasn't lightning or thunder at all . . . someone was knocking at my bedroom door. "Micah, breakfast is almost ready." Relief filled my apprehensive body as I recognized the welcome sound of my mother's voice.

"If you're not ready to eat, I'll just warm it up for you when you come down, but I thought you might like it while it's fresh," she added kindly.

"Yeah, Mom, thanks," I replied tersely through my dry throat. "I'll be down in a few."

"Okay, sweetie," she responded. Her footsteps grew faint as she walked away from my door and headed back downstairs. I sat up in my bed, breathing hard and slightly sweaty. It was still fairly early in the morning, and I was exhausted from a restless night of terrifying dreams and vivid reenactments of the bank that had played out in my mind over and over again while I slept. Trying to go back to sleep seemed pointless. Closing my eyes again would just invite more nightmares to return.

I hopped out of bed, threw on some shorts and a T-shirt, and then made my way downstairs. After the night of unsettling events and nearly palpable dreams, it was a relief to arrive down at our dining room for breakfast and find my home and my parents continuing on in normal fashion. My dad, Paul, sat in his usual spot at our dinner table, sipping at coffee and reading the paper. He brushed his mousy brown hair out of his eyes and pushed his thick glasses down lower on his nose to get a better reading angle.

His tall, thick frame gave him the look of someone who used to be a good athlete, but over time had slowly settled into being a professional bookworm. Just by looking at him, someone would get the impression that he was both loving and stern . . . and trust me, he could be both. He could be a best friend and mentor, but he was also one of my main reasons for staying well behaved in life, because I never wanted to cross him.

As I looked at my dad and wondered if he was thinking about the previous night, I heard my mom, Naomi, rummaging busily in the kitchen. Peeking my head in to watch her work, I couldn't help but chuckle as I saw her jumping up and down, trying to reach something up high, but only gaining a couple of inches on her vertical with each attempt. While my dad was tall like me, my mom's small stature meant that she constantly had to grab a step-stool to reach things from the upper cabinets.

She hastened to the side of the fridge for her fold-up step-stool, but I hurried into the kitchen and easily grabbed the dish she had been stretching for.

"Thanks, Micah," she said as she brushed out of her eyes the light brown, slightly graying hair that had fallen with her last jump. She took the dish out of my hand and gave me a deep hug. I would be quick to tell anyone I had the world's best mother. Her rosy cheeks and kind demeanor would give anyone the distinct impression that she would rather make sure they were properly fed than take her next breath . . . and that impression would be correct.

True to her maternal nature, she promptly poured me a glass of orange juice, and then ushered me back to the dining room to wait for breakfast. I took a seat at the table across from my dad, who glanced up from his paper and into the living room as I sat down. I followed his eyes and realized that he was staring at the television in the living room, which he had conveniently left on, allowing him to watch a news channel from his perfectly positioned chair in the dining room. I laughed to myself as he intently searched the paper and the TV, simultaneously, apparently looking for something . . . or nothing at all, who knew? I guess one could never have enough sources if they wanted accurate news.

Noticeably absent from the table was my little sister, Shelby, who was not awake yet. My parents were strict about a lot of things, but they were also practical people—which I appreciated. They always let Shelby enjoy her summer break; and as every kid knows, the first and most important way to enjoy summer break is to sleep until they are done sleeping. No alarm clock, no rushing out to make it to school on time, just limitless and uninterrupted sleep. I'd probably not see Shelby until 11 a.m. . . . at the earliest.

In fairness to her, this was one of the few things Shelby took advantage of. She was ten years old and was so cute she could probably have gotten anything she wanted out of me—and especially out of my parents—but she didn't try to. She was a great little sister and the sweetest kid I had ever seen. Her golden blonde hair, dark green eyes, and completely innocent temperament could melt any big brother's heart, let alone a mom and dad; but for her age, she was strikingly honest and mature. She was also already proving she was going to be a better student than I had been.

"I knew there wouldn't be anything in the news about the bank last night," my father yelled to my mother, finally looking away from his plethora of news sources. I sat there quietly, unsure what he was going to say, but immediately feeling uncomfortable with the topic.

"Well, Paul, Sheriff Sentry is a fair man and a good police officer, and if the story goes as he said when he called, then the whole thing was just an accident. So, Sheriff Sentry probably thought it was best not to rouse the media, and I'm sure Tonya didn't want to get anyone in trouble, either," my mom replied offhandedly as she walked in from the kitchen carrying a plate of biscuits.

Tonya Newberry, the head manager of our little bank, was always a very caring lady, so it would have been characteristic of her not to make a big deal of a mistake if she thought it might bring a lot of trouble for someone.

"I know accidents happen, but I can't believe Kimberly could be so careless. To leave the door unlocked is bad enough, but to leave the vault open . . . " my dad said with a shocked voice.

"Kimberly?" I asked. "Kimberly Stanfield? It was her fault?" My dad nodded and then went back to reading his paper, a little less intensely having given up looking for a report on the bank incident.

Kimberly Stanfield was one of the few tellers our little bank employed. If she was the reason the vault had been left open, then I knew the whole ordeal must have been nothing more than a huge accident because I knew her to be a very honest person. I wasn't as surprised as my dad, though. Kimberly was nice, but in my opinion she had always been a little flighty.

"They're lucky it was Micah who found the bank unlocked instead of some hoodlum," my mom said matter-of-factly as she carried in bacon and eggs and plopped down into her seat beside my dad. The temperature in my face began to rise. If my mom only knew how close I had come to robbery, she might not think my presence at the bank was quite so lucky for them.

"Think about it!" she continued as we filled our plates with food. "What if some crook had waltzed in there and taken whatever they wanted? They could have had thousands of dollars. I know it's all insured and what not, but still, they could have stolen a bunch of money and then it would have been a *really* big ordeal. Kim would have definitely been in trouble if that had happened. Of course, the camera would have seen everything, but the robbers could have been long gone by the time the bankers came to work in the morning," my mom pondered out loud as she took a few bites of breakfast.

With her words, my stomach dropped to my knees. I was going to be sick. *How could I have been such an idiot? How had I forgotten that our bank had security cameras? What was I going to do when the cops saw me on camera, standing there for who knows how many minutes, quite obviously lusting greedily at the open vault, and then running away like a guilty criminal?* Perspiration began to build on my forehead.

"Oh, that reminds me, Micah, Sheriff Sentry wants to have a word with you about everything, just to wrap stuff up and make sure the stories match, to eliminate any possibility of foul play," my dad said as he began eating his breakfast too. "Not that he thinks Kimberly did any of it on purpose, but he has to be thorough. He wants you to stop by the station before lunch."

My stomach now sank through the floor. *How was I going to explain myself to Sheriff Sentry?* There were no logical reasons for my actions at the bank. My mind raced ahead, doing the thing any person does when they are guilty: search for excuses to explain my way out of trouble. I started to try to think of plausible fibs I could tell—like I had just been investigating the bank to figure out what was going on.

But no, I knew I couldn't lie to Sheriff Sentry—not successfully anyway. He's the type of man who could see through lies. His ability to perceive the inconspicuous was one thing that made him such a great sheriff, and also what made me sure my secret inner thoughts would quickly be revealed to him. No, lies would do me no good. Sheriff Sentry would know exactly what I had been thinking. I was going to have to face the consequences. There was no way around it.

"Naomi, honey, could you pass me some more eggs, please?" my dad asked, interrupting my guilty, isolated train of thought.

* * * *

After I ate breakfast, I decided to go ahead and make my way to the police station instead of allowing the inevitable meeting to hang over my head all day. By the time I left my parents' house, anxiety had pushed everything else out of my mind. Honestly, getting into trouble was not my main concern. I knew I hadn't technically done anything wrong. I had not stolen anything and the bank door *had* been unlocked, so I had not really *broken* in. In fact, I had reported the issue and possibly prevented something worse from happening.

Therefore, I knew Sheriff Sentry would treat me fairly. He was actually a family friend. He had attended the church where my dad preached for as long as I could remember, and he had always been a fair and just sheriff. So, even if I got into trouble, it was not going to be anything major.

No, deep down, I knew what was really troubling me. I was afraid of the disappointment Sheriff Sentry would have on his face if he realized exactly how close I had come to taking the money; and I knew he would figure it out . . . if he hadn't already. His disapproval would be almost as bad as if I had hurt my own parents.

Most small towns have very little crime. Ours had almost none. It wasn't only because Sheriff Sentry was so good at his job, though he was, but it was the respect he commanded. No one, not even teenagers, wanted to be caught doing something wrong by him because no one wanted to disappoint him.

It's like the difference between the discipline styles of teachers in school. Some are feared because they will come down on students with an iron fist, but others keep kids in line because they are so well respected. Sheriff Sentry was the latter type. Even when the occasional misdemeanor occurred, the offender would end up being mentored rather than simply punished.

And that's what was really troubling me. As guilty as I already felt, I didn't want Sheriff Sentry to know how wrong my intentions had been, because if he did, then I knew I would feel ten times worse. I didn't want him to be disappointed in me, and I was positive that he soon would be.

I left my house and decided to walk instead of taking my gas-hog of a car. I made my way down Dogwood Lane toward Main Street. As I turned the corner to head toward the police station, I took a quick glance at the bank. It was open and doing business as usual. I could see Tonya and Kim in there, as well as the other bank workers. They seemed to be continuing on with life as normal. I was sure Kim had received a bad talking-to for her mistake, but she seemed okay. I was relieved about that. Had I actually stolen anything, she might not have gotten off the hook quite so easily.

I tore my eyes away from the bank and resumed walking down Main Street. I walked past the pizza shop, the gas station, the library, and all of the other small businesses and little houses in the town. Despite my unusual walk down the same street just the night before, everything seemed normal now.

I reached the police station after just a few minutes. It was a small building, much like everything else in the town. Its one-story windowed exterior glared back at me as the morning sun rose slowly behind me, barely allowing me to see the words "Police Station" written in white paint across the two large front windows. I walked up the concrete steps and opened the shiny glass door to the sound of bells jingling. Stepping through the doorway, I entered an average-sized rectangular room filled with wooden desks and busy people scurrying about.

Only a few police officers, probably five or six, not including the sheriff, policed the surrounding area, which included several small towns—perhaps better described as villages. The few secretaries who worked at the station clicked busily on their typewriters while the lady at the front desk switched back and forth between phones, presumably relaying calls to officers out in the field.

I peered across the main floor, toward Sheriff Sentry's office, hoping to catch a glimpse of his mood to ascertain how much trouble I was in. I was relieved as I spotted him sitting at his desk and talking on the phone, wearing his typical, good-natured smile. I allowed myself to hope that this might mean I was not in too much trouble.

I walked over to his office and his smile grew as he saw me, but then he signaled for me to wait outside as he finished his phone call. This was the first time I had seen him since I had come home for the summer. I always forgot what a very large man he was. I was pretty tall, but he was several inches taller. I also always got the impression that he had been a body builder earlier in life, because while I was tall and thin, he was tall and massive. Not fat massive; but break your neck if you mess with him, massive.

His black hair accompanied with a natural, year-round tan gave him a still youthful appearance, and he was in surprisingly great shape for a man presumably about forty-five. He was like a large athlete who had somehow only gotten stronger with age. I would liken him to either a very large football player or a slightly small bear.

In spite of his intimidating size, though, he was a calm looking man with a strange internal sense of power, wisdom, and goodness that seemed to radiate from him. His presence alone would make anyone believe that he stood for justice and was guided by a higher standard than other people. Few men were as respected as he was in the community. My dad was probably pretty close, but my dad couldn't haul anyone off to jail or shoot someone if things got too out of control. Not that I could picture the sheriff ever needing to shoot someone, as he could probably wrestle a rhino into submission.

At last he hung up the phone and came out to greet me. He offered his large hand and shook mine with great strength, as he gazed at me with his honest, but intense dark brown eyes. His expression was friendly, but he seemed to be searching me for an answer to a question he had silently asked.

"So good to see you, Micah!" Sheriff Sentry greeted me kindly, in his deep and powerful voice. "How was your school year?" he asked as his piercing gaze continued to comb over me, causing me to want to squirm a little. Perhaps my squirm was the answer he was looking for.

"It was good, sir . . . you asked to see me?" I responded uncomfortably, not knowing what else to say and just wanting to disengage from his stare.

"Right to business then," he said with a small chuckle. "Let's go into my office, shall we?" He ushered me through his office door with his hand, followed me in, and then closed the door behind us.

Light shone through the open blinds that partially covered the large window on the back wall. It was a quaint room, with a filing cabinet and book shelf that stood behind an untidy wooden desk, which was covered in files. Other than that, and a few chairs, the room was quite vacant. I had the feeling Sheriff Sentry wasn't the type to spend too much time cooped up in an office.

He motioned me toward one of two chairs standing in front of his desk. I sat down, and was relieved when he followed suit, sitting beside me in the other chair instead of behind his desk. I hoped that this indicated it would be more of a conversation than an interrogation.

With a big smile on his face, he began first. "So, I guess we owe you thanks for last night. That could have been a huge problem for the police department and perhaps an even bigger problem for the bank had someone with less integrity stumbled upon such a tempting situation," he commended me.

"I guess so," I said, immediately feeling miserable. I didn't want any recognition for reporting the situation. I had barely escaped unscathed and innocent—if I could even be called innocent. I certainly didn't want to be painted as a hero.

"Accidents happen," I said. "I just hope Kim doesn't get into trouble." I added, desperately hoping that we could take the topic away from me.

"Yes, accidents do happen," he responded kindly. "And I think Kim has certainly learned her lesson, so no harm done," he added with another genuine smile. "With that said, Micah, if you are able, I would like to know your account of what happened last night; everything from when you noticed the light on in the bank, all the way to the time when your parents reported the incident to me."

His tone was normal and professional, but his eyes remained locked onto mine in an intent search for the truth. And yet, as he examined me, I was reminded of why he seldom had to use his authority to grill people for information. Even though I was guilty, and even though he wanted to know things that I desperately wanted to hide from him, somehow his face still garnered my trust. It was remarkable really; something about him simply compelled a person to be honest. It might sound ridiculous to say, but lying to him would almost feel worse than telling the awful truth.

Still, something in me resisted. I was not ready to tell him everything. As such, I began my report with what I had been planning to say from the moment I had found out he wanted to see me . . . that is, I told him the same abridged version of the story I had given my parents; which was, and is, the truth. However, I once again left out all the weird stuff, as well as how powerfully I had been tempted by the open vault door. After telling the shortened version of my story in just a few minutes, I sat silently as the weight of Sheriff Sentry's gaze continued to bear down on me.

"Is that all, then? Is that your full report?" he asked me calmly, while he continued to look at me with persistent expectation.

Heat rose to my face. *He knows,* I thought to myself as I avoided his piercingly honest eyes and remained silent. There was no way he knew about all the weird stuff that I had experienced, but the shrewd look on his face made me believe he had already watched the security film and seen how close I had come to stealing.

"It's all right, Micah, you can tell me," he said with comforting words that confirmed my suspicions. I glanced back up at his powerful yet kind eyes. His gaze really was like a spotlight of truth that seemed to shine right into my soul, revealing everything I wanted to hide.[3] My heart pounded as I tried to decide what to do. It was more than I could take.

"Ok," I began solemnly, looking down at my feet in shame. I still was not going to tell Sheriff Sentry, or anyone, about the man in the white robes—that seemed irrelevant and certainly made me look crazy—but I was ready to have the guilt of the night before lifted off my chest. It was a burden I wanted to be done bearing. The time had come. I was ready to confess the truth.

And with that, without any more hiding, I confessed to him my sins from the previous night. After a few minutes of recounting my frustrations with college and basketball, as well as my greed-filled excursion into the bank, I began to wind down my story by describing the unnatural feelings I had experienced . . .

"It was like the thoughts controlled me," I said, "like a thick cloud of darkness that wouldn't let go of my mind. Finally a truck outside backfired, and I snapped out of it, but there were moments when I seriously entertained the idea of taking . . . of taking the . . . " I couldn't finish the sentence, but he nodded in understanding " . . . and it scared me," I ended in complete honesty.

My eyes met his, and I saw that there was no longer inquiry in his face. Just as he always did, he had uncovered the truth, and now he was ready to deal with it. But the disappointment I had anticipated did not come. After everything I had admitted, I expected Sheriff Sentry to be angry, or even disgusted, or maybe I would be getting into trouble after all . . . but I didn't read any of that in his face. He merely seemed deep in thought and concerned.

Finally he spoke. "*Fleeting* thoughts are not a crime or a sin, Micah. We cannot always help what enters our mind for a moment. However, what we can help is whether or not we allow those thoughts and ideas to remain with us.

"You see," he continued in a serious manner, his eyes now looking at me with nothing but kindness, "our real crime, or it might be better said, 'our real sin,' begins when we don't immediately dismiss an evil, fleeting thought. When we let unhealthy ideas linger, when we indulge or entertain the notion of them, that is when we open ourselves up to a dangerous and destructive world that was not meant for us.[4] What you experienced last night is nothing more or less than a temptation. Even though the situation and emotions were very powerful, it was a temptation that obviously already appealed to you, otherwise it would not have held you captive for so long. When times like that come, Micah, always remember the good things you already have. You don't want to throw away your life by making a wrong and impulsive decision, do you?" he asked.

"No sir, I don't . . . I just felt . . . I just wanted . . . " I stumbled, because every way I tried to say it made me sound like a terrible person. "I just could really use some money. It sounds ridiculous now, but when I was tempted last night, it was as simple as that," I confessed.

He smiled. "Have you thought about getting a job, Micah?"

I smiled back. "I'll do little odd jobs around here for the summer, but you know there is nothing in this town that I could do that would be enough to pay for college. That's exactly why the vault was so tempting to me . . . it was like an instant answer to all of my problems," I said with a little too much longing in my voice.

He nodded his head, but looked more serious than ever. "Micah, money is not evil; however, the *love* of money is.[5] People always try to use material things in this world to fill the void in their life. But after we have one possession, we will want another, and then another. People will always want more; a little more money, a little bigger television, a little faster car. These things will not bring happiness," he said seriously.

"Besides, nothing in this world lasts. Do you remember the sermon your dad preached on King Solomon last year?" he asked, catching me off guard. I searched my mind trying to remember, but I could not recall the sermon.

"I probably should, but no, not really," I confessed again, feeling embarrassed.

"Well," Sheriff Sentry began, "in the book of First Kings, chapter three, it tells of a prayer by young King Solomon at the very beginning of his reign. Solomon could have prayed for many of the things that all humans want, such as long life, fame, riches, military power, or anything, but he didn't. Solomon asked only for the wisdom to lead his country well. This request pleased God so much that God not only gave Solomon wisdom, but also granted him long life and incomparable riches, as well," Sheriff Sentry stated excitedly.

"And so," Sheriff Sentry continued, "throughout the Bible, we see that Solomon becomes wise and rich beyond any other, building the kingdom of Israel to the pinnacle of its glory. Solomon goes so far as to say that anything his eyes desired he kept not from them.[6] In other words, Solomon got so rich and powerful that if he saw something he wanted, he simply took it," Sheriff Sentry said, looking as if this were a point of emphasis.

"Think about it, if you or I said that we took everything that we wanted, that statement does not bear a whole lot of authority behind it. For instance, if you had taken the money from the bank, I would have had to throw you in jail," he said with a big grin on his face. "However, if a king says something like this—and not just any king, but a rich, powerful, and wise king—then that means something! He took *anything* that he wanted!" He paused for me to catch up. I wasn't exactly sure why he was telling me all of this. It felt as if he was just trying to make me jealous of King Solomon—and it was working.

"So, wouldn't you think this type of guy would be happy?" he asked, the inquisitive look returning to his face.

"I suppose, yeah," I responded feeling the answer was quite obvious. "I mean, Solomon definitely wouldn't have had to worry about paying for college and stuff, like I do," I said, now feeling very envious of Solomon, and a little depressed.

He laughed. "That is true, although if I could be blunt, I bet the life of a king comes with a little more stress than the life of a college kid. But that is beside the point. The point is, Solomon had everything that this world believes will give us happiness. He had money, fame, fortune, power, women . . . he had everything!" Sheriff Sentry exclaimed dramatically.

"And yet, in Ecclesiastes chapter two and verse eighteen, the great King Solomon writes that he hates all of his labor under the sun because he knew that he would have to leave it to another man after he died," Sheriff Sentry said solemnly.

"Think about that!" he bellowed at me more excited than ever. "Solomon knew that no matter how much he had in this world, when his life came to an end, he could not take anything with him! Do you see, Micah?" he asked. "There will always be more, and bigger, and faster, and better, but even the richest man on earth cannot take the things of this world with him when he dies.

"Don't misunderstand me, people should certainly work hard to provide for themselves, and there is nothing wrong with striving for success and wealth, but we should always view those things with the proper perspective because those things will not last, they will not bring us permanent happiness, and there are so many more important things in life!" he said.[7] "As your dad would say, 'that is why we must invest in heavenly things, because those things are the only things that will last.'"[8]

"So, Micah, even if you had stolen the money from the bank and somehow gotten away with it, which is extremely unlikely by the way, given the security cameras and what not," he added with a chuckle, "all of that money would still not have brought you lasting happiness because the treasures of this life do not last. This is why the Bible asks, 'what is a man profited, if he shall gain the whole world, and lose his own soul?'[9] The answer, Micah, is easily *nothing*! Do you understand?" he asked, still staring directly at me, but now with a gleam of joy in his eyes. His impromptu sermon seemed to have awoken a fire in him.

"I think so, sir," I replied with a very feeble voice, not really wanting to get into a religious discussion with him.

"I hope so," he said with a look of warning. "Because this stuff is so much more important than where you go to college."

"Okay," I responded indifferently, now just ready for the conversation to end. For most people, having their county sheriff preach to them might have been really unusual, but I had known Sheriff Sentry all my life, and this was just how he was. To be honest, though, I would sit through any speech he wanted to give, so long as it meant I wasn't going to be in trouble; but that didn't mean I had to be as fired up about it as he was.

He stared at me with eyes of sadness that I didn't quite understand, but then seemed to decide that he needed to move on. "Well, you are in no trouble as you technically did nothing wrong, and you actually did save us quite a bit of work. However, in the future, try to think these situations through more thoroughly," he said as a last bit of advice as he stood up.

"I will, sir," I answered, standing up, too.

"Tell your parents I said hello," he said, as he turned to walk me out.

Before he closed his office door behind me, I looked back and noticed a perplexed look on his face.

"Sir, is everything okay?" I asked. He was silent for a moment and his eyes were glossed over as if he were in a daze. Then his demeanor suddenly changed as his eyes locked onto mine, more fiercely than they had our entire conversation.

"Just remember, Micah, *that which is born of the flesh is temporary, but that which is born of the Spirit is eternal,*"[10] he said quickly and mysteriously, and then he immediately closed his office door without another word.

*   *   *   *

I left the police department feeling confused at the enigmatic dismissal from the conversation. Still, I was relieved that Sheriff Sentry had not been too disappointed in me, and also that I was not in trouble. Even more, though, I felt that I had been given a second chance. I had heard a lot of Sheriff Sentry's message. The greed was behind me, and if I ever found myself in a situation like the bank again, then I would definitely fight harder to do what was right.

I exhaled deeply, relaxing myself even more as I walked away from the police station. All of the apprehension from the meeting had left me, the temptations from the previous night were gone, there had been no sight of the man in the white robes all day, and I felt at peace. Man, what an emotional roller-coaster I had been on.

I wandered my way back down Main Street and subconsciously headed toward my house. I didn't really have a plan for the rest of the day, so after walking for a few minutes I decided to take a detour. I changed my direction to one of my favorite places in town, my best friend, Brice Jacobs', house.

Besides the basketball game we had watched together the night before, I had not really had the chance to hang out with him since I had gotten home from college just a few days earlier. He had recently come home from college as well, and we were looking forward to spending all of our free time that summer playing basketball and hanging out.

CHAPTER TWO

Within a few minutes, I arrived at the Jacobs' house. Gravel crunched under my feet as I sped up their driveway toward their one-story home, with its odd green roof and brown wooden boards for siding. It wasn't any more impressive than my parents' white, two-story house. While our house was tall and shabby, theirs was wide and shabby, but both had an admittedly friendly and inviting *home* feeling to them.

I hopped up the Jacobs' front porch steps, underneath the large overhang where their family usually spent time when the weather was nice. I knocked on the friendly dark green door that matched the odd green roof perfectly.

Before I knew what hit me, the door burst open, and my face was buried in sandy blond hair as Brice nearly tackled me in a bear hug and gave me a hard punch in my arm to welcome me. "What's up, man?" he greeted me excitedly.

"Dude, you just saw me last night! What on earth is the matter with you?" I said irritably as I rubbed my arm. For a moment I considered socking him back. I was quite a bit bigger than him, but it was already beginning to feel warm outside, so I was in no mood to get into a wrestling match with Brice.

"Hey, can't I be excited to see my best friend?" he asked with a far more obnoxious grin on his face than usual. I had known him long enough to realize that he was up to something. "So, have you done any teleporting lately?" he teased, reminding me of how crazy I had probably seemed to him the night before.

"Oh, shut up," I said smiling back at him.

Before either of us could say another word, someone else walked up behind Brice.

FACING THE TRUTH

"Oh, hi, Micah! I had no idea you were coming over today," said a friendly and excited voice from just inside the Jacobs' house. The door was pulled open wider and my heart skipped a beat as my eyes were treated to the beautiful sight of Rachel Jacobs, Brice's younger sister.

She was only a year younger than me, two years younger than Brice, and I had always considered her to be the most beautiful girl I had ever seen. To me, she was the standard by which all other girls were measured. She was tall and slender, with long flowing blonde hair and big beautiful blue eyes, and she, like the sheriff and unlike me, kept a natural tan all year round. I had liked her as long as I could remember. I was pretty sure she felt the same way, but I will admit I have always been a coward when it comes to girls.

"Hey Rachel," I said nervously as she stepped forward to give me an awkward hug—or at least I felt awkward. She, on the other hand, was beaming with a huge, beautiful smile that made me feel quite inadequate.

"It's so great to see you," Rachel said in continued cheer. I had not seen her since Christmas break and she seemed to have only gotten prettier. We had all been extremely close in high school, but had gone our separate ways after graduation. Brice had given up his plans for playing basketball and was three years into a five-year degree at a nearby university—a university that he desperately wanted me to attend with him. I had gone to the junior college, and Rachel had gotten into Shepherd's College, the private school that I could not afford. Suffice it to say that playing basketball was not the only reason I wanted to go to Shepherd's.

CHAPTER TWO

The three of us stepped through their doorway, into their living room, and Brice closed the door behind us. I peered around the large room, and I noticed a very pretty girl I didn't recognize sitting on the couch. She got up as we filed into the room.

"Oh, you haven't actually met her yet, have you, Micah? This is Katie Spencer, my girlfriend from college that I told you about last night," Brice said to me, barely able to hide the pride in his voice. "She is staying with me for a few weeks."

My eyes widened. It surprised me that Brice's parents would let a girlfriend stay overnight.

Brice noticed my shocked look, laughed, and said, "What I meant was, she is staying with Rachel in her room. Don't worry, man; my parents haven't slacked just because I'm out of the house."

With awkwardness now firmly fixed in the air, I turned to Katie to introduce myself properly. Brice had reason to be proud; she really was very pretty, with her long dark brown hair, almost black, dark brown eyes, and the same perennial tan that everyone seemed to have but me. She was quite a bit shorter than Rachel, but her height actually fit Brice quite nicely. "Hi, I'm Micah Jones," I greeted.

"Nice to meet you, Micah. Brice talks about you all the time," she replied with a big, friendly smile on her face, which I found nearly as intimidating as Rachel's.

I always got uncomfortable when I had to meet new people, and as I have already indicated, girls were not my strong suit. I was hoping that Brice would remember that fact and strike up the conversation again to rescue me from an awkward moment. However, true to his nature, he did the exact opposite. He embarrassed me even further.

"Hey man, we are going to the movies this weekend. Why don't you and Rachel come with us . . . as a *double date*," he said calmly as if this statement would not be awkward to anyone, taking special care to emphasize the "double date" part.

My jaw hit the floor and my eyes once again went wide with shock. I was stunned and unable to speak. I just stood there frozen in silence.

"We'd love to," Rachel suddenly said in the sweetest tone.

"Great; it's a date. You can pick us all up at seven o'clock this Saturday," Brice exclaimed to me happily.

At last I knew why Brice had greeted me so obnoxiously. I was certain that they had rehearsed the whole thing, and I had simply walked into their trap. It was an awkward, but also a wonderful and glorious trap. I was shocked, but elated.

"Oh, hi, Micah. It's good to see you," came a kind voice from just outside of the living room. I looked toward the door that led to the kitchen and saw Mike, Brice's dad, walking into the living room. He was a short, plump, balding man with a very kind face, a giddy smile, and a good natured demeanor. He worked at the high school as the music and band teacher.

"Diane!" Mike yelled into the kitchen, "Micah is here!" He walked over and shook my hand as Diane, Brice's mom, came scurrying in from the kitchen to give me a hug. She was also a small, yet slightly plump, woman, so she fit with Mike quite as nicely as Katie fit with Brice. She had shoulder length black hair and fair skin with a very spunky aura about her. She worked as a nurse at the town clinic.

"It's great to see you, Micah," Diane said as she squeezed me into a deep hug. "How was your school year? Brice tells us that you are probably going to join him at the university next year," she said without pausing for me to answer her first question. I shot a quick evil stare at Brice.

"What?" Brice said with another obnoxious grin. "I just said that you were considering it."

"Yes, I'm *considering* it," I said to Diane while continuing to glare at Brice. Unfortunately, even that was more than I should have admitted because Brice took that as his cue to go into full recruiting mode.

"Great!" he began. "Now, I know it won't be as cheap as your junior college, but I've done some research on student loans and some smaller grants and things you should apply for," he said excitedly as he pulled several papers out of a back-pack that was sitting propped up against their living room couch.

"What is all that stuff?" I asked, realizing how quickly the conversation had gotten out of my control.

"This is your application, man," he responded matter-of-factly. "What did you think, they were just going to let you show up on the first day of fall semester without applying?" Everyone laughed. Apparently no one knew exactly how determined and prepared Brice was to get me to his school.

"Okay, man, I'll look at it," I conceded, feeling slightly annoyed and slightly amused. Either way, I had a funny feeling I would end up going to school with my best friend the next semester, which, despite the expense, actually sounded pretty good to me . . . but there was no way I was going to admit that to Brice.

"You should seriously consider it," he said as he leaned closer to me and lowered his voice so that no one else would hear. "Trust me, there are tons of girls there," he said as he glanced over at Katie who was now chatting with Diane, implying Katie was all the confirmation I should need.

Rachel, however, had overheard him. She quickly cleared her throat, giving Brice a dirty look, which caused him to change the subject immediately. I couldn't help but smile.

*   *   *   *

I stayed at the Jacobs' house for much of the rest of the day, catching up on the different things in our lives; all the while still in awe that I had a date with Rachel. It was a great reunion. I had missed Brice and Rachel's parents almost as much as I missed my own. They were about as good and tight knit of a family one could find. Their family was pretty close to mine, not just because of my friendship with Brice, but mainly because we had gone to the same church for as long as I could remember.

I stayed for lunch as we continued to talk the day away. Brice and I made plans to play basketball with the high school guys for the remainder of the week. We knew this year's team needed a lot of practice, and we were eager to get started, so, we plotted and planned how we were going to work with the team. It felt just like old times.

By about dinner time I was ready to head home, feeling I shouldn't impose on the Jacobs for two meals that day, despite their assurances it was okay. I said goodbye to Brice and Katie and then bashfully said goodbye to Rachel. I was glad when I saw her blush a little, too.

I passed through most of the town without really looking at anything, completely absorbed in my thoughts. Peaceful blurred scenes quickly passed by me, and before I knew it I was home. I strolled through the friendly white gate and hopped briskly up the concrete porch into the quaint, but loving, two-story white house that was my home. Everything about the house and life seemed inviting. If only life could always be that happy.

I went in to greet my parents and my little sister. Supper was already prepared, and they were waiting for me to eat. My father told us about new sermon ideas, as my mother gave little inputs and advice. Shelby told us about all the friends she had played with at the pool that day, how she had swum out past the ropes into the deep end all on her own and jumped off of the diving board by herself, too. She was quite proud of her accomplishments at the tender age of ten.

Life was back to normal. The man in the white robes was so far from my mind that it was as if he had never existed—and I was beginning to think he never really had. I didn't know how to explain what I thought I had seen and experienced, but I was more than ready to move on from it all. As such, I went up to bed that night without a care in the world, excited about the prospect of playing basketball all week, excited about my date, and ready for a dreamless sleep. I sank into my bed and buried myself in my blanket and pillows. If only life could stay that way forever.

When I went to sleep that night in ignorant bliss, I had

no way of knowing that the bank incident was just the first in a wave of many things that would soon occur and change my life forever. I had no way of knowing that the next two weeks would be the most challenging and terrifying weeks of my life. And I had no way of knowing that I was destined to see much more of the man in the white robes.

CHAPTER THREE

THE SECOND TEMPTATION

Tonight it will happen, just as the first,
Stand fast and be strong, don't give way to the thirst.[II]
Integrity and goodness have hold of the key,
To passing the trial, number two of the three.
A new prophecy made and a new secret told,
Up or down in the sea, which way should one go.
A warning for all, of things yet to come,
Caution for all, but especially for one.
A deep drowning pool, yet still they can't tell,
One's good and one's bad; one's heaven, one's hell.

*   *   *   *

SATURDAY, MAY 25, 1985

The long awaited day had finally arrived. It had been years—most of my life, really—that I had liked Rachel, and things were finally working out. As such, despite a poor week of practice with the high school basketball team, I was in a wonderful mood. With my date that night and the fact that the rest of the week had gone by with no sign of the glowing man and his golden ladder, my spirits were feeling extremely high. If I could just get through the entire date without saying anything too stupid, then it was looking to be a great start to my summer.

I crawled out of bed and threw on a pair of jeans and an old T-shirt, then staggered downstairs still feeling slightly groggy from a good night's rest. I rubbed the sleep out of my eyes and yawned as I entered the dining room. The delicious smell of bacon had filled the house, and my stomach growled as I sat down in one of the simple wooden chairs that surround our round wooden table.

My mom was putting the finishing touches on our big country breakfast, which was kind of a tradition for my family on Saturdays, especially on important occasions, and my being home from college constituted an important occasion in my mom's eyes. I certainly wasn't going to complain about that. Shelby was not awake yet, as usual, and I was just getting ready to ask my mom if she wanted me to go wake her up when my dad entered the room.

"'Morning, Micah," he greeted. "I spoke with Sheriff Sentry last night about your interview with him," my dad said cheerfully as he took a seat next to me.

"What all did he say?" I asked, suddenly nervous, having not thought about my meeting with him for a couple days. I hoped the sheriff wouldn't tell my dad everything I had told him.

"Well, he just said things we already knew about you," my dad replied, patting me on the back as he took his seat. "Such as the fact that you are a good kid . . . excuse me . . . a good man, and your first concern was hoping that Kimberly wasn't in too much trouble," he said like a proud father, as he turned his attention toward his morning paper.

"She isn't in too much trouble, is she?" I asked, attempting to divert the subject from me, just like I had tried to do with Sheriff Sentry.

"No, they spoke to her and told her never to let it happen again, and the same old stuff you tell people when they mess up. But she knows what she did, so there is no use in beating a dead horse," my father answered, speaking almost to himself, as he flipped through the pages of the paper.

"Well, that's good. She always seemed nice to me," I said, hoping the conversation would be over.

"Yep, she is," my mother interjected offhandedly as she carried in a bowl of eggs. "Oh, Micah, will you go wake up Shelby? Breakfast is almost ready. Just see if she feels like eating yet. If she doesn't, then she can come down when she's ready . . . crazy kid," she added endearingly.

"Sure," I said as I hopped up from my chair and walked to the steps. I took three steps at a time in a sort of skipping fashion until I reached the top of the flight, and then made my way to Shelby's door. I opened her white wooden door with a slow creak and entered her dark room silently, intending to wake her gently so as not to startle her.

– BANG –

Without warning the door slammed shut behind me and a blinding light filled the room, causing my eyes to hammer shut. I screamed in fear as I was blown off my feet and onto the floor, but my voice was drowned out by a loud rushing torrent of wind that suddenly whipped through the room. The roaring air pressed down upon me, pinning me to the floor as it stifled any sound from the outside world. I could see nothing but the redness of my eyelids and I could not move an inch.

"*Peace be with you, and fear not,*" came a deep and powerful voice, overpowering even the mighty wind.[12] "*I am not here to harm you, only to warn you,*" the voice rumbled. "*The second of three temptations will occur tonight. If you are to stop the evil that is planned for you and for many people in this town, then it is time for you to make a choice. This world has had your heart for too long.[13] You must be born of the Spirit, Micah, because that which is born of the flesh is temporary, but that which is born of the Spirit is eternal.[14] The second temptation will occur tonight!'* exclaimed the powerful voice.

I was silent, still held tightly to the floor by the raging wind and blinded by the dazzling light. Before I could attempt anything, a pulse of power like an explosion radiated throughout the room, and instantly the air became calm as the room turned silent and everything went dark.

I opened my eyes slowly. The bright light had been extinguished, and the violent storm was gone. I looked around. The room was back to normal and Shelby was lying still on her bed, sound asleep. I scampered to my feet and raced to her bed, grabbing her into my arms.

"Shelby, are you okay?" I yelled. She began to stir.

"Did you see that?" I continued to shout. Shelby was coming around, but not quickly enough for me.

Frustrated and frantic, I let go of her and she immediately rolled over and continued sleeping. The bright light, raging wind, and powerful voice hadn't stirred her at all. I looked around the room impatiently, desperate for answers, but found none. Whatever had happened had finished as quickly as it had begun, and it had left no traces. I got up and drew back Shelby's blinds, revealing the sunny Saturday morning and the peaceful and normal neighborhood that lined the street below. There was not even a hint of anything out of the ordinary.

I turned my attention back to Shelby and scrambled to

her side once more. Grabbing her shoulders, I gave her a little shake to wake her. "Shelby, wake up!" I said, my voice unstable with emotions.

"Micah?" she finally responded in a sleepy and unsure tone. "Why do you have a hold of me?" she asked, sounding irritated.

"Because . . . you . . . you didn't see or hear any of that?" I stammered, feeling very alone and still not letting go of her.

"Any of what, Micah? I was asleep," she said, sounding even more cranky. "Will you let go of me?" she added as she fruitlessly tried to bat my hands away.

"So you are okay?" I asked in defeat. Just like Brice, Shelby had not experienced the strange event with me. There was no point pressing her for any more information . . . she had none.

"I'm fine. Except for the fact that you won't let go of me!" she shrieked, now attempting to wiggle free from my grasp. I released her.

"What are you two doing?" asked my dad's deep familiar voice from behind us.

I looked at Shelby's bedroom doorway and saw my father and mother had entered the room.

"Why did you slam the door, Micah? Couldn't you just wake her up nicely?" my mother scolded, clearly thinking I had tried to scare Shelby awake.

"I didn't slam the door! I need to talk to both of you . . . now!" I said, with my eyes wide in a disbelieving panic.

What in the world was going on? I felt like I was about to lose my mind. None of it was natural; the man and his golden ladder, the bright light at the bank, the unnatural feelings and thoughts . . . and now *this*!

Either I was going crazy, or something big and supernatural was happening to me. I didn't know which option sounded worse. I left the room and my parents followed as Shelby climbed out of bed to get dressed. I tore into my bedroom, not knowing where to begin. My parents followed me in, but stopped at the doorway, staring at me in confusion.

"What's this about, Micah?" my dad asked in a concerned tone. His expression made it clear that he still suspected that I had tried to scare Shelby.

But I had no time for that. Terrified, I began telling my parents everything. I told them about blacking out at the game, the man and the golden ladder, the parts I had left out about the bank, all the details I had given to Sheriff Sentry, and his advice and insight. I was speaking quicker than I can ever remember speaking in my life, my voice still trembling. I explained what had just happened in Shelby's room. When I finished, I was as out of breath as if I had just run a race.

I waited, still terrified, staring at them expectantly. What I told them was a lot to take in, but I had always been an honest kid. I wasn't a liar or a thief, and they knew me well enough to know I didn't like attention. I had never given them reason not to trust me, and clearly I was quite serious. Therefore, despite the fact that what I was saying sounded insane, I still expected their support.

"Oh, Micah, it is perfectly natural to want nice things. Lots of people would have had fantasy thoughts and lingered in front of that vault," my mom responded, a little sardonically.

"The important thing is that you did what was right."

"She's right, Micah, and you are probably just tired. It's easy to imagine stuff when you had that much excitement this week," my dad said in an attempt to console me, though I wondered if he even believed what he was saying. Then I saw him glance at my mom with a look of concern, as if I were not there. When he looked back at me, his face was slightly annoyed.

"Still, that's no reason to try and scare your sister," my dad started.

"I didn't scare Shelby!" I yelled. "Aren't you listening to me?!"

Anger now joined my other emotions as I shook almost uncontrollably. I tried to calm myself. I had never yelled at my parents before, and I knew my dad wouldn't stand for much of it, let alone listen to me if I lost my cool. I sat down in a chair by my bed and sank my face into my hands as I let out a sigh.

"Sorry," I said, looking at the floor sheepishly, "but I'm telling you the truth. Something weird is happening to me," I finished, all hope dwindling from me.

I looked back up to see their expressions. It was clear—they were worried, but they still didn't believe me. Perhaps they *did* think I was losing my mind—and maybe they were right. My dad let out a sigh of his own, but unfortunately, his was the sound he made when he disapproved of something. He shook his head slightly and left the room without another word.

My mom stepped forward, kissed me on the top of my head, and left, too. I was crushed. I didn't know what to say. I sat in shock as I listened to them walk down the upstairs hallway, away from my room. My father mumbled something to my mother about the lengths I would go to for a joke. My mom mumbled something indiscernible back to him. They were annoyed and worried, but neither one thought I was telling the truth.

I collapsed onto my messy bed, feeling more terrified and alone than I had ever felt in my life. I knew I wasn't going crazy. There was no doubt in my mind that I had just experienced a very real, extraordinary event . . . and my own parents thought I was making it all up! I knew what I had told them sounded crazy, but I had still hoped they would believe me and possibly offer some reasonable explanations . . . or support . . . or something.

Instead, whatever was after me, trying to influence my mind with targeted temptations, I would have to face it alone . . . and I would be facing it soon. The voice in Shelby's room had warned that a second temptation was coming for me that night, which meant a date wasn't the only thing to be worried about. If the bank incident had almost landed me in prison, what kind of trouble could I potentially get in with another temptation?

Buried in my misery and fear, I tried to think about the advice Sheriff Sentry had given me. I didn't understand everything he had said, but one thing really stood out. When temptations came, he had told me to remember the good things I had to be thankful for. He was right; I had a lot to be thankful for. There were lots of reasons why I shouldn't want to throw my life away by doing something stupid. This thought gave me a small grain of confidence. I was certain I would do better if greed came after me again. I was going to focus on the things I already had to be happy about. Hopefully that would be enough to stop the temptation from getting to me this time; not that my parents' recent distrust would do anything to bolster my defenses.

I continued to lie in worried contemplation until my thoughts were interrupted by the growling of my stomach. Defeated by hunger, I got up and went back downstairs, hoping there was some breakfast left for me. Thankfully, my mother's annoyance would never prevent her from setting aside a plate for me with all of my favorite breakfast foods. My parents and Shelby had finished eating already and were all sitting in the living room watching TV and chatting cheerfully as if nothing had happened, so I quietly ate my breakfast at the table by myself.

Once I finished, I spent the rest of the day attempting to avoid my family by bouncing back and forth between my room and the bench on our porch. I decided to use the time of solitude to try to prepare myself in case the temptation returned to me on my date later that night. It was difficult in my fear and frustration, but I practiced concentrating on things I was happy about, things that were a blessing in my life. I even made a list. Despite the recent distrust, I was still thankful for my family, and they were at the top of my list.

By the time evening arrived, I felt confident I would be able to conquer any sudden attacks of greed that might well up inside me, but I was also certain of another thing: if the second attack was anything like the first, I was not in for an enjoyable evening. My biggest fear was slightly selfish as I hoped whatever was going to happen would not interrupt, or otherwise mess up, my date with Rachel.

I was glad when it turned six o'clock because I felt that it was finally close enough to the date for me to start getting ready. I took a shower, shaved, and threw on some clothes. I wasn't really that fashionable . . . jeans and a T-shirt would do. Besides, it was bound to be hot, so I wasn't going to wear anything with long sleeves.

I actually considered taking off my jeans and throwing on shorts. But deciding I had to look somewhat decent, I resisted the urge. I kept my hair short enough that, despite what my mom said, I never really needed to comb it. At six thirty, I was ready to go. Without a word to my family, I walked down to my car, an old beater with leopard spots of rust. Originally the car had been blue—I think—but by the time I owned it in the latter years of its life, it had become impossible to tell what the color was supposed to be. However, it ran, and the interior was not in too bad a shape, so it served its purpose.

I jumped in, started my car, and then headed forward, making my way slowly to Main Street. Once on Main Street, I took the familiar right turn onto a side road that would lead me toward the Jacobs' house. As I drove, my stomach became inexplicably tense, but it wasn't date related . . . it was something else. With dread, I looked out of my window, expecting the worst. My fear was confirmed immediately.

The outside world was eerily silent, and the sky, though a few hours of daylight were left, was oddly dim. No clouds were in sight, yet the light around me seemed like a large room trying to be lit by a forty-watt bulb. An unnatural fog had been set atop of the world . . . or atop of *my* world at least. Immediately,

CHAPTER THREE

I knew I would soon be facing the struggles that had been promised that night; there was no escaping it.

I drove on slowly, taking the different back roads that led to the Jacobs' house without really concentrating on them. As I drew closer to their house, through each misty and dim trail, my stress was not only fixed on the supernatural, but also on the very real date that was before me. I would probably be awkward enough on any date, let alone if I was waiting to be attacked by something. This night was bound to be a disaster. I considered turning around, going home, and calling Brice to cancel, but I wasn't prepared to do that yet. I had waited too long for Rachel.

Finally, I turned onto the Jacobs' street and saw their house a couple of driveways down, covered in the same dim fog that enveloped everything. Even the trees seemed to droop as if they were wet, though it had not rained all week. *Was nature itself warning me something was about to happen?* I felt as if the angel of death were going before me and darkening the world. Like silence before the storm, at any moment a battle was about to begin. What the fight was about, I didn't know, but a fight was certainly coming.

I pulled into the Jacobs' driveway and got out of my car to the usual creak of my car's large driver side door. I ran up their porch steps and knocked on the green wooden door as quickly as I could, hoping to escape the eerie atmosphere. Brice opened the door before the echoes of my first few knocks had even faded. I could tell he had been waiting by the door to make sure he could talk to me alone before the girls came along. He was smiling at me with a cheesy grin. His happiness seemed extremely out of place, given what was happening to me.

"The girls are still getting ready," he said as he pushed me out to the porch. He closed the door behind him, blocking the path inside and ruining my hope of getting under cover; but at least I wasn't alone in the shadows any longer.

"You look worried. Aren't you excited?" he asked, still grinning like crazy.

"Oh . . . of course," I said, searching for words and trying to act normal. "But I still can't believe you put me on the spot like that. You know I don't react well under pressure. I mean, come on, you played basketball with me all of those years. When I get nervous, I choke," I spouted off to him. I had said it so quickly that it made me realize subconsciously, I had been waiting for a while to say that to him, despite my other distractions.

He slapped his hand on my shoulder and laughed with a chuckle. "I know man, which is exactly why I did it. Rachel has liked you for years and you have never made a move. She came home from college talking about how she had seen other guys—most of them were jerks—but she had yet to find one she liked as much as you," he said, making a puking sound.

"After being around hundreds of guys at school, she still liked you, and a lot at that," he continued. "It was her idea actually. She didn't want to ask you out on principle, but she knew you never would, so she asked me to do it for her. I, of course, was happy to oblige. The look on your face was payment enough," he said, laughing even harder out of sheer enjoyment and then making a dumbfounded look to mock me. It still felt out of place to be having such a normal conversation in such an abnormal atmosphere, but deep down I was trying to ignore the supernatural stuff in the futile hopes that it would simply leave me alone.

I socked Brice in the arm, sort of playfully, yet still solidly enough to faze him. "You should have just told me. I would have asked her if I knew she liked me that much," I said with false bravado in my voice, not really believing any of it myself.

"No you wouldn't have, you coward. You've known she's liked you for years and you never did anything about it," he said, rubbing his arm, yet still laughing at me.

"You're right, man. I guess *thank you* is what I meant to say," I said with a slightly mocking, yet finally submissive smile of my own.

"Oh, don't worry about thanking me," he replied, with a devilish grin. "You owe me now, and you better believe I'll be cashing in. I might demand that you come to college with me," he said with his first serious look of the night, making it obvious he had only just realized what he might be able to demand from me in repayment.

I chuckled. "You need to learn how to negotiate. You already gave me what I want. Now I don't have any incentive to appease you," I said smiling in triumph.

"Hmmm . . . it's curious you think it's a coincidence that I'm coming along on your first date. Perhaps you forget how good I am at saying embarrassing things. Maybe you need a little reminder tonight," Brice said, smiling devilishly again. I knew he was an expert at embarrassing people. He found it hilarious. He was one of those people who never got embarrassed, so he didn't see any real harm in embarrassing others. I knew he had the power to make my date unbearable. I didn't want to admit it, but he still held all the cards in our negotiation.

"I guess I'm not such a poor negotiator after all," Brice said with a satisfied smile as he noticed the defeated look on my face. He had won.

"I suppose I'll be giving your school a little more consideration," I said through gritted teeth, hoping that would be enough to prevent him from embarrassing me too badly.

"I thought you might," he said, laughing fully this time. This was an exact reversal of most of our conversations. Usually I won our arguments, but Brice had the clear upper hand when it dealt with his sister.

Finally, the door opened behind Brice and the girls walked out. Katie stepped onto the porch in front of Rachel. Katie alone was enough to knock a guy off his feet. Her long, flowing, rich, dark hair and dark green eyes gave her an exotic, mesmerizing look. She was indeed a beautiful girl, but I only appreciated her beauty for a moment because my eye caught Rachel as she came through the front door onto the porch. She had gone all out for our date. Her hair was shiny and straight, and it reached the middle of her back. She wore a white skirt and pink top that in my mind made her look perfect. I could not help but stare, and I had a feeling my mouth may have dropped open.

"I take it I look all right, then," Rachel said with a smile at me, and let out a short laugh that awoke me out of my stupor.

CHAPTER THREE

I smiled back and laughed at my own extreme lack of suave for having just stared at her without saying anything. I tried to salvage the moment a little, "Yeah, uh . . . you look very nice."

I looked down at my jeans and T-shirt feeling for once I should have probably put a little more effort into how I looked.

Brice and I escorted our dates down the few porch steps and opened the car doors for them. Rachel sat up front with me, and Brice and Katie sat in back.

"Which movie are we going to see?" I asked Brice, just trying to break the ice.

"Oh, just whatever one looks good when we get there. I didn't call ahead," he replied.

"Sounds good to me," I said, not really caring what we saw anyway. As the others began talking, I took a quick glance at the evening sky. Relief spread over me. Everything seemed to have returned to normal.

I pulled out of their gravel driveway and headed back down the Jacobs' street and on toward Main Street, occasionally glancing over at Rachel. She was stunning. I wound my way through the side roads, onto Main Street, and then headed down it, past the small businesses, past the bank, our church, the pizza shop, the gas station, and finally past the police station. The movie theater was on the outskirts of town. We eventually arrived and pulled into the partially filled parking lot. My car door opened with the usual creak, which was suddenly more embarrassing with people around.

We got out of the car and walked toward the front doors. The sign on the side of the building showed pictures of what movies were playing. None of them looked familiar to me. We had the choice between two chick flicks and a scary movie. When the rest of us said we didn't care, Brice chose the scary movie.

I would have preferred a chick flick to a scary movie any day. I knew Rachel would, too. She found scary movies a little ridiculous, without plot, and sometimes just sadistic—and I certainly did not disagree with her. However, I had a feeling Brice only chose the movie because he hoped Katie would snuggle close to him during the scary scenes. I honestly had slight hopes the scary parts would benefit me as well, although more likely than anything, I would probably be just as scared as Rachel would—especially given how creepy real life had become.

We made our way to the front door of the theater and stood outside in a long line of people as we waited to pay for our tickets. The evening sky was still clear, and while it was darkening more and more, it was just the natural darkening that came as the sun sank into the horizon. Plenty of sun was left to light the summer day. With no dark cloud or weird feelings, I began to feel hopeful about the date again. Perhaps the dark fog would only bother me if I was on my own. I wasn't sure if that thought was comforting, but I was glad for it at that moment.

The line gradually shortened, and when we reached the clear glass front door, I held it open for Rachel, Brice, and Katie as they filed inside. I stepped through the door to follow, but just before I closed it, I took one final glance at the evening sky. Without warning, a blinding bolt of lightning crackled through the air, striking the grass beside the parking lot with an enormous **BOOM**. Its force shook the ground, scaring everyone in the theater's entryway.

Electricity filled the air and the hair on my neck stood on end for the second time that week. The sky dimmed ever so slightly, and an unnatural heat rushed over me. My stomach was suddenly overcome with the all too familiar ominous feeling. It was clear that danger lay ahead. I closed the door quickly, but kept my eyes locked on the outside.

Fear filled me as I peered out of the glass door, waiting for another strike. But nothing else came. No second bolt, no thunder, and oddly enough, still no clouds. I would have welcomed clouds, even a thunderstorm. I would have welcomed almost anything, as long as it wasn't focused on me, alone.

I looked at the crowd of people who were staring through the glass door and windows, wondering curiously about the anomaly that had just occurred. They seemed surprised, but excited, at having witnessed the random lightning. To them, it didn't represent danger. To them it was just lightning. They had no idea it was a warning that something bad was coming . . . because it wasn't meant for them. It was meant for me. If they had felt how I did, they wouldn't have been scanning the sky with such eagerness. The day was still bright for them, but for me, the dark cloud had returned.

"Well, that was odd," Brice said, breaking the silence. "What was that, heat lightning? There aren't any clouds in sight. I wonder if we'll have snow next on this bright sunny day," Brice said coolly, stating the irony of the situation.

With just a few more comments about the lightning from the others, we finally turned inside to pay for our tickets. I was thankful to get away from the door. Deciding we didn't want to wait in line for popcorn and drinks, we headed straight to our seats.

"I'll just go get us something once the movie starts," Rachel said as we entered the room that was showing our movie. "It's not like I'm going to miss an important plot point or something. I imagine I'll get scared at all the right parts without knowing why the psycho is chasing some random innocent woman," she continued sarcastically.

One by one we filed into some seats in the back row, of course taking Brice's lead. He, no doubt, had plans for this movie. I undoubtedly would be too nervous and too distracted to even attempt something as simple as holding Rachel's hand.

I was disappointed when Brice sat down on the far end of the row, leaving Rachel and Katie to sit between us. I would be alone to carry the conversation with Rachel for the few minutes we still had to wait before the movie began. That meant it was sure to be quiet—I never could speak well when I was around Rachel, but I was bound to be especially reclusive given everything going on with me.

My eyes wandered as I sat in silence. An elderly couple sat in the middle of the theater. I found it kind of odd they were at a scary movie. I was young, and I didn't like them. I couldn't imagine being older and sitting through them.

Glancing over at Brice, I noticed he was already holding Katie's hand, which immediately made me feel awkward. I knew he had been dating Katie for a while, but it still felt like he was setting a standard—one that I was not even going to attempt to measure up to. I stared for too long. Rachel caught my eye and smiled at me. I felt the blood go to my face. I had imagined going on a date with her before, but actually being on the date was quite intimidating and uncomfortable.

"I'm glad we did this. It should be a good time," she said, gazing into my eyes.

"Yeah, the movie should be good," I said nervously without thinking.

"Um, yeah . . ." she generously said.

I was an idiot. Could I really not think of anything better to say than that? I knew she didn't like these movies, and she knew I didn't either.

"You do look very pretty tonight," I said while looking at the floor and blushing even more. Still, I was a little proud of myself; that was definitely better than my stupid comment about the movie.

"Thank you. You look very nice, too," she said, blushing slightly herself.

Oh, how I hated awkward moments. I knew I liked her; she knew she liked me, so why did we have to have all these sappy, awkward moments that made me uncomfortable? Luckily, the previews cut on to save me from having to say anything else, which would have undoubtedly not been very clever.

"I'll go get some popcorn and drinks after the previews. I like to see those," she whispered to me and her brother, in turn.

We sat through the previews, and when the movie eventually started, she got up and slid past me to head out to the aisle. "No, wait!" I said quietly as I grabbed her arm and quickly pulled out my wallet to hand her some cash.

"No, you got the movie; I can get some snacks." She smiled at me. I hesitated, trying to think of a way to kindly change her mind. "Micah, you know you won't win this argument," she whispered, smiling her beautifully disarming smile at me. I smiled back and let her arm go without saying anything. She went down the steps and headed through the back door. Brice leaned over to Katie and I heard him say he would be right back. He then climbed past Katie and slid into Rachel's seat next to me.

"How's it going, man?" he asked in a quiet voice as we ignored the movie.

It was normal for a brother to be happy for his sister when he believed she was dating a good guy. However, normally a brother does not want to do too much talking about his sister dating a guy—ever—no matter how good of a guy. Brice and I, however, had talked for years about Rachel, and he actually wanted me to marry her. I was genuinely his best friend, almost his brother, and he trusted me more than almost anyone. He always said it was difficult to find men who respect girls, and Brice knew I did. Even more, I could relate to him. As a brother, I wanted the same thing for my little sister, Shelby . . . though I wasn't in any hurry for her day to come.

"You know me, man; I can't talk to her," I answered him quietly, not wanting to disturb the movie watchers just a few rows in front of us.

"Why not? You never shut up with me," he said, with a smile that told me he was joking and serious at the same time.

"I know, I just get all nervous," I admitted, looking

around to ensure we were definitely out of earshot of all the other people in the theater, including Katie. It was embarrassing enough talking about that kind of stuff with Brice. I didn't need Katie taking my conversation back to Rachel. Fortunately, the movie was loud, and she didn't seem to be listening to us.

"Oh!" Brice said suddenly, looking down at his seat as his foot kicked something. "She left her purse here. Mom and Dad gave her money for the snacks since we were paying the girls' way into the movie. I had better run it out to her," he said.

"Shouldn't I? I am her date," I asked him, kind of hoping the answer was no.

"Better let me," he whispered slyly. "I'll try and work some magic for you."

"What are you going to say?" I asked urgently, now extremely worried.

"Don't worry about it, man . . . trust me," he said obnoxiously as he grabbed the purse and jogged down the steps quickly, and into the lobby without saying anything else.

"Oh, she forgot her purse?" Katie leaned over and asked in an offhanded way.

"Yeah," I answered a little too loudly, startled by her sudden presence. People a few rows down looked back at me in annoyance. I glanced up at the screen to pretend I was watching in hopes they would quit giving me dirty looks. I had no idea what was going on in the movie, but it appeared someone was walking down a dark street, all alone. My recent personal experience told me that would most certainly not end well for them. I decided to watch it a little in case Rachel asked me to fill her in on it, although I knew she wouldn't really care.

However, Katie wasn't finished yet. I could feel her eyes staring at the side of my face as I pretended to watch the movie. She began to say something, but then hesitated for a moment as if wrestling with her thoughts. Finally she spoke again, but this time it was in a soft whisper that I could barely hear.

"Don't be so nervous," she began as I turned my eyes in her direction. "Rachel really likes you. She says you're the man of her dreams. She won't quit talking about you, actually," she said to me with a grin, making me feel more awkward than ever. People didn't realize I felt fine about my chances with Rachel. That didn't mean I was going to be comfortable the whole time. I knew Katie was just trying to be nice, but did I really have to keep talking to everyone about it?

She continued to look at me, obviously waiting for a response of some sort. So I spoke, again without thinking. "I just can't help it. I really do like her, and it's just, different when I'm around her. . . . I'm different," I said to her with an openness that surprised even me.

Katie didn't look surprised at my honesty, though. Perhaps she was just the type of girl who liked gossip, but for whatever reason she suddenly looked eager. Before she said another word, she hopped out of her seat and quickly plopped next to me, into Rachel's seat, ready to talk. "She really does think you're great," she said very quietly. I subconsciously noticed how pretty she looked. "You *are* quite a catch," she added out of nowhere, inching slowly closer as she spoke.

A warning light went off in my head, urging me to retreat, but I was frozen. Common sense and reason should have made me jump in shock, to put a little distance between us. But before I could move, the aroma of her perfume floated to my nose, intoxicating me. I looked up at her and the rich green against the pure whiteness of her eyes lassoed me in, like a vortex in the deepest ocean, pulling me ever closer to her. She was breathtaking . . . and I was helpless.

"You really are very handsome. No wonder she has waited for you," Katie said with a voice as deeply intoxicating as her fragrance.

I was mesmerized, hopelessly enchanted by her. Somewhere deep down in my mind it registered that the dark cloud had returned, but I easily ignored it as it crept in, filling the air and my mind. It blinded my eyes and clouded all judgment. Before I had even begun to register its presence, the world around me was gone—the movie, the people, everything—there was only Katie and her beauty. I was immobilized. I yearned for her, as powerfully as I had yearned for the money in the bank vault—or perhaps even more powerfully. Though she was not mine, I wanted her. *I deserve her. She is beautiful, and I will have her.*

Lust passed over me like an eclipse. I was impervious to everything but her. A switch had been flipped in the world, turning out the light. Only darkness remained, and it engulfed us both completely.

It's just the two of us, alone, like it should be, a silent voice seemed to whisper into my mind.

She put her hand on my arm gently and pulled me toward her . . . to kiss her. I leaned in. *She is mine.*

But as I leaned forward, something inside me hesitated. My mind was not clear enough to know what it was, but something, just for a moment, pulled me away from her. My eyes suddenly came unglued from her. As I looked away, the dark cloud became more noticeable and my situation clearer. Even in the haze and passion of the moment, I knew what I was being tempted to do was wrong . . . but I still wanted it. I continued to look away from Katie, but I could almost feel her, staring at me. She was just sitting there waiting for me . . . and I wanted her. My eyes and my body craved her. They yearned for the pleasure they were being deprived of.

Just one glance, a voice seemed to say. My flesh begged me to look at her. *Just a peek*, it said. In weakness, I decided to give in. My eyes turned back to Katie's face and immediately I was pulled, even more powerfully, toward her.[15] A wave of justifications bombarded my mind.

I had been without a girlfriend for so long. I was a good looking man; *why should I not have whatever girl I wanted? What harm is there in just kissing her?* The answer should have been obvious, but as silent thoughts of longing poured over my flesh and into my mind, it wasn't.

I want to . . . she wants to, the thoughts continued to reason, with increasing power. Justifications swarmed around in my head, as if someone were trying to convince me that what I was doing was right.

Who is trying to convince me? I wondered to myself. *Is someone else here? Is something else influencing my mind?*

Katie was so beautiful, and she wanted me. Her tan skin, her dark hair . . . tempting, soliciting, rationalizing, impure, and inviting thoughts delved into my mind and continued to circle. Shallow, selfish ideas rattled through me. There was no room for deep or moral thoughts, only simple longings.

Yet why do I continue to hold fast? If I want her so badly, why don't I simply lean in and kiss her? Her glossy lips beckoned me, but something inside of me held back. The fog in my mind and Katie's beauty urged me forward, but what was it that prevented me from doing what I so desperately wanted to do?

Then, as if answering my question, a voice seemed to speak into my mind, *Brice is your best friend.*

The words ripped at my heart. This was the reason I was holding on. This was the reason I couldn't lean in to kiss Katie, despite my intense longing to do exactly that. I couldn't do that to Brice!

Who cares? A rebuttal entered into my mind? *Do what feels good*, something seemed to say to me as Katie ran her fingers through my hair and applied slight pressure to my back, gently guiding me toward her. Polarized confusion stole through me. I wanted to do what was right, but I also wanted Katie.[16]

What about Rachel?! Something urgently spat at my heart. As the name "Rachel" pierced my heart, my thoughts cleared slightly and my eyes ripped away from Katie's gaze. Like a breath of fresh air in the midst of a smoke-filled room, I could suddenly see. It was finally clear; I was being tempted. Katie was the next temptation! As if a powerful fan had been placed in front of the smoke-filled fire in my mind, the dark cloud began to lift.

But the temptation was not done with me yet. In a mixture of curiosity, fear, and desire, my eyes fixed onto Katie once again. The effect was instantaneous. Her beautiful dark skin, her flowing hair . . . everything about her drew me in. She was gorgeous, and she wanted me. I could almost feel her heart beat as I stared into her seductive eyes. The dark cloud began to fill the air again, making an already dark theater disappear into blackness. Once again, all I could see was Katie.

You are so close; just kiss her, something encouraged.

She spoke again, in a soft seductive whisper, "Micah, just kiss me." She grabbed a handful of my shirt and pulled me even closer. Too close.

It's not right! It's not right! Don't do it! something in me pleaded in violent, panicked protest. Instinctively, I pulled back a little again, but Katie did not let go of my shirt. She kept me very close to her, and half of me was glad that she did because half of me wanted to let Katie do whatever she wanted. It was like a tug-of-war match between two incredibly strong and equally matched opponents. Principles, morals, conviction, and love pulled me away from Katie, but raw burning desire pulled at me too, drawing me closer and closer toward her.[17]

I continued to stare, now nearer to her than ever before. She was so beautiful. Inches from my face, her warm fresh breath washed over me as she exhaled slowly. My heart pounded. I leaned in slowly, ready to give in. My last barriers were being torn down. I wasn't sure how long I would hold on. I involuntarily closed my eyes, resisting my urges . . . or giving in to them, I couldn't tell which. I couldn't think. I had no control. I didn't know where I was or what was going on. All I knew was that Katie was everything I wanted . . .

All I have to do is lean in a little, and . . . I thought, as I began to close the last few inches between us.

Micah, that which is born of the flesh is temporary, but that which is born of the Spirit is eternal![18] something screamed to my heart, halting me completely once again. I had no idea where the message had come from, nor still did I understand what it meant, but whatever had spoken to me now had my complete attention.

If you do not resist the flesh, much will be lost! something continued. I remained frozen, unable to move, unable to speak, just waiting for more . . . waiting for something to happen.

Rachel deserves better than this.

Where are the messages coming from? . . . My thoughts . . . or from somewhere else? I couldn't tell, but no matter the origin of the words, my heart was finally convicted beyond a point that I could ignore.[19] This was not the type of man I wanted to be. This was not how I wanted to treat Rachel, a wonderful girl whom I was crazy about. *Am I prepared to throw her away for temporary pleasure?*

Suddenly Rachel was all my mind was focused on. Not in an impure way, but in a good way.[20] Everything else began to clear. My desire to be faithful to her acted like a purifying agent, driving away the darkness; driving away the lust.[21] Just as before, like waking up from a deep sleep, my mind was suddenly my own again. Realizing my eyes were closed, I opened them, uncertain how long my awareness would last.

Katie's eyes, barely an inch from mine, were closed, as well. We were face to face, almost touching lips. Determined not to get sucked in again, I seized my momentary consciousness and did the only thing I could think of to ensure I wouldn't be enticed again . . . I fled.[22] I hurled myself backward, away from Katie, scaring her awake in the process.

THE SECOND TEMPTATION

Katie jumped back to her seat. I was relieved that she, too, wanted to put distance between us. We sat and looked at each other, not in lustful longing this time, but in horrified shock and confusion. She had come on to me, I couldn't believe it, and even worse, I had almost succumbed.

People were turned around in their seats, staring back at us, this time looking extremely annoyed. Our jolt back to reality had apparently been quite loud. I tried to look at the movie screen again and ignore their angry gazes, hoping that no one was about to get up and report us for interrupting the movie. Thankfully, everyone gradually turned their attention back toward the movie, satisfied that Katie and I were finished causing a scene. I wondered what exactly everyone else had seen. It was a small town, so gossip channels were notorious for spreading like wildfire. I just hoped no one had seen anything that might make its way back to Rachel and Brice.

Katie leaned back over to me, but with caution this time. "What happened?" she whispered in heartfelt bewilderment.

"I honestly don't know," I answered in equally honest confusion, ensuring my voice was low enough so as to not garner any further attention from our already perturbed fellow viewers.

Katie was blushing and looked extremely ashamed. "I had a strong urge to . . . " She broke off and covered her face.

"I did, too," I admitted with equal shame.

"I didn't mean to," she said, almost crying. "I really like Brice. I don't know what came over me."

"I know, I really like Rachel. I have all my life, actually . . . and Brice is my best friend. I would never do anything to hurt either of them," I whispered to her in shock. "It felt like something was urging me to . . ." I broke off. "For some reason it was way too easy to ignore all of the reasons why kissing you would be bad . . . like my mind was clouded," I frantically explained to her, suddenly realizing that this temptation would be different than the last one. This time I would have someone to believe me.

"I don't think it's our fault. We were in sort of a trance. We couldn't help it," I continued, trying to comfort her and secretly trying to convince myself. Deep down, though, I knew it was my fault. I knew I had allowed just a little thought about her attractiveness to suddenly become so much more. I had let it linger until it had nearly consumed me.[23] Had I stopped it immediately, I would have never sunk so deeply—but I was not ready to admit that.

As if she had read my mind, Katie confessed, "I had one little . . . ," she hesitated " . . . *thought* about you . . . and then I sort of blacked out," she admitted with horror on her face. "Well, I didn't black out, I knew what was happening, but it was like what you said, a dark cloud took over my mind—desire took over my mind," she continued. "It wasn't . . . normal. All of my usual reasons that would keep me from doing something . . . something so *stupid* were silenced. If you hadn't startled me when you pushed yourself back, I don't know what I would have done," she finished slowly in utter disbelief.

Vainly, I couldn't help but wonder what she had thought about me before she had given into her temptation, but I knew it was best to move completely away from the topic. Instead, I wanted to open up to her completely because, for once, I was not alone in my supernatural struggles. All thought of my nervousness around girls was now gone—this was too important. I was not sure how much time I would have before Rachel and Brice came back, but I knew I had to give the short version of everything that had been happening to me.

I quickly recounted the night of the bank incident and made sure to include feeling the same dark cloud that had swept over me and seemed to inhibit or at least dilute all sound judgment. I even went further and told her about the man and the golden ladder, and what I had witnessed in Shelby's room. After I finished, she was silent and was shocked, but amazingly I could tell she believed me.

"Something is happening," she said, looking down at the floor with a look of deep contemplation, as if searching for all the pieces of a puzzle as her eyes welled slightly with tears. "I've been having dreams," she whispered.

"What . . . what kind of dreams?" I asked, as excited intrigue filled my mind. At last, I wasn't alone. At last, I had someone else who knew firsthand that something strange was going on, and perhaps could even give me a few more pieces to my own puzzle!

"Well, I'm not sure; they feel sort of like the stories in the Bible," she began. "You know the stories that are for warnings or something, like something bad is going to happen."[24]

"You mean like a prophecy or something?" I asked.

"Yeah, I think so," she answered, slightly mystified. "I don't understand what it's all about, but it scares me, and it gives me the same weird feelings I had tonight, the same desires. It's as if a struggle is going on . . . inside of me," she said in a way that looked as if she was solving a mystery, but was scared of the conclusion.

"Well, tell me about the dreams. It could all be related," I encouraged.

"Umm . . . I don't know," she said, now looking worried. She was apparently embarrassed or ashamed of whatever she was holding back from me.

"Katie, I almost committed a felony, stealing from a bank. Whatever you've dreamt about surely can't be worse than that," I pleaded with her.

"I suppose not." She laughed slightly, looking reassured.

"Okay . . . well, I've had mainly the same dream over and over, with a little more revealed each time," she began. "They've been going on for a week now. It all starts with me sitting in the middle of a great body of water in this tiny wooden boat that is far too small to be in what I'm pretty sure is the ocean. Nothing happens at first; the waves are calm, and I'm just rowing aimlessly without any course or direction.[25]

"Then out of nowhere, I hear music calling from the horizon. It's a mysterious sound that makes me feel uneasy, yet, for some reason it also pulls me in . . . you know, the same way we were drawn together tonight," she continued. I could tell she was now engrossed in her story, and all shame was forgotten. Undoubtedly, she felt as I did, happy to be sharing a heavy burden with someone else. I was ready for my mysteries to be solved. I wanted answers, and I was more certain than ever that Katie's experiences were related to mine.

She continued, "I get the feeling I'll be happier if I follow the music, like all my fantasies will come true, but then in my heart, I feel a warning like I shouldn't go toward it. The music draws me in, though; I'm curious about it, so I paddle toward the horizon. With each stroke of the paddle, the warning in my heart grows stronger and the waves grow higher. My little boat begins rocking violently as the waves crash into it, threatening to overturn me.

"The music places me into a trance, pulling me ever closer. By the time the warning in my heart and the waves finally wake me, it's too late. I'm being pulled without paddling now. I'm being pulled closer and closer to the music. As I draw nearer, the music gets louder, and the waves rise higher still. Frantically, I try to paddle the other way, but the current is too strong. Then, without warning, a huge wave towers overhead and crashes on top of me, forcing me under the sea," she exclaimed, pausing to draw a desperate breath, as if she had really been capsized and was fighting to stay on the surface.

"I'm swimming for my life," she continued dramatically, "but now something is pulling me down. Cold hands clasp onto me and are dragging me down into the icy depths. Fighting doesn't help. It's something much stronger than I am. Then a strange deep voice speaks over the music.

"'*Join me my beautiful Katie; I have plans for you,*'" it says.

"Then the voice stops, but I continue to be drug toward the bottom. Though I'm terrified, and I should be fighting, I'm torn. For whatever reason, I begin to succumb to the thing dragging me down. It appeals to me. It has a strong hold on me . . . but it's more than a physical hold . . . mentally, or spiritually, it has me. I long for the depths, though I know I shouldn't. I can't help but wonder what plans the voice has for me.

"The music becomes louder than before. It sinks into my body. It appeals to me powerfully. It seduces me to a point where I don't want to fight at all. I'm lost and scared, but excited, and ready to give myself over to whatever it is that's pulling me down. Then, suddenly a voice from above encourages me to fight. It says something confusing, '*that which is born of the flesh is temporary, but that which is born of the Spirit is eternal!*'[26] My eyes grew wide in shock, but I held my tongue and let Katie continue.

"But I don't know if I *want* to fight. I don't know who to believe or who to follow. I look straight up to the top of the water and can still barely see light, and as I do so, there is a small splash and a ripple at the surface. Someone's arm penetrates the water. They are reaching for me," she said in a shocked whisper.

"That's the last part of my dream lately; that same situation, every night. I wake up, unsure which direction I should go. Should I follow the music and the voice, or fight it, and grab the arm that's waiting to pull me up? It's almost like the dream is waiting for me to decide,"[27] she finished, stunned at having vocalized her story for the first time.

I stared at her for a while, unsure what to say. Then finally I asked, "What direction do you want to go?" hoping she would not answer as I suspected.

"Honestly . . . I don't know. The way down seems easier, and I get a sense that I'll enjoy it more, if I follow. Going deeper is what I *want* to do. It's like grabbing a cookie from the cookie jar when you are a kid. Eventually you get tired of hearing 'no, don't go there, don't touch, and don't do this or that.' Sometimes, you just want to grab the cookie . . . to see how it tastes, you know?" she said with a look of excitement in her eyes as she seemed to search my face for agreement.

"The other way, though," she continued when I didn't respond. "Whatever is up, above the water, I get the feeling it wants to protect me from what is beneath. But it seems like I would have to fight to get to it. It seems harder and not as pleasing, as if it is not nearly as easy as just giving up and going down under the water; and honestly, in my dream, I don't desire what is above me nearly as much as I do what is beneath me," she said, searching my face again, seeming to see if I understood.[28]

This time I gave her a solemn nod because in that instance, I did understand. I did not agree with her excitement, but I understood. Recent events made me relate all too well to the dilemma of wanting things that were bad for me, things that were wrong. But Katie did not seem to get the answer she had hoped for from my expression.

"I do get a sense of guilt, though," she went on with a disappointed look on her face, clearly realizing I didn't think the depths of the ocean sounded as appealing as she did, "and a sense of danger when I turn away from the surface toward the voice in the deep. But the depths seem good in their own way. So, honestly, I don't know which way I want, and I always wake up before I choose," she stated with a look of complete confusion on her face.

It was so odd to have such a deep conversation with someone I had only met that week. But now I knew the real reason she didn't want to tell me her story in the first place. She was ashamed of the choice she secretly wanted to make. She knew it was wrong . . . but just like me and the money at the bank, she wanted it. The only difference was, no matter how tempting each situation was, I was afraid of whatever was coming after me . . . she didn't seem to be; not that much at least.

I responded almost immediately because I could not help but draw a connection.

"I think the voice down deep is the same voice that almost made us do what we almost did tonight . . . what we both knew we shouldn't do, no matter how badly we wanted to. I think it's also what almost made me take money from the bank. If I were you and this dream of yours comes true, I would fight with everything I had to swim for that arm at the surface," I said warningly.[29]

I was scared for her. The wild look in her eyes terrified me. She was far too curious about something that was quite obviously dangerous. I understood being caught up in the moment, but looking at my temptations from the outside, with a clear mind, they weren't nearly as tempting. However, even being removed from the temptation, Katie was still clearly being sucked in.

"I don't know," she said. "I guess it could all be related, but if something big is happening, I wouldn't mind seeing what it is," she said with a tone in her voice that matched the look in her eyes all too well.

Before I could give her another warning, I saw Brice and Rachel enter the theater. Katie gave me a slightly worried glance and then turned away from me for good. Rachel and Brice took their seats.

"Sorry it took so long. The line was really long," Rachel whispered with an apologetic smile as she handed me the popcorn to hold.

I knew I had probably said my last piece, but even with Rachel back and the movie playing, I could not help but worry about Katie. She was far too accepting of her dream. If I had dreamt that something was pulling me underwater, I would fight like crazy to get to the surface.

Or . . . at least I thought I would. I obviously wasn't as predictable as I used to consider myself. Almost stealing money from a bank had proven that; and *how had I come so close to being seduced into kissing Katie?* I could have ruined everything between Rachel and me before it had even begun, not to mention how much I would have hurt Brice by kissing his girlfriend and betraying his little sister. *Am I any better than Katie?*

No, I certainly wasn't better than her . . . but it really wasn't a question of who was "better," it was a question of recognizing danger. When I was not in a trance, when I was myself, I could clearly see that going down into the ocean, stealing money, and kissing Katie were all wrong. When I was myself, I could see the danger and turn away from it. Yet Katie was still so curious. Perhaps she wasn't completely herself. That worried me more than anything.

One thing was clear, though. Katie's temptations were quite obviously linked to what I was going through. The last thing I wanted to do at that moment was sit through a movie . . . especially a bad one. There was so much to find out, but my chance to talk with Katie was gone, and Brice and Rachel would probably not be too eager to discuss a topic that included Katie and me almost locking lips.

Frustrated at my inability to deal with something so extraordinary and so important, I leaned back in my seat in defeat and attempted to make myself watch the movie. However, some things are just too weird and too big to shake off.

Whatever was after me had blindsided me. I had never even considered Katie a temptation—but my attraction to her had been powerful. I thought my defenses had been fortified like a castle, only to have temptation glide through easily, like a cannon ball through a gaping window. I had been sucked in just as easily as before, and rendered nearly powerless.

I realized something, though. The second temptation had ended a little differently than the first. This time I hadn't just been startled awake. This time I had made more of a conscious decision to turn from my actions.[30] I might not have kept the temptation out altogether, but at least I had stopped it before it had gone too far . . . before it had passed a point of no return.

The point of no return, I thought again. My stomach started to feel sick and I began feeling very hot. It made me shudder to think of how close I had come to ruining my life . . . with both temptations. *Am I really that weak? Am I really so out of control that I couldn't be trusted around money in a bank, or around girls? Did I really have so little power over my desires?*[31] I wondered.

My body stiffened with anxiety as my heart began to pound and heat and stress continued to rise. Whatever was after me was indeed crafty.[32] *What is Rachel going to think?* I looked over at her as she watched the movie with a bored look on her beautiful face. I had to tell her. She had to know what was going on with me . . . and what I had almost done. I had no idea how I would tell her, and I had no idea how she might take it. But I had to let her know.

Perspiration had begun to percolate out of nearly every pore on my body and I was fidgeting in my seat. I was a nervous wreck. In fairness, who wouldn't be? I mean, I was on my first date with the woman of my dreams while also trying to fend off something that wanted me to hurt the people I cared about as well as get me thrown in jail. It wasn't even fair. I had never been great under pressure, but I felt justified in believing that even the coolest fighter pilot in the world would have been anxious under the enormity of what I was facing.

"I know you are nervous," Rachel's quiet voice suddenly whispered in my ear, "but you don't have to be. I wouldn't have come on this date if I didn't really like you." She must have noticed how stressed I was looking. I smiled at her, fairly certain that my face was red and sweaty, but she didn't seem to care.

Rachel then reached over and grabbed my hand, flashing a big, bashful smile as she did so—which to me was the most beautiful smile in the world—and instantly everything changed for me. With the knowledge that Rachel liked me, and her hand in mine, all of the supernatural stuff was pushed completely out of my mind, and life seemed suddenly good. It felt like a sign that my future might not be that bad after all; that even though I had difficult decisions and some unknown evil waiting for me, perhaps there was happiness on my horizon, as well.

There would be time in the next couple of days to seek

out answers, but right then I wanted to enjoy my time with Rachel. Looking back, I realize there was really never a need for me to look for answers at all. In the end, the answers would find me. In fact, they were already closer to me than I could have possibly known.

A defining moment was coming for me. A moment that would change the way I viewed everything, a moment that would rip apart my reality and forever alter my understanding of the world around me. But all I knew right then was that I had Rachel, and in that moment, she was more than enough.

CHAPTER FOUR

HIDDEN SIDE OF THE WORLD

The mystery has long been hid, its knowledge been concealed,[33]
But quickly, with a glimpse of light, now partially revealed.
Good words, they may be uttered; true paths, they may be shown,[34]
But once the trial's at your feet, you choose all on your own.
Therefore, let him who thinks he stands take heed lest he should fall.[35]
Examining his inner self, and harkening its call.[36]
For He who caused the light to shine hath shined it in our hearts.[37]
Revealing sin and secret things, once hidden in the dark.[38]
So, when there's light and when there's dark;
or broad and narrow roads,[39]
There's still a choice—no victims here—we reap that which we sow.[40]
A conqueror you're meant to be; the world to overcome,[41]
But to the one you yield yourself, their servant you become.[42]
So, sow the seeds of goodness, and prune the tares of death,[43]
Step out of darkness, into light, awake all ye who slept.[44]
The approaching days are evil, with danger and trials unknown,[45]
But be strong, fear not, comfort your soul, for you are not alone.[46]

* * * *

SATURDAY, MAY 25 THRU SUNDAY, MAY 26, 1985

In the end it was a good date. Really, a great date! I said some stupid things, like usual; I had almost been seduced by my best friend's girlfriend; and I was pretty sure there was an evil ghost or something out to get me; but all of that was trumped by my time with Rachel. She was simply amazing. Besides being painfully beautiful, she was the type of girl I could not help but respect. She was simply chock-full of character and integrity.

After the movie we all went out for pizza. We ate and talked for quite a while and when it was getting pretty late, I drove Brice, Katie, and Rachel back to their house. Just as I was getting really nervous, wondering if I was supposed to walk Rachel to the door—even though Brice and Katie were with us—Rachel made it easy for me by staying in the car when Brice and Katie got out. Mystery solved, I guess.

However, being left completely alone in the car with Rachel caused a new awkward nervousness to begin to creep over me. Not helping matters, Brice let out some wild hoots as he and Katie laughed their way up to his parents' house. That was just what I needed. With a subtle glance at myself in the rearview mirror I saw my cheeks had flushed redder than should be humanly possible. Gritting my teeth in embarrassment, I made a mental note that Brice deserved a little payback later.

My nerves aside, I really did want to be around Rachel more. I was hoping that the more time I spent with her, the more comfortable I would begin to feel. I glanced over at her in the passenger seat and could tell by her face she was thinking intently, almost as if she was building up the courage to say something. I waited patiently for her to speak, unsure what she wanted to discuss, but quite sure that whatever it was would only make me even more uncomfortable than I was already.

Secretly, I hoped I was not going to have to talk to Rachel about relationship stuff because my face was slowly returning to its natural color, and I was in no hurry to have it turn bright red again. Still, despite my fear of talking about mushy stuff and occasionally blushing crimson, I was very happy to finally be with her after all these years of waiting and hoping.

"Micah," she finally said feebly, turning her head to face me, "I wonder if . . . well . . ." She hesitated and then said, "Brice has been acting as our go-between for a long time, hasn't he?" She smiled.

"Yeah, I guess he has," I conceded with a smile of my own. "And he is a middle man that I wouldn't mind cutting out of the loop," I added with a chuckle, as I thought of his natural gift for humiliating me.

Rachel laughed, too. "I couldn't agree more." She paused as if still making up her mind how to approach whatever topic she was thinking of.

"Okay, then," she said, taking a deep breath. "Thanks to Brice," she said in a sarcastic tone, "you know that I've liked you for a long time . . ." She spoke very quickly, and then hesitated again. "And I know you've liked me for a long time, too," she said much more slowly. Now it was *her* face that was suddenly red, as her eyes drifted away from my direction.

Though I wasn't thrilled that she had begun our conversation with talking about the mushy stuff, I suppose it was worth it to get Brice out of the picture. However, my throat was suddenly dry, and I could feel the temperature rising again in my face. Unable to say anything, I gave a quick nod, coupled with a shrug of my shoulders, in response.

We each took a deep, involuntary exhale at the exact same moment, which caused us to lock eyes and laugh, as we realized that we were both extremely nervous.

"Well," she began again, "do you know why I've liked you for so long?" she asked, with her usually sweet eyes now bearing down on me. I began to stare at the dashboard of my car like a coward, pretending something on my steering wheel looked very interesting.

Unfortunately, her question forced me to speak this time. "I assume it's for the normal reasons someone likes someone else," I muttered lamely, as I continued to avoid her gaze.

"Well, yes," she said with a small laugh. "But also, no."

I had no idea what that meant, so silence was my only option.

"Well, why do you like me?" she asked expectantly. I braved another quick glance at her. She was still staring directly at me with her disarmingly beautiful blue eyes that pierced right through me, leaving me dazed. I turned away to regain my thoughts, in no hurry to answer her.

"Well?" she repeated gently. I looked back at her gorgeous face with my mouth hanging open like a sap, desperately searching for words and finding none. She left me speechless . . . breathless.

"Why do you like me?" she continued; smiling at my obvious demonstration of at least one reason I liked her. "Surely you like me for more reasons than what you think of my looks," she continued, encouraging me to fill in the blanks.

"'Course I do," I said roughly, trying to get my throat to work properly.

"Well then?" she encouraged gently, yet again. I was still feeling quite nervous, but Rachel had begun to seem more steady—more confident. It was as if she had finally locked on to the path she wanted the conversation to go and was holding on resolutely . . . no matter how poorly I was doing at answering her questions.

"Well," I stammered. I had hundreds of reasons I liked her, probably thousands, but my mind was blank. I turned my attention back to my steering wheel, hoping that if I looked away from her I might be able to think clearer.

"Micah, you are a tall, handsome guy; you could date other girls, but you don't. Brice has told me that you have always held out hopes for me . . . he said that I was the only one you were interested in," she said. "There are prettier girls than . . . ."

"No, there aren't," I said in sincere disagreement, unable to stop myself from interrupting.

"Thank you, Micah." She chuckled in patient amusement at my inability to grasp her point and answer her simple question. "But there are *other* pretty girls who would have dated you, but you didn't. Why were you waiting for me, Micah?" she asked, bluntly.

There was no getting around it, I would have to answer. I was going to have to talk about feelings, and mushy stuff, and all the things I hated to talk about. My face had undoubtedly returned to a fierce shade of crimson. The open windows did nothing to stop the heat from continuing to build in the car—or so it felt to me.

"Okay," I managed to begin. "There are lots of reasons I like you, but I guess the most important reason—the main reason—is the type of person you are. In all honesty, I think you are amazing." My gaze became directed even more intently at my steering wheel, in a desperate effort to concentrate on what I needed to say. "You're kind; you're good to everyone, even the people whom others are mean to. You respect yourself. You are just . . . good; I don't know how else to describe it. When I think of you, I think of . . . almost . . ." I struggled for words. "I guess I would say I think of you as the sort of symbol of what a woman should be."

I risked a quick glance at her, to see how I was doing. Mistake! She had tears leaking down her cheeks. *How am I supposed to deal with that?*

"Exactly," she said, as my eyes returned to their safe place on the steering wheel. "That's exactly what I think of you." She paused to take a sniff, which I mistook for another prompting to speak. I had nothing to say, and naturally when nothing comes to my mind, I say something stupid.

"You think I'm what a good and pure woman should be?" Yep, that's what I said. I was such an idiot—and woefully ill-equipped to talk with women. Thankfully, this woman was gracious.

She gave me a small, courteous giggle, "You know what I mean. I mean you are exactly what I think a guy should be. You are a good man. You are strong, but not boastful. You are humble; you aren't greedy—you've never been rich, but you've always been content," she said, causing a pang of guilt to hit my chest. She was right that I *had* always been content with not having much . . . until my recent run in at the bank. I pushed that out of my mind as she continued.

"You are kind to others, just like you said about me, and you aren't some womanizer like other guys. You could have had a lot of girls in high school, but you didn't go after them. Other guys in your position, they would have."

"I wasn't interested in other girls," I said, continuing to avoid looking at her, now pretending something outside of my driver side window looked interesting.

"You respect girls, and I think you really care for me," she said, with a certain amount of expectation in her voice.

"Pretty much," I replied awkwardly, unable to think of any other way to respond to her. A thought of what had happened earlier with Katie flashed through my mind, and guilt rose up in me again. I knew I was going to have to tell Rachel, especially since she was being so complimentary of my character. It was going to be difficult, but I had to do it.

"We've been around each other almost our entire lives, and I've seen what kind of man you are, Micah. You're a good man with a very big heart. That's what I like most about you. I just wanted you to know because I know you are nervous around me, but you don't have to be—because the real reason I like you is not how cool you are, or how witty, or even how attractive. While I do think you are handsome and there are plenty of other reasons to like you, it's the type of man you are that attracts me most . . . I just thought you should know," she finished.

If I thought I had nothing to say before, it was even worse now. My mind went completely blank. It was useless. Just as before I was speechless, but this time I couldn't even think of anything stupid to say. Once again, though, Rachel broke the silence.

"Unfortunately, I have more uncomfortable stuff to talk about," she said, timidly.

I wasn't sure what on Earth could be more

uncomfortable than what we had been discussing, so I was terrified as I waited for her to continue.

"I want to talk about some guidelines for our relationship," she said, looking even more embarrassed than before.

She immediately began laying out some moral parameters for our relationship, and though most guys probably would not have liked that, it was actually the sort of thing I really liked about her. She stuck to her principles and was not going to sway for anyone, including me. As she spoke, I began to feel a little guilty, realizing that I should have been the one to initiate this conversation.

After she said her piece, and I agreed to all of her "rules" with a simple "of course," she gave me the sweetest smile I had ever seen from her—and that is saying something. It was as if by agreeing to her rules, I confirmed her opinion of the type of guy I was—perhaps as close to the perfect guy as possible, in her mind. It was going to be quite difficult when I had to correct her false impression of me by telling her about Katie; but I knew it had to be done . . . at some point.

"Well, that is really all I wanted to talk about," she said to me in a sweet, yet excited tone. "I wanted us to get started right. Did you have anything you wanted to talk about?" she asked me, considerate as always.

"What, me? . . . No," I said as quickly as I could sputter out. With yet another sharp pang of guilt, I panicked, and decided not to bring up Katie. Mostly, I was simply ashamed of nearly kissing Katie, but I also did not want Rachel to think of me as a crazy person, like my parents had started believing. To properly explain what had happened with Katie, I was going to have to explain all the other stuff going on with me, too, and I was not ready to do that. The evening had been going so well, I shamefully did not have the courage to ruin it with the truth—especially if that truth made me seem both crazy and disloyal.

Besides, I was ready for the awkward conversation to be over. I loved the fact that Rachel cared about me, and I absolutely cared about her, but talking about it all just made me uncomfortable. I was looking forward to other conversations with her that were slightly less intense. I realized, though, Rachel was trying to start us off on the right foot, and I was already keeping something from her. That tore at my heart.

"Well, it's getting late, so would you mind walking me to the door?" Rachel asked, waking me from my guilty thoughts. I pushed the guilt aside and refocused on her.

"Not at all," I replied in a cheesy tone, once again relieved she had eliminated all question of what I was supposed to do by simply asking me to walk her to the door. She gave me another small, courteous laugh.

My door creaked open, and I stepped out into the peaceful, starry night. Rachel did not wait for me to open her door, but got out simultaneously. She walked to the sidewalk that led to her parents' front porch and waited for me to catch up. I hurried to her side and we climbed the front steps together.

Now was the real part of the date I had been worried about—the door—one of the scariest places on Earth for cowardly men like me. I was pretty sure Rachel did not kiss on the first date, and I had not been on enough dates to know what

I did.

Panic fluttered to my stomach. If one did not kiss on a first date, what was supposed to happen at the front door? A hug . . . like I would hug an aunt at a family reunion? Or shake hands, possibly? Sure, how nerdy and awkward would that be to shake hands with my date? Even Rachel, kind though she was, might laugh at me for that one. So, I did the only thing I could think of and followed her lead, as usual.

When she reached the door, she turned to me and had a confused look on her face. "What is it?" I asked, immediately feeling self-conscious.

She took a deep breath and seemed to once again be thinking through something that was weighing heavily on her mind. Finally she spoke, "Just remember, Micah, *that which is born of the flesh is temporary, but that which is born of the Spirit is eternal.*"[47]

I was stunned. My mind raced as I stood frozen, unable to respond. Before I could open my mouth to speak, she leaned in, kissed me on the cheek, and then swiftly opened their heavy green front door, went inside, and closed it behind her in a flash.

That was it. She was gone, and I was left standing alone on the porch, kept company only by my thoughts, which were suddenly zooming in every direction. It's probably a good thing Rachel had hurried inside so quickly because the dumbfounded expression on my face wouldn't have been attractive and was certainly not indicative of the glad look of a person who had just received a kiss—but I couldn't help it, I was completely and utterly confused.

Our parting at the door had been so abrupt. Why had she left so quickly—before I could ask her what she meant? *"Just remember that which is born of the flesh is temporary, but that which is born of the Spirit is eternal."*[48] What a random thing to say to me even under normal circumstances—but my circumstances were not normal, and Rachel was not the first one to say that to me.

Does she know that? I wondered. *Does she know about the weird things happening to me? Has she guessed it? Has she sensed it? If not, then why in the world did she say that to me? Where had it come from?* I wanted to ask her what she meant; I wanted to ask her what she knew; but she was gone.

Defeated and alone, I turned and began a slow walk down the porch steps onto the Jacobs' driveway, and opened my door to the same creak as always. I slid into the driver's seat, slammed my door shut, and just sat there, in shock.

Don't get me wrong, I was ecstatic about the kiss on the cheek and my new "relationship" with Rachel. As great as all of that was, though, it was pushed far to the back of my mind. The supernatural had once again forced its way back to the center stage of my thoughts. How many weird things could happen in one week . . . or one day for that matter?

It couldn't all be a coincidence. The events had to be linked to something bigger; but what? The man on the golden ladder . . . the bank . . . the voice in Shelby's room . . . almost kissing Katie . . . Katie's dream, and the phrase everyone kept saying. *"That which is born of the flesh is temporary, but that which is born of the Spirit is eternal,"*[49] I said to myself out loud. Why in the world did people keep saying that? What did it all mean? What was causing it?

CHAPTER FOUR

Unable to answer my own questions, I decided it was time to quit sitting in the Jacobs' driveway. Before long, they would undoubtedly look out their window and wonder why I had not left. Sliding my car into reverse, I backed out of their driveway, and then threw it into drive, beginning my way home in a reverie, too deep in thought to focus on the suddenly dark and starless night around me.

I wove in and out of the back streets without thinking about the familiar route, completely in my own world. Finally arriving at the long road that led to Main Street, I prepared to turn. As I did so, a silent flash of light flared far off in the distance over my left shoulder. Subconsciously, I slowed my car to a halt, unsure what to think. My eyes peered out into the distance to where the light had been, but whatever I had seen was gone.

It had been nearly a week since the first random light had caught my attention and sent me gallivanting mindlessly into an unlocked bank. After everything I had experienced since then, I probably should have been terrified that this light meant danger, but deep down I was honestly just ready to face whatever was after me. I was tired of constantly worrying about when the next evil influence was going to creep up and try to ruin my life. I wanted it over with.

I continued to stare to my left, out of my driver side window, hoping to see something, but nothing else happened. The night continued to darken, causing the first bit of fear to rise up in me a little, as I felt certain that the darkening was unnatural. Finally with a mixture of disappointment and relief, I slowly took my foot off the brake to drive forward again, deciding I must have just imagined the light.

Just as my wheels began to roll on the pavement, a great **CRACK** echoed through the sky as thunderous lightning erupted in the air off in the distance. Suddenly blinding light illuminated the black night, pouring over the tree tops and bursting out with an overpowering and electrically charged series of powerful strikes—as if it was intent upon clearing away the darkness.

Though I was a good distance from the storm of light, my car suddenly began to shake violently as gale-force wind seared through my open windows. Instinctively, I ducked low in my seat, feeling like a bomb had just exploded and I was feeling the aftershock. Unnatural heat coursed through the air filling my car; and then there was nothing.

The light was gone again. The peaceful, star-filled night had returned to normal as if nothing had happened. Like a beacon that had shown in my direction and then revolved to a different direction, the storm of light had been there, and then was instantly gone. The afterimage from having looked directly into the bright light still darkened a portion of my eyes, providing the only evidence that I had not imagined it all.

Common sense would have made me keep driving, but curiosity urged me to investigate. My heart pounded. Just like when I had entered the bank by myself, I knew searching for the source of the light would be asking for trouble. However, this time, no weird desire motivated me. I quickly counted to ten, assuring myself I still had possession of my own faculties.

I seemed to. My head was clear, and I wasn't dwelling on a particular temptation or desire. This time seemed different.

CHAPTER FOUR

My only motivation was the hunger for answers that burned in the pit of my stomach. If the light had something to do with what was going on with me—and it almost certainly did—then I had to confront it head-on.

I hesitated, breathing deeply and wondering if I should just drive on. My car's humming engine provided the only sound in the otherwise still and silent neighborhood. Everyone was asleep in their quaint little houses that lined the small country streets. The stars sparkled. Both the unnatural darkness and light had dissipated, leaving a completely normal, and even beautiful, night.

Still, the danger was apparent. With everything that had happened in the past week, investigating went against better judgment. For a twenty-year-old, though, impulse and curiosity seemed far more enticing than caution and restraint.

I knew I was probably making the wrong decision, but I made up my mind; danger or not, I had to know. If something was going to keep coming after me anyway, I had to at least try to find out what it was and why it wanted me. I did a U-turn on the road, which was not an easy feat with the big rust bucket, boat of a car that I had. It was better at drinking gas and oil than making sharp turns.

Thankfully no one in this small town would care if I caused minimal damage to the grass in their yard. Grass isn't quite as important in the country as it is in the city. I swerved off the road a little, into a yard or two, and after a few maneuvers backward and forward, managed to head my car in the right direction.

I steered toward where I had seen the light, but it was

still nowhere to be found. After a few seconds of driving I slowed to a halt where I thought the light had originated. I parked on the side of the street, beside a row of dark houses, and waited for the light to return. For someone who had spent so much of the day being extremely paranoid, I felt suddenly fearless.

An eager exhilaration stole through my body. Was I walking into a trap? Perhaps, but it felt good to be doing something proactive. I was on the offensive. No more waiting! It was time to go straight for whatever was attacking me.

However, after twenty seconds had passed without anything happening, I began to doubt myself again. Glancing around at the dark and silent houses on either side of the street, I began to feel a little scared, too. *Perhaps I should just go home*, I thought as fear and doubt escalated. I couldn't tell if my eyes were just playing tricks or not, but as I looked between two houses something seemed to be moving in the darkness. *Yeah, just like at the bank, I should definitely just go home*, I thought, finally deciding to obey my inner warning. I reached down to put the car in drive and looked up one last time . . .

—CRACK—

"Ahhh!!!" I screamed, as blinding light suddenly filled the night sky all around me. My eyes hammered shut as the dazzling light from the storm returned in a fury. Powerful electricity crackled dangerously, encircling me completely. Lightning struck, thunder rumbled, and power disturbed the air. My hands clenched down on my steering wheel as bright light kept my prying eyes ever at bay and heat-filled wind blistered through my car. My car slid on the pavement under the force of the wind. I had driven directly into the storm of light and it was going to destroy me.

Heat bore down on me. My skin felt as if it were too close to the summer sun . . . and then suddenly a strange feeling crept over me. It was something I couldn't quite describe, something very out of place.

But I had no time to focus on feelings. I was alone and defenseless against a supernatural cyclone of light and heat. Panic began to fill me. *What am I going to do?* There was no way out. I couldn't see, so driving away was out of the question. Besides, I wasn't sure if it was safe to move. Everything I heard and felt made me believe that the barrier of lightning that surrounded my car could fry me in an instant.

A pulse of intense heat hit me, and an unusual feeling permeated my body for a second time. *What in the world am I feeling?* It felt so conflicting with such a serious moment; a moment so deadly. Nevertheless, mixed in with my fear and adrenaline was another feeling that didn't quite belong; so much so, that I couldn't quite tell what it was.

Again, there was no time to think. The force of the wind increased. Lightning struck more and more, jolting my car with each blow. Thunder, powerful enough to be an earthquake, shook my car mercilessly.

What is going on around me? I thought in fear. I had to try to see! But my eyes would not open on their own. My eyelids were locked together, protecting my eyes from the brilliant light. I had to see, though! With a great effort I pulled at my brow and cheeks, finally forcing my eyelids to crack open, just a sliver.

What was that?

My eyes slammed shut immediately against the blinding light, but before they did, I had seen something . . . something extraordinary. Excitement filled me . . . I had to try to see it again.

Feeling as if I were staring directly into the sun, I began to struggle to open my eyes to get a second glance, but then, suddenly everything was gone once again. Just as quickly as the powerful torrent of blinding light had come, it was replaced by silence and darkness. I was not going to get a second look, but I knew . . . this time, I had seen it! At last I had seen the source of the light—and what I saw was more unbelievable than anything I had ever experienced.

In stunned silence I sat there, as all the pieces of the puzzle began to fit themselves together. It was what I should have expected from the moment I had seen the mysterious man descend from the sky on his golden, glowing ladder. But now I was certain. All fear was extinguished as I replayed the image in my mind several times. *Surely not . . . surely it could not have been . . . could it?* I suppose I had always believed, so it shouldn't have been such a surprise . . . but to actually see one? I felt crazier than ever, but there was no mistaking what I had seen.

I had only caught a glimpse of the extremely large being, wearing white and blanketed in light, but the image hung in my mind as if it had been nailed there. And what was more, I finally understood the sensation that had accompanied the heat from the storm. The light had not only expelled great amounts of heat, but it had also generated an undeniable sense of purity and goodness.

Just as human emotions can be seen through a person's facial expressions, I had *felt* the goodness radiating from this powerful being. It was this, above anything, that made me believe what I had seen was no ordinary man; I had seen an angel!

However, with the afterimage already lessening in my eyes and the feeling of goodness gone, worry began to creep over me. *What if something more sinister was simply playing a trick on my eyes, hoping to lure me in? Surely something evil couldn't have made me feel such goodness*—I hoped.

I stared into the yard where the angelic figure had appeared, as I contemplated my next move. Fear welled up inside me even more as I realized the angel had appeared in the yard of an abandoned house. *Why did it have to be an abandoned house?* I sat there, trying to decide exactly how brave I felt.

My dad's occupation as a preacher naturally kept me informed of the deaths in the town, even while I had been away for college. He morbidly calls a preacher's secondary job "marryin' and buryin'," referring jokingly, of course, to weddings and funerals.

As such, I knew this particular house had been occupied just months before, but the owner had recently passed away. Mr. Weber had been a kind old man who had attended our church. Had he been alive and living there, the house would have been extremely welcoming.

But now, approaching the abandoned house at night, after having just spotted something that was hopefully an angel, but quite possibly something evil posing as an angel, made the old house more uninviting than a graveyard filled with hungry guard dogs.

Am I about to walk into another trap? I did not feel the dark cloud at all, and I was watching for it. Its presence would have made me give in to my fear and drive out of there immediately! But the ominous dark cloud was nowhere to be found and my mind was as clear as ever. My heart pounded as I stared at the house, trying to decide which was more powerful at that moment, my fear or my curiosity.

Finally, curiosity overruled my fear. I *had* to take a closer look. I turned off my car, took a deep breath, and then grabbed the handle of my car door to pull it open. The moment the usual creak from my car echoed into the air, my door flew open on its own with a **WHOOSH**, as if pulled by a powerful magnet. As I looked up, intense light flooded into my car, illuminating every inch of it.

My eyes slammed shut once again as the same radiating brightness swam over me, filling every sinew of my body with a sense of goodness, purity, and power. It was awesome . . . but also terrifying. The air reverberated with a mighty humming noise. It was as if a switch had been thrown, and pure electricity now crackled through my car like a power conduit.

"Micah," roared a deep and magnificent voice over the electric hum, shaking my car with its force. "*You* have been chosen!"

In fear, I ducked low again. I tried to open my eyes, but they only opened a sliver before they hammered shut again, now watering from the bright light that held them irresistibly shut. Even with my eyes closed, bright redness from the hot, powerful light shone through my eyelids.

"Let me see you!" I screamed, in fear, adrenaline, and frustration.

"Not yet, Micah," boomed the voice. "It is not yet time for you to see me. But I have come to warn you. Every minute of every day, there is a war raging for your soul, and the time for you to decide is running out. The third temptation approaches and if you fail, then you and many others will pay a great price. *You must be born of the Spirit, for that which is born of the flesh is temporary, but that which is born of the Spirit is eternal.*"[50]

Then, like a giant vacuum, a second whooshing sound overpowered all other noise, and instantly the light and the noise were once again gone. My eyelids darkened in the absence of the light, and a breeze of cool air blew lightly over my face. I decided to risk opening my eyes again, but they felt as if they had been glued together, as if the light had caused them to melt slightly.[51]

I tried to force my eyes open with my fingers, but before I could open them, a new humming sound made its way to my ears, but it seemed different than before . . . more familiar. Finally my eyelids unglued and I was able to see again.

"Ahhh!!!" I screamed for the second time that night, as I grabbed the wheel of my car to keep it on the road!

I was driving! My car was moving! I slammed on the brakes in panic, screeching to a halt in the middle of the road. *Where was I?* I looked around to get my bearing. In shock, I realized I was a long way from where I had pulled over by Mr. Weber's house to investigate the light. I was at the stop sign just before Main Street. *How is that possible?* Mr. Weber's house was several blocks away from Main Street. *How did I get here?* It was as if I had never stopped to investigate the light, almost as if I had continued driving the entire time.

I put my car in park. I was blocking the entire road, but even if it had been the busiest time of the day, I would not have cared. I was nearly frantic. *Has any of it been real? Did I just imagine everything? Perhaps I really am losing my mind*, I thought worriedly. No! I knew what I had seen, what I had experienced.

Frustration and confusion coursed through me, but I didn't have any more time to organize my thoughts, because suddenly another light flashed in my eyes, this time in my rearview mirror. My eyes went wide with disbelief and I turned around so quickly my neck tweaked slightly.

Rubbing my neck in pain, I looked at the light behind me expecting to be blinded again, but the light was bearable this time. Its steady and constant beam drew ever closer to me. I stared at the unwavering light, squinting to determine its source, ready for what was sure to be my next encounter with the supernatural. My heart pounded in my chest as I noticed there was not just one light . . . there were two, and they were heading straight for me.

– HONK –

I jumped with a start, my hands flailing in the air in fear. *What on earth could make that kind of noise?*

I looked back at the two lights again . . . *what in the world was it and why wasn't it accompanied by anything crazy this time?* There was no wind, no thunder, and no heat. And then, reality finally caught up with me. These lights were not angelic at all; they were in fact quite *earthly*. They were headlights belonging to a vehicle whose driver was impatiently waiting to get past my boat of a car that was blocking the entire road.

I laughed in relief as the driver of the car honked at me again in annoyance, urging me to move out of the way. It might have been rude, but I was in no hurry to move my car. I relaxed in my seat, feeling very glad that there was another human being around—no matter how displeased they were with me at that moment.

The car finally gave up on waiting for me to pull forward as I continued to sit still, blocking the road. They pulled onto the shoulder and then stopped beside me. To my surprise, it was Sheriff Sentry in his police jeep. I sat up in my seat, now a little worried about what he might say to me for blocking the street this late at night. However, his presence still made me feel safer.

"Micah?" he said, with surprise and confusion in his eyes, "are you all right?"

"Yes, sir," I replied, clearing my throat as I spoke.

"Well, is there a reason you are just sitting here at the stop sign, blocking the entire road, so late at night?" he asked, this time with a mixture of amusement and chastisement.

"Um . . . I'm just clearing my head, sir," I answered, unsure what else to say.

"Why don't you get on home my boy, and clear your head on your pillow," he stated in a caring, yet stern, fatherly fashion. For a brief moment I almost asked him if he had seen the light, but I decided not to. If he had seen it, surely he would have said something—or at least he might have been acting differently. But he was as steady and normal as ever. No, like usual I was all alone in seeing the weird stuff.

"Yes, sir," I finally replied as he began to drive forward. "Good night."

"Good night," he called back with a smile and a small laugh at my odd behavior.

When he had gone, I pulled onto Main Street and headed to my parents' house. Thankfully, no further abnormal encounters occurred. I parked my car in my parents' driveway in front of their shabby, square, two-story house with its little white fence, which looked especially welcoming. After all my run-ins with the abnormal, the familiar sight and safety of my home called out to me like a lighthouse on the shore of a storm-tossed sea. It was my safe haven. Its doors promised normalness and rest for my weary mind. As I ran up the plain concrete porch steps and stepped through the front door, my thoughts longed for the prospect of a good night's sleep—which had never seemed more appealing.

"How did it go?" my mom's voice suddenly asked out of nowhere. Then I spotted her rushing out of the living room and into the entryway, intent upon intercepting me before I could slip upstairs. I should have known. With everything else that had happened, my date was far from my mind, but it wasn't for my parents. Even if I hadn't left the house on speaking terms with them, I should have realized that me dating Rachel was just too big of a deal for them to go to bed without first seeing if it had gone well. Excitement stared back at me from my mom's face.

"It was good," I replied without offering any details, as I began to remove my shoes and avoid her penetrating look as purposefully as I had avoided Rachel's. The truth is, if I could have taken away all of the weird supernatural stuff, then I would have been ecstatic at having progressed into a relationship with Rachel. It was like a dream come true. As excited as I was about Rachel, though, something like a date seemed pretty trivial after having just seen an angel and having been warned about a third trial that would spell doom for me and the people I cared about if I failed.

"Oh, come on," she pleaded, determined to squeeze my already tired mind for as many priceless details as she could. "Tell me more than that," she said, now jumping up and down, not even attempting to hide her eagerness.

Unable to resist my mom's begging, an involuntary smile broke across my face, and my mom knew she had won. My dad, who did not usually get into these types of things, had strangely made his way to the entryway just a few seconds after my mom and was listening intently, too. I suppose he felt his son dating the daughter of a church member was something he ought to know about, no matter how uncomfortable it made him.

"Mom, you know me; I'm a coward with girls," I finally began. "Rachel led the conversation, she had to make the moves, she grabbed my hand during the . . . " I wasn't finished with my sentence, but I had to pause to laugh and roll my eyes at my mom's excited, "Ooooh!" Hand holding was exactly the sort of information she was craving.

"At the end of the night, we had a good talk about limits in a relationship and about respecting each other and things like that," I finished.

"That's my boy," my dad interjected. I knew he would

like that part. Immediately after he spoke, his eyes seemed to disengage from the conversation—as if he'd heard all he needed to and was ready to go back to the living room.

I gave them a few more tidbits even though it was a pretty normal date. Well, the date itself had been normal at least, and I was not about to go into the other part of the night with them. Since they had not believed me about the incident in Shelby's room, they were not likely to believe that I had seen an angel, and they certainly would not think there was a good reason for me to have almost kissed Katie.

When they were finally satisfied, I hurried up to my room, ready to lay my head down on my pillow and fall into a deep sleep. I did not really want to think about the day. There is only so much the human brain can process and I felt mine had reached its max. I was simply overloaded and didn't think staying up into the hours of the night worrying was going to help me any.[52] I undressed as quickly as I could, threw on some basketball shorts, hit the lights, jumped into bed, and was asleep before anything else out of the ordinary could happen.

If there was ever a time when I appreciated a dreamless sleep, it was that night. Based on the events that had been happening, I can only imagine how bizarre my dreams could have been. But I awoke the next morning feeling extremely refreshed, content to just lie on my pillow for a while, and oddly at ease with the unknown threats I was up against.

My confidence grew as I lay there, contemplating the enigmatic warning everyone kept giving me.[53] I didn't really know what they meant with all the talk of *flesh* and *spirit* and what not, but I hoped that their warning was a sign that I could pass the third, and hopefully final, temptation. I had made it through the temptations at the bank and with Katie all right. Why wouldn't I make it through whatever else was coming? One thing I knew for certain, succeed or fail, I was ready for the tests to be over and for life to return to normal. The past week had been like sailing through a hurricane, but I was beginning to feel as if I was almost through the storm.

Looking back, I still find it incredible how naïve and casual I was during this part in my journey, the time before the true battle had even begun. I had no way of knowing that what I was destined to go through would change my life forever. I still did not realize what was at stake; I didn't realize that people's lives depended on me . . . that even my own life hung in the balance. Even more, I didn't realize that if I passed the final test, I would never see the world the same way again.

My naiveté was only partially responsible for my bolstered confidence; what had put me the most at ease was that I was now all but certain an angel was watching over me. It was one thing to approach a battle feeling alone and tempted, to have a dark cloud looming over my mind, constantly frightened of being lured into danger, and distrusting my own ability to resist the temptation of various sins.

But it was an entirely other feeling, an amazing encouragement to me, knowing that while I was about to face darkness, an angel was with me.[54] Up until I had seen the angel, I had felt alone, like the target of something I could not see or understand, and certainly could not hope to defeat on my own. But now I knew I wasn't facing the battle alone, there were quite possibly some pretty powerful good guys who had my back, and that made all the difference in the world.

What a weird week it had been. I had just been a kid at a basketball game, struggling with normal problems like college and money, when the hidden side of the world had suddenly decided to reveal itself to me. Most people go their entire lives unsure about the spiritual world, wondering what is really out there, but for whatever reason, it had shown itself to me . . . and the encounter had nearly been disastrous. Stealing money, kissing a random girl, dating Rachel, being struck blind, seeing an angel, and the ever mysterious warning *that which is born of the flesh is temporary, but that which is born of the Spirit is eternal,*[55] these were the unexpected circumstances I had been presented with that week.

What is going to present itself to me next? If I really had been chosen for something, then *what would I be expected to do? What possible good could I do?* And most importantly, *where can I go to find answers to questions like these?*

Suddenly one man's name entered my mind and caused me to sit bolt upright in my bed—Sheriff Sentry!

"He was there last night. I should have just asked him," I said aloud to my empty room, my eyes now wide with excitement. Even if he didn't see the angel, Sheriff Sentry had believed me—unlike my parents. And he had been the very first one to give me the warning about the flesh and the spirit.[56]

Is he just that wise, or could it be possible he is experiencing something strange, too, like Katie and I are? I thought excitedly. Resolution formed in my mind as my next move finally became apparent. It was time to see Sheriff Sentry again, to find out what else he knew.

CHAPTER FIVE

<u>FLESH AND SPIRIT</u>

If only all days were filled with this bliss,
Then our hero's story would be one you could miss.
However, it seems that this story's worth telling,
To show that a soul is just not worth selling.
The battle is real and so is its prize,
It's seen with the heart and not with the eyes.[57]
For the thief, when he comes, will kill, steal, and destroy,[58]
And an unprepared heart will fall prey to his ploy.
Temptation awaits; the whole world, its offer,
But death and destruction will be its true proffer.[59]
So, love not the world, for it shall not last,[60]
Lust of flesh, lust of eyes, and pride of life will all pass.[61]
For just as the grass always withers away,
And the more beautiful flower can be gone in a day,[62]
This world will vanish, like a vapor of smoke,[63]
And when death comes for men, in what will they hope?[64]
It won't be in treasure, in fame, or in power,
So turn from the flesh and resist the dark hour.[65]
Hear the good news that knocks at the heart,[66]
And choose, because soon, the true battle will start.
For the silence will break, and the storm will come back,
And the calm of the air will have just been a trap.

*   *   *   *

SUNDAY, MAY 26, 1985

I jumped out of bed in a flurry, desperate to speak with Sheriff Sentry. I was not even sure what I would say, but that didn't matter. He was the one man who might have some answers! I threw on jeans and a T-shirt and slipped on some socks and shoes and bolted out of my room. As I sped downstairs, the smell of cooking bacon met my nose, but I was in too big of a hurry for breakfast.

As I flew through the house, I heard my mom rummaging in the kitchen, and saw my dad sitting at the table doing his usual reading of the newspaper while watching the news on the living room TV from afar. But there was no time to tell them what I was up to; my answers couldn't wait! I rushed out of the front door without speaking a word to either of them.

I broke into a fast paced jog through my parents' neighborhood. It was still very early, so none of our neighbors were out yet. I had jogged halfway to Main Street before a realization stopped me dead in my tracks. It was Sunday. I was not going to be able to speak with Sheriff Sentry at work. He didn't go in to the police station on Sundays.

Disappointment stole through me as my desperate search for answers hit an apparent roadblock. I would have to wait until I saw Sheriff Sentry at church later that morning. With no other option, I turned in defeat and began a slow walk back toward my house.

I was frustrated. Like a kid ready to open a Christmas present, only to find an empty box. I was glad I would be able to speak to Sheriff Sentry that day at least, but the thought of waiting an hour or two until church made my answers seem an eternity away. It would be even worse if I couldn't catch him before the service. If I had to wait through an entire sermon before I could ask him anything, I thought my head might explode.

I made my way grudgingly back to my house, through

the white gate, up the concrete steps, and inside the front door, returning to the smell of bacon and eggs. At least there would be time for breakfast now, I attempted to comfort myself. I walked into the kitchen a little sweaty from my jog, and joined my family at the table.

"What on Earth was that about, Micah?" my father immediately sprung on me, glaring over his glasses in disapproving inquisition. The look on his face immediately put me on the defensive. I had enough to deal with; I didn't need *him* to add to my frustration.

"You nearly gave me a heart attack!" he continued, before I could respond.

"Yes dear," my mom cut in far more gently, "what made you rush out of the door without telling us where you were going? You've been acting very strange lately," she added in concern.

Even if they had not believed me before, they were still bound to recall all the odd things I had claimed were happening, making my rush out of the house appear all the more abnormal to them. Unfortunately, my frustration was incited even more as I recalled their previous disbelief.

"Well, if you must know," I said, in an indignant tone, "I was going to speak with Sheriff Sentry again. Things have been happening lately, and I thought he could help shed some light on them." The look of concern was now firmly plastered on my mother's face. She clearly thought I was losing my mind.

"Micah, does this have something to do with that prank you pulled on your sister yesterday?" my father asked in a bored manner, his eyes now roaming back over his paper.

It was infuriating to think that the biggest thing that had ever happened to me was going on right then, and my father thought it was no more than a prank. I tried to keep my calm, but my voice shook as I spoke. "Just so you know, I did *not* pull a prank. I would think my parents would believe me, since I have never given you a reason to distrust me. However, since you're determined not to believe what I say anyway, I'll just keep my thoughts to myself, thanks. Besides, I don't see any reason why you all should object to me asking the sheriff some questions if it will appease my mind," I finished, quite reasonably considering how angry I felt.

My father looked very unconvinced, but indifferent. My mother, however, looked at me with the continued expression of worry that let me know she not only didn't believe me, but she definitely doubted my sanity.

"He is a busy man," my mother said, "but no, there shouldn't be any harm in asking him some questions. Just try and stick to . . . believable questions; no crazy tales."

Crazy tales, I thought. That's what they thought of their son! "Yes, ma'am!" I responded shortly to my mom, my anger now barely controllable. I got up before they had a chance to respond and stormed upstairs to my room, not having eaten any breakfast. It is funny how anger can dull the appetite. I knew my story sounded crazy, but I had always assumed my parents would just believe me no matter how absurd my stories sounded.

Flying into my room and slamming the door, I ripped open my dresser and got out some fresh clothes. I hurried to the shower, determined to isolate myself from my family. Not only were they frustrating me, but I also wanted to sort through my thoughts. My mind had been filled with confusion the entire week, but it was now just one huge mosaic of angry thoughts. Irritation flooded through my veins. A deep burning sensation filled my chest as my worry and confusion were replaced by sheer anger. I felt as if my blood was on the verge of boiling.

Even in the solitude of a nice hot shower, my frustration was making it impossible to concentrate on the actual problems at hand. The puzzle I had been trying to put together all morning was now shooting around in my head like millions of pinballs, impossible to grab hold of. Only one thing was clear to me: I still knew what my next step was. I desperately needed to speak with Sheriff Sentry—at least he believed me.

After a long while, the shower began to run low on hot water, so I decided to get out and finish getting ready. As I dressed, I could hear my family downstairs, opening the front door to leave for church—apparently without me. Ordinarily that would not have been a big deal, since I drove—and even walked—the few short blocks to church by myself all the time. However, right then it felt like a personal insult.

I threw my pants on in even more anger. *How could they not believe me?* I thought angrily. *And now are treating me like they do not even want me to ride to church with them . . . not that I wanted to anyway!* I sat on my bed, my head in my hands pulling at my hair, ready to scream, ready to explode. The confusion, the worry, and now the anger; it was all too much!

Just as I thought I could not take a second more, I heard a knock at my door. I looked up in surprise as my mom peeked her head into my room. I did not want to have a conversation with her at the moment. I looked back down at the floor with my head in my hands again.

"Micah," she said timidly, "we left some food out on the table for you. We are going to head on to church. See you there," she finished with obvious sorrow in her voice. She was too kind hearted to continue fighting with me. Even if she did not believe me, I knew it killed her to have a rift between us.

She hesitated, waiting for me to say something. I kept silent, knowing my anger was too ready to lash out, and as mad as I was, I did not want to lash out at my mom. After a moment, she turned and left without saying another word.

A few minutes went by before I got up to finish getting dressed and then headed downstairs ready to grab a quick snack from the kitchen. I had been expecting the house to be empty, so I was startled when I reached the bottom of the stairs to find that my mom and dad were standing there together, waiting for me.

My mom spoke first. "Micah, I have a strange feeling you are serious," she said to me with a sincere look on her face as she grabbed my hand. "You've never lied to us before," she continued. "Even though your story sounds absurd, I should have believed that you weren't lying," she finished, her words finally faithful.

My father stood speechless for a moment, looking directly at me, seeming to make up his mind about something. Finally he spoke. "Micah, I'm overwhelmed with a feeling that something really big is happening to you. Forgive me for not believing you, Son. I *am* sorry, and you have my full support now. I don't know why, but I think talking to Sheriff Sentry is a good idea," he finished, his facial expression appearing just as confused as I felt.

My mom leaned forward and pulled me down to her height to kiss me on the cheek as my dad squeezed my arm. Then, they turned to head out of the door, but just before it closed, my dad stopped to look back at me and said, "We love you, Son, and we believe you now; just be careful and . . ." he paused, " . . . remember, *that which is born of the flesh is temporary, but that which is born of the Spirit is eternal.*"[67]

That was all he said. Then they closed the door and went to join Shelby, who was waiting for them in the car. I was dumbfounded, shocked, speechless, and completely disarmed. It was almost comical. It was as if two spirits were roaming around our town. One went around tempting me to do bad things, and the other went around getting people to tell me "the flesh is temporary and the spirit is eternal." I didn't even really know what that meant, let alone why everyone felt so compelled to say it to me.

It was bizarre. I no longer had any clue what was really going on, but at least my frustration and hurt was gone. I was still confused and curious, but now my curiosity took a more patient tone. With my parents finally on my side, and their "feeling" that Sheriff Sentry would be a beneficial next step, the day seemed a little brighter.

I grabbed a quick bite to eat and then headed out the door. It was extremely beautiful outside already. It was early enough the dew was still blanketing the lawns as I started my way toward the church. The sun was shining bright, the sky was a dazzling blue, and the summer morning air was crisp and refreshing. In every direction, the rich green of grass and trees highlighted the horizon. The Midwestern humidity was only a few hours away, but right then, the weather was picture perfect, a great day for a walk.

The little town was already bustling. Families were getting into their cars to head to one of the many churches in the small town, others were doing chores in their yard, and like in any small town, I was frequently stopped by people who had not seen me since winter break and simply wanted to chat. By the time I finally reached the church's street, I only had a few minutes to spare. The walk had not provided any new conclusions or epiphanies, but it had done a good job of clearing my head and making the day feel new.

Walking down the last small stretch, our church finally came into view. It was actually a decent sized building considering the small size of the town. It stood high with a steeple of brass, and was elegantly decorated with beautiful antique stained glass windows on all sides. The white outer walls, painted by my father and me in summers past, gave the church a majestic, yet reverent and welcoming feel. I started up the front steps to the church when behind me I heard the deep friendly voice of just the man I wanted to see.

"Hello, Micah. How are you?" said Sheriff Sentry, standing alone at the bottom of the steps behind me. He wasn't married, and I had never heard him mention any family, so he always came to church by himself.

"I'm doing great," I responded with enthusiasm at seeing him. "I actually wanted to speak with you, sir."

"I thought you might," he responded in an oddly

omniscient manner. "Why don't we talk after church?"

"Yes, sir, that sounds great," I replied. As good as my walk had been at clearing my head, seeing Sheriff Sentry caused all the curiosity to come rushing back to me. His words always seemed to carry more meaning than what was on the surface. *Why had he thought I would want to speak with him?* I wondered. Perhaps my dad had mentioned something to him, or maybe he'd had more of the odd insight that seemed to be going around the town. Either way, it gave me hope that he would at least be able to provide some answers to my questions.

"Shall we, then?" he said, gesturing toward the great wooden doors that set atop of the steps.

Pushing open the heavy doors, I stepped through the threshold and into the familiar site of my home church. As far back as I could remember, nothing about it had changed. The large circular auditorium still had its dark wooden floors with row upon row of pews standing erect on two sides of a main aisle, which led straight down the center of the room and up to the pulpit where my father always preached. The bright summer sun flooded in through the stained glass windows, illuminating the entire auditorium. The bright day and the design of the church made for a beautiful sight.

The giant room was already mostly filled with people. I looked around and found my mother and sister sitting in the congregation. It wasn't because I was still frustrated that I avoided sitting by them, especially now that my parents believed me, but it was sort of our church tradition for the young people to sit up front.

When we were really young, my friends and I sat in the

back but we would act up, so eventually our parents sat us up front where they could keep an eye on us, and if we became too rowdy we could also be embarrassed by my dad from the pulpit. Somehow, though, the tradition just stuck with us.

I knew some of my friends probably would not be back from college yet, since it was still the beginning of summer, but Brice and Rachel would be there. Sure enough, I gazed up to the very front row on the left side of the auditorium and saw Katie, Brice, and Rachel, with a space between Brice and Rachel, which they had saved for me.

The whole dating thing was definitely odd. I had sat by Rachel plenty of times in church before, but never had they specifically saved me a place by Rachel, or at least to my knowledge they hadn't. It felt weird and yet great at the same time.

I walked up to greet them. "Hey, guys," I said with a smile as I started to take my reserved seat.

"Whoa!" Rachel and Brice said at the same time as they reached their arms out to stop me from sitting down.

"We're saving this for someone," said Brice, disgruntled with a look of disbelief.

"Yeah, sorry," Rachel agreed, looking far more apologetic than Brice.

I was really embarrassed. I had walked down the aisle and just assumed they were saving the seat for me. Now I felt like a complete idiot standing in the front of church, red faced, with everyone looking at me for the disruption I had caused.

Rachel and Brice waited until they saw the embarrassed look on my face, and then they started laughing.

CHAPTER FIVE

"You dork, we're just kidding. Sit down," Brice said with a light punch in the arm and a big laughing smile.

Rachel and Katie were laughing, too.

"Do you think I'd let someone else come between so new a love?" Brice said mockingly, making a face with his best attempt at puppy dog eyes and then laughing even harder.

Katie continued to laugh as well, but Brice's comment had turned Rachel as bright red as I was. She was still smiling, but rather more sheepishly. *It serves her right for teaming up against me with her brother,* I thought vindictively.

I was glad Brice had set me up with Rachel, but he was getting far too much satisfaction out of our being together. In that moment, I remembered the mental note I had made on my date with Rachel to repay Brice for embarrassing me. Now I owed him two. He was far bolder than I was, but I could be patient.

For right then, I responded the only way a twenty-year-old can respond to one of his friends when faced with an embarrassing situation, by rewarding his light punch with an even harder punch to his arm and a juvenile comment. "You're such a jerk," I said with a smile as he rubbed the spot on his arm.

I guess we had finally gotten to the age between being a child and being a mature adult. We were old enough that we felt we did not need to pay as much attention to our parents anymore, yet young enough we still caused a scene in spite of sitting in front of the entire congregation. The girls were naturally better behaved than we were, but they still did not usually help matters. As we began to notice some of the more senior members of the church giving us looks of disapproval, we settled down and chatted in more appropriate inside voices. While waiting for the service to begin, we also greeted a few of our other friends as they poured into the church.

The first part of the service went along as usual. One of the deacons got up and announced a baby shower the church was throwing for a new mom in the community. He followed with some other announcements for upcoming church events, and a list of people and things to keep in our thoughts and prayers. Then we sang some hymns led by Brice and Rachel's dad, Mike, who was not only the school music teacher, but also the church's choir director.

At last, my dad got up to speak. I had heard so many of his sermons it was impossible to count. Since I was a little kid, every Sunday and Wednesday we went to church, and he would preach. I watched as he positioned his tall figure behind the pulpit.

He glanced down at me and smiled as he began, "What if you were to see an angel and a demon in the front of our congregation, locked in battle?" His deep probing voice filled the auditorium, as he held out his hands, indicating the small space in the front of the church between the altar and the front pews.

"What if they were right here in front of us, visible to us, fighting to the death before our very eyes?" he continued with his fist clenched in the air.

"What if the angel and demon were here, rolling around, taking punches at each other, throwing each other through walls, and trying to destroy each other? Who would you hope would win?" he asked, pausing to give time for people to think about the question.

He continued, "To most people—even non-Christians, I would think—the answer should be easy. They would, of course, want the angel to win." The church was silent. Every single person was listening intently, unsure where my dad was going with this.

"But I ask you," he went on, "if the choice is so easy to decide which of the two sides you would want to win in a battle fought before your very eyes, why then, do we choose the demon to win in our spiritual battles, every day?"

Confusion stole through the crowd and I became nervous for my father. *In what way did we choose demons to win over angels every day?*

"Make no mistake, when you sin, when you succumb to temptation, you are allowing a demon to triumph in a battle for *you*," he said with great emphasis. The crowd was silent.

"Did you know that? Did you know when angels and demons fight, they do not fight for their own survival; they fight for you? You are the prize of the fight; you are the goal they battle for. They fight to influence you, to lead you to follow God, or not," he said holding his two hands out flat, indicating the two options.

"It's the ultimate fight for your life, and for your soul, and your choices declare the winner. They fight for *you*!" He exclaimed loudly, making a few of the older people jump a little. I had never seen my dad so fired up.

"Just because you can't see the spiritual realm to witness the battle does not mean the choice has changed any. When you choose purity, and abstaining from sin, or when you choose to give in to the temptations of evil, you are choosing which side you want to win. You are choosing which side you truly follow.

"So, I ask you, if we would so easily choose the angel to win over the demon if we could see them fighting in front of our church, then why is the choice so hard when we cannot see them? If we would only realize that the battle is real, and that there are real forces which we wrestle against each day, then I believe we would live our lives a little differently.[68] Every time we give sin a foothold in our lives, evil controls us a little more and a little more because sin is never satisfied.[69] It always wants more. Those temptations to sin, which we are presented with each day, they promise happiness, but they really bring destruction—our destruction, and the destruction of people we care about."

The hairs on the back of my neck were standing on end. Of the hundreds upon hundreds of his sermons I had heard, never had I felt my dad's message was so directly intended for me—and he probably had no idea.

It was as if millions of neural connections all pieced together in my mind at one time. My eyes were wide and my mouth hung open in disbelief. Everything finally made sense. What my father had said was exactly what was happening. I was sure of it. I really had seen an angel. Angels and demons were gathered in an all-out, behind the scenes battle in our little town, and I was caught in the middle of it.

Both sides were fighting for something—souls of the town I supposed—and my decisions and actions in the third temptation would play a huge role in determining the victor. My decisions in the final test might have much stronger consequences than I had originally thought.

My mind was racing. *What would happen if I were to fail the test?* The gravity of what I was mixed up in had finally set in. Sweat began to build on my forehead, even worse than it had on my date with Rachel. Sitting in my seat, in an auditorium filled with a couple hundred people, I felt completely alone.

I alone had been chosen. I alone had to face the final test. I was the one who had to choose goodness over evil, and if I failed, who knew what the consequences could entail? If I failed, it would not be just a simple case of messing up my life; other people were at stake.

A large number of our town had already been affected: my family, the Jacobs, Sheriff Sentry, Katie . . . and the bank workers. *How many more souls would be affected?* I wondered in fear. *Could it be like my dad had said in his sermon? Could people's lives be destroyed? Could they be lost?* I was more worried than I had ever been in my life, feeling as if I were on the verge of hyperventilation.

Sitting in mental solitude, the outside world blurred from my sight, spinning on, quite content without me. It was a burden too great for one man, one kid. *How can I contend with the world of angels and demons? How can I make any difference?*

I looked at the people around me, listening, unknowingly, to my father preach a sermon with more relevance than even he could imagine. None of them really knew the dangers my dad was speaking of. Like me, they probably had always "believed" in angels and demons, but had never really given them much thought, never considered them an actual part of our world.

How mistaken I had been. Now I knew it was all true. I had seen an angel. I had been influenced by demons. It was *all* real!

Part of what the angel had said to me returned to my memory. "Many others would pay a price" if I failed. My choice in the third temptation was going to affect other people, the very people sitting around me, perhaps, and I was not prepared to let harm come to them, not if I could help it. I glanced over at Rachel and shuddered to think of anything happening to her.

I have to make a difference. I have to try. I was in this battle already, and it was time to fight. I could not sit by and let evil prevail, not if I had inherited a path already laid before me. I would do whatever I could to keep the people I cared for safe.

The sermon ended without me catching much more of it. My father said his last piece; the pianists played one more song, my dad closed in prayer, and then we were dismissed. As we got up out of our seat, Rachel turned to me and said, "Hey, we are all going out to eat. Do you want to come with us?"

I had to shake my head to process something as normal as a Sunday afternoon lunch. The human part of me almost took over, tempting me to say yes. I really did want to go—both to be with Rachel and because I was always hungry—but I had business to attend to with Sheriff Sentry. "I can't. I have something I have to do. But I'll talk to you later," I said apologetically, as she looked a little disappointed.

"That's fine, call me sometime." Something in her expression made me think she was hinting that she was going to wait for me to make a move for once.

"Okay, I will," I replied with a smile.

"Okay, see ya," she said, smiling back as she turned and walked away to join her parents.

Katie followed, but Brice turned to me and said, "Hey, Micah, are we going to play ball at the school this week?"

"Yeah, I'm sure we will," I responded, not really interested in anything but talking to Sheriff Sentry, now that I had pieced so much together.

"Great. The high school guys want to scrimmage against us all week, again. Tom Reynolds told me he would get the keys from Coach to open the gym for us," he said excitedly. Though Tom Reynolds had a temper, he was a senior, and the coach usually trusted him with the keys to unlock the gym doors for us. Coach had done the same thing for us when we were in school, to allow us to practice on our own in the off season.

"Sounds good, man," I said to him.

"Okay, see ya later," he said, running to catch up to Rachel, Katie, and his parents.

"Later," I replied.

Soon the Jacobs and Katie joined the large crowd of people filtering out of the church. My father was at the main door shaking hands with everyone as they left, so I walked over to my mom and Shelby, who were still sitting in their pew, waiting for my dad to finish.

"You all can go home and eat lunch without me; I am staying to speak with Sheriff Sentry," I told my mom.

"All right, honey, I'll save you a plate," my mom answered back.

"Thanks," I replied, now turning to find the sheriff. My

eyes found him waiting for me near a side door that led out of the auditorium and into a hallway containing smaller rooms used for Sunday school classes. As I approached him, he greeted me with a warm smile.

"Hello, sir," I said. "Thanks for staying."

"No problem at all, Micah. I always enjoy a good conversation," he replied in a friendly manner. "Shall we go have a seat in one of the classrooms?" he suggested.

"That sounds good," I replied.

We walked through the dark wooden door, into a small hallway with off-white Berber carpet and wood paneled walls, the same shade as the door. We picked the first classroom on the left and entered. Sheriff Sentry closed the door behind me, and we took seats on opposite sides of a study table.

"Now, what seems to be troubling you, Micah?" he said, with the same sort of wise paternal air he always commanded.

I sat there silently. I had not been able to decide where I actually wanted to begin. It just seemed to me in all the chaos, Sheriff Sentry had been the only one who had given me any real answers. Therefore, I had hoped, just by meeting with him, questions and answers would flow magically. Now that I was with him, though, I wasn't sure how to proceed. I finally decided to start with where it had all begun.

"Sir, I am sure you remember the bank incident," I said.

"Naturally," he replied in a kind tone.

"Well, that wasn't an isolated incident," I said slowly. "All sorts of strange things have been happening to me." I stopped to look for any change in his expression, but he simply nodded his head, encouraging me to continue.

CHAPTER FIVE

"It's going to sound weird, but I've been feeling that something greater than we can see is going on . . . almost as if something spiritual is happening." I paused again, feeling embarrassed. It sounded so absurd saying it all out loud. Here I was, talking to one of the busiest, most respected men in our community, and I was about to tell him what would probably sound like ghost stories. I was certain he was going to think I was crazy. But if it was all true—which it was—then it really didn't matter how I sounded. I just needed help.

"Why don't you give me some examples?" he said kindly, with an expression of genuine interest.

"Okay," I began, but then immediately stopped yet again. I wasn't sure if I wanted to tell Sheriff Sentry about the angel, or the man and the golden ladder—they were exactly the sort of thing that made me sound crazy—but I had to tell him something. Otherwise there was no point talking to him. I began again. "Well, I told you about how I had felt the night at the bank, as if something had clouded my mind, how there was some sort of foreign influence," I said.

He nodded, indicating he remembered.

"Well, it sort of happened again. . . . Not exactly the same, I didn't mean I was at the bank again," I said quickly to answer his shocked wide eyes; undoubtedly he was concerned I had been trying to loot banks again.

"This was a different situation, but everything felt the same. Last night, I almost did something I never would have done if I were completely myself. It was nothing illegal," I reassured him once more, just in case he was still worried. "But it would have been huge in my life," I said. Then I paused for a fourth time, feeling the conversation was proving more difficult than I had anticipated. Sheriff Sentry wasn't going to know how to help me if I just continued to talk around the subjects. After all, what nearly happened between Katie and me in the second temptation had been one of the main reasons for wanting to talk to him, but now that I was speaking to him, it felt too personal . . . too embarrassing. I froze in contemplation over my dilemma, trying to decide how I might be able to explain the temptation without giving him specific details.

"I take it you do not want to tell me what this particular incident is," he said with a grin. I nodded. "That's fine," he said, reassuring *me* this time. "You say it was nothing illegal, and you also said you *almost* did it; so I take it that just like at the bank, you stopped before you actually committed this act?"

I nodded once again.

"That's good enough for me. Please continue with only the details you feel comfortable sharing," he encouraged.

"Okay . . ." I began. However, I knew that sharing only the details I was comfortable with would not be enough. If I was not going to tell Sheriff Sentry about the angel, the man and the golden ladder, or Katie, then there was really nothing else to say. I hung my head. If I wasn't going to give him the full story, then I was just wasting both of our time. *Why shouldn't I tell him?* I thought. He had believed me before. Besides, I had told Katie everything, and I barely knew her . . . *why not Sheriff Sentry, who I had known for years?*

"Okay," I began again, feeling I had no other option than to tell Sheriff Sentry the whole unbelievable truth, "but this is going to sound crazy, sir," I said apologetically.

"Micah, I'm a police officer. You wouldn't believe the stuff that I've heard," he said with a laugh. "Besides, you are a good kid; I trust you," he finished sincerely.

"Here goes nothing, then," I said with an exhale, looking down at my shoes as I began. "It all started almost a week ago at the high school basketball game, the night of the bank incident. As I got up to leave the game, I sort of blacked out. Only, instead of waking up inside of the gym, I woke up outside, and I was all alone. And then, out of nowhere I saw a bright light descend from the sky, and a large man dressed in glowing white robes slid down what looked like a ladder made of light.

"I never saw the man's face, and he walked away from me quickly toward the top of the hill on the road near the school. However, before I could chase after him, I was suddenly surrounded by people again, and when I looked back toward the hill, the man was gone."

I looked up at Sheriff Sentry again, searching for signs of disbelief. If he thought I was making the story up, he certainly wasn't showing it. Feeling more confident, I resumed my story. "I went chasing after the man, but he was not on the other side of the hill. So, I gave up my pursuit of him and decided to walk home. However, on my way home, I began to feel like someone was watching me. And what was even more noticeable, I began to feel as if something were attacking my mind. Just as I was really beginning to panic, I saw an abnormally bright light on in the bank, and my curiosity was reawakened. I thought it might be the glowing man, but to be honest, I was drawn to the light in a more powerful way than just mere curiosity.

"Well, you know the rest of that story," I said. "But then there was this second situation that I mentioned," I hesitated again, still not wanting to admit that I had almost kissed Katie. I just felt that it tarnished my character more than I wanted to.

"Like I said, Micah, only tell me the details you are comfortable sharing," he said kindly.

Relieved at his perpetual generosity, I decided how I wanted to proceed. "It's just that in these two instances, the feelings were so appealing, they felt almost . . . normal. What I mean is, even though the thoughts and feelings felt foreign—as if an outside force was influencing me and clouding my judgment—they were still temptations that I found natural, and quite powerful, and enticing," I said, looking down again, this time in shame.

Sheriff Sentry silently waited for me to continue. "But that's not all. The second event I just mentioned, well, I sort of knew it was going to happen. Well, not exactly what was going to happen, but I knew something similar to the bank was going to happen because I had been given a warning. Earlier that morning, I had walked into Shelby's room, to wake her, when I was suddenly struck blind by a bright light. Then a deep and powerful voice spoke to me, warning me that a second temptation was going to happen that night."

I had no idea how Sheriff Sentry believed any of this. I thought my story sounded crazy, and I was the one who had seen it all. Faithfully, though, Sheriff Sentry remained silent, listening to every word I spoke.

I went on, "Then on my way home last night, right before you drove up behind me and asked what I was doing . . .

well, I was sitting there because I had just seen what I think was . . . an angel. I know it sounds crazy, and I only caught a quick glimpse because my eyes were hammered shut by a blinding light, but I'm certain it was an angel. And then, the angel spoke to me. It said that a third temptation was approaching and if I failed, then there would be a great price to pay.

"It also said the same thing that you did," I continued, looking into Sheriff Sentry's non-judgmental eyes. "The angel told me *'that which is born of the flesh is temporary, but that which is born of the Spirit is eternal.'*[70] Actually, a lot of people have been saying that exact same thing to me—you, Rachel, my parents, the angel, and even Katie mentioned it." I stopped myself from continuing, remembering that I didn't want to divulge too many details about Katie.

"It can't be a coincidence," I resumed. "I know this all sounds insane, but you have to believe me," I finished, feeling a little shaky with emotion.

I stared at Sheriff Sentry, desperately hoping he would believe me. We sat in silence for a minute while he sifted through all I had said. Finally, he broke the silence with a question. "Micah, do you think it is a strange concept that a spiritual war could be occurring in our little town?" he asked.

"I don't know . . . I guess not. That's what my dad was talking about in his sermon, right? I mean, we go to church, and believe in God, and the devil, and angels, and demons, and stuff, but we never really see things happening. I guess that is why it just seems strange," I answered.

"Exactly! We claim to believe in God and with that belief we get angels—and unfortunately for now we get the devil by default, too. Yet, if we actually experienced things that seemed extraordinary, or out of the norm, most people wouldn't believe us." My thoughts drifted to my parents' initial disbelief.

"I can't answer for certain why that is," he continued. "But I think you are right. I think it's because we don't see obvious miracles very often. We definitely don't feel like we see miracles as often as they seemed to happen in the Bible. To the minds of modern people, our beliefs have become more of a tradition, or even a fairy tale or a myth, than they are truth," he said with a sad expression.

"However," he said, "I do have faith in God, and I believe the devil is real, and so are angels and demons. So, while your story is unusual, it doesn't seem crazy to me at all. I believe what you are saying is *entirely* possible," he finished simply.

I sighed in relief. He actually believed me . . . again. But before I could fully appreciate the support he was showing me, his words registered in my mind. "So, you think it's Satan and his demons that are coming after me?" I asked, feeling suddenly frightened and insignificant compared to what I might be up against.

"Certainly they are coming after you, Micah. Even if everything you told me today was a lie, Satan and his demons are still coming after you. He's out to destroy all of God's creation. Satan is the great deceiver, able to deceive nations.[71] This struggle goes far beyond your own recent temptations. Since the fall of man, there has been a war for the souls of people. None of us are immune to this war. Is Satan coming after you more powerfully right now than he usually does? *Perhaps*. But the battle still hasn't changed. I believe angels and demons can be found in the midst of almost any human struggle.

"Satan tempts a person with desires that they already have. His temptations are appealing, so giving in feels natural. However, if you give in, then before you know it, you'll be in deeper than you realized and you'll be unable to find your way out. He'll lead you down a path of your own destruction, hurting everyone you care about along the way," he said as he stared at me as intently as ever.

"Micah, I believe this is how people are tempted, every day. It starts with just a small influence, a small message of temptation from a demon. When a person gives in to that temptation, they fall deeper and deeper into sin. The deeper the person becomes entrenched, the more destructive and evil the sins become.[72] In my job as a police officer, I have seen people at their worst. I have seen thieves, rapists, murderers, and more. Most people look down on these people, even hate them, but I have pity on them. Do you know why?" he asked.

I shook my head.

"I have pity on these people because I realize they didn't start out this way. They were fearfully and wonderfully made by our awesome God. They are part of the crown of God's creation and meant to be so much more.[73] But as they gave in to small temptations, they gradually sank deeper and deeper into sin, until eventually even horrible things didn't seem so bad anymore.[74] People don't start off as thieves. They begin with envy, jealousy, or pride. They begin by wanting something more than they should—fame, success, power, money, whatever it might be—they indulge, just a little at first, then they want more, until they are buried in greed or hunger for what they do not have, and they take what is not theirs.[75]

"People don't start out as murderers. They start out with little dabs of selfishness. That can escalate to envy, or jealousy, or pride, or even hate, and these things can escalate to violence, and violence to murder.[76]

"People don't start off as rapists," he continued seriously. "They start off with lust, and as they feed their lust, their sin grows until their desire is never satisfied. They need *more*, they need *different*, and they don't stop until their desire is appeased.[77]

"Not everyone falls all the way down to the level of a rapist, a thief, a murderer, or whatever other crime people consider heinous. However, everyone who sins begins exactly where these heinous criminals begin—with indulging in small sins that they never thought could lead so far. It always starts the same, Micah; *every man is tempted when he is drawn away of his own lust and enticed. Then when lust has developed it brings forth sin, and sin, when it is finished, it brings forth death.*[78]

"Sin is a shackle," he continued.[79] "It ensnares people, pulls them in and will never let them go if they don't listen to the conviction of the Holy Spirit, and turn from their sin. Sin is so effective because it appeals to us, and it is careful not to offend our sensibilities too quickly. It starts out slowly, by finding an opening, a chink in our armor, and once we let it in, it wants more, and like a wildfire it spreads. If we let it in, and never deal with it, it eventually consumes us completely," he said.[80]

I swallowed nervously and my heart was beating heavily.

Heat spread throughout my body. Sheriff Sentry could have been talking about anyone, but I felt like he was talking about me—even if he didn't know it. I had never been a bad kid, but I had certainly been okay with little sins my whole life. *Surely they couldn't be as dangerous as he made them sound*, I hoped.

"So," I finally said, ready to move on, "the reason I wanted to speak to you is that I hoped you might have some advice for me. If what the angel said is true, and I have one more temptation to go, then I'm afraid that I'll fail. If I fail, then both the angel and my dad's sermon make me believe that other people might pay the consequences; perhaps a lot of people. What if I don't choose what is right? I just don't see how I'm going to know what to do. The only advice I've really gotten is what everyone keeps saying *'that which is born of the flesh is temporary, but that which is born of the Spirit is eternal,*[81] but to be honest, I don't really even know what that means."

"Oh, well that part's simple, actually," he said matter-of-factly.

"It is?" I asked in surprise.

"Sure," he responded. "Well, I say it's simple, but that doesn't mean it will be easy to hear."

"What do you mean?"

"Well, let me ask you this; do you think everyone is God's child?" he asked.

"Umm . . . I guess, sure. I mean, God created everyone didn't He?" I answered, thinking this was kind of obvious.

"God certainly created everyone. However, the Bible teaches that there are two types of people in the world, those born of the Spirit, and those born of the flesh.[82] According to

Scripture, those who are born of the flesh actually aren't God's children, and because they are not God's children, they cannot enter into heaven," he said.[83]

"Okay . . . so what does it mean to be born of the flesh?" I asked, feeling confused.

"Well, the reason there are two types of people in this world, those born of the flesh and those born of the Spirit, is because there are two people we can be born from," he said enigmatically.

"You mean our mother and father," I said, scratching my head, now in utter confusion, feeling as if we had gotten terribly off topic.

He laughed, "I can see why you think that, but no, that's not what I'm talking about. The first person we are all born from is Adam."

"You mean, Adam, as in Adam and Eve? You're talking about the story of creation?" I asked skeptically, hoping that Sheriff Sentry was not going to spend the whole time preaching to me. I had real problems that I was dealing with. I didn't need lectured on old Bible stories. I needed answers.

"Yes, I'm talking about Adam from the creation story," he answered with a little edge to his voice, seeming to notice the tone of skepticism in mine. He continued, "Adam was the first man, and every single human who has ever existed since him has borne his nature.[84] Humans exist in the flesh, like Adam was flesh," he said pulling on the skin on his arm for effect, "and just like death came to Adam, all humans eventually die, too.[85] This is our birth of the flesh. Yes, it's a birth to our mom and dad, but ultimately it is being born in the earthly image of

Adam. This is what it means to be born of the flesh.

"Now," he said importantly, "if there had never been sin, then this birth—the birth of the flesh, the birth of Adam— would be sufficient. However, because of sin, Scripture teaches that *if* this is the only birth we ever have, then we are not God's children, and because we are not God's children, we cannot enter into heaven," Sheriff Sentry stated seriously.[86]

"Okay," I cut in, hoping to summarize everything he had said, "when someone says the flesh is temporary, they are referring to the temporary nature of this life. Just like you said about King Solomon when he recognized that he could not take his wealth and his power with him when he died, he was recognizing that everything that is of the flesh, everything that is of this world, it is all temporary and therefore cannot be taken to the next world; to heaven," I said.

"That's mainly right, but the most important part is not about the materials and riches of this world. The most important part is about our soul. If a person is only born of the flesh, if they are only born of Adam, then they will not inherit eternal life; they will not enter into heaven," he said staring pointedly at me.

"Okay," I said, "I think I understand that, but what does it mean to be born of the Spirit, then?" I asked, now feeling we were at least on the right track toward answering the riddle everyone was so fond of reciting to me.

"Well, Scripture explains that just as all humans were born of Adam, and have worn the earthly image of Adam's flesh, they must also bear another image . . . the image of heaven. To do this, there is a second man that we must be born of. This second man is Jesus Christ.[87] Unless a person is born of Christ, they cannot inherit heaven.[88] I'm sure you've heard preachers use the phrase 'born again,'" he said.

I nodded.

"Well," he continued, "this is what it means. All people are born of Adam, the flesh, but not all people are born of God, the heavenly," he hesitated. "Are you a Christian, Micah?" he suddenly asked me directly.

"Uhhh . . . I mean, yeah. I go to church and everything. I'm a pretty good person," I responded, feeling the heat rise to my face. I was suddenly very nervous. I knew that answer wouldn't fly, but I had just said the first thing that popped into my mind. I had been in church my entire life, but to be honest, I had doubts about whether or not I was really a Christian. On the surface, I'm sure everyone thought I looked great, but underneath was an entirely different story.

Sheriff Sentry frowned, causing me to feel even more embarrassed. "The Bible says that everyone has sinned, and even more, it says when we sin, we earn death,"[89] he said seriously. "You say you are good, but Micah, have you ever sinned?" he asked pointedly.

I hung my head. Sheriff Sentry knew the answer was yes.

"You're a preacher's kid, you know what the Bible says about our sin. It teaches that if we sin even once, then we are as guilty as if we have broken God's entire law.[90] So you see, Micah, if you have not been born of the Spirit, if you are only born of the flesh, then even a single sin in your life would make you guilty before God, and guilt before God earns only one thing—death. This death is both physical and spiritual. The first death is the death of our physical bodies; the second death is separation from God for all eternity in hell.[91]

"There will be many people who stand before God in the end, people who believe they are Christians just because they attended church, or because they did good deeds.[92] However, unless a person is born of God, they will not inherit eternal life,"[93] Sheriff Sentry continued gravely. "A person must be born of God, and that only happens when they accept Jesus Christ."

"I believe in God," I said almost involuntarily, as if trying to regain Sheriff Sentry's approval.

"The book of James says that even the devil believes in God, Micah.[94] Do you think Satan's belief in God is enough to get him into heaven?" he asked rhetorically. Obviously the answer was no. "You see, placing our faith in Christ means more than just believing that God exists. The existence of God is a given, we *must* believe it,[95] but that is not where we stop. No, we go beyond belief and on to faith. True faith is not simply believing that God exists, but *since* we believe that God exists, faith is trusting in God's promises to us.[96]

"And there is one promise in particular that is fundamental to the Christian faith.[97] I've told you that Scripture says we are all sinners," he continued, "but the next part is realizing that Jesus died in our place.[98] If sin causes death, then that means something had to die for our sins. Picture it this way; if we were on trial, God is the judge, and perfection is the standard. All of us are guilty of breaking God's perfect standard, right?"[99] he asked me. I nodded my head. It was obvious, every person who is honest with themselves would have to admit they are not perfect.

"Well, if we are all guilty, and the penalty for our guilt is death, then for God to be a good judge, He has to sentence us to death, right?" he asked me again.

"What about mercy?" I responded, trying to grasp onto some sort of hope in this dreary speech. "Surely a good judge could show mercy," I demanded.

"Ah, yes. You would think so. Let me ask you this, though. If a man murdered someone in your family and the judge let them off with a warning, would you call him a good judge?" he asked.

"No, I'd obviously be angry," I admitted.

"That's right. When we want God's mercy and incorrectly believe that nothing has to pay the price, we are seriously underestimating our guilt in sin. You see, God is a good judge in every sense of the word. God is holy, therefore, His standard is, and must remain, perfection.[100] People forget that sometimes, but God doesn't. People usually only remember verses from the Bible that teach God is love—which He is— but He is also holy.[101] As such, anything short of His holy standard cannot enter into His kingdom," Sheriff Sentry said.

"But as you know, Micah, God really does love us, therefore, He wanted to show us mercy, but He had to show mercy in a way that wouldn't go against His holy standard."[102]

"And that's where Christ came in," I inserted, the Sunday School answer springing easily from my lips. Although it sounded trite when I said it, there was no doubt that my heart was feeling newly convicted of the truth that Sheriff Sentry was saying.[103]

"That's right, God the Father sent God the Son, Jesus Christ, to die in our place. Because of sin, something had to die, so He sent His son to die for you, and for me," Sheriff Sentry said solemnly.[104] "So how is a person born of the Spirit?" he asked rhetorically. "A person is born of the Spirit when they confess their sins to God, accept the sacrifice of Jesus Christ, and they place their faith, their trust, in Him to save them from their sins.[105] The Bible says that if we confess with our mouth the Lord Jesus and believe in our hearts that God raised Him from the dead, we will be saved.[106] And when we accept Jesus Christ as our Lord and the Savior from our sins, then Scripture teaches that God literally adopts us, we become His sons and daughters—we become His children," he said excitedly.[107]

"And when this happens, the promise of God for eternal life is sealed in us by the indwelling of the Holy Spirit—meaning, we are born of the Spirit. This is what it means to be born of the Spirit, and this is why you have been repeatedly told, *that which is born of the Spirit is eternal*, because once you accept Jesus Christ, you inherit eternal life," he finished happily.[108]

I was a preacher's kid. It was all stuff that I already knew, but in all honesty, I had never heard it laid out the way Sheriff Sentry had just explained it to me. I'd be lying if I said my heart wasn't feeling extremely convicted. However, I didn't feel like I had time for this sort of thing. I was being attacked by demons for crying out loud! I'd have plenty of time in my life to get religious. For now, though, I had other matters to attend to. I didn't want to call them more important matters, but they certainly seemed more pressing.

"Look, sir, I appreciate what you are telling me, but I just really need help with passing this third temptation. People's lives are at risk, and if I don't focus on this, who knows what could happen?"

"Micah, I'm telling you that accepting Christ *is* the key to the third temptation. Christ is the key to passing *all* temptations," he responded emphatically.[109]

I just stared at him, with no idea how to respond. I wasn't against what he had to say, but I didn't see how it was the key to stopping me from succumbing to the next temptation.

"You're not quite ready, then, are you?" he said sadly.

"Sir, no offense, but I am facing Satan here . . ."

"Oh," he interrupted, "you think you can do battle with Satan and his demons on your own, do you? That is folly," he warned with his eyes wide. "If this were a battle of your power versus their power, they would win. They are far more powerful than you.[110] But this battle has never been about *your* power. If anything, victory in spiritual war is all about our ability to depend on God.[111] Micah, what power or ability do you have apart from God? What do you have that He didn't give you?[112] Do you think He needs your strength to fight against Satan? It's not our abilities that God needs. In fact, God often chooses the weak things, simply to show how mighty He really is![113] His strength is made perfect in our weakness.[114]

"This is why," he continued, "when you are tempted, it is to *Him* that you must flee.[115] *He* is your refuge when you are in danger. *He* is your deliverer when you need help.[116] *He* is your rock, your strength, and your fortress.[117] It is in *Him* that you must trust.[118] It is to *Him* that you must run when temptations are more than you can handle. It is behind *Him* that you must hide when an enemy is greater than you. It is on *His* stable ground that you must stand when doubt comes for you.[119] It is in *His* arms that you must rest when your pain is too great to bear.[120] There is only one victory over Satan and death, and that is the victory that Jesus Christ has won for you on the cross.[121] When evil comes for you, the only hope you have of surviving is to turn to Him, and to once and for all place your faith and your hope in Him.[122] If you don't, then you will surely fail, and even more, you cannot have eternal life," he said with finality in his voice.

"So, what of it, Micah?" he said, looking directly at me. "If you died tonight, where would you go?" I didn't answer, but just looked down at the floor. "Do you have hope for eternal life?" he continued. "Have you been born of the Spirit through Jesus Christ? Or are you still stuck in the flesh, born only after the image of Adam, destined for hell, and lost in your sins, trying to face the temptations of this world all on your own?" Sheriff Sentry asked boldly, his eyes bearing down on me, making me feel as if an interrogation light had been switched on.

I continued to stare at the floor and the oddest of sensations arose within me. Sheriff Sentry's entire message was truth . . . I knew it was. But something in me resisted. It might have been fear, or pride, or something else, but whatever it was, something in me was not prepared to just turn it all over to Christ. There was no doubt that I was deeply convicted of my sins, but a spirit of rebellion was in me as well. Perspiration built on my face as I knew I was facing a point of decision. I remained silent. My heart hammered away, and yet it felt hollow. It was too much for me right then—it was all too heavy.

"Okay, Micah," Sheriff Sentry finally said after what seemed like an eternity. "I am not going to force you into a decision. That wouldn't be right, and it wouldn't be real. Just know that I'm always here to talk, my friend. I hope you'll consider everything we've discussed today, and when you've had some time to think, I hope you'll make the right decision," he closed with a smile.

I nodded my head, and with that we both got up, he patted me on the shoulder, and we headed out of the room in silence.

The lights had already been turned off in the sanctuary, but plenty of light shone in through the giant stained glass windows to allow us to walk easily to the front doors of the church. Sheriff Sentry offered me a ride as we stepped out into the bright, hot day through the front doors, but I wanted to walk. I needed some time alone, to think about all he had said to me.

We said goodbye, and I began my walk home in the warm summer sun as he drove off in his police jeep. Church had never been so informing . . . or convicting. My heart was heavy and my mind was greatly burdened. I felt prodded, perhaps by my conscience, or maybe it was by my own soul, but something was eating away at me.

I had been very close to giving my life to Christ. Turning away from that opportunity had filled me with a guilt that was almost harder to deal with than anything I had dealt with in the few weeks of weirdness since I had been home.[123] I just wanted to turn it off, to ignore it, and to go back to normal. But everything I had heard made me believe life would never be normal again. I knew a third temptation was coming for me. And while Sheriff Sentry had warned me that I couldn't face demons on my own, I had to at least *try* to resist this final temptation. Too much was depending on me. Who knew what could happen if I failed? Whatever came my way—greed, lust, whatever—I had to be ready for it because Satan and his demons were not going to make it easy on me. They were going to do all they could to ensure I ruined my life or other people got hurt, and I had to do my best to stop them.

Satan and his demons, I thought. What a bizarre world I had been exposed to. Between my dad's sermon and my conversation with Sheriff Sentry, most of my questions had finally been answered. However, the answers had not provided the relief I had hoped would come at finally learning the truth. It was probably good to know what I was up against, but ignorance had been a comfortable enemy. And now, ignorance was gone. Now, I felt like not only was a fight ahead of me, but so was a choice . . . and I didn't really want to think of either right then. I didn't want to deal with such serious stuff. I was only twenty years old. I hoped to have decades before I needed to get serious about life and death and heaven and hell. As unlikely as I knew it was, I just wanted life to get back to normal.

The gorgeous day was a welcome distraction as I continued my way home, trying to push everything out of my overburdened mind. The sun having already passed straight overhead was just beyond the top of its swing through the sky and on its way back down. Though significantly warmer, everything was just as beautiful as it had been on my way to church that morning.

When I arrived home just a few minutes later, I found my family outside sitting in lawn chairs on our concrete porch enjoying the day. Though we didn't have an overhang, the sun was slightly behind the house, giving the porch a nice, cool bit of shade.

"Hey, Micah," yelled Shelby in excitement, as she ran down the front steps to give me a hug, which was her customary greeting for me. She leapt dangerously into my arms trusting I would catch her—which I did—and gave me a huge hug. Little did she know, but that was exactly what I needed at that moment.

I slid her to my side so that she was sitting on my hip the way mothers often carry their toddlers. She wasn't much heavier to me than a toddler. I carried her back up to an open lawn chair next to where my mother was sitting, and spun Shelby around in the air so that she could sit on my lap. My father had his rocking chair out, which he liked to sit in while he read his paper and drank lemonade.

"So, did you have a nice talk with Sheriff Sentry?" my mother asked sweetly.

"Uh, yeah," I answered quickly, hoping she was not in the mood for details. "He definitely answered a lot of questions for me," I added.

"Oh, good," she responded. "I saved you some lunch; it's wrapped up in the refrigerator, if you are hungry," she said, transitioning easily to her favorite topic—ensuring her family was well fed.

"Thanks, I'll probably heat it up in a bit. I'm not really hungry yet," I answered honestly. She gave me a look of shocked confusion. Not being hungry was unusual for me. Normally, I was a bottomless pit, and my mom knew that, but I was still feeling too overwhelmed to think of food. Shaking off this abnormality, my mom moved on to a topic of even more importance to her than food.

"So, have you talked with Rachel about a second date yet?" she asked. I was momentarily caught off guard. It was difficult to continually have so many normal conversations with people in the midst of such abnormal circumstances.

"Oh . . . no I haven't yet. But actually, I was thinking about calling her this afternoon," I said, hoping that my cluttered brain would have enough room in it to get through an entire conversation with Rachel.

"So you're going out with Rachel again?" Shelby asked, even more excited than my mother. "I *love* Rachel!" she cheered. Shelby had always viewed Rachel as a sort of big sister, so she was naturally elated with the news—and I was thankful that Shelby's happiness was contagious.

"I don't know; I guess I am . . . if she says yes," I said, laughing at Shelby and feeling less stressed every minute.

"Oh, she'll say yes," Shelby responded, jumping off my lap and beginning to dance around the yard while we all laughed at her.

Dating Rachel was about the best news of my life. However, it had the unfortunate coincidence of being coupled with what was probably the most terrifying, mysterious, and burdensome few weeks of my life. The darkness and uncertainty in my future meant that anxiety seemed to continually eclipse my jubilation.

Yet, sitting there with my family, in the home that I loved, in the town where I had been raised, on a beautiful summer day, and with a date with the most beautiful woman in the world on my horizon, the day was suddenly seeming a little better. The heavy weight that had plagued me since my first encounter with the man in the white robes had only been increased by my conversation with Sheriff Sentry. However, right then, all the weird stuff, all the spiritual stuff was being pushed from my mind, and I was feeling lighter by the second. It was as if the warm summer sun were melting the stress and guilt away from me. Shelby's good natured, sweet, and innocent excitement helped more than anything. She made all evil and fear seem like a problem for another day.

In fact, with Shelby and my mom's excitement, my relationship with Rachel suddenly seemed more real to me. Over and over again Shelby sang the "sitting in the tree" song there in our front yard while she danced around in circles. My dad laughed, and eventually my mom actually joined in with her. Shelby brought much needed cheer to my wearied heart, though I admittedly laughed a little less when they got to the marriage and baby carriage part of the song; but what young man wouldn't?

We enjoyed the afternoon, sitting and talking about normal things and the spiritual world was feeling further away from me than it had all summer. My mom couldn't stand that I hadn't eaten, so she eventually brought me out some food.

Then she and Shelby began giving me unsolicited advice about girls. I was feeling so much better that by the time we vacated the porch in search of cooler air inside the house, I decided it was finally time to make my first ever phone call to Rachel. As nervous as I was to call her, I knew she was ready for me to wipe the yellow off my belly and make a move.

I ran upstairs to my room, closed the door, and jumped onto my bed, grabbing my bedside phone as I did so. I was dialing the numbers before I knew what I was doing. Perhaps I should have thought of a plan, but I wasn't really the planning type of guy. If I planned, I would get myself too worked up and end up being too nervous to call. It was better to just rip the bandage off. The phone was ringing. My heart started to pound.

"Hello," said the unmistakable voice of Brice. Man, I had hoped I would not get him first.

"Hey man, it's Micah," I reluctantly admitted.

"Oh, hey, we missed you for lunch, man," he said to me.

"Sorry, I had some stuff I had to take care of," I answered.

"Oh, that's cool, so what's up?" he asked. I was fairly certain he knew what I wanted. The only reason I would be calling him would be to confirm our plans for basketball for the week, but Brice knew I didn't do that. In all of our years as friends, Brice planned everything and I just tagged along. He knew why I was calling. I was sure of it.

"Actually . . . I was hoping to talk to your sister," I said even more reluctantly than before.

I had said precisely the line that he had been waiting for and I could almost hear a big, obnoxious smile spread across his face.

Brice instinctively lowered his voice to a tone that he wanted to sound like his father's, and unfortunately for me, it did all too well. "Now Micah, I think it's time you and I had a talk about my sister. You've been seeing an awful lot of her lately. It's my job as a brother to make sure you have purely good intentions for her. I don't think we're looking for more than a friendship here . . ."

I cut him off. "Oh, will you ever shut up?" I said. I had to stop him early; once he got going, I knew he wouldn't stop.

"Excuse me. If I am going to let you date my sister, I don't think you should be taking that sort of tone with me," he said, continuing his charade in a deeper voice than normal.

I didn't want to stop him this way, but he left me no choice. "My apologies, *sir*. You said you wanted to talk about my relationship with your sister. Well, did I tell you that your sister kissed me last night? I have been waiting to kiss her for as long as I can remember . . ." I said, knowing Brice would not listen to too much of that. It worked.

"All right, man, come on! I don't want to hear that stuff. What are you trying to do, make me vomit?" he complained, his voice returning to normal.

"May I speak to Rachel now?" I asked, enjoying my victory.

"Yeah, hang on," he said in a discouraged tone that I found far more amusing than anything he had said to that point. "Rachel, Micah's on the phone," I heard him yell. Then I heard him mumbling something about me messing up a good joke. I couldn't help but laugh to myself.

CHAPTER FIVE

"Hello," Rachel's beautiful voice called out, before I was ready.

"Oh, hey, how's it going?" I asked, as awkward as usual, surprised by how quickly she had picked up the phone.

"Not too bad. Did you do what you needed to after church?" she asked pleasantly.

"Yeah, I did. I had a long talk with Sheriff Sentry," I answered.

"Oh! About what?" she asked, in a surprised tone. "You're not in trouble, are you?" she said, half joking.

"No, no, nothing like that. I just wanted to talk to him about some stuff that's been going on. You know . . . I just needed his advice on some things," I said cryptically, hoping she wouldn't inquire further.

"Well, that's good. He's a wise man. I hope he helped you," she responded, and to my relief, let it drop.

"So, why did you call?" she asked in a voice that let me know that she too knew exactly why I called, but she wanted to hear me say it anyway. I could almost hear her face form a huge beaming smile, just like Brice's undoubtedly had. Her sense of humor was a lot like her brother's, but in this instance, I think she was just genuinely excited to finally be having this conversation.

That was much the opposite of how I felt. I would rather have everything set up for me and avoid all of the awkward talks. Some people would probably say having to do things like this was good for me. However, besides the cardiovascular workout I usually got from increased heart rate, I was not sure how being uncomfortable was good for me at all.

"Well, I was wondering what you were doing this Friday night?" I asked.

"Why don't you tell me?" she responded in a slightly flirty manner.

"Oh," I said, slightly taken aback. "I actually haven't thought about that part of the conversation yet," I admitted, slapping my hand to my forehead, feeling quite incompetent. It would have made sense to anyone else to have had a plan before they called, especially since my mom and Shelby had given me so many suggestions, but I had been so preoccupied that I had completely forgotten that to go on a date with someone, you had to actually *go* somewhere.

"Well . . . " she began graciously, "we could go out to eat, and then maybe just go and talk somewhere, or whatever," she said with an attempt at sounding casual, but she had responded with such readiness that I could tell she *had* been thinking of this part of the conversation.

"Sounds good," I said. "I can pick you up at seven."

"Great! Then if I don't see you before then, I guess I'll see you Friday," she said in a very happy and sweet voice.

"Sounds good," I replied.

"All right, then if that's all, I guess I'll talk to you later," she said, waiting to see if I had anything else.

"Yep, that's all I had, so talk to you later," I answered, excited for the first time.

"Bye," we both said, as we hung up.

That had been extremely easy. I had finally worked up the courage to ask Rachel out on a date. Granted, her eagerness and gentle guidance through the conversation had definitely made it less difficult for me, but I had done it! It was such a contrast to the guilt, defeat, and stress I had felt just a few hours earlier. Now, I felt victorious! I felt like jumping in the air and screaming in celebration. I had finally overcome my fear . . . with a lot of help from Rachel . . . but it was done! We were finally going on our first date alone!

I went downstairs with a little extra spring in my step and enjoyed the rest of the evening with my family. It was an astonishingly uneventful night, which was a very nice change from the norm. Like usual, I went to sleep that night with a million things on my mind, but it was nice to add something happy to my list of thoughts. With school, money, demons, and everything else I was trying to ignore, a date with Rachel was a wonderful counterbalance.

I laid my head on my pillow and had another good night's sleep. Now no matter what was in store for me, no matter what clouds darkened my horizon, it was nice to know that I had at least one good thing to look forward to.

CHAPTER SIX

<u>SOLO</u>

It's patient and kind, it's honest and true,
It cares not for me; it cares only for you.
It's not proud or unseemly, nor easily provoked,
It doesn't despair, but through faith does it hope.
It gives jealousy no power, nor evil its way,
When love is the choice, through all things does it stay.[124]
But just as life seems it could never be better,
Wisdom foresees a quick shift in the weather.
For the dream of serene does not hang by much,
And the absence of clouds will be gone in a rush.
With a feeling of fright, and a sense of unease,
The storm leaves behind its first wave of debris.
But when the peace of this life and the calms we hold dear,
Are gifts that are robbed by trial and fear.
When chaos rips at our heart, and tears at our soul,
When our pain is so great, and we feel all alone,
It is then we should cling to our only real friend,
The Alpha and Omega, the Beginning and End.[125]

*   *   *   *

MONDAY, MAY 27 THRU FRIDAY, MAY 31, 1985

It turned out I did not have to wait until my date on Friday to see Rachel. She and Katie came to watch as Brice and I played basketball with the high school team several days that week. I always seemed to play worse on the days Rachel was there.

It wasn't just me, though. Having two very attractive college girls watch our games had a noticeable effect on the high school guys, too. It wasn't exactly the best way to make them focus on practice. Normally Brice, who is always overly serious about basketball, would have pointed this out and asked any spectators to leave—but neither of us were about to tell our girlfriends to leave.

It would have been better if Brice had stuck to his guns in this instance, because Rachel and Katie's presence actually caused a bit of an issue we had not foreseen. The first day they showed up, the high school guy who had let us in the gym—who also happened to be the guy with a hot head, Tom Reynolds—went up to Katie and started hitting on her right in front of Brice. Tom persisted, even after Brice made it quite clear that Katie was unavailable.

This surprised me because while Tom was a tall guy, Brice was older and much stronger. The tension reached its max when Tom asked Katie to stop by the local pizza restaurant, where he worked, to come see him sometime. Brice erupted in anger at this, and we had to separate the two before they came to blows. Tom left Katie alone after that, but I could tell he didn't like being told what to do, especially when girls were involved.

What was even weirder to me was that Katie seemed to enjoy Tom's attention a little too much. Fortunately, Brice did not notice Katie's interest, or the situation might not have diffused so quickly. Nothing else happened between Brice and Tom that day, though all throughout the week, I could tell that neither of them particularly cared for the other.

I tried not to let their situation bother me because I was happy that my life was finally getting back to normal. With basketball, Rachel, and the freedom that came with summer, I felt as if I were in heaven.

Surprisingly, my parents had not asked me a single question about any of the weird stuff I had told them about. I had assumed that once they believed me, they would want to know everything; that was usually the case. However, despite all the things they had heard me claim and their assurance that they truly did believe me, they acted as though nothing out of the ordinary had happened.

Though I was a little surprised at this, I was also relieved. Like any problem, deep down I sort of hoped if I ignored it long enough, perhaps it would never return. Obviously, that is not the case or my story would be over and you would have found something else to occupy your time. But no matter what else was coming for me, at that moment, life was really good. What more could a twenty-year-old ask for? Pretty much every day I was playing a sport that I loved, and I had a date to look forward to with the girl of my dreams. It's amazing how quickly we humans can push bad or difficult things out of our minds when good things are there to distract us.

When I got out of bed that Friday morning, as usual, and went downstairs for some breakfast with my family, I had no reason to suspect that my happy bubble was about to burst. After a bowl of cereal and some orange juice, I headed down to the high school where Brice and I met every day around 10:30.

I arrived at the school and found that the side door had been left unlocked, as it had been every morning that week. I stepped into the gym and saw Brice was already there, and he and the other guys were already lined up, shooting for teams. I glanced around the gym and was a little thankful I did not see

Rachel and Katie. Perhaps I would play better without Rachel watching and I hoped Katie's absence might ease the tension between Brice and Tom.

I walked across the gym floor and set my stuff on the stage, changed into my basketball shoes, and joined the line waiting to shoot free throws, which is how we always decided teams. The first five to make it were on one team, the second five to make it were on another team, and anyone remaining had to wait until the next game to play. Fortunately, there were only ten players so far, so no one would have to sit out.

"What's up, Micah?" Brice greeted me.

"Hey man, who's made free throws so far?" I asked, trying to determine who I would be playing against, since I generally missed my free throws—not on purpose, they just were not my specialty.

"Just Tom and that sophomore, so far," he answered, pointing over at two tall high school guys who were waiting at half court for the rest of the teams to be decided.

"I'll just miss mine so that we can be on the same team," he added matter-of-factly. If he were not my best friend, I might have taken that personally, but we had played ball together since we were kids; so he knew I was probably going to miss my free throw, and if we wanted to be on the same team, then he might as well miss his shot.

"Sounds good," I responded.

After the three freshmen missed their free throws, and Brice missed his on purpose, the three remaining high school guys made theirs to round out the teams. We played a couple of games, which were pretty evenly matched. Brice and I were quite a bit better than any of the high school guys, but only one of the three freshmen on our team was any good, whereas the other team had two seniors, two juniors, and a sophomore, all of whom were fairly decent players.

The morning continued to progress in a normal fashion. Brice and I tried to score just enough points to keep us in the game until the end, but made sure we were giving the other guys their opportunities as well. It was working out okay. We won about half of the time and lost the other half.

We were about six games into the morning when the other team realized they needed to slow Brice and me down to increase their chances of winning. The two seniors were guarding us, and the other three players began helping them out quite a bit, leaving their guys open. This made it a little more difficult, but we were still scoring with relative ease—which was not making the other team very happy.

As their frustration increased at their inability to stop Brice and me, the game turned uglier. The high school guys began playing more physical, bumping us harder and playing a little dirty. Then, one trip down the court, something happened that made me realize that my week of peace, my five days of nothing bad happening, was about to come to an end.

We were playing to twenty. Our team had fifteen and the other team had thirteen. Brice had been hot all game. He had hit two threes and had driven to the basket for a layup three times, giving him twelve of our team's fifteen points. He was, unfortunately, being guarded by the senior who already didn't like him, Tom Reynolds.

Tom was getting frustrated at not being able to defend

Brice well. With his long, tall body, Tom was not nearly quick enough to guard Brice. He should have been guarding me, but Tom was the arrogant type who believed he should always guard the best player, even if it was not a good match-up. As such, he had switched back and forth between Brice and me all morning, depending on who was scoring more that game, and he was simply no match for Brice's quickness.

Finally, one trip down the court Tom decided he had seen enough. Brice performed a really quick crossover dribble and left Tom standing in his wake, but just before Brice jumped to take a shot, Tom grabbed him from behind, pulling him to the floor with a lot of force. In football, they call it a horse collar. In basketball, they call it a flagrant foul. In pick-up ball, like we were playing, they call it a good way to get punched in the nose.

If Brice had been a big guy, he would have probably hit his head on the floor. Luckily, he was nimble, so except for bruised elbows, he escaped relatively unharmed. He was mad, though, and so was I. Anyone familiar with basketball knows this type of foul is nothing more than a cheap shot. I waited to see what Brice was going to do.

Fortunately Brice, being a nice guy, got to his feet and just shook it off, pretending the foul had been an accident. I was mostly glad Brice kept his head, but part of me also wanted to teach Tom a lesson. I breathed deeply to calm myself. We certainly didn't need to get into a fight with a high school kid— no matter how much he had it coming.

The game resumed. We all started playing again, hoping the situation would diffuse naturally. However, Tom continued playing rough with Brice. Every trip down the court, Tom threw an elbow or purposely bumped into him. I suspected Tom hadn't forgotten about their disagreement over Katie, and with being outplayed as well, it was more than his ego could take.

Brice quit shooting the ball and just passed to the rest of us, hoping the rough play would stop. It didn't. Tom seemed intent upon escalating their feud, and continued running into Brice every chance he could. Then, he finally went too far.

Tom had been saying things to antagonize Brice all morning—typical trash talk that we were used to and could have ignored . . . until he crossed the line and said something crude about Rachel.

We were already too close to our boiling point before his comment, but that was it, for both of us! Brice shoved Tom backward with surprising strength, making him fall hard to the court floor.

"Back off, Tom!" Brice yelled in frustrated anger. "And you better shut your mouth about my sister!"

Tom struggled to regain his feet, and I started forward ready to defend my friend, and equally ready to teach Tom the proper way to speak about Rachel.

At that moment, time stopped for me. I sat frozen in thought. Anger began to rise in me like I had never felt before. I was like a petrified spectator. I wasn't petrified because I was frightened. I had been in small scuffs with bullies before and I knew either of us could take Tom, let alone both of us. But I was frozen because of what accompanied the anger. I had spent most of the peaceful, enjoyable week in fear of one thing happening, and right then it happened. The treacherous dark cloud had returned.

This time it was not making me jealous, or greedy, or lustful. No, it was acting upon another emotion—a strong one. This time it appealed to my *anger*. The dark cloud's slow, numbing effects on my mind were immediate, blotting out all normal inhibitions, and blurring my vision to all of my surroundings, except for one thing . . . Tom. I wanted to make him pay. I knew what was happening, but that didn't make the temptation any less potent, because I didn't need a dark cloud to be angry with Tom.

I was genuinely and rightly furious with him. It felt only too natural as I began to let the anger have me, to let it soak through my skin. It was empowering. It felt good to be mad at Tom; I enjoyed it. My blood boiled with rage and would only relent if I let my fury erupt and my wrath pour out on the object of my aggression, Tom. His was the only face I could see.

Tom, the one who had insulted Rachel, the one who had tried to hurt my best friend; his pride and his arrogance had turned even his own team against him. None of them stood at his side ready to defend him the way I was prepared to fight for my friend. Tom!

I hated everything about him. I knew bullies like him. He was the kind of guy who took whatever he wanted, from whomever he wanted. He was the type of guy who treated no one with respect. To him, nothing was sacred—not even Rachel. Well, he had finally picked the fight that all bullies eventually pick—the fight they can't win—and he was about to pay for it.

Then, as if hit by a bus, random thoughts forced their

way into my mind; things unrelated to the situation, but things that made me even angrier. I thought of my parents, and how they had not believed me at first.

What? It took some sort of revelation for them to believe me?

More thoughts came as if they were being shot at me by an arrow, attacking and penetrating my skull, setting my mind ablaze with anger, and making my temperature and my hatred continue to rise uncontrollably. The attacks were personal—everything was personal.

Like a cruel joke, I was just a loser who made a college basketball team, but had no money to actually go to the college. What I needed was someone to take out my anger on, and I have Tom!

His *stupid*, angry face glared at me as all the injustices of my life came flooding into my mind, like an avalanche of memories, stored up for one purpose—to help me remember exactly how badly Tom deserved to pay. I felt powerful. Hatred boiled impatiently in my veins, ready to be funneled into violence. I was ready to act.

All of this happened in an instant and Tom had just barely gotten back to his feet, ready to attack my best friend. But he didn't move. Perhaps he was surprised at how easily Brice had thrown him to the ground and was wondering if he stood a chance to win the fight. He didn't!

Tom didn't know, but I would be there in a split second to help Brice rip him to shreds. He wouldn't know what hit him. My eyes remained locked on Tom as I waited for him to move. I was ready to strike. He was my target. He would pay for what he'd done . . . and he'd pay for everything else I was angry at in my life. I took a step forward.

CHAPTER SIX

For a second, I noticed subconsciously Brice had not done anything else. He had pushed Tom, told him to back off, but Brice hadn't lunged, he hadn't struck when Tom was down. He could have. Tom would have been an easy target lying on the ground in shock at having been thrown there by a smaller guy. *Why did Brice stop?* I wondered.

I shook the thought out of my head; it clouded my anger, and I wanted this. But the moment's hesitation had caused something else to happen. Suddenly and finally repercussions entered my mind.

If I hit Tom, I will be in trouble—they don't just let grown men punch a high school student in the face.

While that seemed sane enough, when a person is angry, sanity is not always what they want to hear. If that had been all, I would have probably taken another step toward Tom, but immediately, more good thoughts entered my head just as quickly as the angry ones had. Rational thoughts . . .

Break up the fight, something seemed to say to my heart. *Don't mess up your entire summer for one stupid fight*, it continued.

However, rebuttals flooded in, too . . .

Tom deserves this. He can't talk about Rachel like that!

There I stood, still glaring straight into Tom's eyes; my anger subsided only slightly. No one, besides me, had moved an inch. The time to make a decision had come. I looked at Tom's face, with his eyes of scorn staring at my best friend.

His unwarranted threatening look towered down at the smaller Brice, though Brice had done nothing to deserve it. The dark cloud formed thickly around me and my anger started to peak, but even then, more good thoughts pelted my mind and my heart, as if purposefully attempting to calm me down. I was torn.

I should attack Tom, now! Make him pay for what he did! I thought as furry rose up in me, urging me to strike him.

Just break up the fight—grab Brice and leave, something countered, immediately causing me to feel calmer.

Back and forth, my mind waged war. A decision had to be made. The inner battle was ready to reach its climax . . .

"Hey, what are you kids doing!" exclaimed a voice from behind us, breaking me out of my stupor.

We turned toward the doors that led into the rest of the school and saw the school custodian, Billy Thornton, bursting through the doors, storming toward us with a mop in his hand and his eyes wide with fury. The appearance of our school's custodian cleared the air in an instant. The dark cloud left my mind like a cockroach fleeing before light, and my anger abated immediately as life resumed at its normal speed. I shook my head and regained my composure, taking my eyes off of Tom for the first time since Brice had pushed him to the ground.

As I returned to my old self, I stepped forward and pulled Brice back because he was still ready to defend himself, and Tom still wanted to fight. Some of the high school guys followed my cue and came to hold Tom back.

"What's a matter, you little *girl?* You can't handle a little physical play?" Tom jeered at Brice.

"What's your problem?" Brice retorted.

"Let's go," I said loudly to Brice, interrupting before Tom could say anything further.

I pushed Brice over to the stage, where we grabbed our

stuff and then headed out of the gym.

"Run away then, coward. I'll see you around," Tom bellowed after us while we were leaving, apparently undaunted by the presence of school staff. Perhaps Tom felt with Billy as a witness, there was less chance Brice and I would retaliate, so he was safe to start talking trash again. He wasn't wrong. I wanted out of there before we got into serious trouble.

We left the gym just as Billy Thornton started yelling at the high school guys, "Wait until the principal hears about this! You will *all* lose your gym privileges!"

Just before I was completely out the door, I looked back and caught a glimpse of Tom's face. Where there had been anger before, there now was a look of bewilderment. He seemed completely unsure of what was happening. Fear swelled in my stomach. The darkness was back, and I had a feeling whatever was going on with me, Tom had just become another pawn.

"What's his problem?" Brice spat at me as the gym door closed behind us.

"I don't know man, just forget it," I said.

"That's going to be hard to do," he answered sharply. "He's going to be around all summer, and that's going to ruin ball for us. I doubt we'll even be able to get into the gym now, once Billy tells Mr. Peterson," Brice said, sounding really disappointed. Mr. Peterson was the school principal and I knew Brice was probably right. If Mr. Peterson heard there were fights between high school students and older guys, undoubtedly there would be a universal ban on anyone not in high school. That was typically how Mr. Peterson handled situations, and in this instance, I couldn't blame him.

"What a *jerk*!" Brice yelled in continued frustration. "And what did he mean, 'he'll see me around'?" he questioned.

"I don't know, man, just keep a look out for him," I said in all seriousness. "And anyone else acting weird," I said under my breath.

"I think I'll head home," I added, not really sure what else there was to do.

"Oh yeah, big date tonight, huh? You better get home to get prettied up," he said mockingly, but with a slight smile.

I didn't feel the need to respond with words, so I just replied with a roll of my eyes and my own, half embarrassed grin. I was glad for the change of subject, and I could tell it lightened Brice's mood a little. We headed down the road from the school and took our separate ways once we reached Main Street.

As was so often the case, once I was alone, my mind began working in worried overdrive. Having the familiar cloud of doom linger over me was not the way I wanted to kick off my evening with Rachel. For a moment, I allowed myself a fleeting feeling of hope, as I foolishly wondered if I had just completed the third trial. But I knew better. This was just a warm-up. Whatever was coming for me would not be that easy.

No, not only was the third temptation not over, but I had also probably almost failed it. A chill went down my spine as I realized I had nearly done exactly what I swore I wouldn't do. I had been so close to giving in to the temptation. I had almost ruined everything. All it had taken was one week of quietness for me to forget the threat that constantly waited for me to let my guard down.

Just five days earlier at church my eyes had been opened to the enemy that was after me, but now, the world had seemed so much safer. I had almost deluded myself into thinking the threat was gone. Who knows what that mistake could have cost? This wasn't over. I couldn't let myself forget again. I would try to enjoy my date with Rachel, but I had to be ready to resist whatever temptation was thrown at me.

When I got home, I took a shower and then spent the rest of the afternoon with my family watching television and just talking, trying to distance myself from the guilt I felt at having so narrowly avoided failure. It was good to be home. Being around Shelby always lightened my heart, even when things seemed so serious.

When six o'clock rolled around, I went back upstairs to get ready. I put on my nicest T-shirt and jeans, and well . . . that's pretty much all I do to get ready. I did not need to shave; though I was twenty, my face was still smooth as a baby's. I thought about putting some gel in my hair, but I kept it so short it would not have mattered, plus I had no clue what I would do with gel anyway.

As such, I only spent a second or two critiquing myself in front of the mirror before I lost interest in that as well. Not really caring what I looked like, I decided to sit on my bed and do a little thinking about the date. That was a mistake!

In addition to the dark cloud that was sure to be an unwelcome chaperone on my date, my nerves started getting worked up as I thought of all of the typical date anxieties that made me so uncomfortable. Teeming with nervous energy, I jumped off the bed and tried to find something else to occupy my mind, but found nothing and gave up again after about two minutes of searching. With my options exhausted, I decided to head back downstairs to sit with my family again, instead of remaining upstairs, alone in my nervousness.

My parents and Shelby were getting ready to eat supper, which made me it impossible to ignore my own hunger. Since I was taking Rachel out to eat, I would have to sit there, starving, and endure the smell of the delicious dinner. Of all the things I could show restraint with, my mom's roast beef and potatoes was not one of them. Nervousness waited for me in my bedroom, painful hunger was there with my family. I had no idea what to do while I waited. It was torture and my anxiety grew as each tick of the clock drew me closer to my date.

At six thirty, I decided I had waited long enough. I begged my mom and dad not to wait up for me this time, assuring them I would provide sufficient details in the morning—*if* they left me alone that night. Mildly content with their half-hearted promise to not wait up for me, I threw on my shoes and scurried out to my car, saying goodbye as the front door swung shut.

I climbed into my car and headed for Rachel's house. My double dose of discomfort continued as I drove down the street, with my stomach growling every five seconds and anxiety over the date increasing every second. The drive went by in a blur and when I pulled onto Rachel's street, I realized I was about twenty-five minutes early, so I decided to circle the block for a while. After about ten minutes of that, I felt I was just wasting gas, plus I was pretty sure people were starting to notice as my rust bucket of a car made several passes in front of their house.

Feeling self-conscious, I relented and pulled into the Jacobs' driveway, fifteen minutes early. That was respectably punctual, I thought. I looked up at their usually inviting square brown house, which now stared back at me with a symbolic aura of fear; not because of dark clouds, but simply because I was so nervous about my date. My stomach had quit growling because it had tied itself completely into a knot.

As I got out of my car and walked up the porch steps, I realized I was extra nervous because I would not have help on this date. There would be no Brice to spark up conversation, or any help from anyone. I was on my own this time, alone, oh-so-alone. This was bound to be a catastrophe.

The house appeared more intimidating with each step, causing my heart to beat heavily and sweat to build on my forehead. I knocked, and the door flew open immediately. Brice and Rachel were both waiting there for me. Rachel looked annoyed at Brice's presence, but Brice had a huge, beaming smile plastered across his face.

"Hey Micah, are you ready for your date, or would you like to take another few laps around our block?" he asked mockingly . . . right in front of Rachel.

It occurred to me that perhaps I should have let Tom sock Brice . . . at least once. On an ordinary day, I would have shot a comeback at him before he had taken his next breath, but around Rachel, my head was as empty as ever.

"It really does amaze me how quick witted you are," he said, beginning a second round of jeering. "Around Rachel you're about as clever as a rock," he said, thoroughly enjoying himself.

I continued to stand there as mute as the afore-mentioned rock, just glaring at my *former* best friend. I made my third mental note, in just the two short weeks I had been home, that Brice would one day be repaid for all of the fun he was getting out of my relationship with Rachel.

"Will you get inside?" Rachel hissed through her teeth at Brice. "You ought to tend to your girlfriend; she's been acting weird all day," she finished as heatedly as she looked.

I wasn't quite sure what she meant about Katie, but Brice's face went suddenly serious and he turned and went back inside without another word.

"Shall we?" I said with a smile, finally able to speak.

"We shall," she said back with a smile.

I loved when she entertained my cheesiness with her own cheesy dialogue.

We walked down to the car and I opened her door for her. Fortunately, the passenger door didn't creak, but opened nicely. I went back to my side, opened the door to its usual creak, climbed in myself, and we headed off.

We didn't have reservations. There was nothing fancy enough in our small town to require reservations. I had decided to take her to a little family restaurant in town that I knew she loved. We pulled into the parking lot, and we both got out and began the short walk up to the front door. Without Brice around, I finally got a chance to appreciate how nice Rachel looked.

I'm sure she had probably wanted to dress up more, but

she undoubtedly knew I would be wearing my usual jeans and T-shirt, so she had gone with jeans and a nice shirt. She still looked amazing, stunning really. I once again stared a little too long because she started to blush. I tried to cover it up with a compliment, but my words sputtered as my already worked up nerves were heightened by getting caught staring. "You look . . . um . . . your hair . . . um . . . your face looks . . . uh . . ." I started getting hot and nervous. *Why couldn't I finish a stupid sentence?*

Rachel laughed and said, "Thank you. I will *definitely* take that as a compliment." Then she added, "Micah, quit being so nervous. I'm with you; I like you. You don't need to impress me; you already have."

Wow, I did not know how to respond to that. It was very nice to know, and the effort on her part was appreciated, but it, like most comforting sentiments in these situations, had next to no effect on me, only steadying me enough to say "thank you" and actually finish my intended compliment, " . . . and you look very nice tonight."

We made our way to the entrance of the restaurant, which had a Christmas color theme that it kept all year around. I opened the door, and the little golden bell attached to it gave a ring to let the greeters know someone had come in. A middle-aged woman came up to us with a smile. I recognized her as one of the women who went to our church.

"Hello, you two," she said smiling ear to ear. "Is it just the two of you tonight?" she asked, obviously tickled to see us on a date together.

We answered that it was, and she led us to a little two-person table in one of the back corners. The place smelled great as we wove in and out of the different tables. We waved at people we knew as the smell of chicken and pasta and other great things passed my nose. My stomach came unclenched as it awoke and once again realized its real passion in life: food.

We sat down at the small, dimly lit table. When the server came a few minutes later, Rachel ordered some soup and a small club sandwich, which are both wise choices on a date. I was not so wise and got a huge plate of spaghetti, which was delicious, but terribly messy, making it impossible to seem well mannered or show any sort of etiquette.

When the food arrived, I did something that should almost be forbidden: I cut my noodles with a knife, in a futile effort to make it a little less messy. It should be known I am entirely against cutting spaghetti noodles. It just should not be done. Spaghetti should be consumed in the manner in which it was intended, rolled up around your fork and, no way around it, messy!

Nevertheless, our first date alone demanded an exception. But even with my blasphemously cut noodles, I still got plenty of sauce on my shirt. Fortunately, I had grown up with Rachel, so she already knew what a barbaric moron I was.

Apart from the spaghetti, we began to have a very nice evening. I actually started feeling a little more relaxed with her and was able to talk about things, such as how we enjoyed school, but how glad we were it was summer.

The night was flying by wonderfully. All other thoughts, worries, fears, and challenges ahead were gone. I was happy eating with, and talking to, Rachel. It was wonderful . . . that is, until she started on the one topic I did not want to speak about.

CHAPTER SIX

Despite all of the events that had happened, and despite the fact something had almost happened that very morning with Tom Reynolds, I was still secretly allowing myself the naïve hope that the trouble would not come back, that it was over. At the very least, I had hoped it would leave me alone on my date. Therefore, I had absolutely no desire to discuss any of it with Rachel.

"You know you can tell me anything, right?" she began cautiously.

"Well . . . sure," I replied, resistant to go where I suspected she was heading.

"I don't mean that as an empty statement, Micah," she added, "like when people say that just to comfort someone. I mean I will absolutely be there for you, for anything." I had no idea what to say to her. She was amazing and caring, but I was not ready to make her think I was crazy by telling her everything that was going on with me.

"I really feel you have something bothering you," she continued, in response to my silence. "Something is going on with you . . . isn't there?" she inquired further in a sweet, non-accusatory tone.

I sat speechless for a second. I still didn't want to discuss the topic, so I decided not to encourage her. I awkwardly tried to delay her. "What do you mean?" I said as I looked away from her in shame.

"I think you know what I mean, but if you don't want to talk about it, then I won't push you," she said simply and honestly. She looked down at her sandwich and poked at it, not really wanting to eat, but just wanting to talk. Not that she was mad, but for once, she was the one who did not know what to say next. I could tell it was my move to either change the discussion or let her in on what was going on in my life.

"Okay," I said slowly, still trying to make up my mind. "You want to know what is going on with me?"

"Only if you want to tell me, Micah," she responded quickly. "I know it's something big and different. I can feel it. All I want to do is help," she replied so sweetly and maturely that I could tell she would be happy with me whether I told her or not—even if she would still be worried.

I'm not sure there are very many people like her in the world. Lots of people will help a person out, but they subconsciously just want to be in on the secret. It's a subtle difference, but an important one. Rachel knew it was not her secret and would have let me keep it to myself so long as she didn't feel I was in trouble. Her concern was not the secret; it was me.

She stared at me intently with her innocent, loving, and completely gorgeous blue eyes as I considered whether to tell her or not.

"It's not that I don't trust you," I said to her in continued shame. "I do trust you, more than almost anyone. But I'm afraid of what you'll think of me after I tell you everything."

"Micah Jones," she responded sternly, "none of us are perfect. I *know* who you are. I know that any mistakes you've made, you are sorry about them. You have a wonderful heart. Making a mistake does not change that. If your only reason for not telling me is that you are afraid of what I'll think, then you might as well tell me now because I don't care about what mistakes you've made. I care about you, and I want to help," she finished, with fire in her eyes.

My heart tugged as my defenses began to crumble. Only one thing kept the walls up at all; I liked her so much. Bringing up crazy spiritual stories—stories where I almost commit crimes and sin—was a terrible way to do well on our second date; but lying to her would be even worse. I looked deep into her eyes and I realized in that moment, Rachel was not going to flinch away when I told her my story. She was a girl who would gladly meet any trials with me, head on. It was time to be honest with her, even about the ugly parts.

When I finally spoke, I opened up to her completely. Her honesty and compassion seemed to compel the truth from me, similar to Sheriff Sentry—but with Rachel it was much more personal.

Relief rolled over my body as I spoke. Sharing all of my stresses with someone who cared for me so much caused all my tensions to simply ease away.[126] I told her everything. I told her about the bank, and about the weird thoughts I had; how my mind had been all clouded, and how I felt I was in a trance. I told her about the bright light and the voice in Shelby's room, and then, with only a slight hesitation, I even told her about nearly kissing Katie at the movies.

I immediately apologized, but to my continued surprise, I received another example of how mature Rachel was and how much she trusted and cared for me—and believed me—because there was not even a hint of jealousy on her face.

I paused, waiting for a reaction, but she stared at me,

unflinchingly, encouraging me to continue. I continued to pause, but this time it was to appreciate the wonderful woman listening to me, the woman whom I adored.

She nodded again for me to continue. So, I told her about the angel I had seen on my drive home and about the upcoming third temptation. I told her about my parents' unexpected turnaround to suddenly trust me, and I finished by recounting that morning at the high school gym. It may have seemed like a regular fight to everyone else, but to me it had transcended the physical realm. It had been so much more.

In just a few moments I had told Rachel everything that had been haunting me the whole time I had been home—well, I should say I told her *almost* everything. Guilt and conviction were not strong enough in that moment to bring up everyone's favorite phrase to say to me—*that which is born of the flesh is temporary, but that which is born of the Spirit is eternal.*[127] As good as it felt to tell Rachel everything else, I was not ready to get into a discussion that might end with me having to admit to her that I had never truly given my life to Christ. She had been around me my entire life and no doubt assumed that I was a Christian . . . just like I assumed she was. I was hiding that topic and that choice as far back in my guilt-laden mind as I could. I was running from it.

"So . . . what do you think?" I asked nervously when I had said my last words.

She sat thinking for a moment, just looking at me as if searching me, then she spoke, "Of course I believe you . . . " she began, but still seemed to be thinking about something.

"It might seem bizarre, but everything you just told me is

what I sort of sensed was going on. I believe some sort of spiritual battle is going on in this town. I've felt something different, too. Well, I've felt different, almost more guarded, and I've noticed changes in my parents and Brice . . . and definitely in Katie," she answered in a tone of contemplation.

"So, you really believe me then?" I said in shocked relief.

"Of course I believe you, Micah," she said, looking at me kindly. "I trust very few people as much as you," she continued. "Plus, why would you make all of this up, especially the part about Katie, when you and I are just starting off. And no, I'm not mad at you," she said, predicting my worry.

"It wasn't you, or at least not the normal you. I think you were being acted on by some sort of demon or something evil, and from what you said, that was the only trance you were really able to break out of on your own. I guess that means messing it up with me is even scarier to you than getting charged with a felony for robbing a bank," she said with a small laugh and a flattered smile, which I returned, though my smile was still more out of relief than humor or flattery.

"I've had a feeling for a while I was supposed to talk with you, and about more than just the two of us. Something big is going on, and something bigger is coming . . . and I think it all has to do with you," she said, squinting in slight confusion as if she knew her words were true, but she didn't know their source.

She was in deep thought, and I waited for her to speak again, as she twirled her spoon in her soup absentmindedly. Then with a CLANK she suddenly let her spoon drop into her bowl, and her eyes became wide with fear. We both gasped and grabbed our chests in pain—emotional pain, not physical. My heart ached, almost like I was lovesick, but it had nothing to do with Rachel.

Looking at her, I knew she felt the same sense of fear and pain that I felt. My stomach gave a lurch completely unrelated to food. Horror overcame my senses. We stared each other in the face and we each had a look of fear.

"Something has happened!" she said in shock.

"I know! I feel it too!" I agreed. "We need to get back to your house, quickly!" I said with wide open eyes. Something terrible had happened, I didn't know what it was, but somehow Rachel and I had both felt it.

I didn't wait for a check. I left more than enough money on the table, and we ran outside as fast as we could. We sprinted to my car and jumped in. No time for opening her door now; something was wrong, and somehow I knew it had to do with Rachel's family. Whatever big event was supposed to happen, it was happening that night . . . or it might have already happened. I started the car and we buckled in.

"Drive," she said in a panic. "Fast!"

I threw my car into drive and sped off toward her house. A feeling of dread crept over me as I zoomed from side street to side street, closer and closer to the Jacobs' house, barely stopping at the unoccupied stop signs. I felt as if death were waiting for us. I turned onto Rachel's street, and in the distance I saw the familiar, ominous dark cloud hovering above their house.

Before, the cloud had felt like it was part of me—like part of my mind was clouded—but now I could actually see the entire house was covered in a thick, dark, and very real cloud. It was not a rain cloud. To put it simply, it looked like a cloud of evil. I glanced over at Rachel, but she didn't seem to see it. I was sure I was the only one who would be able to see the cloud, but I knew that *everyone* would be able to feel its presence.

Flashing lights from police cars and an ambulance illuminated the night sky.

"Oh, no, Micah! Get there quick!" Rachel cried. I glanced at her quickly and watched as her eyes welled up and tears streaked down her cheeks.

My heart tore in pain as she began to cry in fear. I put my hand on her hand and squeezed gently as we rushed down her street. We stopped on the side of the road just before her house. I slammed the car into park and we scrambled out to see what was going on. We ran up through the yard, and Sheriff Sentry spotted us. He jogged down to meet us, with a look of sadness painted on his face.

"What happened?" Rachel cried, panic and despair thick in her voice.

I put my arm around her for comfort and she leaned into me. Tears splashed down her beautiful cheeks, as we both stared at Sheriff Sentry, waiting for an answer. His face was grim, and I could tell the news he was about to relay was something he wished he didn't know. He looked sick with sorrow as he put his hands on both of our shoulders. He closed his eyes, fighting back his own tears of compassion and said in a heavy voice, "It's Brice and Katie."

CHAPTER SEVEN

THE THIRD TEMPTATION

The wind sweeps past, a storm creeps in,
An impending clash is about to begin,
Let the battle commence, and the allies declare,
Let the enemy come forth; no more time to prepare.
Two fronts collide, but neither gives way,
A push from each side, but neither will sway.
Darkness surrounds, will this be the end?
Will evil devour, or a shield defend?
A shock and a fright, a hit close to home,
A treacherous night leaves the one all alone.
First it was greed, next it was lust,
The senses all gone, in God one must trust.
Frustration and fear, igniting in rage,
Consumption by hate is the pivotal stage.
Pleasure or light, it's time to decide,
But where is the truth that so easily hides?
A flash and it's gone. It's here, no it goes,
The good rises up, but so does its foes.
A rip and a tear, a mind rent in two,
The time is right now, what to do, what to do?
A jolt of the truth and a motive is seen,
Peer through the veil, peek through the screen.
The truth is right there, just reach out and grab,
The enemies fighting, a soul will they have.
From darkness to light, from hatred to grace.[128]
Remove the dim glass, come see face to face.[129]

* * * *

FRIDAY, MAY 31, 1985 (EVENING)

Silence and dread filled the air. Rachel buried her head in
my chest and began to bawl.

CHAPTER SEVEN

"What's happened to them?" I asked with a shaky voice.

"Honestly, we aren't sure yet," responded a deputy who had come over to join our conversation.

"What do you mean? Have they been hurt?" I asked, fearing the worst.

"Well, Brice has been attacked. He's stable, but unconscious," answered Sheriff Sentry with heartache in his voice, staring at me with great watery eyes. Rachel squeezed me a little tighter, tears now blanketing her cheeks. "He received several pretty serious blows to his head. His heart rate and breathing are stable, but we aren't doctors, so I can't really say how he is. I wish I had better news, but we'll know more when they get him to the hospital."

Neither Rachel nor I knew how to respond to his statement. Our gut feeling at the restaurant had been right, but even expecting something terrible, we still didn't know how to process this. With all of the weird things that had been happening, we should have been ready for anything, but we weren't. Can you ever really be prepared for someone you care about being seriously injured?

"And how is Katie?" asked Rachel in a very weak voice.

Sheriff Sentry hesitated. "Well, that's troubling, too . . . we can't find Katie," he replied as he fought back his own tears.

"Let's go inside," he said as his strong arms embraced Rachel and me in a fatherly hug.

As we walked up the steps to enter the house, Sheriff Sentry was forced to usher us to the side of the porch to make way for the ambulance crew who were leaving the house. To my horror, I saw that they were carrying Brice on a stretcher. That was more than Rachel could handle. She buried her face deep into my chest again, trying to hide her eyes from the sight of her brother as she cried and called out his name.

I, however, was unable to look away from my best friend's deeply battered face. The gashes on his forehead, swollen eyes, and dark wet spots in his hair—almost certainly blood—made him almost unrecognizable. He had been severely beaten. Whoever had done it to him had been brutal and unrelenting. I squeezed Rachel tighter and gave her a kiss on the top of her head while my heart sank in fear and helplessness.

As the crew made their way down the steps, my gaze remained fixed on my best friend's gruesome appearance, and it was then that I became suddenly aware of something even more alarming than Brice's physical injuries. Not only did I notice that Brice's eyes were twitching erratically beneath his eyelids, but right then, something cold and dark crept down my spine. It was evil . . . the presence of evil surrounded us all! Brice was enduring far more than a mere physical attack. He was in a spiritual battle.

The crew made their way through the yard, and then they carefully placed my best friend into the back of the ambulance. As they closed the doors behind him, the cold darkness was suddenly gone. After a moment, they drove away with their sirens blaring and lights flashing. In surreal shock, I watched as the ambulance and several police vehicles turned the corner and drove out of sight, leaving only the reflection of the flashing lights still visible off the trees, but they soon disappeared as well.

In that moment, the fight was absolutely real to me. I

had never viewed the situation as a joke and had often feared what I was up against. But now, the spiritual war had inflicted a personal casualty. Now it was real in a way that theory and theology could never be. My best friend was hurt, perhaps permanently, by a very real enemy. His life and his fate hung in the balance and were quite possibly tied to my upcoming decision in the third temptation. I had to resist whatever Satan threw at me. Perhaps if I did, then Brice might be okay. If I resisted, it might prevent others from meeting a similar dark fate. I just hoped I was strong enough.[130]

Mike and Diane Jacobs came out of their house and joined us in the front yard. Mike had his arm around Diane, supporting her as she cried and appeared to be on the verge of fainting. I turned Rachel around to see her parents. She did not let go at first, but then she quickly grabbed her mom and dad, switching between us in a way that made me know she felt that if she were not holding onto someone, then she might fall forever. The family hugged and cried as I stood in disbelief.

What else is going to happen? I wondered in sadness and fear. *Will it get worse? Are more people in danger? Is Rachel?* I felt terrified and frustrated. I was tired of it all. I was tired of being tempted to do things I would normally never do, actions that would ruin my life. I was tired of being on my guard, simply waiting for my world to fall apart. Now, my best friend was hurt, and I had no idea what was coming next, or who else would be hurt. I *hated* whatever was after me. I hated the oppressive game that the spiritual world seemed to enjoy subjecting humans to. I hated it all! I wanted it to be finished. I wanted out.

THE THIRD TEMPTATION

"You can all ride with me to the hospital, and I'll make sure someone takes you home when you're ready," spoke the kind voice of Sheriff Sentry, breaking me from my dejected thoughts.

We all walked down to his police jeep and got in. Mike got in back with Diane and Rachel so that they could all be together. I climbed in front with Sheriff Sentry. I was glad to sit up front; I knew nothing I could do would console the Jacobs. They needed to be with each other.

Mike put his arm around his wife and Rachel, as they continued to cry. Except for quiet sobs and the occasional muffled conversation over the police radio, the car was silent. As we drove, I peered enviously out of my window at the peaceful and unaffected town, jealous of their ignorant bliss. Although I knew it would not be long before the gossip channels had spread Brice's news to everyone in the small town, even then I still knew that none of them would have to face what I was going to face. The spiritual world was just a Sunday sermon to them. Tragedies were causeless in their mind. They had no idea what we were up against, not really, and I envied them for it.

It seemed to take an eternity to get to the hospital. When we finally arrived, we pulled up to the emergency entrance. The ambulance had already dropped Brice off and left again. Sheriff Sentry parked in a close parking spot and we all walked to the emergency room door together.

We entered the hospital and found that a friendly looking nurse was waiting for us. She led us to the waiting area outside of Brice's room, and then she went in to assist. We waited for a while, sitting in silence, with just the whimpers of Rachel and Diane echoing in the hallway.

Finally, the nurse returned. We all looked up at her, desperate for news. "He's not out of the woods yet," she said with a solemn expression as she entered the hallway. My heart sank and a lump began to build in my throat. "He'll be under close observation until we are certain that he'll pull through, but they are done tending to him for now, so the family is free to go in."

Rachel and her parents got up and trudged together toward the door to Brice's room. Rachel looked back at me with a face of despair and then went in to be with her unconscious brother. Sheriff Sentry and I sat alone. My stomach felt hollow. My best friend was fighting for his life, and I had to just sit there, unable to help him. It was pain beyond measure. My heart ached and my eyes filled with tears. It was more than I could bear.

"I'm sorry this is happening to your friend," Sheriff Sentry turned to me and said.

"Thanks," I responded in sadness, looking at the ground and not knowing what else to say.

After a pause, he spoke again. "Be strong, Micah. When bad things happen, our only true comfort is in God."[131]

"That's not much comfort, then, is it?" I spat back hatefully. Sheriff Sentry went silent, just staring at me through sad eyes. I had never been disrespectful toward him before, and I had not meant to even then, but at the mention of God my anger suddenly spiked. I had heard empty words of comfort my entire life, people claiming that God takes care of us. They'd tell stories of how He had performed some miracle to protect them, or to heal them and make them healthy. Perhaps I was cynical, but what was their answer for when bad things happened? Where was God then? Did God just not love Brice enough to protect him? Did He simply love others more? Or worse, were God's benevolent interventions simply capricious acts, based merely on whim instead of merit? I had always hoped not, but in my life I had seen no evidence to the contrary, so I was done listening to empty words of comfort. I was done with foolish hoping. Bad things happened to good people all of the time, so how could Sheriff Sentry expect me to find solace in a God who may or may not decide to help Brice?

"Don't be angry with God, Micah," Sheriff Sentry finally replied. "God didn't do this. Whoever attacked Brice made a choice," he said in a calm, but sad voice.

"But God could have stopped it!" I responded angrily, my rage flaring yet again.

Sheriff Sentry responded with something else, but I ignored him. I felt his eyes still staring in my direction, but his words were lost on me. I didn't want to talk to anyone right then, not even him. I was tired of it all. A hopeless realization had overcome me. Life was just some big dumb game, and we were mere pawns. Brice was just a pawn; I was just a pawn. The past two weeks had been proof enough of that.

Why is God allowing Satan to come after me over and over? I thought angrily. *Why do angels and demons care so much about us? Why do they fight for us? Why do they involve us at all? Why do they seek to harm us, and most importantly, why does God allow it?!*

None of it was fair! I was just a normal guy, and all of

these things were happening to *me!* I didn't want to fight. I didn't want to do anything great, or important . . . or sinful. I just wanted to be left alone! I wanted my best friend left alone. I wanted my town left alone. I didn't want anyone else hurt.

Will they come after Rachel next? Will they come after my family? I thought in worried frustration.

It all seemed so stupid and yet so terrifying, and now my best friend was in the hospital and his girlfriend was missing. Anger pulsed through me. I was helpless against something that wanted to ruin my life, something that didn't care if it hurt the people around me, and God was just sitting by, content to watch me be destroyed. I didn't want *anything* to do with whatever was happening to me, to this town, and to my friend. I just wanted us all to be left alone!

"Hold on, Micah!" I thought I heard Sheriff Sentry say.

He can hold on! I didn't want any more of his stupid advice. I was sick of it all.

The dark cloud was thick over me now, and I had not even seen it coming. I stewed in my own rage, which was now being fed and supernaturally amplified by the surrounding darkness.

How am I supposed to place my trust in God if He will allow things like this to happen? What kind of loving God would allow Brice to be so brutally attacked? I thought in continually growing rage.[132]

Like an insatiable fire, my anger feasted on the pain I felt and the disappointment I harbored toward God, devouring them, roaring higher and higher, consuming every thought like gasoline ignited by a flame. It felt good to let my anger burn as I dwelt on the injustices of life—the merciless charade that we helpless humans were forced to endure. Being good didn't matter, bad things happened to us anyway. Evil chose random targets. There was random cruelty and random suffering![133] None of it mattered, none of it made any sense. Brice was just an unlucky ant, squished beneath the feet of mightier beings—and so was I!

I could tell Sheriff Sentry was still speaking, but I was determined not to listen to him. I didn't want to hear any more of his *lies!*

"It will be all right, Micah," I thought I heard him say.

It will not *be all right!* I thought. *Life is* never *all right! There is always more pain. There is always another bully. There is always injustice or failure or disappointment. Lies!* My frustration had escalated to anger, my anger to rage, and finally, my rage to hatred.

I hated God. I hated Him for the game He was putting me through, for the pains He allowed humans to endure.

"God loves you," I heard something say; perhaps it was Sheriff Sentry . . . perhaps not.

He sure has a funny way of showing it! I thought to myself. *Death, destruction, sorrow, disappointment, and pain; were these the acts of a loving God?* I questioned.

"No," something said again, "these were the results of human choice."

Enough! I thought in response to this unwanted excuse. I knew where this line of thinking was going, and I didn't want anything to do with it! I was not about to sit there and indulge justifications made for an almighty God who could prevent *everything*, but seemed only too happy to prevent absolutely *nothing!*

Without really knowing what I was doing, I rose from my chair and ran outside before the sheriff could say another word. I didn't care what he thought of me; I wanted to be away from him—away from everyone. I stumbled my way to the sidewalk outside and stood there, looking around for something to take out my frustration on.

And then I saw him. The one person who could set my feverous hatred ablaze completely, and the one person whom I desired to take my anger out on more than anyone else . . . it was Tom Reynolds. He was standing in a dark area nearby, covered with trees and bushes; it was as if he had been gift wrapped for me. He had showed up just in time to be the object of my fury and the appeasement of its hunger. Taking my anger out on him would feel good.

Is he the one that hurt Brice? The thought crossed my mind. Perhaps, but I had no idea. That didn't matter, though. He was such a *jerk*, he deserved it anyway! *He always deserved it!*

The dark cloud was so thick on me now that I could barely see my surroundings; the only exception was Tom. Just as the light in the bank had been, Tom was somehow unnaturally highlighted in the night. And then I heard him speak, as if he was talking to someone. I couldn't see anyone else, but he definitely was not alone. Although I was ready to chase after him and attack, I paused, impatiently hoping that whoever was with him would leave quickly before I had a chance to cool down.

And then, although I was at least a hundred feet away, I suddenly and clearly heard Tom say, "Katie," as he began laughing.

In that moment, I knew . . . he had caused it all! He had taken Katie! He had attacked Brice! Hatred welled up in me. A murderous fever overtook me. Whether he was with someone or not, Tom was going to pay! I was going to chase him down and beat the life out of him. I took a step forward and the dark cloud thickened over me, denser than ever. Tom's face remained the only thing I could see, and my eyes were steadfastly targeted onto him as I prepared for my assault.

But then, before I could take another step, I suddenly collapsed. My legs gave out and I felt my body hit the ground with a thud as I began to shudder involuntarily. As terrible as that might have seemed to an onlooker, it was nothing compared to what had begun in my mind.

Like a movie reel that had been switched on in my head, my mind was bombarded with an onslaught of rage-inducing memories. If my anger with God had been focused on general injustices before, now it was personal. As if something had been waiting for just such an occasion, every pain and frustration I had ever felt suddenly flooded into my mind. Memories of miserable times, times when I had felt helpless, and times I had been wronged; every injustice, every hurt, every pain, every sadness I had ever experienced in my twenty years came rushing into my mind all at once.

Each sensation, each memory was as real as it had been the moment I had experienced it. Each sorrow was more heart wrenching than the one before it, each moment of anger more potent. Bullies from my youth, deaths of family members, disappointments, pains, trials; I remembered them all as if they were happening right at that moment. Memory after memory coursed through me like palpable images, quite literally veiling my eyes, and completely blinding me to the outside world.

All was darkness; both my sight and my mind. A desire for unrestrained violence overtook me. I wanted to hurt people. It didn't matter who, almost everyone I knew had done something bad to me at least once; and I wanted revenge. I wanted to hate them. It felt good to hate them. Everything was against me. God was against me. God could have stopped all of this from happening, but he hadn't. Over and over God had allowed terrible things to happen to me, and I wanted to know *why!*

And then, for no particular reason, I suddenly thought of Rachel. Rachel was the antithesis to all of the anger and hate that was boiling in my veins. I couldn't hate her. If truth be told, I loved her. *Love*—the thought disarmed me. It was so contrary to what I was feeling. *Love*—half of me stretched for it, clung to it; the other half of me was repelled by it, even disgusted.

Something in me tried to push it away, but then a happy memory of Shelby fluttered through my mind, reminding me of how innocent and precious she could be. *What about my parents? They were not perfect, but they loved me. They did all they could to raise me properly and provide for me.*

Then an image of Brice and his parents swam into my mind. *They are good people. I cared about them, too. I can't hate them*, I thought.

Soon, as many good memories jolted into my mind as angry ones had just moments before. Like lightning strikes, the thoughts hammered at my heart, beating back my indwelling anger. My rage was lessening, and the battle within me was turning a new corner. However, evil would not be abated so easily. Suddenly, the memories of anger and injustice redoubled their efforts, rushing into my head and causing spite and malice to rise up in me again.

As if anger were not enough, though, like magical imagery of the most horrifying kind, I was raced back to the night of the open vault. I felt all the same feelings that I had experienced that night. I imagined all the people in the world who had money and did not deserve it. *If I could only take some money . . . I deserved it!*

Then more memories and more feelings rushed over me. Lust-filled fantasies, insatiable greed, hate-fueled violence, and more, all poured into my mind, all of them strong, and all things that I wanted, but things that I had been deprived of. I had an unquenchable urge to take anything and everything that I felt should be mine. My anger was now being fueled by greed, jealousy, lust, and pride—to name a few. Anything and everything that I had ever desired, I knew in that moment that I *should* have it, and no one would stop me!

Then more good thoughts flooded my mind. Happy memories with my parents, and Shelby, and Brice, and Rachel; playing basketball; graduating high school; entering college—those, and many more good times all came into focus, but they were not enough. I was being overrun by evil, and it was far more powerful than me. With all my might, I focused on all of the good things in the world, faith, hope, love, and more, but evil fought on.[134]

"Hope for what? There is no hope. Get what you can in life.[135]

There is nothing else," shot a menacing thought throughout my consciousness as though it had been announced on a loud speaker.

Thoughts raced in and out of my mind like bees in a hive. As the torrent of emotion whirled in my head, a war was raging for my heart; conviction versus desire, love versus hate, they tore at my very soul, threatening to pull me apart completely. I was being ripped in half by polar opposites. My eyes were still blinded, but I began to feel the world around me shaking and pressing in on me. I felt cold and dark, and then warm and light. My fury climbed to an all new peak, but as my anger climbed, so did thoughts of goodness.[136] I was stretched, far beyond the normal limits of human emotion.

I felt like I was the rope in a tug-of-war match, being pulled by two sides, both more powerful than me. They threatened to snap me in half at any moment. I was angrier than I had ever been—consumed with hatred; but yet, somehow in the same instance, I cared and loved deeper and more fully than I had ever thought possible.

I felt as though I were two people, with two different minds, who had long shared one body, but were now being forcefully severed from each other.[137] Images and memories, both good and bad, continued to flood into my mind as if they were being sprayed into my ear with a fire hose.

All this time, I saw nothing of the outside world. I saw nothing of the violent convulsions that I knew were shaking my body. I saw nothing of the concrete sidewalk that I lay strewn across. Like Brice, I was trapped inside my own mind, a target of spiritual battle, fighting for my life. But unlike Brice, my situation was about to come to an end, one way or another.

As I thought of Brice's condition, rage pulsed through me as I had never experienced before. My body shuddered as if my anger were a physical thing, trying to erupt out of me, kept at bay only by my skin; but my skin would not hold for long. Soon the wrath that boiled in my veins would be set free to be unleashed upon anyone who crossed my path.

The only thing that stopped me was my momentary incapacitation, which only served to frustrate me further. There I lay, immobilized on the sidewalk, forced to watch as painful, enraging memories replayed in my mind, each thought driving me toward an all-consuming fury. *Why had I collapsed? Why couldn't I see?* I was ready to rise up and give Tom the beating of his life, but I was stuck, blinded to the world.

"Is that really what you want, Micah, to hurt Tom Reynolds?" spoke a gentle voice out of nowhere. *Was it a real voice speaking, or was it in my mind?* I couldn't tell.

"Who's there?" I cried into the night, blinded by the dark cloud and the deluge of memories.

"Would attacking Tom satisfy you?" the voice asked, ignoring my question.

"It'd be a start!" I yelled in anger.

"And then what?" the voice replied quickly.

I was silent. I didn't have an answer. *Would Tom be enough?* I thought, temporarily sidetracked from my rage. As I paused to think, the memories suddenly stopped flowing through my mind. Now, there was nothing but darkness.

"Once you've hurt Tom and destroyed your own life in the process, what will quench your anger next?" the voice continued, its message bearing down on me more powerfully in the sudden absence of all other memories and thoughts.

"I don't care, I'm tired of it all! I want to give Tom what he deserves!" I screamed blindly.

"Don't you get it?" the voice asked. "Attacking Tom will not satisfy you. Sin can never be quenched. Once it takes root in your heart, its cravings are *never* satisfied. Once it has you, it will consume and destroy you. Sin only leads to one thing, Micah, and that is death."

"Death? You mean like what's happening to Brice?" I fired back, into the darkness. "I'm tired of this game. I just want out. Everything is empty and pointless.[138] Life is pointless! We think there is meaning, but there's *not!* We could be here one day and dead the next! I'm done with this stupid game! I'm done caring!" I continued to yell.

"Life is only pointless if you invest in the temporary, Micah," the voice responded. "This world is indeed like a vapor. It's like grass that withers away. If only you have hope in this life, then eat, drink, and be merry, for tomorrow you die," the voice said soberly.[139] "But . . ."

"Let me guess," I interrupted. "*I need to walk in the spirit, not in the flesh?*[140] I said bitterly. "Well, no thanks. I'm done playing God's game. Why would I give my life to *Him*, when He just stands by and watches bad things happen to me? He lets my dreams get crushed. He lets demons attack me. He lets my best friend get hurt. God doesn't care about me! He has done *nothing* to help me," I accused.

"God sent His Son to die for you, Micah,"[141] the voice began, but I didn't want to hear a sermon.

"And how exactly does that help me *now!*" I yelled, angrier than ever.

"Now?" the voice questioned. "How does it help you *now?* Micah, this war is about eternity. It's about your soul."

"My soul's just fine, thanks," I spat angrily.

"No, Micah, it's not!" the voice replied. "Your soul is one heartbeat away from hell. You are a son of Adam, but not a son of Christ. Your spirit cries out for you to place your faith in Jesus, but you have allowed your heart to become hardened by unbelief.[142] For years you have heard your father proclaim the Gospel of Jesus Christ from his pulpit at church, but for years you have turned a deaf ear. You have mistakenly believed that your life was good enough, that your sin was not bad enough, and that you were somehow exempt from God's judgment. Know this, Micah, no man shall enter into heaven, except he be born again through Jesus Christ."[143]

"Is that all that matters?! Heaven?! What about the pain we have to go through in *this* life?" I yelled at the nameless and faceless voice!

"You said it yourself, Micah, humans can be here one day and gone the next, so certainly heaven is more important than this life. However, do you really think that God does not care about your pain?" the voice asked. "He certainly does! God cares about the pain of all His creatures."

"Then why doesn't He stop it?!" I demanded.

"He will, Micah," the voice answered, gently as ever. "All of creation is waiting for the day when God lifts the curse from this world.[144] But God will do it in His *own* time."

"What's He waiting for?!" I cried. "Is the pain of this

world not great enough yet? What will it take for Him to stop it all?"

"He's waiting for people like you," the voice answered. "Humanity is in open rebellion against God. Since the sin of Adam, all humans have chosen, one by one, to reject God, by choosing sin instead of Him. Death and destruction don't exist because of God. They exist because of Adam's sin, and your sin, and the sin of *all* humans. In the beginning, there was no sin or death. Everything was good.[145]

"However," the voice continued, "sin has always been possible because of one thing—God offered humans the freedom of choice. Sin was possible because to have true choice, a person has to have the option and the ability to say *no;* and that is exactly what sin is. It's saying *no* to God and *yes* to self. God has written His law on the hearts of all men, to know what is right and what is wrong, and as mankind betrays this law, as they give in to their own selfish desires, they are willfully choosing to rebel against the very one who created them—God.[146] And realize this, Micah, God could have ended it all in the Garden of Eden. After Adam and Eve sinned, God could have destroyed creation and started over, but He didn't.[147] God could have even forced people to choose Him.

"But this is not what God wants," the voice said, "because real love is not forced, it is chosen. God hasn't stopped the evils of this world because he is patiently waiting for people to *willfully* turn back to Him.[148] God endures the sin, which has caused all of the death, destruction, and pain, which you so vehemently hate, because He is still hoping that people like *you* will repent of your sins and turn to Him.

THE THIRD TEMPTATION

"He is waiting for *you*, Micah," the voice said slowly. "Right now you are at enmity with God. If He were to do as you asked and stop all of the evil and pain of this world, that would require Him to judge it, and that would mean judging you. But he waits, Micah, because He's hoping that people like you will realize that apart from him, your fate is death. He's hoping that you will reject Satan's lie, which you have bought for far too long. He's hoping you will wake up from the sleep that Satan has so craftily lulled you into.[149] It's the lie that believes happiness is found in earthly possessions, in revenge, in lust, or in pride. None of these things will last, Micah. They are temporary, doomed to be destroyed. Only God and His kingdom will endure forever. To take part in His kingdom, to find true satisfaction that will last for eternity, it is time for you to give your life to Christ; it is time for you to be born again. The war is real, Micah, but the choice still rests where it always has . . . in your hands. And so, I ask you, will you continue to vainly pursue after the temporary satisfactions of this life? Will you continue to place your happiness in a world that is corrupted by the curse of sin, and can therefore only end in death? Or, are you ready to fully and finally turn your life over to Jesus Christ and allow Him to save your soul for all eternity!?" the voice resounded.

I was speechless. I still had no idea who, or what, was speaking to me. For all I knew, it was simply a voice in my mind. But no matter the origin of the voice, my defenses had finally been broken down, and I was overrun and overcome by the truth of its words. I had no argument, nor struggle left within me.

CHAPTER SEVEN

I lay on the ground feeling defeated, blinded and silent, contemplating everything I had heard. The voice was right. The spiritual world was far more important than the physical world. Basic math should convince anyone that the infinite breadth of eternity was immeasurably more valuable than the finite span of a human's physical life. That equation was simple, and almost comically unbalanced. Eternity was worth more—I understood that.

However, that didn't mean that my hurts weren't real. That didn't mean our present sufferings didn't matter. I had no argument against the logic of the faceless voice, but I still had pain. The truth of eternity had been revealed to me and there was no denying it, but my afflictions were still real, and they served as the final barrier between me and God.

"But . . . what about Brice?" I asked with tears leaking out of my blinded eyes.

"Micah," the voice began softly, "I'm sorry, but Brice's fate is not in my hands. I don't know if he will recover. But let me ask you this, if Brice were to die, would hating God make his death any less true?" the voice asked.

I didn't answer. Obviously, hating God would not change Brice's fate, but Brice's fate certainly might change the way I felt about God.

"This is important to understand, Micah, because *truth* is what matters. The truth is, Brice has an immortal soul, which is far more valuable than his temporary flesh. God cares very much for Brice, just as He does for you, but even if God chooses to heal Brice from his current injuries, one day he will still face a physical death. This is the fate of all mankind.[150]

Your sins have made you mortal. So, whether Brice were to die tonight, or in one hundred years, your greatest concern for him should not be the fate of his physical body, but whether or not his soul is ready to face his Creator—because one day he will," the voice said.

I didn't answer. Suddenly a new fear crept into me. I had no idea if Brice was spiritually ready to die.

"Death is a reality," the voice continued solemnly. "God never wished it to come upon man, but it did. Hating God will not change that. But physical death is not the end for man. Your death is merely the beginning of eternity in one of two places—in heaven or in hell. While physical death seems like a tragedy on this side of eternity, the only true tragedy would be dying apart from Christ because dying *with* Christ as your Savior means inheriting *true* life for all eternity.[151]

"*Truth* is what matters, Micah," the voice said again. "Death is coming for all men. You can be angry with God about it; you can hate Him, and reject Him, but death is still coming for you anyway. Sin was the risk of choice, and death was the price of sin, but life is the gift of God through Jesus Christ our Lord.[152] Because of Jesus, it is not an empty hope to seek God's comfort during our times of grief. This is not to say that all pains will be spared—they won't—but the true comfort of God is to view life through His eternal perspective because *His* perspective is the only hope that humans have. If there be no Christ and no heaven, then death is indeed a devastating tragedy, unequalled by any loss which man can suffer. However, if Christ be real, and His gift of salvation true, then while death is still inevitable, it is but a temporary parting for all who have placed their faith in Him. And if this is the truth—as I know it is—then there is nothing more imperative in the life of a human than to accept Jesus Christ as their Lord and Savior."

I was breathing heavily. I still could see nothing of the outside world, but ironically, as blind as I was, for the first time in my life I felt that I was actually beginning to see.[153]

"And so, Micah," the voice continued, "the real truth you must come to accept is this, God is God, no matter the circumstances. He is no less loving in affliction than He is in blessings. He is no less sovereign in trials than He is in triumph. God is no less gracious in poverty than He is in prosperity. This world has fallen due to the choice of sin, but God is still God. Brice is badly hurt, and his life is certainly at risk, but God is still God. You have faced disappointment, trials, and temptations, but God is still God. No matter how hurt you're feeling right now, and no matter how angry you are with God for the bad things that have happened, God is still God, His love is still unconditional, and His offer of salvation is as necessary as ever because eternity is still what matters.

"So yes, your pain is real, but to hate God is to hate the only one who can offer you hope. It is a sobering truth to realize that you cannot cling to this world because until Christ returns, every person who passes through this terrestrial realm is destined to leave it through death. But I pray that this realization evokes not foolish and fruitless rebellion against the God who can save you, but instead, I hope this realization guides you to acceptance of the truth. The truth is that God loves you and He sent His Son to die for you so that you can be set free from the curse of this world and find the hope that only

He can offer—everlasting life. And so, whether Brice lives until he's an old man or dies on his bed tonight, the truth of *your* eternal situation will not change. No matter what happens to him, Micah, *your* sins have still separated you from God for all eternity. While his death would be tragic, physical death still pales in comparison to death apart from Christ, and the only way to reclaim your title as a son of God is through placing your faith in Jesus. You need Jesus Christ, Micah, and you need Him now," the voice finished. And then all was silent.

Lying in the darkness, my mind raced and my heart beat swiftly beneath my chest. Life had seemed so meaningless to me before, but at last I felt I understood God's plan. I wasn't just a pawn to God, I was a *soul*. And while God cared about my life, He cared infinitely more about my soul. The reality was that bad things were going to happen in this world because this world was not my home. It was temporary. It had been contaminated by sin and death, and therefore was not meant to last and would never be able to fully satisfy. Even the richest man on earth could not take the things of this world with him when he died—and death was coming for us all.[154] I understood that now. However, there was no use fearing death because we had been given a way to prepare for it.

"*That which is born of the flesh is temporary, but that which is born of the Spirit is eternal,*" I said aloud.[155]

"That's right, Micah," responded the unknown voice. "So, in which are you going to invest?" it asked. And at last, I was ready.

"I'm ready to invest in the eternal," I said, finally allowing the submissive spirit within me to break through. "But

I don't know what to do," I cried desperately.

"Yes, you do," the voice replied.

I had prayed my whole life, but for the first time ever, I didn't really know what to say. I didn't have any powerful words or a magnificent speech prepared. All I had was the truth; I hoped that would be enough. And with that, I began to pour my heart out to God.

"God, I have heard the message of the Gospel of Jesus Christ all of my life, and up until now I have rejected it," I confessed out loud, still blind to the outside world. "I'm sorry for my hate, my lust, my greed, my jealousy, and my pride. I've been so angry and so frustrated with my life. I've sinned against you. I've cared about all sorts of things that have nothing to do with you, and I've put this world before you. Can you forgive me, God?" I cried into the night. "I believe that Jesus Christ is your only begotten Son, sent here to this world to live a perfect life and die for my sins. I believe He rose on the third day and is alive. I put my trust in Him! And I ask you now, God, to save me from my sins. Make me whole, and help me to live for you. Amen."

As I finished speaking, my disposition changed immediately. All thought of chasing after Tom Reynolds was long gone, as I lay on the sidewalk barely conscious and unaware of where I was. Anger had left me completely, and suddenly I felt as if a curtain was lifting from my eyes as they struggled to open.[156] For a moment I thought I saw . . . but no, surely not. My eyes closed again. I was too weak to keep them open. In fact, I suddenly realized exactly how weak I was. My hold on consciousness was quickly slipping away. I had been pulled too hard, and I thought I might just allow myself to slip into a deep sleep and never wake up. Just as I was starting to lose all awareness and fade into oblivion, an image of Sheriff Sentry flashed through my mind, and I grabbed hold of it.

At first, I thought I had grabbed hold of the image, figuratively in my mind. But then, I realized my hands were gripping something real.

"Micah, wake up," I heard a deep, majestic voice say, as a charge of warmth and power surged through me, as if someone were reviving me with electrical paddles.

The world around me began to solidify. I felt the warm concrete beneath me, and then I shivered. I was cold, as though I had been lifeless. I tried to open my eyes, but I was still too weak.

"Micah, wake up," I heard the voice say again. More warmth surged through my body, as though the breath of life was being breathed back into me.[157]

"Micah, wake up," I heard the voice say a third time, strengthening me even more.

Finally, enough strength had returned. My eyes slowly opened and saw the friendly, smiling face of Sheriff Sentry standing over me, but he was somehow different. A bright light was shining all around him.

"Micah," he said, reaching a strong arm down to help me up. "It is time."

THE MAN IN THE WHITE ROBES

If I shall know the truth, the truth that makes one free,[158]
Then I shall fear no evil thing because you walk with me.[159]
The invisible now clearly seen, the way is paved with care.
The eye now sees, the ear now hears, God's path has been declared.[160]
The enemy, he must be faced—eye to eye with evil's glare.
For once I had been blind and entertained angels unaware.[161]
But the veil has been removed. The truth has been made known,
This world's prince has come to take God's glory for his own.[162]
Just like a lion he roams about, seeking whom he may devour.[163]
He carries with him sin and death. He strikes at any hour.[164]
So, now, oh man, the time has come to walk the Spirit's way.[165]
It's time to put your armor on, to withstand the evil day.[166]
It's time to leave the easy road, where evil treads therein.[167]
The choice is made, it's time to fight,
The battle now begins.

* * * *

FRIDAY, MAY 31, 1985 (LATE NIGHT)

Adrenaline coursed through my still weak body as I gazed up at this being that resembled Sheriff Sentry, but who seemed somehow less touched by the world. He was clean, bright, pure . . . good! He was still in his uniform, but now it glowed with a certain whiteness. His arm remained outstretched, offering to help me to my feet, but I retracted my hand in fear.

Sheriff Sentry smiled, withdrawing his hand slightly, too. And then, in the same voice I had always known, he said, "Fear not, Micah.[168] I am not here to harm you . . . but perhaps an explanation is warranted," he added, as I continued to look apprehensive.

He then paused, noticing that I had begun examining him. *How can it be?* I wondered in awe. *How can he have the voice of the man I have trusted all of my life, and yet look . . . how he looked?* And yet, beneath the glowing aura, I could see him, the same man I had always known. He was there, covered in radiance, and as I studied him, something within me knew . . . I could trust him. Still stunned, but slightly less fearful, I reached my arm out and took hold of Sheriff Sentry's hand, noticing his normally dark brown eyes seemed to be lit with fire. As I gripped his hand and he helped me to my feet, a warm sensation began to flow throughout my tired and worn body. Inexplicably, I felt strength and power returning to me.

"Where to begin?" he said, looking down in thought and releasing my hand before my strength had fully returned.

"How about, what are you?" I suggested, as I staggered to keep my feet and continued to gaze at his awesome appearance.

"Oh, right," he said with a small chuckle, which sounded far too human to be emanating from this majestic being.

"Well, I'm an angel," he exclaimed simply. "The common human name for me would be a 'guardian angel,' I suppose. I'm in command over all the angels who guard this town, and right now I'm specifically assigned to you," he said, his blazing eyes now locked onto me.[169]

"You're . . . you're an angel!?" I questioned in a choked voice. He nodded and then was silent, allowing me time to absorb this revelation. My brain was spinning into overdrive.

CHAPTER EIGHT

Sheriff Sentry was an angel . . . *how was that possible?* At least all of his unusually insightful advice for dealing with my recent spiritual activity finally made sense. For all I knew, he might have even had a front row seat, behind the scenes at each trial. Questions began pelting around, rattling my already sluggish and weakened mind.

"Wait," I finally said, feeling that something wasn't adding up. "How can you watch over me, and also be sheriff of the town at the same time?" I asked, still fighting to keep my balance.

"Let's just say that angels have ways of being *where* we are needed . . . and arriving exactly *when* we are needed," he said enigmatically.

I gave him a look of confusion, but he didn't elaborate.

"Well, shouldn't you have wings?" I blurted out without thinking. The moment the words had escaped from my lips, I began to feel very silly. There I was standing with an angel, and the most intelligent question I could ask was about his wings. But in my defense, I was still quite groggy.

A familiar, deep chuckle sounded from him. "We appear in many forms,"[170] he responded. "I could reveal my true form to you right now—wings and all—but I actually haven't."

"What do you mean?" I asked, feeling thoroughly confused. "You look quite a bit different than you usually do. Humans don't glow . . . " I contradicted in a mesmerized tone, still feeling ready to collapse at any moment.

"To you I look different," he began. "However, believe it or not, I have not changed forms. You are simply seeing more clearly than you ordinarily do," he said, as a proud smile spread across his face. "In the form I am in right now, I would look exactly the same as I have always looked to any other human . . . except for you. Because it is not me who has changed; it's you.[171]

"You are seeing me as I actually am. You are . . . shall we say . . . seeing through my disguise," he added, with a continued smile. Then he waited, allowing me time to collect my thoughts once again. I wanted to respond with another question, but it was all I could do to remain standing. I was stretched thin, my energy drained. To learn that a man I had known for years had been an angel all along would have stretched my mind to its max even on an ordinary day, but after enduring such a fierce spiritual battle, it was proving impossible. I was overwhelmed and my weakened mind refused to focus.

Noticing I still felt faint, Sheriff Sentry placed a hand on my shoulder. The instant he touched me, warmth and power radiated throughout my entire body again. However, this time he allowed his hand to remain on me. As if I had been plugged into an electrical outlet, energy surged through me, almost as if I were being charged like a battery. I felt my torn and weary mind—and perhaps my soul—begin to mend. After just a few short minutes, my strength had fully returned. I felt steadied, and my mind sharpened, allowing me to finally focus. I had so many questions for Sheriff Sentry, and I knew exactly where I wanted to begin.

"It was you all along, wasn't it?" I asked, now standing steadily under my own power. "You were the angel I saw last week on my way home from the Jacobs' house, weren't you?" I felt like I was an outsider finally being let in on a long standing joke.

CHAPTER EIGHT

"Of course," he answered with a giddy smile.

"And you were the man I saw on the golden ladder two weeks ago when this all started. You were the voice in Shelby's room . . . and it was you that I heard just moments ago in the midst of my struggle, wasn't it?" I asked, the pieces of the puzzle clicking together in my mind.

"Who else?" he responded, still smiling brightly as if nothing pleased him more than the conversation we were having.

"Sheriff . . . actually, what do I call you now?" I asked awkwardly, unsure if angels carried titles.

"My proper name is what you already know to be my first name, Quentin," he began happily. "However, angels do not have last names because we have no lineage. I was not born; I was created, just as Adam, the first man, was created.[172] My earthly last name, Sentry, means guard, so it seemed to be a good choice for my occupation as a sheriff and as a guardian angel. I know it's not creative, but it has suited me well," he said, ending in another small chuckle.

"Okay . . . Quentin . . . you said that you are in charge of the angels who guard this town, but what does that really mean? Do you go around and stop car wrecks and stuff?" I asked, as my thoughts continued to catch up with the situation.

"Well, the first thing you must know is that we carry out God's will at all times.[173] Sometimes that involves protecting humans physically, but most of the time we are here to minister to you spiritually, which is far more important," he finished.[174] Something in me felt like he was only telling me half of the story. His answer was vague, and quite honestly, I was tired of it. I had been through too much. I was ready to know everything. I was ready to know why Brice had been attacked, and why evil spirits wanted my life destroyed. I wanted answers.

"Can you please just tell me what this is all about?" I pleaded. "If you really watch over me, then you know how tired I am of the games. Please, just tell me why all of this is happening." I said in an exasperated tone.

"Okay, Micah," he said with a look of understanding. "If you want to understand what has been going on, then it is necessary for me to start from the beginning, and that will require a little patience." He then stared at me, seeking my agreement. I gave one quick nod indicating he could start wherever he wanted, if he would just give me some answers.

"Why don't you take a seat then?" he said, pointing to the sidewalk. I plopped down quickly and returned my gaze to him as he began. His deep voice reverberated in the quiet night as he spoke.

"There was once an angel in heaven, wiser, more beautiful, and more powerful than all the rest. Chosen, he was, from amongst his kind to be the greatest of all angels. Blessing and honor were freely given to him. His future was to be as bright as the sun and he was destined to excel beyond any other created being." Goose bumps began to form on my body as I listened to this magnificent being speak.

"Yet somewhere along the way," Quentin continued, "this angel lost himself. He became consumed with an overwhelming desire to be like the most-high God.[175] Corrupted, he turned on his creator and waged war in the heavens. Unsatisfied with all the glory and blessings before him, he sought to overthrow the very one who had made him—God. This angel's name was Lucifer, now more commonly known as Satan, or the devil."

I nodded my head. I knew this story well . . . although hearing it told by an angel certainly gave it new relevance.

"Sadly," Quentin continued, "one third of my brothers fought by Satan's side—drawn to him by their own sinful desires.[176] Decisive was God's victory over Satan and his followers, who would forever be called demons from that day forward. They were struck down out of the heavens. Judgment and darkness await them for all eternity," Quentin continued, his voice now somber.[177]

"However, the war did not end that day. For his own reasons, God has allowed Satan to endure until the great last day when God shall judge all of creation.[178] As Satan waits for his impending judgment, he continues to wage war against God. Yet the battles are no longer fought in heaven; instead they are fought in the realm of humans, here on Earth," Quentin said, spreading his arms out to indicate the world around us.

"Humans take it for granted," he said, as be began to stare intently into my eyes, "that there is an entire world behind your world—a world beyond your sight, filled with powerful allies and powerful foes who surround you at any given time, but who always remain completely invisible to you. Or, almost always, I should say," he added with a smile returning to his face.

"You, my friend, are one of the few exceptions there have been to that rule. And because of this, you have witnessed what *many* suspect, but *most* ignore. You know the truth! The truth that there is far more to this universe than planets and stars, matter and physics, life and death.

"However, *this*," he said as he extended his arms again and the serious expression returned to his face, "is the only portion of our universe that most humans will be allowed to experience until they either face their mortal death, or until the universe is revealed to *all* men at the coming of the great and dreadful day of the Lord.[179] At that time, everyone will see that there is so much more than meets the eye. The entire world will realize that what they cannot see is far more important and far more dangerous than what they can see."[180]

"But for now, Micah, the world is blind to the spiritual realm. Because of this, Satan and his demons remain an enemy more dangerous than most humans will ever imagine," he continued. "Ever since Satan and his demons fell, their primary goal has been to destroy all of God's creation.[181] And from the moment that God created humans, humans became their primary target.[182] They seek to destroy you, but not just your bodies; they are after your souls. 'How can they harm you?' many people might ask. Can they touch you? Can they force you to do things you don't want to? The answer is simpler than most would guess, yet more powerful than almost anyone realizes.

"They don't nab you in an alley or break into your home to steal your things, and without God's permission they cannot physically harm you at all, not directly at least.[183] No, their true power comes through suggestions, or what we like to call messages."[184]

"Messages?" I questioned, the confused look on my face

prompting him to continue.

"You heard me right, *messages!*" Quentin repeated with emphasis. "A message is a powerful thing, Micah. The proper words delivered at the proper time can save a life. Then again, the proper words withheld or delayed can cause great harm and even risk the loss of life. A message can cause inspiration, courage, adoration, and even love; or a message can tempt, it can provoke fear, wrath, anger, or uncertainty. A message can warn of danger, or it can seek to harm. A message can be the truth, or it can be a lie! Oh, the difference a message can make. They can be amazingly powerful things, for good . . . or for evil.

"Unfortunately," he continued in a sad voice, "the terrible truth is that most people are scarcely aware of the most important and most dangerous messages they will ever receive. You see, Micah, every person alive has areas of weakness in their lives, areas where they are less resistant to sin, areas where temptations will be more alluring and more potent," he said, giving me a knowing stare. "Your own recent trials, with greed, lust, and anger are evidence of this," he stated, continuing to pierce me with his burning gaze. I remained silent. I was not really eager to talk about my own impurities in front of this clean and good being, no matter how familiar with him I was.

Noticing my silence, he continued. "Though Satan and his demons cannot touch you without God's permission, they have the ability to influence you and deceive you through their messages.[185] Aiming for your weaknesses and vulnerabilities, they tempt you, hoping you will stumble into sin.[186] Satan lures you in and tricks you. He invites you into his clutches, has you believing you are merely chasing your own desires, when suddenly he strikes like a serpent that has been lying in wait.[187] To him, you are just mice, being baited by your own favorite flavor of cheese, wandering ignorantly into a trap ready to snap upon you.

"He leads Christians down paths of sin in hopes that they will become indifferent, ashamed, or even angry toward God.[188] Through sin he separates you, leaving you stagnant and hiding in guilt, unable and unwilling to partake in your daily walk with Him. Likewise, he leads lost people in a pursuit of earthly desires and away from salvation in Christ in the hopes that one day, when Satan faces God's judgment and wrath, most of God's creation will be destroyed as well.[189] Each and every day he does this—simply by using *messages*." I raised my eyebrows and nodded my head in understanding. It was all true. I could see it clearly. All humans were in danger because not only did we all have areas of weakness, but we were also all blind to Satan's deadly game. We were easy targets—most of us at least.

"Fortunately," Quentin continued, "there is one good thing that all messages have in common, and that is choice." I nodded my head again in understanding. Having just made my own choice to accept Christ, I could at least *begin* to see what Quentin meant. Suddenly he paused, smiling down at me, looking for the second time as if he was quite proud.[190] After having just reminded me of my sin and weaknesses, it was odd for this pure being to give me any look of approval. Somehow, he made me feel both safe and terrified, victorious and guilty all at once.

After a few seconds, he looked back up and then

continued. "Just as in your own struggle, Micah, once a message has been delivered, the choice still rests with the hearer. A message can be heeded or ignored. It can provoke; it can influence, warn, or tempt; but the message itself *does* nothing. All a message really does is influence an individual toward a choice, but in the spiritual world, the choice is *always* in the hands of the individual. Whether good or bad, pure or sinister, a message itself is not what actually brings harm. True danger comes when the wrong message is received and the wrong information is acted upon. This is why humans must be very careful of the messages they receive, discerning who, or what, they listen to.[191]

"So, do you help other people listen to the right messages . . . the way you helped me through my battle?" I asked.

"Of course," he said smiling again. "You see, Micah, it's not just Satan who sends messages. God knows the power of messages, too. That's where we come in," he said with an even bigger smile. "Angels are often thought of as mighty warriors in shiny white robes, and we indeed do *many* things to serve God. However, when you get right down to it, the word *angel* means *messenger.* What else could we be doing, then, besides delivering messages from God, hoping to help humans choose Christ over sin? We do the opposite of Satan and the demons. When the dark clouds of temptation come, we guide you to the light; we point you toward Christ.[192] As I said, we do many things for God, but our primary role in the war for your souls is ministry," he said.[193]

As Quentin finished talking, he turned and started

walking away from the hospital toward his police jeep, which was still parked in the same place as when we had arrived there with the Jacobs a short time before. I scrambled to my feet and followed his glowing figure instinctively. "So, Quentin," I began my next question as we walked, still uncomfortable saying his name, "all of these messages and all of this stuff I've seen and experienced, it's all been just to influence me?" I inquired, not taking my eyes off him, as if I feared he would disappear should I look away.

Quentin stopped by his police jeep, and then turned toward me. "Not just you, Micah. This whole town is under attack; all the people in it. Satan has special plans for this town," Quentin said, being enigmatic once again. "He has also sensed the Holy Spirit's movement in your life. Because of this, he has rightly concluded that God has appointed a special role unto you. This is why he has tempted and tried you beyond normal, because he will do whatever he can to stop you from interfering with his plans," Quentin said in a serious tone.

I was silent for a moment as I swallowed in fear. For almost two weeks I had known that I had been chosen for something, but I had secretly hoped that passing the three temptations would bring an end to my part in this struggle. From the way Quentin was speaking, it sounded like it was just the beginning.

"Okay," I said as I exhaled, realizing it would be foolish to ignore a fight if it was going to come for me whether I acknowledged it or not. "Why is our town under attack? I mean, what could Satan possibly want with this small, insignificant town? And what could God want with me . . . I'm nobody!" I pleaded, feeling a little desperate.[194]

Quentin sighed and said, "I don't fully know why Satan has chosen this town, and I don't know why God has chosen you. In the same way, it was unclear why God chose Abraham, Moses, Gideon, Paul, or any other hero that you've heard of from the Bible.[195] He has *His* reasons, and His ways are always right, but many times we'll never know why.[196]

"However, we do know a few things. First, we know that God indeed *has* chosen you, or I would not have been revealed to you tonight. Second, the question of 'why' might seem the most pressing, but in reality, asking 'why' doesn't change the fact that your town and the people you care about really *are* in danger," he said seriously.

"But what danger? What could Satan possibly have planned for us?" I asked, still trying to understand why we were singled out. "Surely Satan could carry out his plans without us, without Brice," I said sadly.

Quentin sighed again. This time he looked a little worn and a little sad. The cool air of the night had begun to settle around us, and the air felt motionless. Not a single car passed, not a single person had come or gone from the hospital. It was as if the universe had halted to allow us time to talk.

"It's the same danger that all humans are in," he resumed, "It's the same war that has been going on since Satan first fell. From the moment he first desired to be like God, he has waged war with God and the heavens, and all of creation."

I got the feeling he was once again talking around my questions with generalities, as if he did not want to give me the specific details that I was seeking about our town. However, as he spoke, another question popped into my mind. "Actually, why did Satan go to war with God?" I interrupted out of sincere curiosity. "Surely he couldn't have expected to win, could he?"

He looked at me with eyes that told me that I should already know the answer to this question, but my mind was blank, so I remained silent until finally he spoke. "Micah, when you were tempted at the bank, or tempted to fight Tom, or tempted to kiss Katie, weren't the consequences pretty easy to ignore? Didn't the things you desired nearly make the warnings and common sense disappear?" he asked wisely, now leaning against his police jeep. It looked incredibly odd to see him lounging in this way, while glowing pure, bright white. He looked up at the clear night sky as I considered his question. The bright moon and shining stars overhead seemed to reflect Quentin's essence.

I nodded my head. I got his point. Satan didn't think about whether or not he could defeat God, he was just consumed with his sin. The consequences were irrelevant to him. It was kind of sad actually; to think of God's most beautiful angel falling so far . . . it really demonstrated the power of sin.

"No human or angel has ever been as consumed by temptation as Satan. The brightest of all of us, yet he turned on God in pursuit of his own unholy desires. He forgot about purity, goodness, and the honor of his position, serving our King. He let his lust rule him, and eventually ruin him.[197] Both he and one third of my brothers fell into temptation, and they were cast out from heaven forever." Quentin ended with a very heavy expression.[198]

CHAPTER EIGHT

I studied his sad face. The war of the angels was only hinted at in the Bible; how fascinating, and yet tragic, the full story must be. Growing up in church as a kid, I had heard of the war, but I had never considered that the fall of Satan had actually been difficult on the angels. In my mind, they had always seemed like mythical creatures, not as beings with emotions, compassion, and feelings. It was quite obvious that Quentin's memory of the angelic war brought back just as many emotions and just as much pain as any memory of mine could have. It was personal to him.

I did not want to be insensitive, but I had my own battle to worry about, so I pressed the conversation forward. "I still don't get what all that has to do with us," I said apologetically. "I get that Satan wants to destroy God's creation, but that doesn't explain why he is focused so specifically on this town. Why are we so important?"

Quentin shifted, causing his police vehicle to rock under his enormous weight. He had always been a large guy, towering over me by several inches and massively strong, but he seemed even bigger now. His eyebrows lowered and his nearly celestial face formed a slight frown as he considered how to approach what I knew to be the heart of the issue.

"Satan is still chasing the very sin that made him fall," he began. "To this very day, he desires only one thing; he wants to be like the most-high God.[199] He hates everything about God and God's kingdom because it is a reminder of everything he is not; everything he so desires, but cannot have. Because of this, he and his fallen angels are always working to mimic God. It's madness, but he's trying to create his own kingdom." He paused again. I remained silent, now hungry for the answers that felt just a breath away.

Quentin sighed and prepared to speak, and I could tell this was it. At last, this was the moment I had waited for. For two weeks, I had wondered why all of these weird supernatural events had been so abnormally concentrated on our town and on me. Anticipation pulsed through me as I silently waited for the answers I had long been searching for.

Quentin began. "Angels can appear in human form any time we need to, but we aren't primarily physical beings.[200] Our normal form is spiritual.[201] Humans are terrestrial, but we are celestial.[202] Because of this, we were not gifted with reproduction like humans . . . at least not in the normal sense; and we aren't supposed to reproduce at all.

"As I said before, angels are created, not born. I have no heir, no son, and no daughter.[203] There are no more and no fewer of us today than the original time when God first created us. One third of our kind fell, but they did not die when they fell.[204] They are condemned, waiting in judgment, but they are still alive.[205] So, our numbers remain unchanged, even though one third of our kind is now evil," he said, as he pushed himself up from his jeep to look me more fully in the face.

"But Satan and his demons love the idea of increasing their numbers because no matter how impossible it might be, Satan hopes to one day fight against God. And that's why he needs a human. He needs a human vessel because other than God, only physical life can create life. Specifically for Satan, he wants to find a human vessel . . ." Quentin paused, as if he had to force the final words from his tongue. "He needs a human vessel, to help him create a son of his own," he finished solemnly.

My mouth hung open wide and my brow lowered in dismay. It was more bizarre than anything I had ever heard, anything I could have imagined. Angels and demons were extraordinary enough, but to think of creating a new fallen angel . . . a new Satan . . . it was inconceivable.

I stared at him in shock. "Have a son?" I repeated, hardly able to believe my ears.

Quentin nodded. "As I told you, he likes to mimic God. Since God the Father has God the Son,[206] Satan wants to have an offspring, too. In setting up his kingdom, he wants someone like *him* to be seated on the right side of *his* throne. It's delusional and mad, and in no way would he and his spawn be like the Father and the Son—the first two persons of the Holy Trinity—but that is Satan's plan nevertheless. And even if he fails, he will undoubtedly cause much destruction and possibly death along the way," Quentin added as his sad eyes glanced over toward the hospital, undoubtedly thinking of Brice.

As horrendous as the story was, something was not adding up. "If angels aren't capable of reproduction because they aren't primarily physical, then how will a human help Satan? He's nothing more than a fallen angel, right?" I asked.

Quentin bowed his head. "Demons don't reproduce in the way humans reproduce," he continued slowly. "Their reproduction with a human is a conception of pure evil, with a willing host who has completely succumbed to temptation and sin and allowed the spiritual being to inhabit them. The result is being possessed by the demon, or in this case by Satan, and used as a vessel to bring forth the new life."

"Is that even possible? I mean, can that even happen?" I asked, feeling there was no end to the bizarre new world to which I had been exposed.

"Yes," he began to respond. "It is possible. It has happened before with other fallen angels, but never with Satan."

"It's happened before?" I yelled; my level of shock at an all-time high.

"Yes," Quentin responded, hanging his head. "The fall from heaven was only the first angel battle. There was another battle between us, but one that is not as well known. I am sure you have heard the story in the book of beginnings, although you likely do not recognize it for what it is," he said.

"The book of beginnings?" I asked in confusion.

"Ah," he said, realizing his mistake. "It's what you would call the Book of Genesis. In Genesis chapter six, it tells the story of a very dark time in our history, second only to the fall, and to be overshadowed in the future only by the final judgment. So, the story goes . . .

> . . . *When mankind began to multiply on the earth and daughters were born to them, the sons of God saw that the daughters of man were beautiful, and they took any they chose as wives for themselves. . . . The giants were on the earth both in those days and afterwards, when the sons of God came to the daughters of man, who bore children to them. They were the powerful men of old, the famous men.*[207]

I had never been more confused in my life. "So, the sons of God . . . were angels, I assume," I said. Quentin nodded. "And the angels mated with humans and . . . "

"Not mated," Quentin interrupted. "As I told you, it is a spiritual joining, a nearly complete possession of a human soul by a demon. But God's angels would never do that—nor can we. If it were possible for me to do that, then I would immediately change from what I am," he said and then paused, looking both sad and angry.

Looking away, he spoke again. "If any angel were able to commit such a heinous act, then they would cease to be angels and forever join the fallen ones. That's who did this, fallen angels, demons. They took wives because they wanted them. Demons are perverse and evil and did not mind twisting and destroying the female humans they overtook," he said with disgust in his voice.

Pain filled his fierce, burning eyes. It was, again, very personal for him, completely dispelling the mythical view I had always held of angels. Quentin was personal, loving, and even emotional. It was bizarre to witness, but it was also quite moving.

"As I said," he finally continued, his throat sounding slightly choked up, "all created beings have weaknesses. Angels are no different. We are not perfect.[208] The purity and beauty of some human women was a real attraction to even some . . . " he cut off, " . . . but to do what the demons did is unthinkable . . . impossible," he said in a sad whisper almost to himself.[209]

"You say it is impossible, but if it happened before, then it's possible, isn't it?" I asked, not wanting to offend, but just hoping to gain a clear understanding.

He cleared his throat and continued. "It is impossible for an angel who did not fall with Satan on that terrible day. Angels fully belong to God now. We made our choice, and two-thirds of us chose rightly. Besides, an angel cannot possess a human.[210] God designed us to protect humans. It's written into our most basic instincts, like drinking water is for you. We see and feel both good and evil more fully. This is why the actions of the fallen ones were so horrendous. It went against their designed nature, and it was only possible because their sin had already changed them into something else entirely," he said, looking down at the pavement with a slight shake in his deep and powerful voice.

It was weird enough to be standing in the presence of an angel. Even stranger still was seeing the pain that Quentin felt as he spoke of the sins of fallen angels. I could tell this part of the subject bothered him more than most, and I was still very confused, so I moved the conversation forward. "Okay, so, demons possessed human women and had some sort of . . . giant?" I asked, recalling the passage from Genesis he had quoted, and uncertain why Satan would want a giant for a son.

Quentin looked grateful to continue, and began again immediately. "The word for 'giant' is actually *Nephilim* in the original Hebrew text. Humans have disagreed as to what exactly this means and have called the Nephilim 'giants' for lack of a better word. But they were not giants like a human would normally think. They weren't just tall, big men, though that is certainly one attribute they possessed, much like angels in our regular form . . . some people might even say that I'm close enough to being a giant in my human form." He laughed, smiling for the first time in a while. I couldn't disagree with him. I was tall, and he made me feel as if I were tiny.

"No," he continued, "the Nephilim were powerful new creations. However, they differed from any other created being. The Nephilim were unique because they were fully part of two worlds. They existed in both the physical and spiritual realms, like angels are now and like humans will be one day.[211] Therefore, upon creation, the Nephilim were much closer in nature to angels than they were to humans or demons. You see, demons can no longer become physical the way we angels can,"[212] he said, looking me full in the face, unblinkingly.

"When they fell they were stripped of that right. When God cast them down from heaven, he also took their ability to become physical. He has bound them to what is known as *Tartarus*."

"Bound them to what?" I cut in.

"To Tartarus," he repeated. "Three realms exist in this universe, Micah: heaven and earth, and also Tartarus," he said slowly.

"What is Tartarus? I feel like I've heard of it before," I said.

"You might have," he continued. "Tartarus is mentioned only one time in all of Scripture.[213] It is the entire spiritual realm that exists outside of heaven, including the spiritual realm surrounding Earth. Angels travel in and out of the three realms freely. However, demons were restricted to Tartarus when they fell. Satan has on occasion been granted access to heaven, but only to speak before God.[214] It is no longer his home, and he is no longer allowed access to Earth, to enter the physical realm—not bodily that is.[215]

"This is why demons try to possess humans, or even

animals.[216] They seek to be physical once again, but they can't. They will never again become physical. They remain bound in Tartarus, spiritual, and waiting for their final judgment," he finished solemnly.[217]

"So, these Nephilim help the demons somehow?" I asked, still unclear how the Nephilim fit into Satan's plan.

"Yes, Genesis does not call them mighty men for nothing. When the demons controlled the Nephilim the first time, they brought destruction upon this world in a much more powerful way than demons are capable of doing because the Nephilim are able to wreak havoc in both realms. They can interact physically like giant, brutal men, and they can also tempt, manipulate, and seduce spiritually like demons. This makes them extremely potent and an extremely dangerous ally of the demons," he said gravely.

"So you see; Satan wants an evil Nephilim son. Although God's Son is, in fact, God, Satan wants his own son, in a vain attempt to rival God's Son. To explain Satan simply, he mimics God and adds to his own false kingdom, causing nothing but death and destruction along the way. This is what he does. This is his plan. And as of right now, this town is where he's focused," Quentin stated, with graveness in his eyes.

I was dumbfounded. It all seemed impossible. It seemed like it should be in a sci-fi movie, not in real life. But I knew it wasn't fiction. While some of it was new and bizarre, the war between God and Satan was nothing new. It was a story I had heard and largely ignored my entire life. But the time for pretending that the spiritual world didn't exist was over. I was in it now. Then, as if reading my mind, Quentin spoke.

CHAPTER EIGHT

"So, the question I have is the same question that we always must ask in our war against Satan. What will the humans involved *choose* to do? Without humans, Satan wouldn't have power over anything," he stated.

"But how is it up to us? I mean, if Satan is going to possess someone, what can we do? Surely you can't expect us to withstand him, to stop his plans," I repeated, getting louder with each statement.

"Why can't we expect you to withstand him?" Quentin asked. "You stopped his plans for you, so far, didn't you?"

"I suppose," I answered sheepishly.

"And how did you do it, Micah?" Quentin prodded. "Was it because you were so strong that you were able to overcome Satan by force? Was it because you were wiser or more powerful than him? How did you overcome Satan?" he continued to question, the fire in his eyes burning brighter than before.

I hung my head, unsure what to answer. I hadn't done anything special. All I had done was give myself over to Christ.

"Well?" Quentin asked.

"I turned to Christ," I answered, sheepishly again.

"Yes you did," Quentin said, a victorious smile immediately springing to his face. "And that's what everyone must do. You see, we don't defeat Satan on our own, Micah, we defeat him by fleeing from sin and turning to God.[218] It's not our might or our power that claims the victory. Victory is only found in Jesus Christ.[219] The more we prepare, the more we study, the more we pray, the more we should learn that we *must* depend on God.[220] If we turn to Him in our times of trouble, then we tap into a source of power which never runs dry. For a human then, it *always* comes down to choice. Will you choose to turn to God in the difficult times, or will you trust in your own strength?

"We *always* have a choice, Micah" he stated with fierce emotion in his eyes. "Satan had a choice. The angels who fell with him had a choice. I had a choice. You have a choice, and the person whom Satan chooses to use will have a choice."

"But if we really have a choice, then who on Earth would let Satan possess them and have his *heir?*" I asked. "No one would do that," I stated in response to my own question. It was absurd to think anyone would help this type of thing happen.

"Didn't we already cover this, Micah?" Quentin asked bluntly. "We don't fall into sin thinking of the consequences. Satan certainly didn't when he fell from heaven. Temptation is very powerful and Satan is very crafty. He doesn't announce himself or his intentions. He's known as the great deceiver for a reason. Would you ordinarily steal from a bank? Would you ordinarily kiss another girl while on a date with Rachel? Would you ordinarily attack the many people that I *know* you were so angry with and so wrathful toward just moments ago?" he questioned, pausing to let his point sink in.

"Satan sends humans subtle little *messages* of temptation. His temptations attack at a person's weak points," he continued. "Satan isn't going to introduce himself, explain his plan, and get informed consent. No, he twists the truth. He attacks weak points. He'll find someone who is vulnerable, and he'll gradually, but effectively, convince them to let sin in. And as they let in the sin, the sin gains control of them, and as the sin gains control, so does *he*." Quentin hesitated again. "Can you think of no one in your life who has seemed quite open to sin recently?"

"Katie!" my mouth spit out in involuntary horror, almost before I had thought it. Then my mind caught up with my mouth. Katie had confessed how curious she was about the dream she had been having. Now she was gone. *Has Satan already taken her?* I thought in fear.

"Through her own choices, Katie has begun down a dark path of destruction," Quentin responded sadly. "If she does not give her life to Christ, then I believe she will find the temptations that await her too strong to resist. If she is unable to turn back from her own temptations, then yes, I believe she will be the host." He leaned against his jeep once more, causing it to shift under his massive weight yet again.

"But to allow herself to be possessed by Satan? She wouldn't!" I protested. Even though my instincts had just guessed that she was the target, I still wasn't ready to accept it as a possibility.

"Micah," Quentin responded, "demon possession is not the intrusion that people think it is. It's not like a thief smashing open a window to break into your home in broad day light. It's more like a person opening the door for a robber believing they are letting in someone harmless. When the person opens the door, they do so for their own selfish or dishonest reasons. They open the door to gratify a temptation. The problem is, people never expect the robber to be evil. They ignore warnings and convictions of things they know are wrong, and slowly they let the robber in. As a person makes one small, selfish wrong decision, and then another, and then another, and so on, they gradually invite the robber in more and more until finally the robber is a permanent resident.[221]

"That's what they do, Micah," Quentin continued. "The demons tempt people; they send their messages—fiery darts of influence—at a person, and if a person lets enough of those in, they become enslaved to sin by their choices.[222] They become consumed by them. Why do you think addictions can have such strong holds on people? Not only can addictions be physical, but also spiritual; people literally let evil inside themselves, and evil does not leave without a fight! Taking full control—full possession—is a rare case because most of the time, a demon simply wants a person to be addicted or dependent on something. They don't even try to fully possess the vast majority of humans because their main goal is to keep you away from Christ—and while something else has your heart, Christ certainly won't.[223] Do you see how deceptive and how powerful that is?" Quentin asked.

I stared at him blankly. I could not speak just yet, so I nodded my head. He remained silent while I thought. Shock was searing through me. I had felt those same influences more times than I could count, not just at my recent trials, but all throughout my life. To think that all of the times I had succumbed to small temptations, I had actually been allowing evil to influence me, perhaps to even develop small footholds in my life.

I shuddered as I stood there in the warm summer night. I knew now there had been demons after me my entire life and they were very good at hiding their assault. It had taken a series of supernatural events to force me into a decision. If I hadn't been exposed to more than the normal person, I have no idea if anything would have ever awakened me from my sinful slumber.[224] Then another thought hit me.

"Does it work the other way? I mean, if we become a Christian, are we *possessed* by . . . goodness?" I asked, unsure if I was saying it right.

"Sort of," Quentin answered, "As I said, though, angels don't indwell people, only God is supposed to do that.[225] When you accepted Jesus Christ just moments ago," he said with a smile, "you were indwelt with the Holy Spirit.[226] While demons can still tempt you and gain footholds in your life through sin, they cannot possess you because God now lives inside of you. You have been sealed unto the day of redemption by the very Spirit of God," he said with a smile.[227]

I looked around at the night sky, trying to clear my head. My mind was once again racing. The evening had been a complete whirlwind. It seemed like forever ago that my date with Rachel had been abruptly cut short by our sudden intuition that something was terribly wrong. So much had happened since then that I had barely noticed how late it had become.

The stars were out in full force, and the weather outside was perfect. The air was calm, and the unnatural chill had been warmed out of me completely by Quentin's supernatural touch, leaving behind only the mild outside temperature. As I thought of my newfound stronghold in Christ, and the Holy Spirit who now lived in me, acting as a sort of impenetrable barrier between my soul and the demons, I felt myself relax a little for the first time since earlier that evening when the date had been going so well with Rachel. I leaned up against Quentin's police jeep, taking my place beside my glowing companion, the man in the white robes who had found me in my darkest hour and pulled me from the depths of sin into the salvation of Jesus Christ. Despite everything going on, I felt at peace.

"We still need to talk about the one thing that I know you aren't eager to discuss," Quentin said, interrupting my tranquility.

"What's that?" I responded, selfishly hoping it wouldn't be anything too unpleasant.

"Your role in this," he answered. I simply nodded. I wasn't exactly excited about being "chosen," but I was ready to listen anyway.

"You have been chosen for a special honor. You've been given a temporary gift. Well, we'll call it a gift for lack of a better word; but make no mistake, this gift will come with immense difficulties. As evidenced by the way you see me now, you will be able to see other angels . . . and you will even be able to see demons."

I instinctively looked around in fear.

"You can't see any now. They fled when you accepted Christ," he said.[228] "But they'll be back, and when they come, they will no longer be hidden to you," he resumed. "You'll be able to see the spiritual battles behind the temptations, the sin, and even the angels at work. When you submitted yourself to God, He gave you this temporary gift. I don't know how long you'll have it, but you have it now because of what is coming. The greatest fight is yet ahead of us, Micah, and to defeat it, I want you to always remember how you overcame your own struggle. You must remember that a person can always choose to return from sin. As long as a person lives, God is able and willing to forgive them of their sins and receive them unto His own.[229] It is never too late to choose Christ for anyone who still has breath in their lungs.

"As for you, much more will be asked. You will face greater and more powerful temptations. Since the beginning of time, there has been a war between good and evil. By choosing Christ, you are no longer a bystander or a victim, you are now truly part of the fight," he said, staring at me and then hesitating . . .

"Yes," he suddenly said aloud, almost as if he had been speaking to someone else. And then, he reached out his hand to me slowly, seeming to accent the weightiness of the moment, and smiling eagerly as he did so. He had apparently just realized something . . . something good and exciting.

"What is it?" I asked, hopeful for some good news for a change.

"Micah, I have just been given permission . . . My heart can hardly believe it," he said, barely able to contain his joy. "There have been many miraculous visions, and revelations, and prophesies in human history, but something like this? . . . Oh no, something like this has only happened to man a few times in history.[230] But, enough talk," he said with glee now radiating from his bright essence as he reached out his hand for me to grab, "it is finally time for you to see for yourself . . . "

CHAPTER NINE

A VIEW FROM ABOVE

He makes his angels spirits, ministers of flaming fire,[231]
With power they protect us from the threat of our desire.
Divine purpose is their mission; for righteousness they burn.
They fight to keep the dark away, which longs for our return.
For angels aren't the only ones with interest in our soul.
There is a foe who walks amidst a deep and darker road. [232]
It wants to know what tempts you most, what lies you have concealed.
What weaknesses it might exploit,
What wounds have not been healed.[233]
Oh gluttony; just one more bite, your hunger to fulfill.
Oh avarice; I want what's yours. Why work when you can steal?
Oh jealousy and anger, oh pride, oh wrath, oh spite.
Any sin can overtake you when you don't put up a fight.[234]
So choose to take the narrow road. It's rarely ever used.[235]
But it will lead from death to life, from emptiness to truth.[236]
And so, the choice is in your hands. It's victory or loss.[237]
There's a price to pay for all we do,
So always count the cost.[238]

*   *   *   *

FRIDAY, MAY 31, 1985 (NIGHT) THRU *EVERLASTING . . .*

The moment I touched Quentin's hand, the world around me fell away like a curtain dropping to the ground, taking with it the sky, the stars, the buildings, and the trees. But what replaced the natural world I could not see, for suddenly everything darkened and a mighty, irresistible force snatched me from where I stood, hurling me into the unknown with blinding speed.

I was not walking or running, jumping or climbing, or

anything of the sort, but somehow I moved—or maybe it was the universe that moved; I could not tell. Silently, streaks of light—possibly stars and planets—flew past me in a blur, as if I were traveling at warp speed; yet somehow, no wind disturbed my hair or clothes. I was suspended in motionless motion—if indeed there is such a thing.

I glided through space and time with the universe unfolding effortlessly beneath and around me. For minutes I traveled—or perhaps it was days or years, it became difficult to know which. Time seemed to have no meaning. My journey lasted forever . . . and yet it took no time at all. In fact, I grew quite certain that time was irrelevant.

If, in that state, it had been possible for me to experience a moment of joy, and I had desired for that moment to last forever, well I feel quite certain it would have. I no longer played victim to the clock, that tyrant which cruelly trudges on, mercilessly bringing an end to life, loved ones, and everything we wish we could hold on to. In our world, time is always our captor and there is no escaping. But, in that moment, I did escape. Somehow I knew *time* had left me altogether. I was simply *there*. Where "there" was, I had no idea, because the forms that flew past me traveled too swiftly to be recognized.

Then I felt my body change too; or perhaps it was the atmosphere changing. Everything was impossible to know for certain. But what *was* certain is that everything grew lighter; I was lighter, weightless. In fact, it was as if I had no body at all. Looking down at my arms and legs, I saw they were becoming somehow less tangible. Their wispy appearance was nearly ghost-like in the empty chasm through which I sailed. Soundless images of light continued to soar past me, swiftly and silently as the weight of the world steadily departed, stripping away my physical existence more and more, until eventually I felt I had become nothing.

Just as I was adjusting to my new timeless and weightless reality, everything began to change once again. With a rush, the feel of the world suddenly returned to me; not its weight, but its time and place—a specific time and place, in fact. Yet somehow I knew neither the place nor the time had a hold on me, as if I could leave them both at any moment.

I had no idea how I would leave, but it felt entirely possible to do so. Like a visitor in a moment of history, I was not really an inhabitant wherever and whenever I was arriving. I was outside of all time and all moments; neither here, nor there, nor when nor where; I simply *was*. How I knew? I do not know; but I knew.

The images and light began to slow around me until they eventually stopped altogether and the darkness lifted, causing the world to rematerialize into a familiar setting. Interestingly, after all I had experienced, I appeared to not have traveled very far at all. While it was true that I was no longer beside Quentin's police jeep in the parking lot outside of the hospital, whatever had happened had merely transported me from the outside of the hospital to the inside. Looking around, I realized I was standing in the hallway just outside of Brice's room.

My eyes glanced down to observe my body, which continued to radiate a faint ghostly glow, just as it had while I had sailed through the empty chasm. I was wearing the same jeans and T-shirt that I had put on hours before in preparation

for my date with Rachel. I had two arms, two feet, and two legs
. . . everything seemed to be in its proper place, only . . .
weightless. I was bound to nothing, and I felt absolutely no
density or interaction between my body and the laws of physics.
I didn't even feel hungry—which was certainly unusual for me.
I started to raise my arms to touch my wispy skin when I saw
something out of the corner of my eye.

"Hello, Micah," bellowed Quentin's deep and powerful
voice, which caused me to jump in fright, having forgotten he
was with me. In fact, I was not entirely certain he had taken the
same unusual journey that I had. I tried to calm myself, but
Quentin's appearance was not helping matters. He was no
longer in his police uniform, but in brilliant white robes with a
white, misty aura that encompassed him even more completely
than before. In fact, if I had to guess, I would have said that his
entire essence was comprised of the white mist. And, although
his face bore the same kind expression and appearance it always
had, he was larger and looked even more terrifying than usual.

Power and purity emanated from him like electricity,
surging through the very air around us. Instinctively, I took a
step back from him in fear.[239] For reasons unknown to me, I
could sense that he was safe and good, but at the same time,
being near him was terrifying, for I could also sense that his
might was unparalleled. He was awesome, in the truest sense of
the word.

"Do not be afraid, Micah," he said to me in a voice that
continued to exude power, yet somehow rang familiar. "It is still
me, Quentin," he comforted as he held out his massive glowing
arms in a welcoming gesture. "I am your friend, and I have long

been your protector and *messenger.*"

He waited for me to gather my thoughts as I struggled to find my voice. Finally I choked out a sentence. "Before . . . you looked different, but you were still the same person . . . but now . . . " I trailed off, ever astounded by his breathtaking appearance.

"As I said, Micah, what you saw before was not a change in me; it was your gift allowing you to see the essence of my true nature. I was in the same form I always appear in when I am with humans. This, however," he said, holding his hands out again and looking down at his body, "is my normal angelic form. I could have appeared to you like this earlier, but I thought it might be easier to see me in my human form first," he said, smiling at his correct assumption.

"You were right," I replied, still very intimidated by him. "But . . . if this is your normal angel form, shouldn't you have wings now?" I asked rather stupidly, for the second time. I was not sure why I cared so much whether or not he had wings, but like most things, when an idea popped into my mind, I simply blurted it out unfiltered.

He laughed his normal deep, hearty laugh, which immediately made me feel much more comfortable with this new, and more terrifying, Quentin.

"I don't need wings to travel, but . . . I can appear as a winged beast, if you think that would be easier for you," he said laughing again, knowing that I would definitely prefer he not turn into a winged beast.[240]

"No, this will be fine," I responded quickly. He laughed again, and smiled.

CHAPTER NINE

"So, why did we have to go through all of that just to go across the parking lot?" I asked curiously, as my comfort level continued to rise. "Not that I'm complaining, but we could have just walked in here if we wanted to see Brice."

"Micah, you are not *in* the hospital in the normal sense. You are absent from your physical body, my friend,"[241] he said, continuing to smile in delight. "You are *spirit* right now. Examine your hands and your feet. Touch your face. Does it not feel different?" he asked.

I reached my hand toward my face, noticing my continued bright and wispy appearance was not all that dissimilar from Quentin's appearance; just less bright and infinitely less terrifying—to me at least. I touched my hand to my face and the sensation immediately gave me chills. It felt different; I was different. I was there, I could feel my own touch, but I could also tell I did not have to be there—I felt like I could be anywhere . . . or nowhere. I felt sturdy enough to stand there and do anything I could normally do, but also like vapor, ready to vanish at any second. There is no other way to describe it.

"Do you see, Micah?" he asked, with a broad, excited smile. "You are not bound by space or time. You still exist, but you can exist anywhere at any time—not all at once of course, but your spiritual body can exist anywhere and as we angels like to say, any-*when*. And so, my friend, you are in spiritual form right now because a normal walk across the parking lot would not have allowed you to see all the things you need to see and would not have brought us to Brice's room exactly *when* we needed to arrive," he said mysteriously, although I thought I could see a slight grin on his face.

"What do you mean, *when?*" I asked, intrigue now overtaking my fear.

"I wanted this portion of your experience to happen uninterrupted. So, I brought you back in time, just a little before you and I arrived with Brice's family at the hospital. We will have a brief window before the doctors and nurses go to work on him. As such, when we see Brice, he will be all alone . . . from a *human* perspective at least," he finished mysteriously yet again. *Now* there was definitely a smile on his face. He was enjoying the experience far too much.

"What do you mean?" I asked again, rolling my eyes jokingly and cracking a slight smile of my own.

"What you are seeing now and what you are about to see is a perspective that only a few humans in history have been privileged to glimpse—without death that is.[242] This is the world as we angels see it. You are in the spiritual realm. You are in Tartarus."

"We're in Tartarus?" I shrieked, my joking demeanor vanishing immediately. "But I thought you said Tartarus was the demons' realm?" I questioned frantically, once again looking around for demons in fear.

"They are in this realm," he began, now serious too, "but they do not own it. This is just where they are bound.[243] As I said, angels were created to go between Heaven, Tartarus, and the physical realm freely, but the third that fell were stripped of their ability to travel between the three realms. They are indeed trapped here, but this is not their realm. Tartarus was created for angels . . . but that is another story for another time," he said, the smile returning to his face once again.

"Besides," he continued, "you have to be in this realm with the demons if you want to *really* see," he said mysteriously, for the third time, now not even attempting to mask his enjoyment.

"What am I about to see?" I asked, hoping that I sounded casual, despite feeling a mixture of curiosity and fear.

He raised his hand and pointed toward the door to Brice's room. "When you step through that door, you will see everything I see and feel everything I feel. In this world, the physical realm is the backdrop. In this world, we fight the spiritual battles. Those pains, emotions, and temptations which you humans endure in the physical realm, they are felt more powerfully and seen more fully by angels here in Tartarus. We sense and see the true evil or goodness of a human's intentions, desires, and actions. In this realm, it is your spiritual health that matters, and as you will see, your spiritual health affects our entire atmosphere quite powerfully.

"When you step through that door, you will see Brice and the spiritual battle he is engaged in. Let me warn you, you might want to help him, but you must resist this urge! Even we angels do not help unless it is God's will. We do not fight under our own power, and you, who are presently much less powerful than we are, must never try to *physically* engage in the struggle.[244] It could be disastrous for you. Do you understand this?" he asked warningly. His eyes locked onto mine as he waited for a response.

I stared at him with my mouth hanging wide open, now scared beyond measure. I was unable to say anything, so I simply nodded. It was too much to take in. I was barely over the fact that Quentin was an angel—my guardian angel no less—but to have been pulled out of my normal world and into some sort of spiritual time travel, for the purpose of seeing my best friend engaged in a dangerous demonic battle; it was all too much to absorb. It was simply unbelievable. How could any of it be real? I was about to be in the presence of demons, demons that wanted to destroy me, and were perfectly capable of doing just that.

Noticing my trepidation, Quentin spoke, "Micah, you have always believed in God and angels. Is it really so shocking when we present ourselves to you?"

"Yes, it really is," I said, allowing myself to laugh a little as I exhaled. Quentin chuckled, too.

"But when I think about God and angels, I don't normally think about going face to face with demons," I added, feeling more insignificant by the second.

He smiled. "You are with me, Micah. Trust me, my friend. Nothing can harm you, so long as you do not try to interfere *physically*. Remember that and you will be safe, right by my side. I promise you that."

I studied his voice. Though masked in supernatural power, it was the same calm, reassuring, good voice that I had heard my entire life. Even his face, while radiant and ghostly, still bore the image of a person I had trusted all my life. His presence meant safety now, just as much as it had before I knew he was an angel. He was Sheriff Sentry, a man who I knew would protect me with his life. I could certainly trust him now. After all, how many times in my life had he protected me without me even knowing?

I nodded again, feeling more relieved.

"Then let us proceed," he said as he made his way toward the door to Brice's room. I expected him to reach for the door handle, but to my surprise there was not one. As I focused on the door, I suddenly realized I was not looking at a physical door at all. It was a barrier of some sort, and it appeared to be made entirely of light.

Its bright surface rippled like water as Quentin's hand approached it, almost as if the barrier sensed his touch was coming. Quentin paused before touching the door, looked back at me with a serious expression on his face, and said, "This will not be pleasant for you . . . Brice's struggle is particularly contested. So, brace yourself, because this will be powerful."

I nodded again, which seemed to be the only thing I was capable of doing. Then Quentin pressed his fingers to the top portion of the door, and instantly it began to dissolve. For a moment, nothing else happened. Then, as the last bit of liquid light melted away, *"WHAM!"* a mighty gale of the hottest and yet coldest wind I had ever felt smashed into me, blowing me backward off my feet.

A volcanic storm and a blizzard, all in one, rushed around me, continuing to force me backward toward the hallway wall. Pain seared over every inch of my body as the wind gushed over me like a sandstorm, ripping and scraping its way into the hospital corridor. Only my spiritual state kept the unnatural mixture of frigid and sweltering air from freezing and burning me simultaneously. I struggled to regain my feet against the storm's immense power. Quentin, who had not moved at all, reached out his hand and grabbed me by the arm. With an effortless motion, he pulled me, launching us both through the door frame, and resealing it behind us the moment we made it through.

Now trapped inside Brice's room, the storm of fire and ice roared in every direction, like a hurricane with nowhere else to go. It violently raged, blurring my vision to within an inch of my face. Each scalding gust boiled the air, each freezing flurry ripped mercilessly over my entire body, threatening to disperse my wispy existence.

Then, a great electrical surge overtook the room, sending the hairs on my ghostly body standing on end. It was as if the vicious storm had become supercharged upon our entry.

– CRACK –

"Ouch!" I screamed as tiny shocks began painfully attacking every inch of me, rapidly emitting from the turbulent wind that seemed to have attached itself to me like a jelly-fish. It wrapped around me, clung to me, and engulfed me entirely as sting after sting pelted against my ethereal skin.

Fire and ice, electricity and power, all unnaturally and chaotically focused on me. Only Quentin's grip prevented me from being overcome. His strength pulled and guided me steadily forward, toward the far side of the room, where I assumed Brice's bed would be. At last, through the haze and pain of the storm, my eyes finally rested on Brice and instantly all of my own discomfort was whisked out of my mind. I stood still, no longer merely held fast by Quentin's unshakable hand, but now frozen in utter dismay as my eyes rested on my best friend lying lifeless on his bed and covered in the same unnatural torrent of wind as I was. Light and darkness moved in erratic, supercharged patterns, sending visible shocks up and down Brice's barely discernible body.

My heart became unbearably heavy. But just as it did so, somehow I began to feel immune to the sting of the electrical shocks. As my burden for Brice grew, even the freezing and burning gale became less noticeable. My compassion seemed to shield me from the supernatural storm. In my pain I felt stronger, as if Quentin could have released my hand and I might have been able to stand against the wind under my own power.[245] All that mattered to me in that moment was Brice, and he was in grave danger.

Everything inside of me yearned to take a step forward to help my friend; to grab him and run away from this violent affront that his defenseless body was being subjected to. Seeming to read my thoughts, Quentin squeezed my hand tighter, as if to remind me of the dangers of interfering. Assuming my voice would have been drowned out by the fierce wind, I looked at Quentin and nodded sadly, indicating that I understood.

As I returned my gaze to Brice, a small break in the wind opened in front of me, and the reason for the extreme hot and cold sensations became apparent. The wind on Brice was not wind at all, but distinct flashes of fiery, white hot light and cold streaks of dark, prowling smoke. Like serpents, they crawled hastily over every inch of Brice, unencumbered by gravity, space, or the laws of physics. They flowed in all directions, out of control, yet somehow still supernaturally magnetized to Brice. He looked as if he was being engulfed by unnatural, chaotic fire intent upon consuming him.

Still firmly held by Quentin, I stared in disbelief as the white hot light and smoky darkness moved frantically over the entire surface of Brice's body. The two forces battled each other, blocked and attacked each other, like birds in an erratic quarrel, unconcerned with direction of flight, only concerned with victory.

Yet, as erratic as this battle seemed, the two forces remained amazingly and terrifyingly locked onto Brice, as if incapable of escaping his gravitational pull. He was their target, their goal, their prize. Both darkness and light appeared to be searching his body, as if looking for a weakness, a gap, shocking every inch of him as they did so.[246]

A strand of the dark smoke momentarily cleared away from Brice's face, and I caught a glimpse of his expression; he was in agony. It was agony beyond anything I had ever seen. Though his eyes were closed, his face was somehow far more expressive than normal. I had never seen pain like this. I instinctively took a step forward, unable to resist the urge to help my friend. Quentin gripped my arm tighter, holding me back. I relented.

Reluctantly obedient to Quentin's wishes, I was forced to watch, in horror, as my best friend cringed in pain. I looked up at Quentin, pleading for help, but he simply shook his head. There was nothing I could do. The consequences for interfering aside, I would never be able to break Quentin's powerful grip.

Just as I thought I could not take any more, the look on

CHAPTER NINE

Brice's face suddenly changed. Even if Quentin had not been holding me back, Brice's expression would have been startling enough to stop me in my tracks. *How could his face be so expressive?* I wondered. It was as if his face was a projection of his very soul. What he was feeling, or thinking, was clearer to me than if he had walked up to me and told me exactly what was on his mind. Though his eyes remained closed, his face told me all I needed to know . . . he was being consumed by greed. All agony was now gone, and it had been replaced with a deep, rapacious desire for something, something that I could not see, but it was all too real to Brice, and he wanted it badly.

But Brice's animated expression was only part of what let me know he had been struck by a powerful wave of greed, for the atmosphere in the room suddenly changed, too. The dark, probing smoke on Brice had become thicker and more aggressive. The room had become colder and darker, too, like a sudden eclipse of the sun. The ever oppressive windstorm was more powerful and more unpleasant, ferociously whirling about, knocking me from side to side, as the electrical shocks returned with increased intensity. Only Quentin's powerful grip allowed me to remain standing.

And then, inexplicably, my emotions changed as well. I *felt* disappointed. Not disappointed in Brice, at having seen greed on his face; no, I was simply in a state of disappointment. Had I not even seen Brice, had I turned my back to him and been unable to witness his greed-filled face, I would have still felt disappointment pervading the air, even sadness.

It weighed on me like a tangible anchor tied around my heart. The entire atmosphere was darker, harsher, less comfortable, and depressing. But just as I thought I could no longer stand the despair, a gush of fiery white light surged through the room, breaking and scattering the darkness. The light became more prominent and the dark smoke on Brice thinned. His demeanor changed again as well. Now his face bore the unmistakable sign of sorrow and sadness, not the type of sadness that comes with loss, but the type that comes with sincere guilt. If I could have called it something, I would have called it a look of repentance.

Just as before, Brice's overly expressive facial characteristics made it obvious to me that he felt bad about something he had done, or perhaps something he had thought. With the change in Brice, the entire atmosphere changed again as well. The probing wind of fiery light and black smoke that had been whipping around me now eased their intensity as the room became more pleasant. The darkness was somehow being suppressed, and I began to feel more protected from its electrical shocks and turbulent force. Even the air became lighter and warmer, as though an eclipse of the sun had passed. I felt my attitude lift. I felt joyful! Brice's spirit of repentance had brought with it a feeling of victory.[247]

It was clear; the shift in my attitude, the change in the room from darkness to light, and the intensity of the smoke and light were all directly linked to what Brice was thinking, or feeling . . . or perhaps it was what he was experiencing. I knew once again that even if I had turned my back to Brice and had not witnessed his face of repentance, I still would have felt the joy in the room. Whatever he experienced, the room experienced.

CHAPTER NINE

For what felt like an eternity, I stood there and watched as the fiery, white streaks of light and the dark, deadly smoke twisted and turned over every inch of my best friend in a frantic torrent of motion. They each jockeyed for position, causing Brice's face to twitch from expression to expression, somehow displaying so much more meaning and emotion than human faces are normally able to convey. With each change, Brice's inner experience emanated outward for the rest of the room to feel. The joy was a deeper, more jubilant joy than I had ever experienced; the anger, a more sincere and righteous anger; the sorrow was more heart wrenching and desperate.

I chanced a look at Quentin, and I could tell he was feeling everything I felt. By the extreme expressions on his face, he apparently felt everything more strongly than I did . . . or at least it looked like he did. I could not see what I looked like, but perhaps my spiritual face revealed just as much emotion as Quentin and Brice's did. It was apparent that emotion, sin, and goodness had a far greater effect on our souls than I had ever considered.

Then, as my eyes returned to Brice's face, Quentin suddenly took a step to the left side of the room toward the head of Brice's bed, pulling me over with him. As we moved, a streak of white fire shot toward us like a beam of light reflected off a mirror. Quentin stopped as I prepared to shield myself, but before I could even blink the figure of a man had materialized in front of us.[248]

He was an angel, quite as large as Quentin, but he looked younger. He wore the same brilliant white robes as Quentin, and his blond hair seemed alive with electricity. He turned his serious expression and piercingly blue eyes toward Quentin and they began speaking in a language I could not recognize.[249] With the wind, I would not have been able to really understand what they were saying anyway, but I could read their faces, and both expressions showed grave concern.

After a few seconds of intense conversation, Quentin stepped back, pulling me with him once again. The angel gave a courteous nod and then dissolved back into fiery white lightning, bolting back toward Brice to reengage in the chaotic struggle. I looked back down at my best friend's face, and he wore an expression of complete and utter confusion.

Quentin squeezed my hand to get my attention. I glanced over at him, and he nodded toward the door, indicating it was time to leave. He then gripped my arm tighter and pulled me with him, moving slowly with the wind now at our backs. It seemed to have given up probing me and was instead attempting to force us out of the room. Quentin blocked the door with his massive body as he unsealed it. I stood behind him waiting.

Finally, the barrier opened, and Quentin grabbed me quickly, pulling me through with him, and immediately resealing the barrier behind us. Instantly, the blinding wind ceased and the atmosphere returned to normal, leaving behind only a quiet and vacant hospital hallway. I stood silent and shocked, staring around at the hallway waiting area, which appeared as physical and natural as any hospital wing ever could. It was bizarre to take in, impossible to absorb, after everything I had just seen and experienced. I was dumbfounded, not to mention the fear I still felt for my best friend who was in the room just a few feet away from me, battling against demons, all the while still struggling to hang on to his natural life as well. It was like stepping into a terrible nightmare.

After a moment, Quentin broke the silence, "As you saw, Micah, I was given a report of Brice's status." I nodded, only now realizing that was probably what the other angel had been doing.

"That was my friend Brimm. He is Brice's guardian. He informed me that Brice is fighting hard, but his struggle is particularly powerful."

"W—what do you mean?" I stammered. "I thought Brice had been attacked physically; why is he being attacked spiritually, too?" I asked frantically, although as the question left my mouth I immediately recalled the presence of evil I had felt as Brice had been carried out of his house on a stretcher.

"Everyone is tempted, Micah," Quentin answered seriously.

"But why is he going through such a powerful struggle now . . . is his soul okay?" I asked in fear, recalling Quentin's question during my third temptation—whether or not I knew if Brice's soul was ready if he were to die. Quentin had not divulged whether it was or wasn't, and the answer to that question had never been more important to me than after having witnessed what Brice was up against.

"Brice is saved, if that's what you mean. He gave his life to Christ several years ago, so in that sense, yes, his soul is secure," Quentin answered reassuringly.

I exhaled audibly, experiencing the first sense of relief I could remember feeling all night. I obviously wanted Brice to live a long and happy life—he was my best friend after all—however, live or die, with all I had seen, it now meant everything to know that my best friend would go to heaven when his time on Earth was over.

"Wait," I said as something else occurred to me. "If Brice is saved, then what was going on in there?" I asked, now feeling very confused.

"That was war, Micah," Quentin answered simply.

"But if Brice's soul is safe, then isn't the war over?" I asked in continued confusion.

"The war for his salvation is over, but the war for how he lives his life is *never* over," Quentin responded, and then hesitated.[250] I stared at him as I waited. Something in his face made it clear that he had hit another one of those moments where he did not want to tell me all of the details. After a moment of contemplation, he resumed.

"Brice has been living with a secret sin in his life, and it has a strong hold on him. He loves God, but he is struggling against a real weakness, which is currently being exploited by the demons in that room," Quentin said, pointing at the door to Brice's room. "Brice both craves this sin and hates it all at once."[251]

"What is he struggling with?" I asked out of nothing more than a deep concern for my friend.

"Unless Brice divulges that information to you, then that is between him and God," Quentin answered in a tone of finality.

"Okay," I said as I nodded. "But then what were they doing to him in there? What was all that wind about?" I asked, drawing my thoughts back to the spiritual storm I had experienced just a moment before.

"What you witnessed was a particularly heated struggle of demonic temptation versus angelic ministry. Angels and demons were probing Brice's spirit searching for weaknesses, openings to shoot in influence and suggestions—*messages*. You saw those streaks of dark smoke that probed every inch of Brice—those were demons. They have other forms they can change to, just as we do, but when they are influencing, they find it most efficient to exist as cold spirits of darkness. As such, when they are in that form, we find our best way to fight them is to become flaming spirits of light, like Brimm was,"[252] he said. "Both sides were probing you as well," he added.

"Yeah, I noticed," I replied, my mind recalling the discomfort of the hot and cold wind, as well as the little shocks.

"They were searching you and Brice for vulnerabilities. The angels probe for vulnerabilities to defend. We sense weaknesses in your spirit and desires, and when we find them, we try to reinforce them. Demons, however, try to attack them," he said gravely.

"The small stabs of pain you undoubtedly felt—or perhaps they felt like electrical shocks to you," he said as I nodded my head. "Well, each little shock was one side or the other trying to send messages of influence to you. Had you been in your normal physical state, instead of being shocked, you would have felt the influence of both good and evil. But you were not able to feel their influence the way a human normally does because you were in the spirit, not in the flesh.[253] You felt as we angels feel and you saw as we see. Humans only notice the influence, but in this spiritual state, you sensed everything differently. It felt like they were shocking you because your spirit notices the intrusion of a foreign and dangerous message. It notices when evil tries to penetrate it, much like a human's skin would notice the poke of a hot knife," he said, raising his eyebrows in sincerity.

"But why did they come after me?" I said looking down at my ghostly body. "Couldn't they tell I was different?"

"You are certainly different, but they could tell you were not an angel. No offense, but you do not yet radiate the same essence and power that we do.[254] And so, when they saw you, they tried to influence you. My brothers had been made aware that you might be coming, so when they tried to protect you, they immediately recognized that you were in a spiritual state and couldn't be tempted like normal. They only remained on you to help shield you from the shock of evil temptation and to balance out the cold," he explained.

"The demons, however, did not know you were coming to Tartarus, and they are not familiar with humans being allowed to enter into the spiritual world. They could not understand why you had no weaknesses to attack, so they sent what we call *fiery darts* indiscriminately at you, shocking you everywhere.[255]

"But that's all they could do to you. As I said before, you are safe while you are with me. You'll be perfectly protected so long as you do not *physically* interfere," he finished sternly, repeating his old instructions with a look of fatherly discipline in his eyes. Clearly Quentin wanted to ensure that my step toward Brice in the room would be my last such attempt at intervening.

CHAPTER NINE

I was ready for his powerful gaze to be off of me, so I quickly nodded my head and changed the subject. "Do spiritual wars always *feel* that strong? I know you said they were attacking Brice with particular aggression, but does it always *feel* that powerful?" I asked. Part of me was once again thinking of the potent wind that had constantly threatened to knock me off my feet, but most of me was reflecting on the powerful emotion that had stirred my heart beyond anything I had ever felt.

He looked into my eyes; the jovial expressions that his face normally wore had long been replaced by seriousness and passion. My question did nothing to change his intense demeanor.

"We are much more powerful than humans currently are,[256] so it will always feel powerful to you . . . but no, most of the time it is not nearly as intense as with Brice. There were hundreds of angels and demons in that room influencing him," he explained.

"Sometimes demons don't even have to show up to a fight," he continued. "Much of the time, humans give in to temptation all on their own, without any demonic influence. You are vessels of freewill, with your own desires that you often succumb to. Demons are all too happy to let humans destroy themselves without any interference . . . there are, after all, twice as many angels as demons,[257] so it is more efficient for them to go only where they feel their presence will wreak the most havoc and cause the most damage," he said sadly.

"When angels are involved, most of the time it is just one, or a few angels," he continued to explain. "During stronger or more important instances, there might be a dozen or so of us and *them*, but almost never will there be anything this powerful for one person. But this town is under siege. The hearts and souls of every human living here are in danger. They are attacking anyone and everyone who they think will play an important role in their plan," he said with a sad sigh. He looked at me with eyes of fire that were also somehow filled with pain.

"So, what can I do?" I asked in a defeated tone, thinking of my inability to help Brice. "I'm just a human like anyone else," I continued, before he could answer. "You don't want me to interfere, so why drag me along, and why show me all of this?"

"My warning was to ensure you refrained from *physical* engagement with demons. But after our journey together through Tartarus, *much* will be expected of you," Quentin responded in a continued serious tone. "That's why you're being shown all of this. You have a special role in what is coming; otherwise, you wouldn't be here with me now," he stated.

I looked at him completely confused at how I could help. "Okay, so I can see demons . . . "

" . . . and angels," he interjected.

"Right, I can see demons and angels and I'm supposed to help, but not interfere physically. . . . I'm not sure I really understand that," I responded, confused at the apparent contradiction.

"Micah, you just saw that angels don't fight physically with demons, not unless we are specifically commanded to," he responded. "We weren't probing and wrestling each other in there . . we were engaged with the human, with Brice! If this were a physical contest, God would just put an end to all evil and be done with it. No one would be able to *choose* anything. God would just destroy anyone who has not been born again.[258] Some people might think they want that, but then they'd be surprised how many people haven't given their life to Christ.[259] And God certainly does not want to destroy a single human soul, if it can be helped.[260]

"However, many souls will be destroyed because, as I told you, God has chosen to give humans freewill. He gives humans a choice to accept Him or reject Him," he said.

"But is choice worth the cost?" I asked. "God gives us choice even though He knows most of us will choose wrong . . . most humans will reject him," I stated sadly.

"It's true," Quentin began to respond. "By giving humans a choice, God knows that some people will choose to turn from Him; many people, in fact. However, that's not what God wants. God gives humans a choice in the hopes that they *will* choose Him. If you come to know Him, He wants it to be because you wanted to. He wants humans to find the truth and then freely accept Him. Think about your own relationships . . . think about Rachel. Do you want her to care for you because someone makes her, or because she chooses to?" he asked rhetorically. The answer was obvious.

"It's the same way with God. He wants humans to choose Him freely.[261] Because of this, a spiritual battle is really a battle for choice. Humans have choice because that's how God wants it. The work of an angel is about influencing that choice. That's what we do. As I told you before, we are *messengers*. We send humans messages, in the hopes that we can help people search for good and ultimately choose Christ. And if someone has already chosen Christ, then our ministry to them is to help them obey God's will. That's what angels *do*," he said, holding out his arms wide for emphasis.

" . . . and so, to answer your question, that's what *you* can do, too," he said, pointing at me. "As a human, there *are* ways that you can help. You can pray to God on behalf of other people.[262] To anyone who would dismiss prayer as silly or unhelpful, I'll remind you what it was like in that room when the atmosphere changed.[263] Anything and everything can tip the balance of a battle for one's soul, but when people cry out in faith for the power of God to help in their struggles . . . well, let's just say there is nothing equal to it,"[264] he said smiling.

"But that's not all you can do," he continued. "You can also guard your own soul, through the choices you make, the time you spend in prayer, study, and service; these things affect the spiritual world in a very powerful way.[265]

"Do you remember the atmosphere back in Brice's room? Every time Brice lingered on an evil thought it caused the whole atmosphere to change and the battle swung in favor of the demons. Every decision that a person makes affects the battle for their own soul in the same way. Every choice and every action affects other people around them. An atmosphere can be one of evil or one of goodness. As a human grows closer to God, as their faith increases, as they prepare and purify themselves, then it cannot help but affect those around them. The light of Christ will not be hid within a soul in which it has been ignited,"[266] he said, looking at me even more intensely.

"And so, Micah, this all leads to one thing . . . your

ability to influence other people for the cause of Christ. Never underestimate the power your prayers, your decisions, your actions, and your words can have on those around you.[267] I'm not talking about anything mystical or supernatural. I'm talking about the completely normal, yet utterly powerful influence that one human life can have on another human," he preached.[268]

I hesitated with Quentin still staring at me intently. I was slightly taken aback at the simplicity of it all. It was not what I had expected. When he had said I would be involved, I had thought I would be doing some specific mission or some special task.

"So . . . so, that's it?" I asked.

"You expected more?" he replied wisely.

"Well, it's just . . . I thought . . . I mean," I stammered, " . . . you said I was chosen for a special role. I'm not disappointed or anything, but it just seems so simple. Anyone could do what you're telling me, so, why me?"

"Why not you?" he quickly replied.

I didn't have an answer.

"The special role appointed unto you might be simple in concept, but simplicity does not imply easiness. Did you have an easy time resisting the temptation at the bank, or with Katie, or keeping yourself from fighting with Tom Reynolds?" Quentin asked bluntly.

"No," I said, sheepishly ducking my head in slight embarrassment, though Quentin had not said it to shame me.

"No, you didn't. And now that you have experienced this world," he said, raising his hands again to indicate the spiritual world around me, "the enemy is going to come at you harder than ever before. As such, obedience will be more difficult than ever. Darkness will try to blind your sight and twist the truth, but now you know the truth, so the only question is, can you cling to it?[269] When darkness comes, you must learn to turn to God and rest in *His* power, abandoning your own desires, and instead, submitting to His will," he finished.

I didn't respond. I simply stared at him, now certain that a physical task would probably be easier than facing whatever blinding and deceptive temptations awaited me. I nodded to let him know that I understood his point, but in understanding, my confidence was at an all-time low.

"Good," he said, as a smile finally returned to his face. "Now, for you to fully grasp the vastness of this battle, there is much more for you to see. If you are ready, take my hand," he said as he stretched forth his hand once more.

I slowly reached out and grabbed Quentin's hand, expecting the world to darken and revolve around me once again. I braced myself in the hopes that I could try to observe more this time . . . but nothing happened. Quentin pulled me a few steps deeper into the center of the hospital hallway and suddenly a bright, golden white ladder materialized before us. Its blinding rungs extended from the floor all the way up to the ceiling, and I suspected that they did not stop there.

The ladder hummed as if powerful energy were coursing through it. The whole thing looked like a beam of bright plasma. Even in the spiritual realm I did not have the slightest desire to climb a ladder that looked so . . . non-solid; no matter where it went.

CHAPTER NINE

Quentin pulled me toward the ladder and smiled at me as I continued to observe it, certain I was about to have to climb. If he really was my guardian angel, then I was positive he knew that I hated heights. Could I have climbed a ladder to change a light bulb? Sure! No problem. However, this was clearly no ordinary ladder. *How high would it take me?* I wondered. *All the way to heaven, perhaps?*

Quentin noticed my apprehensive look, and it amused him. "You were just in a room with hundreds of demons, but you are afraid of a ladder?" he said, laughing his familiar laugh.

"I'm just not a big fan of heights. Isn't there another way to get where we need to go? Perhaps we could go back to your jeep," I suggested hopefully.

"Oh, my jeep can't go where we are going; and yes, there are other ways for *me* to get there, but they aren't nearly as efficient . . . and they aren't nearly as fun," he said with excitement in his eyes. "So be brave, Micah." An impish grin now spread across his face. ". . . Because it's time for something new."

Without warning, his free hand grabbed the golden ladder and with a jolt we were hurled toward the ceiling—and as I had guessed, right through it. To my surprise, though, I felt nothing. In fact, we passed through anything and everything that stood in our way, completely unencumbered, as if nothing were really there . . . or perhaps we were the ones who were not really there. We rocketed upward on the golden ladder, ascending through each floor of the hospital in a catapulting blur, and in an instant, we erupted out into the clear night sky and continued traveling upward with blinding speed, as if fired from a cannon.

In exhilaration and fear, I looked down and saw my entire town far below us and getting even farther by the second. My head spun as I tried to take in my surroundings against the rushing wind. And then I noticed that we were not the only ladder of light accelerating into the heavens. Hundreds of beams of light filled the sky, stretching endlessly upward into the starry night, but each stopping abruptly at different locations in the sleepy town below.[270]

Just as I began to wonder again if we were going to climb all the way to heaven, the ladder slowed to an unceremonious stop. Quentin kept one hand on the ladder and one hand holding mine, while our feet dangled freely over the world, as if we stood on an invisible platform.

We were now high enough to see surrounding cities and countryside. I looked down at my extremely small town beneath us, and could not help but notice far more golden ladders descended to it than any other town, though the other towns had several as well.

My eyes were wide in amazement at the sight. I knew my heart should have been pounding—I had just traveled through a building and nearly into outer space after all—but oddly, in my spiritual state, my heart remained silent as ever. Still, the view was breathtaking.

"We didn't travel this way last time," I finally managed to say. "To get to Brice's room we seemed to go outside of time and space and all of that stuff."

Quentin did not respond, so I continued, "I couldn't understand what was going on when we traveled last time. It was a lot weirder. But this time . . . " I stopped, uncertain how to finish my sentence.

How in the world could I even hope to articulate the way I was feeling? How could anyone go through what I had and be anything other than dumbfounded? My mind was blown! Beyond Quentin being an angel and witnessing Brice fighting with demons—which were enough to call my sanity into question—I had just ridden on some sort of angelic transportation. I had traveled on a ladder of light through ceilings and walls and furniture, and I was sitting thousands of feet up in the air. It was almost more than I could take in, let alone describe.

I opened my mouth to try to explain again, but Quentin, still gripping my hand tightly, looked at me and spoke first. "Last time you were not in spirit yet. To take a human from the physical realm to the spiritual realm is a lot different and significantly more complex than simply traveling once you are inside the spiritual realm," he explained.

"For a human to cross into the spiritual realm any way other than death is almost unprecedented," he continued. "As I have said, what we did earlier has only happened a few times in the history of mankind.[271]

"But *this*," he said, indicating the ladder of light with a nod of his head. " . . . this is how *we* travel. And it is much more versatile than flying with wings," he added, almost as if he expected agreement.

"You'll remember me saying angels can travel anywhere and any-*when* . . . well, this ladder is how," he said, once again indicating the golden ladder that held us suspended above the horizon.

"These ladders can take us to any point in the world at any time in human history . . . or, if we are commanded to, we can also go into what you would consider earth's future," he said with another excited smile. I looked into his glee-filled face and realized that he was genuinely enjoying getting to share his amazing world with me.

"But not only are you unbound by time," he continued, "having just traveled through a building, I'm sure it's quite clear that the world has relinquished its physical hold on you as well," he said, his excitement mounting.

"Now that you are spirit, you and I will be able to take this ladder anywhere and any-*when*, together, to see anything that we need to see," he said, now barely able to contain his joy. I'm sure angels rarely get a chance to speak so openly with the human they guard. For me, it was learning of a spectacular secret; for him, it was getting to share that secret with someone he clearly cared so deeply about, *me*.

My mind raced with questions, but Quentin had other things on his agenda. Before I could say anything else, he pointed toward the ground and said, "You will notice below us that there are odd concentrations of light and dark."

I looked down from the great height, and sure enough, some areas seemed to have greater amounts of light or darkness engulfing them than others. Most places had a mixture of light and dark, but a few buildings were so covered in light that even from the great height they were easy to see because they almost glowed. Yet many areas were so covered in darkness that they were indiscernible.

"Each of the areas below us is a battlefront. Some areas are more occupied by us, while other areas are more occupied by *them*," he said, emphasizing the word *them* with an obvious distaste toward the demons.

"We are going to view several different places in town, at several key moments in time because my mission for you is to ensure that you witness the struggle behind human choices. We will start with something . . . familiar," he finished mysteriously.

As if his thoughts commanded the ladder, the moment he quit speaking, it started to vibrate slightly. I prepared for a quick thrust up or down, but it did not come; we seemed to be remaining in the same place. I looked down at the town toward the bottom of the ladder, and to my surprise, I saw that although we were not moving up or down, the base of the ladder was gliding swiftly throughout the town beneath us. It swung steadily, moving through houses and buildings like a finger through water, completely uninterrupted, until eventually it rested at a place that was entirely covered in light.

"Now, to one of my favorite places in town," said Quentin with a smile.

Before his words had faded, the bottom dropped out of the ladder's invisible barrier and we were shot toward the earth with blinding velocity. Yet, even with the sudden and tremendous speed of the fall, somehow I did not feel like I was falling. It was more like I was aboard a train on a vertical track; fast, but not reckless.

Equally interesting, my spiritual form felt no gravitational effects. The free fall inflicted no sickness or momentum on my massless existence. Had I closed my eyes, I might not have known I was falling at all. Like the wind itself, I traveled on a ferocious, yet precise course.

However, that precise course propelled us toward the earth with such speed that a violent crash seemed imminent. Instinctively, I braced myself for the impending collision as the town grew closer and closer and the houses more detailed. Matter and time might have left me, but my earthly fears were still fully intact, and the game of chicken we were about to play with the ground was bound to be one we would lose.

The rungs on the golden ladder whizzed by as we reached a speed that would surely be impossible to halt before impact. However, just as I thought we had descended beyond the point of no return, the ladder began to slow with the smoothness and softness of air. With no effects of inertia, we stopped easily and gently on the ground, directly in front of a place I knew all too well.

"Welcome home, Micah," Quentin said happily.

My mouth hung wide open in shock, as there in front of me stood my parents' house. The sight of their house in the midst of this supernatural experience felt more abnormal to me than anything had all night. Nothing had changed physically with the house. It was the same white fence and the same concrete porch. It was still a small shabby two-story white structure, just as it had always been. But what made my mouth hang open was the fact that the entire house was ablaze with fiery white light. It was completely engulfed, like staring at the sun, yet somehow without over-stimulating my eyes.

Every inch of the house shined so bright that every surrounding house should have been bathed in its light . . . but oddly, only some of them were.[272] To my surprise, impenetrable darkness lined much of the house's exterior, forcefully blocking the light from shining onto several of the neighbors' houses. Only occasionally did the light break through to other houses, and even in those instances, darkness seemed to be trying to suffocate the light.

In fact, as we stood there, the darkness began moving. It was circling my parents' house, seeming to look for a weakness, just as it had done with Brice.[273] With a slow surge, little bands of dark smoke began rapidly striking the light. However, the wall of light was impregnable. The darkness retreated immediately as the light reacted toward it. Even more curiously, as the dark cloud retreated, little bursts of fire shot from the dark smoke toward the house like an arrow. When this happened, the light reacted urgently, ricocheting the fiery darts back toward the dark clouds with great force.[274]

I started to ask what the fire was, but Quentin spoke first. "Darkness never relents," he said simply, apparently having seen what I had. "Shall we?" he asked, motioning me toward my parents' house.

He stepped through the white gate, and I mean right through it, and then hopped up the concrete porch, leaving me standing in awe. I took a step forward and attempted to open the gate, but my hand passed right through it.

"Quit being a coward, Micah," Quentin goaded me with a smile and a laugh.

Not really looking forward to it, I stepped *through* my parents' white gate, expecting to feel odd sensations course through me, but I felt nothing. Quentin stood at the top of the steps, waiting for me with an amused smile as I stood still, assessing what I had just done. I was not sure how long I would be in the spiritual world, but it was going to take a while to get used to walking through solid objects.

After my brief pause, I joined Quentin on the porch by the front door. To my disappointment, we were not greeted by a natural door, but once again it was the same weird, bright liquid barrier that most-likely promised another confrontation with a turbulent storm.

"No need to worry, Micah; this will be much more pleasant than the visit to Brice's room," Quentin said, in response to the clear apprehension on my face.

With that, he touched the top center portion of the barrier, and I watched it dissolve just as before. This time, however, we weren't greeted with the brutal, harassing wind, but instead, with warmth and joy. It was easy to follow Quentin into my parents' house; the environment seemed to beckon my very soul.

We walked through the door frame and once inside, it sealed behind us automatically. I glanced back at the barrier in curiosity.

"Barriers help keep the darkness out," Quentin said simply, in response to my look of inquiry.

"How?" I questioned. "Did angels put it here?"

"No, this barrier is your parents' light," he said simply, again.

I looked at him in confusion. "I don't really understand. How did my parents put this barrier up?" I asked, pointing toward the bright, plasma door.

"Think of the barrier as an atmosphere," he answered. "Your parents' faith, their choices, their habits, and more, all promote an atmosphere of holiness, which helps keep the darkness away. This does not mean that darkness can never enter; it only means that the atmosphere fosters holiness. Take, for example, prayer, or reading the Bible, or going to church; all of these activities help people live the life that God has planned for them. They protect people, shield them from allowing evil to enter into their hearts and lives. Your home has been based on these practices. As such, the atmosphere of holiness is very strong," he said seriously. Then a thought entered my mind.

"But how have I been allowed to live here?" I asked. "I lived in this house for years before accepting Christ—didn't I seriously weaken the defense? Was the house less bright and the barrier weaker with me here?" I asked, suddenly wondering what our house would have looked like just one night ago, before I had been saved.

"Yes, and no," Quentin replied. "Certainly you invited darkness into this house on occasion, just as anyone does from time to time . . . "

"But how was I allowed into this 'holy atmosphere' at all?" I interrupted impatiently. "I just saw darkness bounce off the barrier outside," I said, once again pointing toward the door. "So how have I been allowed to live here all these years?"

"A person can be lost in a house of light just as much as a person can be saved in a house of darkness. This is not a question of who can live here. It is more a question of exposure. The atmosphere of a home can either expose people to darkness, or it can expose them to light."

The look of confusion remained fixed on my face.

"Imagine a child who is raised in the home of a drug addict. Can they find salvation in Christ?" he said in response to my expression.

"I imagine they can," I responded in uncertainty.

"Certainly they can!"[275] Quentin replied. "Salvation is available to all who put their faith in Christ.[276] However, here is the difference; there is no question that a child raised in the home of a drug addict would be exposed to far more sin and evil than a person who was raised in a home with two parents who *truly* follow God. The more a person is exposed to darkness, the more it tries to ensnare them. On the other hand, the more a person is exposed to Scripture, prayer, and love, the more likely they are to follow in it. A home can expose you to Christ, or it can expose you to a world of sin. A person's atmosphere, then, does exactly what angels and demons try to do—to influence humans," he said.

"So the barrier doesn't really keep evil out, then?" I asked, pointing yet again at the barrier of light that we had just passed through.

"Once again, yes and no," he said with a smile. "The barrier is nothing more than a spiritual representation of your family's habits, their choices, and most of all, their faith. These things, by their very nature, help to keep the evil out of your lives. This is not so different than our interactions with every human that we meet. People can build you up, or they can tear you down; they can guide you to Christ, or they can guide you to the folly of the world. In the spiritual realm, it is all about influence. So, even though your soul was in darkness while you were lost, this home was still a beacon of light in your life," Quentin finished.

And without another word, he turned and started walking. I followed silently as he led me past my home's familiar stairs, through the quaint hallway, and toward the living room, where my parents would usually be found reading or watching television. Before we entered the room, I could already see light radiating out of it. As we stepped inside, the glowing figures of two men stood with their backs to me. More angels, and in my very house. Each angel stood over one of my parents, who were knelt down at the couch, on their knees praying.

"Is this happening tonight . . . I mean is it the same night as the hospital?" I asked, unsure how to associate time with a timeless experience.

"We will be going forward and backward in time throughout our journey," he said. "You should be less concerned with time, and more concerned with moments," he added, as unclear as ever. My eyebrows lowered in a confused frown as I continued to look at the two angels standing over my parents.

"With that said," he continued, noticing I was not satisfied with his answer, "much of what you see on this journey will occur on the same night in which you went on your date with Rachel. We will focus on this night because so many important things have already happened, and because so much is yet to come," he finished with his usual mysterious ambiguity.

My eyes had not flinched away from my parents since Quentin and I had entered the room. How weird it was to see them unknowingly caught up in the spiritual world. I knew they believed in God, and angels and demons, but I also knew that they had no idea two angels were standing watch over them, and that their house was surrounded by their own barrier of light, which was constantly being circled and attacked by a storm of evil darkness.[277] It felt surreal, even though I knew it was all quite real.

There my parents were, dressed for bed, probably waiting as long as they reasonably could, hoping to catch me when I got home from my date—despite their earlier promise to refrain from bombarding me with questions. They clearly did not yet know what had happened to Brice; otherwise my dad would have been at the hospital with the Jacobs. Being a preacher, my dad would undoubtedly be getting a call about Brice in the morning and would go to visit the family right away. But for now, they were doing their regularly scheduled nightly prayers together. As far back as I could remember, prayer was the last thing my parents always did together before bed, and for whatever reason, they always prayed by the living room couch.

The angels standing over them were a brilliant white and they seemed to pulse with energy, which formed a sort of circle around each of my parents, similar to the one surrounding the house. Standing behind them, I could not see their faces, only their robes, which were white like Quentin's, and I felt a sort of extra goodness that permeated the room. It was so peaceful . . . and safe. As a human, it's hard to imagine ever feeling so serene. All of life's troubles seemed to melt away in the atmosphere of joy that radiated from my parents' prayers.[278]

"You see, Micah, your parents, who are in prayer, are

deeply protected. These two angels are here to watch over them, and as you saw, the house is very secure.[279] That is because your parents have decided to lead their home in ways that follow after God, and are actively serving God.[280]

"With that type of intentional pursuit of God's will, evil will still sneak in occasionally, as it did when your parents didn't trust you, or when evil sneaks in through other vulnerabilities," he said, pointing at the television. "But for a heart that intentionally pursues God and actively seeks His truth, the truth will be found and evil will be revealed and quickly rooted out,"[281] Quentin explained.

He looked down gravely and said, "Unfortunately, far fewer examples of homes and people like this exist than other examples I am going to show you. Every soul is precious, but so many souls choose to walk the path of darkness rather than the path of light."

Quentin turned out of my parents' living room, leaving the two angels watching over my parents, without having spoken a word to either of them. I followed Quentin back down the hall, past the stairs, out of the door's protective barrier, and into the yard. Just past the gate, the golden ladder was still waiting for us, but before I went through the gate I paused and turned to look back at my parents' house.

How bizarre it all was. All this time, angels had been watching over our home. *Had they seen every bad thing I had ever done?* I wondered. *How could Quentin still seem to care so much for me if he had seen how selfish, proud, and sinful I could be?*[282] It was embarrassing, shameful even. Despite the goodness I had just seen, I could not look Quentin in the face because I felt my own guilt weighing me down. I wanted to hide from the light because when it shined on me, it revealed how impure I truly was.[283]

"Micah," Quentin said softly, "I know what you must be thinking. It seems almost like an intrusion to have angels watching over your every move, but God only sends us to you to help stop the darkness from having a free reign. Angels are not here to judge; we are here to minister. We do not wish to make humans ashamed of the mistakes they have made. That's not our job;[284] but sin is certainly something to be sad about. It's an affront to a holy God,[285] and it destroys what you were created to be.[286]

"However, remember this," he said more strongly, "godly guilt is not intended to weigh you down or hold you back; it is intended to promote change in your life. When the Holy Spirit convicts a Christian of sin, sometimes people like to hide in shame. This is a mistake. It does you no good. You have been set free of your sins through Jesus Christ. There is no longer any reason to let sin weigh you down or destroy you.[287] When guilt or conviction comes, humans should turn from their sin, and choose to obey God's will for their life. That is what God wants! That is living in victory through Christ Jesus."[288]

I remained silent as I watched the glowing barrier around my home continue to keep the darkness at bay. I had nothing to say to Quentin, still feeling quite somber, so I just nodded. With that, Quentin led me through the gate and toward the ladder.

"Now I will show you something familiar, but terrible," he said, gravely.

He grabbed my hand and the ladder simultaneously, and

instantly the ladder swung over the earth like a pendulum. Only a few inches off of the ground, we quickly ran out of room to glide, and were heading directly for a neighbor's house. Again, I braced for impact, but just as before, we passed straight through the physical obstacle as if nothing surrounded us but open space. We traveled through fences and yards, houses and cars, mail boxes, people, cats, and dogs—anything and everything that stood in our way. We moved so rapidly that I could barely catch glimpses of people still awake in their homes.

Despite Quentin's suggestion to be more concerned with moments than time, I could not help but be curious. I tried to calculate what time it might be as we traveled silently throughout the town. I could tell by the sky that it was definitely late at night.

"How much later in the night is it now?" I asked Quentin as we continued to glide throughout the town.

"What makes you think this is even the same day?" he said as he smiled at me. There was no question that he loved the mystery of it all. It was so confusing to not be certain what day it was. My date with Rachel seemed like a lifetime ago and for all I knew, it could have been. *Is it still Friday? Are the people I am zooming by experiencing their Friday night? Or, is this some other point in human history that I am supposed to see? Is it even 1985 anymore?* I thought in continued intrigue.

We continued to glide throughout the town, passing through the business portion, if you could even call it that in such a small town. I knew we had to be getting close to our destination because we were running out of populated area to sail through. Finally, the ladder came to a halt between two of the city's larger buildings—the pizza restaurant and the grocery store.

The street lights illuminated the surrounding area and only the after-hour lights were on in the stores; including the pizza shop. If it was closed, I knew it must be late because the pizza place was one of the few places to eat in the town, so it always stayed open later than other stores.

Quentin released my arm and the ladder at the same time, and the ladder disappeared instantly. I stood there and stared, wondering where it could have possibly gone, but Quentin ignored it and began walking toward the alley between the two buildings. I followed in his wake with slight trepidation rising in me, as I noticed that the alley was just out of reach of every single street light.

As if the lack of street lights were not enough, I could tell that something was different about the darkness that filled this alley. Something about it seemed unnatural. Pure blackness blanketed whatever lay concealed beneath the canopy of shadows only a few yards away from us now. No light penetrated it whatsoever. I had an ominous suspicion that Quentin had started me with my parents' house to see what an area occupied by goodness looked like, and now, I was about to experience a place controlled by evil.

CHAPTER TEN

<u>WALKING IN DARKNESS</u>

Children of darkness, born in the curse,[289]
No pain and no suffering will ever be worse
Than the judgment that comes for the chaff among wheat,
For great will they weep and gnash with their teeth.
When the angels go forth, they will gather the crop,
They will bind and burn tares. They cannot be stopped.
For to gather the harvest, it all must be severed,
Then the lost will be thrown into judgment forever.
They'll be cast into darkness, where the worm dieth not.
Where the fires won't quench and the carcasses rot.[290]
So who among men would choose such an end?
It is only by sin to these depths they descend.
For the way of the wicked is blinded by night.
Their feet often stumble on things out of sight.[291]
They pursue all that's folly, for they're naught but seduced.[292]
But they dabble in death, and they'll have no excuse.[293]
For in fire and ash all the wicked shall fall,[294]
When the trumpet shall sound and the Lord comes to call.[295]

* * * *

FRIDAY, MAY 31, 1985 (NIGHT) THRU *EVERLASTING . . .*

Quentin strode briskly and confidently toward the dark
alley as if he were approaching nothing more than a parked car
that he needed to get to. I, however, followed cautiously in his
wake, terrified about what we were walking toward, and ready to
be attacked at any moment. My eyes remained fixed onto the
dense and ominous shadows, which appeared to be swirling
ever so slightly, as if moved by the wind . . . or something far
more sinister.

"Is something in there?" I asked as Quentin trudged on

ahead.

"Yes," he responded simply while continuing to walk.

I swallowed deeply and continued to follow him. *CRACK!* Suddenly a thunderous crash reverberated above our heads without warning. I dove to the ground as two bolts of lightning flashed overhead, and then hammered into the darkness as if trying to smash their way through. Unable to penetrate the alley, the lightning ricocheted with a mighty *BOOM*. I braced myself for yet another impact. The bolts of lightning now flashed directly at Quentin and me, but before I could even blink, two men materialized out of the lightning. They soared through the air and then landed gracefully on their feet no more than an arm's length away from us. Both men were angels.[296]

They gave me an amused glance as I took my arms off my head and ceased my futile attempts to cower on the ground. I picked myself up in hurried embarrassment and turned my attention to the two angels. With their added presence, the atmosphere of goodness and purity increased exponentially. Being in their company compelled from me the same sense of awe that I had felt when I first saw Quentin in his angelic form. They, too, were massive, and they wore the same dazzling white robes that seemed to emit light and energy.

Just like Brimm and Quentin, each angel had his own distinct features. One sported a dark beard and had unusual symbols carved into his short dark hair. He looked very seasoned compared to the other angel, who bore a completely different appearance. His long brown hair and baby face were youthful and happy . . . almost naïve looking.

CHAPTER TEN

They both radiated warmth and goodness, but their eyes were fierce with fire and purpose. I could sense their alarming power and strength. If I had not been with Quentin, I would have feared them. Even with Quentin, I was still daunted by their presence; like a tiny mouse among immortals.

"Quentin, we are sealed out," the long haired, baby-faced angel said in plain English. While his voice was powerful, slow, and heavenly, it bore noticeable hints of desperation and sadness. "We are slipping messages through, but they are becoming unresponsive to our suggestions. They have given in almost completely, and as we feared, it is the demon type *Hallucinogen*," he finished with a worried look in his eyes.

"They will undoubtedly come out when they are ready," Quentin responded; his tone was sad as well, but not nearly as desperate. "We must keep trying, but I believe in the end, Micah will get through to them. Not now perhaps, but in the end he will," he said, glancing at me expressionless, and then back to the angels.

The angels nodded and stepped to either side of us to face the alley. We stared into the darkness as my mind began to race. *What did Quentin mean I would get through to them? Who is* them? I wondered fearfully. *What spiritual battle is going on that I don't know about?*

Without another word, Quentin and the other two angels started walking toward the alley, so I followed suit, terrified that my questions were about to be answered. We reached the alley in just a couple of steps and stopped a few feet from it. As close as we were, the street lights should have provided plenty of light to give at least slight visibility to any normal alley, but this alley was covered in an unnatural blackness. It was tangible, a thick cloud of ash that no light could penetrate.

Quentin reached his hand out to probe the alley. At first, I thought he would reach inside, but as soon as he touched the surface of the dark cloud, his hand was repelled forcefully backward. I looked at him in shock to see if he was hurt, but he simply dropped his hand to his side, apparently not having felt any pain or discomfort; or at least not showing any.

He ignored my concern and continued staring into the blackness. "You see, Micah, much the opposite of your parents' home, this ground is occupied by evil because the people here have given themselves over to sin. We cannot enter."

"We can't enter *yet*," interjected the baby-faced angel beside Quentin, ever hopeful.

"I don't understand . . . who's in there?" I asked with wide eyes.

Quentin hesitated, so the baby-faced angel spoke instead. "Tom Reynolds and Katie Spencer," he said gravely.

"No!" I cried. "They're covered in that . . . that . . . darkness? Covered in evil? We've got to help them!" I said, as I started forward.

The angel with the short dark hair grabbed me and easily held me from moving. "Not now, lad," he said kindly, in his own powerful voice that somehow seemed older than the others. "You can't go in there when you are with us. Even in your normal state, to enter this alley would be dangerous—but to enter now, in your spiritual state, we cannot allow it."

"Besides," said the baby-faced angel with obvious pain in

his eyes, " . . . they chose this. They are doing what they believe they want to do."

"But . . . what are they doing?" I asked desperately.

"Listen for yourself," Quentin said as he pointed toward the dark alley.

Then, as if their voices had been amplified for my benefit, I suddenly heard someone in the darkness.

"I've never done this before," Katie's familiar voice rang out from the shadows.

"I know, but you'll love it," Tom responded. "You're the one who said you were looking for something crazy to do. We already finished all the beer. This is all I have left . . . and trust me, it's way better than alcohol," Tom said, with the sound of excitement in his voice. "It will help you forget all about that punk, Brice. I showed him what was up," Tom said with an arrogant laugh.

"Ha ha," Katie said mockingly, though she didn't sound the slightest bit remorseful. "Okay, give me some," she added in a lighthearted manner.

Then the sound of something small rattling inside what sounded like a plastic container filled the air surrounding the alley.

"You'll feel better in a minute," Tom said. And then, as if the alley's volume had been turned down once again, there was complete silence.

"I don't understand. What just happened?" I asked, looking at Quentin first and then the other two angels in turn.

This time Quentin answered my question, and his voice was filled with sadness. "Katie has taken a very dark step in her life. For her, this was not just one action, it was much more than a teenager experimenting," he hesitated. "For her, this was a first step toward a very different lifestyle that she has been desiring for some time. As she once told you, Micah, she's tired of being told not to take the cookie from the cookie jar. She's tired of being good. She wants to see what it is like to live life without restrictions. Tom has been doing drugs for months, but for Katie, as you heard her say, this was her first time. And unless something changes, it won't be her last."

I gasped as I looked back toward the alley in sad disbelief. My heart became heavy once again. If what the angels were telling me was true—and I knew it was—then it appeared Katie had given in to her wild desires after all. Compassion and frustration stole through me simultaneously. I could not sit there and do nothing while Tom and Katie destroyed their lives. I knew I could not physically interfere, but Quentin said I could influence; I had to try!

Making up my mind to help, I yelled their names into the alley, "Katie, Tom, stop!" but I was the one who stopped, in shock. As I had spoken, a bolt of light had fired out of my mouth with each word, forcefully penetrating deep into the dark alley.

Before I could ask what had happened, there was a ripple in the darkness. And then terror seized me as red eyes peered out from deep within the alley. I stood frozen in fear. The darkness rippled again, and then it was moving. Quentin and the two angels took several steps back in unison as Quentin put his arm in front of me, guiding me back as well. About ten feet of space separated us from the alley when two massive figures stepped out of the darkness, engulfed in black smoke that was identical to that of the alley. It covered their features completely. As the two figures stood, towering before us, the smoke gradually descended upon the massive figures, thinning into dark, cloak-like coverings and revealing the monsters beneath the darkness.

My breath caught in my throat as I stared in horror at the two hideous, winged creatures that stood before me. Like the offspring of giants and dragons, these beasts were enormous, far bigger than the angels. Their faces bore identical deranged and distorted expressions. Their blood-red eyes glared at me menacingly, as if they were thirsty for me. Like monstrous shadows, their wispy black essence yielded no discernible texture. If my eyes had been my only sensors, then I would have believed a strong gust of wind could have blown them away.

However, I knew they weren't going anywhere. Just as I could feel the warmth, the goodness, and the power of the angels, with these creatures I could feel their cold, evil nature, and unfortunately a power that quite easily rivaled that of the angels. Only the continued sense of goodness, joy, and love from the angels kept me from being overcome by the despair, insanity, and sheer evil that radiated off these terrible demons. Their red eyes remained fixed on me; they wanted me.

"Ah, we heard you had brought one of them with you into Tartarus, Quentin," one of the two demons said, in a sadistic and chilling voice as he continued to gaze at me hungrily. My body tensed. My vulnerability and inadequacy had never been so apparent. My safety rested completely in the three angels who stood beside me. There were only two demons, but

I suspected the alley contained a few more of their brethren. *Would three angels be enough?* I wondered in fear.

"Well, where are our manners? We wouldn't want to scare this little one," the same demon said, still glaring at me as if he wanted to devour me. He gave a loud psychotic laugh that even his silent counterpart did not echo, and then he and the other demon transformed again. We stood in silence as their huge figures shrank into the smaller, but still large figures of two *men* . . . for lack of a better word. You could call them men only as much as you could call the angels men.

The change in form did nothing to diminish the fear I felt of them and the continued coldness and evil they emitted. They now had the appearance of two handsome men, but not handsome in an attractive way. Rather, they were handsome with looks of arrogance, cunning, and deceit on their faces. However, the most prominent feature of either face continued to be the extremely deranged expression that each creature wore.

Their skin was pale, as if they had never been exposed to light. A deep midnight black filled the portion of their eyes that should have been white, but the pupil remained the sinister red that had locked onto me since I had first caused the treacherous alley to stir. Black slicked-back hair and equally black cloaks completed their human looking attire, but their evil spiritual essence continued to cling to them like a dark, poisonous smog. A chill went over my body as I observed them.

"You are too late, brothers. They are ours. They have made their decision, and there is nothing you can do," said the same demon, breaking the silence. Neither demon would look at Quentin or the other two angels. They only had eyes for me. I could sense both of them examining me with a lustful greed. Their evil desire spread through the air. Claiming Tom and Katie as their victims was not enough for them. They were determined to get me next.

Without warning, a wisp of fiery smoke shot out from the silent demon's head and darted toward my face like an arrow. Quentin reacted with such swiftness that my eyes were barely able to capture his movement. He caught the fiery substance in clean air as if catching a rope that had been thrown at him. As his hands grasped the streak of fiery smoke, the silent demon immediately began screaming in horrific agony. The trail of black fire was still firmly anchored to the demon's mind. He grabbed his head and bent over double, wailing hideously in pain.[297]

The other demon stepped forward and yelled in a cold and menacing voice, "Enough! We are done here. Release him and we will go." His blood-thirsty eyes had at last left me, but they were now piercing Quentin with a look of pure hatred.

Quentin calmly relinquished his hold on the black, fiery substance, and it instantly soared back inside its owner's mind. That demon now also glared at Quentin with sheer vindictive rage. And then he and the vocal demon took one step backward into the darkness of the alley and were gone.

Quentin leaned down and spoke to me quickly and quietly, "You will not be able to do anything, so please do not try. They will not even know you are here. It is too late for this battle, but you *will* have a chance in the future . . . "

He cut off because the dark cloud covering the alley had

begun to move once again. This time, the darkness was thinning like water being sucked into a drain. The air cleared, more and more, until only two figures remained—but the two figures were not the demons we had just seen. Rather, standing in front of us were Tom Reynolds and Katie Spencer, the unbeknownst hosts of countless demons.[298]

Even though Quentin had just warned me not to do anything, I could not help myself. In desperation, I began shouting at the top of my lungs, "Katie, what are you doing?" Once again, the words shot out of my mouth as light, but this time the darkness was ready for it, swatting my light away instantly. My words reflected off Katie and were lost in the night, just like the darkness had ricocheted off the light at my parents' house.

Neither she nor Tom made any indication that they had heard my voice. Oblivious to our presence, Tom handed Katie something small, but I could not tell what it was.

"Here," Tom said. "Last one."

Katie immediately put whatever he had handed her into her mouth.

"We're out, but my guy at the hospital said he could get us some more if we go see him tonight," Tom said, dropping something as he did so. It fell to the ground with a light clack. With that, Katie nodded and Tom wrapped his arm around her as they headed out of the alley together, completely ignorant to their spiritual peril.

They walked right toward us, unaware that we were watching them go down their dark path, unaware that they were destroying themselves, and unaware of the foothold that evil demonic forces now had on their life. They knew none of it. But as clueless as they were to our presence, I suddenly felt as if I had never been more aware of theirs.

This was because I felt them. Not physically of course, but just as I had experienced Brice's innermost feelings while watching his spiritual struggle, now I felt Tom and Katie. The environment changed in an instant. It hit me powerfully, and all at once. I closed my eyes, but I knew there was nothing I could do to escape the atmosphere. Tom and Katie's souls were crying out to us for help. Not that their souls actually spoke, but I felt the design of their souls, the purpose of their spirits being perverted and defiled. Beyond the drugs and the danger that I could sense, from the view of angels, I could feel the delusion and distortion in the atmosphere. Nothing was hidden. Intentions, emotions, secret motives, I could sense it all.

Sadness overwhelmed me. I was sad for my best friend, Brice, at what his new girlfriend was doing while he lay unconscious and locked in a battle of his own. I was sad for Katie and Tom, not in a judgmental way, but I felt genuine sorrow at the decisions they were making. They knew drugs were physically dangerous, but they had no idea of the evil spirits that were behind the scenes, fighting for their spiritual destruction as well.

But the veil had been lifted for me; I could see and feel everything. I had felt the lust and hunger of the demons as they glared at me with their evil red eyes. And now I could feel sorrow for Tom and Katie, these two members of God's creation, who were willfully committing violent acts against themselves, harming what God had created to be wonderful.[299]

There was no way to shut it off . . . I had to feel it all, no matter how painfully my heart was wrenched. This is what I had been brought into the spiritual world to see, because I was meant to understand the destructiveness of sin. Now I knew who my real enemies were, and now I knew how important God's mission was.

Just before Katie and Tom passed us, I looked up and saw the red in their eyes. For the second time, instinct made me take a step toward them, but again Quentin held an arm out impeding my way. As he did so, a wisp of dark smoke shot from the side of Tom's head and began to circle Tom and Katie as if forming a perimeter, daring me to cross, daring me to take another step. I stood where I was, accepting that this was more than I could handle; there was nothing I could do. Tom and Katie walked away from us, out of the parking lot, onto the sidewalk, around the corner, and out of sight.

"Quentin, it is time for us to go," said the dark haired angel, breaking the silence. "We have been called to meet with Roland. To try to stop the decision that will soon be faced."

Turning to me, his flaming eyes came alive with urgency. "Micah, be strong and stand fast.[300] We will see you again before your journey is over. You have much to do and much depends on you. Remember what you have seen. Evil seeks to destroy you and those you love, but *you* can make a difference when you turn to God for your strength. Remember that!"

With that, both angels turned their backs to Quentin and me and then each one held up one of his arms. Instantly, two ladders of light appeared. Within seconds, the angels grabbed hold of their ladders and then they too were gone.

CHAPTER TEN

Standing alone with Quentin, I stepped into the now vacant alley, foolishly hoping to find something to disprove what I had witnessed Tom and Katie doing. I wanted my senses to be wrong. Sadly, I received immediate confirmation as I reached down and picked up the unmarked pill bottle Tom had dropped. It was empty. Sorrow bore down on my heavy heart even more. Quentin patiently waited for me to finish my futile and tragic investigation.

"Can't you do something to stop them?" I asked Quentin sadly.

"They're blocking us out. They've made their choice. They won't hear us now," Quentin replied sadly.

"Can't you force your way in? Can't you make them hear you? Can't God do it; can't He make them choose right?" I rattled off desperately.

"Of course He *could*, but He won't. We've already discussed that God gives people freewill," Quentin responded tiredly.

"But they were possessed, weren't they?" I asked in vexed disbelief.

Quentin nodded.

"But that's not freewill! Can't you all stop them from being possessed?" I pleaded. "If Tom and Katie knew what was really happening, they wouldn't choose to be possessed."

I was frantic, but Quentin was quite calm. "Micah, don't you see?" he replied to me. "Katie *did* choose this . . . not to be possessed, but she did choose evil. When the demons came to tempt her tonight, instead of resisting, she was all too ready to allow sin to take her over," he said.[301]

"Katie wouldn't have invited a demon into herself . . . " I began to protest.

Quentin cut me off, "But she would invite sin in," he said seriously. "Sin is like an infectious virus, and for demons it is a gateway into the life of a human. When a person makes a choice to sin, they are opening themselves to the very real possibility of inviting a demon into their life. That does not mean that a person is possessed just by committing one sin. But one sin *can* give a demon a foothold of influence in a person's life."

"What do you mean?" I asked.

"Once a demon finds a weakness, a chink in your armor, they exploit it.[302] They use that weakness to make you sin more and more, until your sin becomes a habit and before long, it doesn't fulfill your desires as much as it once did. Then you need something else to appease your sinful cravings. When that happens, they lead you on to the next thing, and then the next thing, until eventually a person is comfortable committing sins they would have once thought were impossible and despicable, sins they had never dreamed of. If they give themselves over completely, then the demon can take control of their life.[303]

"This is real demon possession. It occurs when a sin takes over one's life completely," he said, pointing his hand in the direction that Tom and Katie had just left. "When someone becomes dependent, engulfed, addicted, or obsessed with a sin, then they could also be inviting in the demon behind the sin, like a Trojan horse.

"Drugs are a quicker method to possession because they are more addictive and more powerful," he went on. "Users surrender their consciousness, and before they know it, they are hooked . . . both physically and spiritually, and trust me, that is a tough enemy to defeat. Tom and Katie took drugs wanting a good time, but they received far more than that. Real possession, then, is not being overwhelmed by force; it's the willful opening of the heart's door to evil, one sinful step at a time, until sin takes over completely. Sin only has control because a person allows it to; and since the sin controls the person, the demon controls them. Once controlled, their life becomes intent on fulfilling their sinful desires, even if it means their own destruction or the destruction of loved ones," he finished sadly.

"It still seems like it is the demons' fault we sin," I stated in defiance. "If they are so good at finding our weaknesses, and they know exactly where to poke and prod, it seems impossible to expect us to resist."

"No, Micah," Quentin responded with a serious tone in his voice. "Demons are just messengers! They tempt; they do their best to influence, and one day they *will* pay for their role in sin,[304] but each human still makes their own decision to sin or not. Humans *always* have a choice. You must remember that! You've heard it said, 'Resist the devil, and he will flee.'[305] That truth is going to be very important soon. When God blesses a created being with intelligence, He also gives them choice," he continued, now very fired up. His eyes burned bright. "No matter how powerful the temptation seems, you *always* have a choice. Humans are vessels of freewill!"

Quentin spoke with finality. I was sure he was right, but it was still difficult to believe because it shook me to the core to think that each time in my life I had chosen to sin, I was potentially giving a demon a foothold into my life. Had I allowed enough sin in my life, who knows, I could have been right there with Katie and Tom. It could have easily been me.[306]

"So, what will happen to them?" I asked, feeling hopeless.

"Their journey is not over," Quentin answered, smiling for the first time in a while and speaking with genuine hope and confidence in his voice. "They still have breath in them. While they have life, there is always a chance. We do not give up until the battle is over, and neither should you. And trust me, their battle is far from over."

His reassurance was sincere, but it did not do much to ease my feelings about what I had just seen. And then another question occurred to me. "What about the jet of fire that shot at me from that one demon? Was he trying to kill me?" I asked, thinking that an arrow of fire to the head would have certainly done the trick.

"Fiery darts are not designed to kill humans. They are the method used by demons to send messages of corruption, evil, and temptation at their targets.[307] We try to block as many as we can. We don't catch them all, so that's when *you*, humans, need to hold fast to what you know is good and true.[308] That's when you need to turn from evil," Quentin answered in the tone of a sermon.

"What about that light that came from my mouth . . . what was that about?" I asked in increasing curiosity.

"Ah, believe it or not, when a human is ministering to another human, their words always look like that to us.

However, when a human is lying, or being crude or evil with their words, they look more like the demons' messages. As I told you, a human's words have more effect on others than most people can possibly imagine.[309] Fortunately, *you* don't have to imagine any longer," he said smiling.

"And . . . who were those other angels?" I asked nervously, wondering if I was asking too many questions.

"You'll meet them again soon enough," he responded with another smile. "They had somewhere else they needed to be. As a matter of fact, we have somewhere else to be, too."

With that, Quentin reached out his hand and the ladder of light appeared out of thin air. He grabbed hold of the ladder and my shoulder simultaneously, and we were off. We swung through the town again, this time stopping at nearly every house along the way. Every home had a moment in history when darkness sought it with targeted fervor.

Demons used anything and everything to draw people to sin. Through the loss of loved ones they drove people into deep despair; through financial struggles they divided families. Seemingly innocent desires were twisted into addiction and pain. Truth was mutilated and lies were propagated. Scene after scene, moment after moment, demons turned sorrow into hate, happiness and success into pride and greed. They turned unity into division, temptation into sin, and more. Their pursuit of destruction was endless.

Quentin and I witnessed people struggling through nearly every trial and temptation imaginable. The demons fed on human suffering, craftily targeting their temptations to exploit weaknesses, and relishing the spiritual ruin of men, women, and children. No one was safe. The demons were sick, sadistic, and merciless . . . but sadly, they were also quite effective.

To comprehend the full danger of temptations, Quentin guided me through history to show the ripple effects of sins throughout generations. The work of demons could destroy entire families. The choices of one individual might affect their children's children's children. Sin was catastrophic. Every single person in my little town had been affected by evil exploits at one time or another. Not a single home went unscathed. The angels fought hard, trying to defend the people of the town, but everything really did come down to human choice. People either turned to God, or they turned to sin. They either made God and *His* things a priority, or they served other things.[310]

Some people sent the demons away simply through their choice to resist and flee to God,[311] though the demons always returned to fight another day. Other people put up a fight, but eventually succumbed. Many people did not resist at all, and by the time we left their houses, they were as completely covered in darkness as Tom and Katie had been.

The only silver lining was that not every sin completely consumed a person in darkness. In fact, the most common choices were to capitulate to a few temptations only. Unfortunately, even something small allowed the demons a window to keep working on the person. For Christians, this ensured that their life would never be everything it could have been. For unsaved people, it gave them a world of excuses and obstacles that kept them away from the forgiveness of Jesus.

However, occasionally we came across homes that were

protected like my parents had been. Their houses were completely filled and surrounded by light. This did not mean that darkness never found its way in, only that if the house continued in its habits, choices, and faith, then the darkness would never be able to rule over the home completely because God already ruled there.[312] Though trials and difficulties would certainly come, they had a firm foundation that could not be shaken and would not crumble so long as they held fast to it.[313]

Each scene delivered the same deep, palpable feelings. I did not simply see people sin, I felt them sin. I felt the exact thoughts and emotions that overtook them as they resisted temptation, or gave in to it, changing the atmosphere to darkness or light with each decision.

We saw one man at home alone by himself in his living room. Initially, the environment seemed peaceful. The man was completely alone on his couch watching television.

"Who is this?" I asked Quentin upon our arrival.

"His name is not important for now. All you need to know is that he is a Christian who struggles with a secret sin," Quentin responded. "Although this man is saved, you'll notice that his house is unprotected. This is because he is not leading his house in habits and choices that promote holiness. He has the Holy Spirit in him, so he is frequently convicted of sin, but his lifestyle does not help him or his family pursue a proper walk with God.[314] As such, there is no barrier of light keeping the darkness at bay," Quentin said.

"Where is his family?" I asked, looking around to see if I was about to see sin rip apart yet another home.

"They are out of town," Quentin answered. "This man is

all alone, so sin is about to greatly test his integrity. Let's watch," he finished as he pointed at the man.

Then, out of nowhere, an inappropriate image appeared on the man's TV screen, and as it did, a dark, flaming dart shot from behind the screen directly into the man's mind. I could sense the guilt the man felt at what he was thinking, but he was also being sucked in. His flesh and his spirit were at war with each other.[315] He wanted to do right . . . but he also wanted to do wrong.

The atmosphere was changing slowly, but noticeably. Before, the air had been clear and undisturbed, but now the room was being filled with a feeling of lust. The lights dimmed as the familiar but ominous dark cloud moved in. Suddenly, I felt myself sliding backward as I was forced away from the man by the darkness that was spreading throughout the room. I could not occupy the same space as evil.

In the next moment, three angels arrived on the scene and immediately began shooting bolts of light toward the man, but most were blocked by the dark cloud that had now fully overtaken the room and they ricocheted away uselessly into the unknown. Only the occasional bolt of light reached the man. When that happened, and the thoughts of goodness reached his mind, he purposefully ignored them. He justified his decision in his own mind. I felt his sense of guilt lessen. He was shutting out the ideas that convicted him and allowing himself to sink into gratifying desires.

Abruptly, the man reached for the remote and turned it to a different channel, one that he knew he should not view. The dark cloud lingered over him thicker than ever. My view of him became almost completely obscured by the cloud. The angels lobbed another wave of godly messages, but it was no use. We were shut out. The darkness engulfed him completely. The angels continued to shoot beams of light, but now none of them made it through. The man was likely not possessed by demons, but that particular battle was over; he had made his decision. Evil now controlled the spiritual atmosphere.

Quentin and I moved on to another house where we found a young girl dressed in meager clothing sitting at her grandmother's kitchen table. She was poring over a fashion magazine. Depressed and insecure thoughts emanated from this girl, filling the room. Every few seconds, she glanced up and looked across the room. When she did this, her eyes would lock onto her grandmother's purse, and when they did so, I could sense an internal struggle that I didn't quite understand.

"Her friends at school have nice clothes," Quentin said quietly. "She desperately wants to fit in. She believes she is inferior and ugly. Right now, she is defining herself by what she does not have, and in her mind, that purse contains the money she needs to begin to fit in."

I looked from Quentin to the girl. His explanation matched perfectly the emotions I felt from her. But I also sensed something else. There was a deep love there as well. She loved her grandmother very much. However, this love was weighed against a very powerful desire to fit in with her friends—to feel good about herself.

This pain and longing was so great that I knew she would not need much persuading. Her desperate eyes looked through the fashion magazine as a palpable rush of envy surged through the room. Fiery darts shot from its very pages. Someone had written and designed the magazine with the intentions of delivering a message, and sadly the message was being readily received. To the girl, it said, "You're not good enough. You need this or that to make you pretty." Words and images could have such power, such influence. A lone angel appeared and immediately began blocking the darts and sending silent messages of light toward the young girl.

None of the bolts of light made it to her. A single fiery dart shot across the room from her grandmother's purse on the kitchen counter. The effect was instantaneous. She looked up at the purse and then her eyes glanced to the living room just ten feet away. There on the couch and fast asleep was this girl's grandmother. She was in no danger of being caught. The only barrier was her conscience, and that barrier could be hurdled easily enough. Her heart pounded in excitement and guilt as she got up, walked over to the purse, and took out the money that she so desperately wanted.

The transaction happened so quickly, I had not noticed the dark cloud's arrival. It was already thickening to a dense, charcoal colored fog. After the girl took the money out of the purse, she hesitated for one guilty moment while she decided if she was really willing to take from someone who had always loved her so much. She glanced over at her grandmother, still fast asleep, and then she decided. Stuffing the cash into her pocket, she was immediately covered in darkness and veiled from sight. As usual, the angel continued to fight, but the darkness permitted no trespassers once the human had made up their mind.

CHAPTER TEN

We traveled to another house with a woman collapsed on her kitchen floor, alone, and crying in despair. Sorrow permeated the atmosphere.

"This woman's already low view of herself has recently been delivered a fatal blow," Quentin divulged. "Her husband, who was both physically and verbally abusive, has just left her for another woman. She hates nearly everything about herself: her appearance, her weight—everything," he said in sadness. "Right now, she is measuring her worth, not by what God cares about, but by what she sees in the mirror, and by what the people in her life have seemed to care about. She does not realize that her true worth comes from God; that she was created in *His* image and is greatly loved by Him."[316]

As usual, everything Quentin briefed me on echoed exactly what the emotions in the room told me. The lady felt all alone, abandoned. Depression filled the air around her. Her angel was already on scene, sending messages of love, support, and comfort to the woman, and pointing her to Christ, but they all glanced off of her. She was wounded too deeply.

Pain poured from her face and her anguish was perfectly reflected in the face of her angel as well. I could understand why; I had been there but a few seconds and my heart already ached for the woman. Her pain was real, her sorrow deep, and her self-image all but destroyed. Years of abuse had assured her of her worthlessness. She viewed herself through the world's distorted lens, which placed importance on all the wrong things, all the temporary things.[317] The angel tried desperately to remind her of her worth to God, but her mind was already made up.[318]

WALKING IN DARKNESS

A dart of fire shot out from the refrigerator, which began to darken with black smoke. I knew a demon lay hiding in there, silently waiting for its moment to strike. The demon sent a lie to the woman. It tempted her with comfort, as if food would make her feel better about herself; it tempted her with self-destruction, as if she had nothing else to turn to.[319]

Then another fiery dart sailed through the air and the woman was struck with despair. In that moment, the demon easily convinced her that she would never look the way she wanted to look, or be who she wanted to be; that she could never be happy again. It exploited her sorrow, her feelings of inferiority, self-consciousness, and solitude. Evil wanted her to give up, to give in and collapse. Sadly, she did, and the scene blackened before my eyes as her angel continued to fight desperately, but to no avail.

House after house, we watched as demons tempted people, flawlessly targeting and exploiting areas of weakness, again and again. The spiritual victories were few and far between. Only a handful of people recognized their weaknesses and proactively sought to guard against them.[320] When people knelt and prayed to God, they were miraculously protected.[321] Equally effective, some people fled from the temptation altogether, ending the fight almost as soon as it had begun.[322] However, those instances were rare. Most people gave in to sin, enabling evil to have a continued foothold in their life.

Everything seemed darker and more deadly than I could have imagined. Little white lies, gossip, and other things that normally seemed so small were nearly always accompanied by truly sinister, evil forces; and it was shocking how often humans gave demons the victory. We left a final house on the ladder of light and glided to an empty adjacent field, lit softly by moonlight.

"Do you see now, Micah?" Quentin began as the ladder came to a halt. As soon as it stopped, the ladder disappeared, leaving us in the solitude of the dark field, with Quentin's angelic glow providing nearly as much light as the moon and the stars. "Do you see how demons use ordinary insecurities and common thoughts as a way to entice and manipulate people into choosing darkness and sin? They make humans think sin will comfort them or make them happy, only to find that sin will leave them far worse off than they were before. It is a terrible cycle of destruction. It's a cycle that trades the important things, the eternal things, for cheap things that won't last."[323]

"That is what *we* are up against," he said putting his radiant hand to his chest. "And that is what *you* are up against," he added, pointing directly at me. "We can only try to show people the truth and help them turn to God, but the choice is *always* up to humans," Quentin said, as he glanced over his shoulder as if looking for something. As he did so, a silent bolt of light came out of nowhere, streaking across the field, and striking Quentin in the head. He didn't move.

I was about to ask if he was okay, but stopped myself as he turned his back to me and began looking out into the field. I stood there quietly. After a few seconds, he turned back to me and his face was filled with sadness; he looked sadder than he had been all night. "One more thing is still left to be decided," he finally said, his voice heavy with sorrow.

"Are *you* willing to fight in the battle that is coming? You will have a chance to help your friends," he continued before I could respond. "Your decisions will affect Brice, Katie, and perhaps even Tom. In fact, you will have the chance to help more than just those three," he said, his eyes glancing down as if he were thinking of someone specifically. "But you will be tempted and tried beyond anything you have ever experienced. No one is tempted more than they can handle, but Satan and his demons will appeal to your weaknesses.[324] They will come after you with all they have. Will you still help in the face of such a potent adversary?" he asked simply.

"Like I really have a choice," I replied with an incredulous scoff.

"Micah, if you have learned anything tonight, I hope it is that we always have a choice," he answered.

"Well then, my choice is made. If I can help, I want to," I said in sincerity.

"I want you to understand, events have been set into motion . . . " he paused, " . . . things are going to happen tonight that will shake you to your very core. You will be tempted, you will be scared, sad, and up against a foe mightier than you; a foe that believes *nothing* is sacred, and will use anything it can to attack you. You have witnessed what he can do; don't make this decision lightly," he said.

"I'm doing whatever it is you want me to do," I answered, thinking of Brice. "I have to help."

Ordinarily, a show of selfless bravery would have earned a satisfied or even proud smile from Quentin, but for some reason, his mood was one of lament. "Very well," he said with a heavy voice, "I have one more thing to show you. This will be the hardest thing you have seen yet . . . perhaps the hardest thing you will ever see," he said as he turned to peer across the open field.

It was clearly very late in the night. I was not sure how late, but it was later than I would have expected to see anyone driving around in our small town. That's why I was surprised when headlights appeared far on the other side of the field, across from where we stood. The car slid to a reckless stop and remained still. The motor continued to hum and the headlights shined bright across the field in our direction.

Suddenly, a **BANG** echoed through the night as someone burst out of the back passenger door of the car and began sprinting through the field as if running for their life. Immediately, the driver and a second person rushed out after them. The first person headed straight toward us with the other two in hot pursuit.

The shadow of their silhouettes became amplified by the car's headlights as the three people drew closer. The two pursuers were quickly gaining on the person who fled. Then, in their haste, the escaping person tripped and fell facedown. Realizing their defeat, the person rolled onto their back to face the two people who were chasing them. It was then that terror filled me, as the voice of a young woman cried out to her pursuers in fright, "No! Why are you doing this?"

A chill blanketed my ghostly body. The girl's voice was unrecognizable from panic and fear, but who she was did not really matter because she was in trouble and needed our help. Even if my spiritual body proved worthless in defending this girl, I had to try to do something. I could not just stand there, no matter what it cost. I took a step forward, ready to rush toward the pursuers, but Quentin stuck out his arm, once again stopping me with ease.

"Micah, I know this is hard, but if you wish to help, then you must see this, and you must not interfere yet," he commanded. I froze in my tracks, like a hungry dog forced to stay away from a steak just inches from its nose. I was barely able to contain myself.

My heart pounded as the pursuers approached the fallen girl and laughed mercilessly, ignoring her desperate pleas for them to stop. Their laughs rang out in the night, revealing a young woman and young man, delirious in their sadistic capture of this poor young girl who sat helpless in the field, awaiting her fate—and I could do nothing but watch.

Without hesitation, the male pursuer reached his fist high into the air and brought it down swiftly, striking the girl with a violent blow. With a terrible thud, the girl whimpered and then was silent. Instinctively, I started forward again to try to help the girl; Quentin was going to have to use force to stop me. However, this time it was not Quentin who restrained me. In the darkness of night, the treacherous dark cloud had silently surrounded the field, undetected, and was now impeding me from moving even one step toward the girl.

I pushed and clawed at the dark barrier, desperate to reach the girl, desperate to help her, but the barrier was unyielding. Anger pulsed through me. *If I could only reach the attackers, they wouldn't know what hit them*, I lied to myself, ignoring the reality that they wouldn't even be able to see me, let alone be threatened or stopped by me. I continued to fight, but it was no use. I could not save her. Defeated, I was forced to watch in horror as the girl on the ground was kicked and beaten several more times by the male aggressor. As fear and sorrow welled up in me, I stared longingly at the helpless girl, and it was then that I noticed something very odd. Light was emanating from her.

In fact, she was the only source of light in the midst of the black and sinister field. Suddenly, there was movement in the darkness. Demons had most certainly arrived on the scene. I feared for the innocent girl now more than ever. *How could we leave this lone source of light, this defenseless young woman, alone in the darkness with demons?* I thought in a panic. I waited for the angels to show up, but none came. She was completely alone.

The demons began to pelt the girl with fiery darts, but surprisingly, none of them sank in. While she was physically weak, the girl was as spiritually strong as anyone I had seen on my journey with Quentin. She was as unyielding as the dark barrier surrounding the field. Each dart from the demons ricocheted unsuccessfully off of her and into the night sky. Miraculously, only light shone from her. She was impenetrable to evil.

Frustrated, the demons increased their intensity, trying harder and harder as the male attacker continued to abuse her and the female attacker mocked her. The lone girl writhed in pain. I was beyond afraid. Tears blurred my vision. I was helpless, forced to witness the brutal attack of an innocent woman and unable to save her. My heart felt as if it were hollow, as if the wind had been taken out of my sails. I felt weak, defeated. The fight in me was gone. There was no hope.

My life force seemed to be draining out of me. The despair and fear were more than my spirit could withstand. *Where are the angels? Where is the cavalry? Isn't anyone besides me even going to try?* I looked at Quentin and saw tears leak down his face as well, as he stood watching.

"Can't you do anything?" I said to him in a terrified whisper, barely able to produce a sound.

"She is safe spiritually; she follows Christ. We have been given no mission for her right now. I can do nothing," he returned in a sad, heavy whisper of his own.

The darkness had almost completely covered the area where the girl lay on the ground, an island of light, surrounded by a sea of darkness. She stirred slightly, and in the light that emanated from her, I caught a glimpse of her hair; it was a very familiar golden blonde hair. Suddenly she rolled to her side so that her face pointed directly toward me.

I gasped. It was Rachel! I couldn't speak, I couldn't move. The world was closing in around me. My heart ached beyond repair and every ounce of me stood frozen in shock and horror. Then . . . somehow . . . even though I was spirit, Rachel's eyes locked onto mine. Impossible though it seemed, she saw me in the distance, through the darkness. With barely any energy left, she whispered a few faint words that I should not have been able to hear from such a distance, but somehow, it was all I could hear, "Micah . . . it's Tom and Katie."

With that, the guy standing near her, Tom Reynolds, picked something up from the ground, held his arm high, and swung down, hitting Rachel solidly and causing her body to go limp. For a brief moment, I saw Rachel lying on the ground, completely still. Her light flickered ever so slightly, and then went out. Immediately, the field was engulfed in darkness and I could see nothing.

CHAPTER ELEVEN

<u>TAKEN</u>

Mine eyes do fill with tears. The joy of my heart has ceased.
My sight has been dimmed, and my soul turns to faint;
Oh, where is my relief?
I've been led into the darkness and not into light.
My path is blocked by fear and snare; I feel alone tonight.
My dance has turned to mourning, my happiness to grief.
The comfort for my heart's travail is far away from me.
Am I alone in sadness? Does it mean nothing to those who see?
With my hands and my heart and my voice lifted high,
Does anyone care that I weep?
Where is the judge who will bring all to right?
When will this price be repaid?
Does no one else seek? Does no one else fight?
Does no one keep evil at bay?
But it is good for me to have hope, and it is also good that I wait.
And with steadfast trust I should never forget,
God's mercies are new every day.
Though my cry and my prayer feel shut out,
He hears every word that I say.
When my foe is too great and my strength is too small,
I have hope, because great is God's faith.
So, I stand even though I'm alone. I walk tall even though I'm afraid.
With your rod and your staff I am safe on this path,[325]
And Your lamp lights my feet all the way.[326]

* * * *

FRIDAY, MAY 31, 1985 (LATE NIGHT)

A flame ignited in my heart. Fight returned to me with such vigor that even the demons in the field seemed but a small obstacle separating me from Rachel. I sprang into action immediately and lunged toward the dark field, ramming it with sheer hatred and panic as adrenaline fueled my veins . . . but the dark barrier would not budge. Again and again I rushed at it, to no avail. Quentin did not even try to stop me from physically assaulting the wall. He knew I would not gain an inch against the darkness.

I punched at it; I clawed, kicked, rammed, but nothing would work. It was as if the barrier were not even there. I could not feel it, but I could not go through it either—almost as if I had reached the edge of the world, and there simply was nothing past that point. Desperation or not, reaching Rachel was impossible. I couldn't get to her, I couldn't see her, I couldn't save her; and she needed me. She was knocked out . . . or worse . . . no! I couldn't think like that; she would be fine. She had to be fine.

"Rachel!" I screamed over and over as I fought against the wall of evil separating me from her, but nothing moved. I was helpless, shut out completely. Rachel was unguarded and in mortal danger, and I could do nothing. Tears leaked down my face as I fell to my knees in hopelessness and began to scream and sob uncontrollably. I was shaken, but I could not give up on her. I had to save her.

I got back to my feet, ready to begin fighting and clawing the dark force field again. However, just as I restarted my efforts, everything vanished before my eyes and my wispy existence was pulled with a jolt back into the unknown. Light began to flash around me as I felt my spiritual essence separate from space and time, just as it had before. I was once again apart from everything, outside of all things. I looked around purposefully, this time intent upon seeing what was happening.

I was alone; Quentin was not with me. I was completely by myself, and yet . . . everything surrounded me; and I mean everything. The entire universe was at my feet, soaring relentlessly beneath me. I was its fulcrum, and all that ever was revolved around me in a torrent—the sun, moon, stars, planets, galaxies, history, things great and things small—everything. I soared through the whole of creation, and yet I did not move at all.

And then, a new but familiar sensation returned to me. Instead of the atmosphere growing lighter in weight as it had the first time I had rocketed into nothingness, this time everything suddenly grew heavier. All of my senses were awakening. Even my bones . . . yes, I had bones again. Looking down at my hands, it seemed my wispy essence was solidifying. I was becoming physical again.

Before I could observe anything else, my body was rocked with a second jolt, as my feet landed abruptly onto the ground. I tried to look around to see where I was, but my mind and my eyes were still catching up to what had just happened. After a few blinks, my dazed eyes readjusted, although my mind was still whizzing about.

I was back outside of the hospital, next to Quentin's police jeep, and I wasn't alone. Quentin's serious face stared back at me. He was once again in his police uniform, and more resembled a normal human, although his angelic brightness and goodness still radiated from him. He spoke quickly before I could, no doubt knowing I would be frantic.

"Micah, we are no longer in Tartarus. We are back in the

physical realm. We have arrived not long after your third temptation," he said, apparently trying to catch my mind up to speed, but there was only one thing I cared about right then; Rachel. My travel through space and time had not erased the frustration and terror I felt at having been unable to penetrate the black barrier to get to her. If anything, I now felt that there were *more* obstacles separating me from Rachel. I opened my mouth to speak.

"Micah," he began again, cutting me off before I could speak, "I must ask you . . . you must tell no one about what you have seen, especially about me, or I'll have to leave, and I'm supposed to be here," he said quickly, as if he had meant to say it earlier. Certainly, the message would have been better received had I not just seen Rachel surrounded by demons and being beaten and tortured by Tom and Katie.

"That's what you care about?!" I yelled at him. "I don't care about that . . . fine, whatever. Where is Rachel?! Was that real? What we just saw, was it real?" I spouted off, breathing hard in increased panic.

Quentin weighed his words as his saddened face continued to stare back at mine.

"Quentin! Has that already happened, or is that something that is going to happen in the future . . . ? Is it something we can stop?" I demanded of him. I was desperately clinging to the hope that none of it had been real. Perhaps it was something I was supposed to prevent—maybe stopping Rachel from being attacked was my purpose in all of this. His silence was maddening.

Quentin opened his mouth to speak as his eyes welled

with tears. "I'm sorry, but everything I showed you was real . . . and everything I showed you has already happened."

My mind raced. I could not comprehend it. There I stood with a mighty angel before me, but I had never felt more alone. Quentin had been right there when Rachel was attacked, and yet he had not lifted a finger to save her. There were countless angels in our town, and none of them had come to her aid when she had needed them most. Anger rose in me approaching the levels of my third temptation, and then something clicked in my mind.

"Micah," Quentin began to say, "you must underst . . . "

"*This* is why those other angels had to rush off," I interrupted, my eyes wide with shock at my sudden realization. "The angels who were following Tom and Katie at the alley . . . they said they had to go meet some . . . what was his name . . . "

"Roland," Quentin interjected.

"Yeah, Roland," I repeated, "Those angels knew Tom and Katie were about to attack Rachel . . . *didn't they?*" I yelled. Anger, blame, and accusations all rushed through my mind. No demon was tempting me; I was angry on my own, and I was ready to fight the man in front of me, angel or not.

Quentin began to answer. "They met Tom and Katie here, at the hospital, to minister to them one last time, to try to stop . . . "

"So, you knew this would happen to Rachel?" I accused, interrupting him again.

"At first, no," Quentin began. I opened my mouth to speak, but he held up his hand, almost begging me for a chance to explain. Looking at the pain in his eyes, I went silent, feeling he at least deserved an opportunity to acquit himself, though my patience would not last long. "Micah, beyond all the things I've already shared with you on our journey, God had only let us know two other things that were going to happen tonight," he said, ceasing the small break in my tirade. "We knew that Tom and Katie had a big choice ahead of them, even bigger than when they chose to take drugs. And we also knew that Rachel would probably be involved. We did not know that she would be hurt, but given what Tom did to Brice, it was always likely."

"But," he started again, just as I had opened my mouth ready to accuse again, "I did not find out that Tom and Katie had taken Rachel until you and I arrived at the field, and by then it was too late. Once Tom and Katie had her, I knew our attempts to minister to them had failed. We tried to influence them, to change their mind, but unfortunately, they have made their decision . . . " He finished slowly.

I didn't know what to say. I felt betrayed. They had kept this from me. Even worse, they had let Rachel get hurt.

"Micah," he began again. "Micah, I'm sorry. I know how hard that last scene was for you to witness. Please believe me, it's hard for us as well. But I had to show it to you because ignoring a reality does not make it any less real. Don't forget who the real enemy is here," he said sadly, looking me deep in the eye with pain plastered across his face and tears running down his cheeks.

I turned my back to him. I didn't want to hear anymore. If they would not defend Rachel, then I would. Demons or not, I had to find Tom and Katie and get Rachel away from them. It was time for action! I looked up and saw the hospital. A thought entered my mind, *I have to check for myself, to see if Rachel is really gone.* I desperately hoped she would still be sitting inside, waiting with her parents. I had to go and see.

Before I had taken a step, Quentin grabbed my arm to hold me back.

"Let go!" I yelled. "I need to go see!"

"Micah, you know where she is. You just saw her," he said as I continued struggling against his mighty grip. Just like the dark barrier, Quentin would easily keep me from going where I wanted to go. "You saw me receive a message just as you and I entered the field, didn't you?" he said. I hesitated and then momentarily relented my struggle to hear what he was going to say. "The message told me that Rachel came out here to check on you when she noticed you were no longer in the hospital. When she came out here, she spotted Tom purchasing drugs from his dealer and she went to confront him, so he grabbed her," he said calmly, trying to appeal to my reason.

"Well, what do we do then?!" I demanded, throwing my free hand up in the air in exasperation.

"You know where we saw her last," he said, remaining calm. "That is where we must start. She is still alive, but she is in the hands of a merciless enemy, so we need to get moving." He then released my arm and climbed into his jeep without waiting for me to respond.

"Well, let's go!" he prompted. Quentin's abrupt change from inaction to action took me a second to catch up with. But then I too sprang into action. As I took my first step toward the jeep, a great **CRACK** erupted in the air, and a streak of lightning zoomed toward Quentin, striking him in the head, just as I had seen it do before. I paused, waiting for instructions.

"Correction," Quentin said. "Tom and Katie have taken Rachel to the high school. *That* is where we must go."

I nodded my head and ran to the passenger side of his jeep, opened the door, jumped in, and we were off.

My mind raced as we rushed down the small country roads, heading toward the school on the opposite side of town. First, my best friend had been attacked . . . and now Rachel, my Rachel. I was sick. I bent double with my face in my hands as Quentin continued to drive. I had always believed in the idea of angels and demons, God and Satan, but never had I considered their involvement in the world as something to actually worry about. It had all seemed like something we just believed in, but never thought about because it did not really have anything to do with daily life.

But the veil had been torn from my eyes. I had been completely and utterly shaken awake and made to recognize the reality and the danger of the spiritual realm. I had been thrown into the middle of a war, a war in which the casualties were my closest friends.

Neither Quentin nor I spoke as we zoomed through the streets of the small town, furiously approaching whatever awaited us. My heart pounded in anticipation. *Will this be it? Will this be the moment the events of these past two weeks have all been building toward?* I wondered apprehensively.

After we had been driving for a few minutes, the school parking lot came into view. It was late in the night, or early in the morning, whichever you prefer. The sky overhead was starry and clear, but looking at the school, one would have thought a storm was coming.

An ominous thick, black fog had settled over the school. The entire building seemed to have been overtaken by demons, the sinister evil spirits bent on my destruction and the destruction of everything good in God's creation. Never before had I feared to go into my school, the place where I had grown up, learned all the basics, played sports, met Rachel, and more. But now, even though I knew who needed me, I could not help but wish we would not have to go in. The enormity of the situation weighed in on me. *How can I be expected to make a difference? What if I am not able to do what is expected of me? What if everyone is lost, because of me?* I thought in fear.

Quentin finally broke the silence as we pulled into the school parking lot. "The foe seems pretty insurmountable, doesn't he, Micah?"

With wide eyes, I nodded my head slowly in terrified agreement.

"That's okay," he said with a smile, "because greater is He who is in you than he that is in the world.[327] You won't fail, Micah, because of *Him*," he said pointing up. "You have already overcome the wicked one by turning to Christ.[328] All that is required of you now is simply to walk in that victory. As I have said from the beginning, all you must do is resist the flesh, and walk in the Spirit.[329] The temptations will still be extremely powerful and extremely appealing, but *you* can turn from them, and turn to God instead."[330] He continued to look at me with reassurance in his eyes as he pulled into one of the many vacant parking spaces in front of the school.

I looked back at him confused as we came to a halt.

"Did you know what I was thinking?" I asked.

He gave me a another small smile. "You know I feel the environment."

"Even now . . . in physical form?"

His eyebrows contracted in a slightly confused look of his own. "Micah, your temporary gift should let you know that I'm never fully in physical form; I'm spiritual. Even in my human manifestation, your spirit can see that my essence is made of something entirely different, right?"

I looked at the wispy, yet powerful essence that blanketed his body, and then nodded my head again.

"Good," he said. "And the fact that you can see me as I really am should be a great comfort to you, my friend. God has awakened your spirit for precisely this moment," he continued in excitement. "He has given you everything you need to succeed. All you must do is walk how He would have you walk, and depend on *His* strength, not on your own."

Quentin continued to stare at me with a face of encouragement. Unable to say anything, I simply nodded for a third time. "Good," he replied again, "now it is time to begin. Let us go."

Quentin opened his door and got out of the jeep. I climbed out too and followed cautiously as he walked toward the dark and ominous school. Perhaps Quentin had confidence that I would succeed at whatever God had planned for me, but I had never been more scared in my life. I would do my best to resist the demons, but if I had learned anything from my journey that night, it was that they hit humans exactly where we were weak. They knew how to get to our soft spots and work them, overcoming people with cunning, rather than force. As such, I knew I was about to be greatly outmatched. I only hoped that Quentin would be able to protect me.

Quentin and I continued to walk closer to the school entrance, which was concealed beneath the evil smog. We were quite alone. Despite our solitude and our hostile destination, Quentin marched on in fearlessness akin to a military general with an army by his side. I, on the other hand, cowered behind him, as if waiting for a demon to jump out and grab me at any moment.

CRACK! A blinding light suddenly filled the night sky. I dove to the ground in fear, expecting the anticipated demonic attack had finally come . . . but nothing else happened. Like the spotlight of a helicopter, light continued to flood in from everywhere, illuminating the earth around me brighter and whiter than the sun could have.

Deciding I was not about to be attacked, I squinted and lifted my head toward the light. I inhaled in shock as my eyes met a multitude of angels—thousands of them . . . perhaps hundreds of thousands.[331]

Quentin grabbed my hand and helped me to my feet. He then resumed walking toward the school without commenting on my fall to the ground, or our new and glorious spectators. I glanced around as I followed Quentin, staring in awe at the incredible sight that surrounded me. Inexplicably, I began to feel strengthened. The light from the angels began to pulse as if in rhythm with a song, and I realized that they were ministering to me. They were sending me messages, messages of triumph and of courage. They were influencing me, preparing me for the great trial that approached.

Quentin and I walked up the sidewalk that led to the school. *BANG!* With another pulse of light, three bolts of lightning suddenly struck the ground beside us. I jumped again, but this time I kept my feet, landing behind Quentin, who had continued walking forward, steadfast as ever. I looked back as I recommenced walking and saw that three angels were now walking beside us. Immediately, I recognized two of them as the ones I had seen with Tom and Katie in the alley, but I had never seen the third angel before. Quentin did not pause for introductions. He marched on toward the school in determined fashion as the four of us followed him in silence.

At last we reached the entrance steps, and stopped as I stared up at the familiar building. A place I would have normally enjoyed revisiting, it now loomed before me as a dark and sinister edifice, concealing dangers and tragedies unknown. I turned from it and looked at the angels who had joined us.

The younger looking angel with the brown hair and baby face caught my eye first. He stepped forward and spoke to me. "This is an odd place for introductions, but now is really our only opportunity. My name is Erasmus. I guarded Katie when she was just a little girl, and I have been called back here for this battle.[332] She has changed quite a bit since she was small," he said sadly. I could not help but notice his appearance seemed to age as he spoke. The normal baby face was now worn and tired. It was as if Katie's recent decisions had affected his very health.

"And I am Joshua," said the other angel from the alleyway. He nodded his head to me as he spoke. His dark hair and beard along with his general rough appearance, especially for an angel, gave him the look of a man who had been through war. He looked more dangerous than any of the angels I had seen. I could tell he was good, but he was also terrifying. If angels bore the scars of the spiritual battles they had been through, then I was certain that Joshua had been through some dark assignments.

"I guarded Tom as a child, and like Erasmus I have been called back to help in this fight," he said, and then he paused as if he were not finished.[333] "I will request one thing of you, Micah . . . please have compassion toward Tom. Remember that he has not had an easy life. You have seen his father. You know a little of what he's like," he said as I immediately recalled the actions of Tom's father at the high school basketball game the night this had all started. I nodded my head.

"Tom has been through very much for such a young boy, and it has taken its toll on him," Joshua said. "He has also made his share of unwise decisions. He could use a friend like you," he finished. Clearly Joshua's terrible assignments had done nothing to diminish his capacity to care for the humans placed in his charge. If anything, his hopeful demeanor suggested he would be able to see light in almost any darkness. My eyes then looked toward the angel whom I did not recognize.

"Hello, Micah," said the third angel as he stepped forward to greet me. "My name is Roland. Let me first say that we rejoiced for you tonight when you trusted Christ as your savior.[334] What a glorious decision, my dear boy. As you might have guessed, I'm Rachel's guardian angel," he said. "I have been honored to watch over her for nearly her entire life and I can freely tell you that few women have walked the earth who were more godly than she is.[335] Her compassionate heart stands alone. She is a precious treasure worth more than I can say." Roland then hung his head in even deeper sadness. "I have ministered to other humans who have caused me so much more difficulty and disappointment, but rarely have I felt pain as I feel now."

I knew his words were true. Roland, the pure and powerful being who stood before me and seemed as if he could wrestle a lion into submission quite easily, was experiencing a pain far greater than I had ever witnessed. Not only were his words heavy, but his sorrow was thick in the air.

The young angel from the alley placed his hand silently on Roland's powerful shoulder to comfort him. These two mighty creatures were a stark contrast to each other. They were certainly both bright and powerful, but the rich brown hair and youthful appearance made the young angel seem like he had shouldered far fewer burdens in his lifetime despite his recent difficulties with Katie.

Roland, on the other hand, looked more seasoned; possibly even more so than Quentin. If I could have compared him to anything, I would have said he looked like a grandfather. Not in a sense that implied weakness, but in a sense that implied experience. Angels did not exactly show age, but there was something about Roland's appearance that suggested his years had been hard on him, and that his wisdom and experience had been purchased through great pain and trials. His heart had almost certainly weathered many more battles and storms than the young angel.

"But shouldn't you be in the school, right now, helping Rachel . . . protecting her?" I said to him, unable to restrain myself.

"God commanded me to stay out, so that is what I'll do," he said simply and sadly. "Believe me, there are few in the universe who want to protect her more than me. But Rachel is spiritually secure, and God has given us no other mission for her . . . not yet at least. Tom and Katie are the ones who need spiritual help . . ."

". . . and they will not let us in," Joshua finished for Roland, gravely.

"So you aren't going in there either!? To help Tom and Katie!?" I asked in shock, desperately looking from Joshua to Erasmus.

They too shook their heads. Finally, I looked at Quentin in fear. He was my one last hope.

"No, Micah, God has told us to stay out. This is something He has called you to do," he said with a look of confident determination on his face.

I couldn't return that look. I was scared out of my mind. I was completely disappointed, too. These angels claimed they cared about the humans they protected, yet they were unwilling to help now. Their obedience was insanity. If someone I cared for was in trouble, I'd fight for them, no matter what!

I couldn't take it. "You all say you care about them and yet you won't go in there to help them now, when they need you most?" I spat at them in a poisonous tone. As I spoke, four fiery darts issued from my mouth, striking each angel in the face. At once, all of their demeanors changed to that of heartbreak. At that same moment, the intensity of the light above us increased as the host of angels began to minister to me.

As the light reached me, I was suddenly overcome by a new realization, which changed my demeanor as well. The fear and frustration that had plagued me now evaporated and to my surprise was replaced with admiration. I studied the sad faces of Quentin, Roland, Joshua, and Erasmus and in that moment I understood to my very core, their obedience had nothing to do with their lack of concern for the humans they guarded. Rather, they were simply trusting in God. They obeyed, not necessarily out of their *temporary* desire, but out of their greater desire to please God, and above all, they obeyed out of faith. They believed all things would work out best if they obeyed God's commands; it was as simple as that.[336] They believed that no matter how they felt about this situation, or any situation, their best chance was to trust God.

I could see the faces of the four angels changing again. They sensed that I understood.

"You see," Quentin spoke, "this still isn't about physical power. As I told you once before, if this were about power, then God could end it all. No, this is about choice. Though we had one thousand angels, which we easily have," he said gesturing above, "we cannot change a heart that does not want to be changed. Rachel has chosen Christ, but Tom and Katie have shut us out. It is for them that we wait and for them that we hope. But they have not shut you out, Micah. That is why you must go into the school alone. Do you understand?" Quentin asked.

I nodded that I did, although, with the dark school lurking behind me, I was still terrified. Fear crept over my spine, and my forehead began sweating in apprehension. I was about to face Satan, all alone.

"You are never truly alone, Micah," Quentin said, undoubtedly sensing my emotions.[337] "Remember, we serve One greater than us all.[338] Just because *we* are not with you does not mean you are alone. You were meant to go in there without angels, but God is with you, and we are no help compared to God.

"And so, as I said to you when we stood in that dark field awaiting an unknown evil, there is only one question left that needs answered . . . what will the humans do? What will you do, Micah? You told me once that you would fight. Well, the time to fight is now . . . *if* you are still willing," Quentin fired at me.

The four angels stared back at me with empathy, but resolute in their stance, waiting for my response.

"Of course I'm willing," I finally answered in a defeated tone. "I'll go in there for Rachel. You all aren't happy about obeying in this instance; I guess I don't have to be either," I said jokingly, trying to force a smile through my fear.

Immediately, I saw a beam of light shoot from Quentin's mind and a voice in my head said, *"No temptation can take you, above that which you are able to handle.[339] Cling to what is good and turn from what is evil.[340] Every word of God is pure: he is a shield unto them that put their trust in him."[341]*

Quentin's encouraging message of light was followed immediately by a shot of light from Erasmus. *"Please help Katie if you can. She, like a sheep, has gone astray.*[342] *Help guide her back to the light, my friend.*"[343]

Another bolt of light hit me, from Joshua this time. "*Have pity on Tom. He has been through things that have scarred him permanently. Be quick to mercy and grace; be slow to anger and wrath.*[344] *Tom is a life worth saving, too.*"

Lastly, Roland sent a thought of light toward me. From him, though, my mind coursed with only one message, "*This is for Rachel!*"

That was all I needed. My panic abated and was instantly replaced by sheer determination. *This is for Rachel.* What did it matter if I had to face something more powerful than me? Rachel was in danger and it was time for me to act. The emotion of the angels filled me. Each angel was genuinely concerned for the human he protected and loved. They were commanded to sit on the sideline, helpless as they sent me forward into uncertain dangers, where I was to battle not just for myself, and not just for Rachel, but for Katie and Tom as well. I had to succeed.

Whether I was just particularly overcome with compassion, or whether the angels were still sending strong waves of influence toward me, I did not know. But I thought of Katie, and her dangerous decision to give in to drugs, and it broke my heart. I thought of Tom, whose anger had so clearly been cultivated by exposure to a dark and destructive atmosphere of pain. My heart hurt for him, too.

I took one step up the stairs that led to the entrance of the school. I had initially stepped forward for Rachel, but in that moment, I also stepped forward for Tom and Katie, because they were souls, too. They were souls that evil was trying to destroy through lies and deceit. I did not know what I could do to help, but apparently I was supposed to try. I was supposed to fight; and I was going to.

I started walking up the remaining steps to the school entrance. The door was covered in the dark sinister smoke that accompanied anything evil, anything sinful. For a moment, I wondered if the dark cloud would impede my path and stop me from entering the school. Just as I had that thought and reached the top step, the cloud parted like a curtain that had been drawn back. I reached for the door handle, my hand sweating along with the rest of me. I gripped the handle and looked back at Quentin, Roland, Joshua, and Erasmus. They each gave me a nod of encouragement. The door was unlocked. I pulled it open and stepped inside.

CHAPTER TWELVE

THE GREAT DECEIVER

All those who walk inside the vale, where shadows lie therein,[345]
Where faith is lost and doubt is found, where joy will meet its end,
Where hope is crushed by fear and gloom, where happiness turns grim,
Where love goes cold and strength is faint, ensnared by death and sin.
You walk a walk of solitude. You play a winless game.
You bear for treasure, filthy rags, with spots and full of blame.[346]
You have not life, for it is found in none but Jesus' name.[347]
But if you'd give yourself to Him, then sin would miss its aim.
He'd give you hope and save your soul,
He'd cleanse your sinner's heart.
He'd wash you off, and clear your guilt; His righteousness impart.[348]
But on your own, then from the vale you never will depart,
For only He can save you from the rulers of the dark.[349]

*   *   *   *

FRIDAY, MAY 31, 1985 (LATE NIGHT)

I stepped into the entryway and let the door close behind me. The dark smog that had parted to admit me into the school now closed behind me silently, blotting out all outside light as it did so. Frigid air filled the entryway, sinking deep into my bones. I stood in absolute, chilling darkness.

Normally, the street lights would have been sufficient to light the entrance of the school, but now nothing was visible. The extreme darkness was even more pronounced having just left the dazzling angelic light outside. There was nothing but blackness; cold, dark nothingness. Not even shapes were discernible.

I held up my hands, just inches from my face, but I

couldn't see them. I had never experienced life completely without sight. I breathed out the cold air and was certain I should have seen fog from my breath, but I saw nothing. Even more noticeable than the cold darkness was the inexplicable inner certainty that something sinister surrounded me. Just as I had felt the goodness of angels when I was with them, now I felt the presence of evil.

I started forward, hoping I might be able to stumble my way through the many hallways that I still knew so well from my years of school, but I feared that even my familiarity with the building might be thwarted by such a dense darkness. However, as I took my first step, suddenly a thin streak of fire ignited above my head with a whoosh, forming a perfectly straight line down the center of the ceiling.

Startled, I ducked away from the fire, but kept my sight locked onto it, certain I would be attacked if I let my eyes wander in any other direction. It roared and crackled as if irritated by a great wind, yet somehow—almost magically—it was restrained to a perfect ember line, suspended on the high ceiling. Its dim light glowed just bright enough for me to see a few feet in front of me, but everything beyond the entrance hall remained veiled in total darkness.

Fire should have been a welcomed companion, my only light amidst the otherwise pitch black atmosphere; but it was not the kind of fire that filled a hall with warmth; if anything, I felt colder. There was no question about it; just the like the cold darkness, the fire, too, was evil.

A shiver ran down my back, breaking my concentration away from the fire and urging me to move forward. Every moment I lingered was another moment Rachel was in danger. I took a second hesitant step toward the end of the entrance hall. Nothing happened.

I took a few more steps, but then a realization entered my mind; so much courage had been expended simply trying to get inside of the school, but now that I was there, I had no idea where I needed to go. Not to mention, the fire on the ceiling only lit my way a few paces more. Once past it, I knew I would be in complete darkness once again. Although it was not a huge school, it still had several floors and wings that would take a while to search even in daylight, and would be next to impossible to explore without light. I would have given anything for a flashlight, but if the light from the outside world could not penetrate the dark corridor, then perhaps a flashlight would not have done me any good either.

It was almost ironic that the supernatural sight intended to help me and warn me of the presence of evil was also making it impossible for me to see anything. Had I been unable to see the sinister dark clouds that filled the school, I felt certain that I would have had very little difficultly navigating the dark hallways of the school. It was spiritual blindness of a different sort.

As I walked, I continued to glance around in front of me with a cautious eye, but then always immediately back to the threatening fire above. I took my final few steps to move past the sinister light and expected to step back into perfect darkness, but to my surprise, the fire on the ceiling began to move with me. I took a few more steps and the streak of fire on the ceiling stayed one step ahead of me, as if guiding me where I needed to go.

Both common sense and my heightened spiritual awareness warned me that the fire was nothing more than a traitorous guide that would only lead me to greater danger. Yet there was no escaping the fact that this light was my only help against the darkness. The fire would prevent me from having to stumble through the entire school blindly, but its presence also meant that I was expected. Danger was not only there, but it knew I was coming, and it was waiting for me.

I followed the fire slowly, deeper into the dark school. The thought of Rachel was all that prevented me from running back to the door behind me where I knew there would be light and safety. I pressed onward. Soon I reached the main hall. From there the fire turned right, so I did, too; following my burning guide faithfully to whatever end. It was both friend and foe, ally and enemy. It blazed and spit chaotically as it traveled down its perfectly straight line. It consumed nothing, though looking as if it should destroy everything; but steadfastly, it traveled on, determined to reach a location yet unknown to me. Silently, I followed, waiting for evil to pounce.

Though the darkness prevented me from seeing beyond a few feet, my familiarity with the school told me that I was approaching a split in the hallway. If the fire guided me to the right, there would be a staircase that led to the second floor where most of the high school classrooms were. If the fire went left, I would be ushered through a small hallway that ran underneath the staircase and led to another wing of the school where the gym was located.

After a few more steps toward the fork, the ferocious

streak of fire blazed past the stairs. I followed as it continued on through the small hallway, and then finally to the gym's exterior corridor. I paused and stared into the darkness that filled the larger hallway before me, wondering what I was about to walk into. If the gym was my destination, then danger was not far away. The fire crackled and flared above my head, waiting impatiently for me to move again, but I could not move; fear paralyzed me.

I took a deep breath, filling my lungs with the cold, cruel air. My hands and toes were beginning to feel numb. Nearly every part of me longed for the safety and summer warmth that I knew was just outside of the school—except for my heart. That part of me still longed for Rachel. It pounded in my chest as I stood there attempting to garner the courage it was going to take for me to move forward to try to rescue her.

As I stared down the hidden corridor, the fire continued to roar and twist above my head, but remained locked in place on the ceiling, waiting for me. I glanced up at it and watched as its light flickered violently, but was swallowed up almost immediately by the dark ash in the air, which was so thick that even the few feet of visibility it provided still remained extremely dim. *Would the fire take the entire journey with me?* I wondered. No matter how little I trusted it, complete darkness would be worse.

I returned my gaze to the long, dark hallway, but as I did so, the fire suddenly sprang to life. With a ferocious roar, it cracked like a whip and shot out at me, intent upon devouring me. I closed my eyes and dove to the floor with my hands over my head, ready to be engulfed in flame.

Cradling myself on the floor, I waited; but nothing happened. The great hall was filled with silence as I remained curled into a ball, anticipating the ensuing inferno. Slowly, I reopened my eyes, petrified at what I might find . . . but the fire had disappeared, leaving me in total darkness, once again.

A mixture of relief and dread filled me. Though the traitorous fire had not devoured me, it had abandoned me at the point of no return. Finding the gym through the darkness would be easy enough now with such a short distance to go, but I had never felt more vulnerable in my entire life. With no sight and no companion, my heart sank. I was ready to crumble, ready to cower in fear. I was all alone.

You are never truly alone.[350] The words of Quentin rattled randomly through my mind out of nowhere.

I sure feel *alone*, I thought to myself in disagreement. It did not matter, though. Alone or not, I still knew what I had to do. Rachel was waiting for me, and if I was going to save her, then I would need the courage to face far more than a dark hallway.

I took another deep, cold breath and forced myself to get back up. After several more deep breaths, I took a few steps forward, making my way to the opposite side of the hall. Reaching out, I found the gym's exterior wall. It was not a huge accomplishment, but it was a start. With the wall as my guide, I would be able to easily find my way to the gym, perhaps only thirty feet away. There was nothing left for me to do but put one foot in front of the other and confront whatever was waiting for me.

However, as I leaned against the surface of the wall for

support, solitude and the reality of what I was about to face began to bear down on me more than ever before. I was not ready for the gym yet. Fears pressed in and my senses began to dim as my heart beat heavily against my chest. This was it. All the weird stuff, all the influences, seeing angels, seeing the temptations behind the struggles of all the different people in the town, it had all led me to this moment; but I was not ready for it.

My breathing and heart rate continued to increase. At the very least, I was probably about to confront Tom and Katie, who were in some sort of drug-induced stupor. Tom was violent enough under normal circumstances, but who knew what he and Katie would be like now? I had already witnessed them attack a defenseless woman I cared for. However, worse than either of them was the fact that I would likely be facing demons all by myself; and most terrifying of all was the possibility of coming face to face with Satan.

I stood clinging to the wall, gasping for breath, completely lost in a panicked trance. I did not want to move. I wanted to turn back. This was bigger than I was. *What can I do against Satan and everything else facing me?* a foreign thought said in my head.

It was true. I was no match for a fallen angel. I had watched human after human fail against their tricks. *Why would I be any different?* something said again.

I knew Rachel needed me, and I was still clinging to the hope that she would be okay, but *what if I could not help her?* another foreign thought spoke for the third time.

Fear and an unnatural sorrow overwhelmed me. My

chest became unbearably heavy, and the world began to close in on me. Negative thought after negative thought pelted my soul, tearing me down until only hopelessness remained. Trapped in my own mind, despair and defeat threatened to paralyze me forever.

Just as I thought I would collapse to the floor, my subconsciousness detected something. Though the hallway was pitch black and what I saw should have been easily discernible, my eyes barely noticed a small streak of fire shoot at me from the wall. I stood still, unable to react to this clear attack because accompanying the fire strike was a single thought, almost like a voice in my mind . . .

What if Rachel isn't okay?

In response to the thought, a surge of panic and worry rushed through me. I had seen the fiery dart; deep down I knew I was being attacked, but right then it did not matter because the question was exactly what I was thinking on my own. *What if Rachel was not okay?*

Despair sank in. Hope fled. It was over before it had begun. All was lost . . . but then something seemed to speak to my heart. It was a counter argument that resonated just as powerfully as the fiery dart had.

She WILL be okay. The angels did not send me in here to fail.

Immediately, my spirits lifted. All was *not* lost. Rachel was still waiting and I had to get a move on.

However, darkness would not be put off so easily. Another barely perceivable streak of fire hit me. *The angels were more concerned with Rachel's spiritual welfare. They did not care if she survived physically.*

CHAPTER TWELVE

Like a roller-coaster, I was drug down again. Somewhere deep down I knew the thoughts were not my own. Subconsciously, I knew that a foreign entity had spoken directly into my mind, but the words tore at my heart nonetheless. The message was right. What did the origin of the words matter if what they said was true? I cared about Rachel's physical well being just as much as I was concerned with her spiritual health. I had seen Tom hit her. I had seen her fall to the ground, and that mattered to me.

Another fiery dart—*What if the angels' mission did not include saving Rachel? What if I was not supposed to save her?*

Paralyzing dread filled me, and depression froze me to the wall. I felt tricked, lied to, abandoned.

Another indiscernible dart—*The angels never cared about her, not really.*

I wanted to turn around . . . to give up. I was blind, cold, and helpless against powers far greater than me.[351] The cold darkness buried me in despair . . .

Just as my eyes began to close and I felt myself sag, ready to collapse to the floor, another counter thought forced its way into my mind like a beacon of light.

You were sent here for a reason; do not despair before the battle is over.[352] You have work to do. Rachel needs you, NOW!

The last word echoed in my mind as if it had been screamed into my ear, awakening me out of the deep trance I had so quickly fallen into. Courage, strength, and purpose returned to me as quickly as they had previously fled. But as I regained normal thought, a new fear lurked in my mind. The negative messages had overtaken me so swiftly and so easily. I had completely lost touch with reality without ever realizing what was going on.

How could I be so susceptible to foreign thoughts, especially when I had expected them to come? I had peeked behind the veil. I had seen the demons' secrets . . . so how had they still sucked me in so easily?

Am I more susceptible because of the darkness surrounding me? I wondered. *Is it making the barrier between consciousness and unconsciousness so incredibly thin that I will not be able to realize when I am sinking into a trance?* The dark cloud that had always blanketed my mind in the previous temptations was now filling the entire hallway, making it nearly impossible to know when my mind was being invaded. This was an advantage the demons were certainly going to exploit.

I shook my head as if clearing out dust. I felt sluggish, like I had been doused with medicine that was causing drowsiness. Even my normal thoughts felt weightier than usual, like dreams, threatening to suck me into a deep sleep each time they entered my mind. I shook my head a second time, for good measure, determined to keep out any thoughts that would hinder me from moving forward.

Finally, I decided my mind was clear as it was going to get; I needed to get moving again. I took a step and then another. Slowly, I inched along the side of the hallway toward the main entrance of the gym, continually dragging my hand along the wall to guide me. My eyes were wide, spinning in all directions; watching, but seeing nothing; waiting for something, anything, to happen.

With scarcely more than my sense of touch, I analyzed

the cold wall and the frigid, dark atmosphere that surrounded me. The frosty air continued to painfully fill my panting lungs as I moved steadfastly forward, nearly hyperventilating in paranoia. I longed for the end of the hall and yet dreaded it all the same.

As I progressed forward, I prepared myself for the next wave of attacks that would surely come. The temperature continued to drop and the air grew steadily thicker. My hands and toes were now completely numb, but they were the least of my concerns. I was certain that evil would rear its ugly head again at any moment, and I had to be ready. The environment continued getting worse, harsher, as if the entire hallway were anticipating the next act of evil. Even the wall to which I so desperately clung was not a regular bare wall . . . it was a wall covered in evil.

"Covered in evil," I said to myself, stating aloud my inner thoughts.

As if alerted by a warning siren, my mind was suddenly awakened to crystal clarity. "Covered in evil," I said to myself, again.

My brain began to spin, as if someone had placed it into overdrive. For no apparent reason, I was trying to recall something, but I could not tell what. The thought *covered in evil* had triggered a hidden memory and my mind was working of its own accord to recall it.

I stood frozen in place as my mind began to search back to my recent encounters with demons. Facts began to click in my mind and a terrifying picture began to form, but I was still missing something . . . *what was it?* Interaction after interaction flooded through my mind, but the answer was just out of reach.

Then, at last, the final puzzle piece popped into place, though it took me a second to realize exactly what it meant.

It was the memory of the two demons who had materialized in the alley where I had seen Tom and Katie taking drugs. The demons had transformed into dark vapor as they possessed Tom and Katie . . . *dark vapor*. That was it; at last the final puzzle piece clicked in my mind.

I let out an audible gasp . . . the misty fog was not simply something that accompanied evil; it *was* evil. The smoke was the demons! My eyes widened in horror and I remained completely still. A shiver went through my body yet again, but this time I knew the shiver had nothing to do with the temperature and everything to do with the realization that something living, something intelligent was in the hallway with me.

The darkness was not just a marker of the enemy, it *was* the enemy. I was not merely headed toward demons; like a nightmare, I was surrounded by demons at that very moment, walking in and through them. The very air I was breathing was a cold, cruel enemy, there to do more than just inhibit my vision; it was also the very thing determined to destroy me.

I snapped out of my paralyzed fear and sprang into action immediately; my legs came alive and catapulted me down the hallway. I was no longer concerned with dragging my hand along the wall to guide me forward through the darkness; terror propelled me quite adequately.

Then, as I sprinted, a flash of fire shot toward me. It was barely discernible in the darkness, but my mind was clear and I knew I had seen it. Sure enough, the moment the fiery dart hit me, a thought entered my mind and my demeanor changed automatically. An unnatural fear welled up inside me that I knew had not originated from *actual* fear, but was instead tied solely to the unsolicited thought that had just entered my mind by way of the fiery dart.

Tom hit Rachel and that was only while I saw. What else did he do to her?

It was out of place, just another angle; another temptation the demons were attempting. I refused to play their game. I merely countered with my steadfast argument, without even breaking stride . . .

God sent me here for a reason; I am here to save her. With that thought, I immediately felt encouraged. The fear that had come with the fiery dart faded away instantly.

I took another step and saw another dart. . . . *You can't save her, you can't fight against demons, against rulers of the dark.*[353]

No, but I can resist![354] *Just give me the strength, God,* I thought back defiantly.

With each bad thought I countered with a thought of God, or of Scripture, and each time I was able to take another step.[355] They acted as my fuel, driving me forward against the evil deterrent, which was determined to crush me with fear and doubt.

I continued on and another fiery dart was fired at me. . . . *You will be destroyed trying to save Rachel; you know that.*

"God will be my refuge," I said aloud in triumph as my confidence increased, and my purpose for being there fixed firmly in my mind.[356]

Then I noticed something else happen. Another fiery dart shot at me, but instead of sinking in, the dart deflected off me and shot back into the darkness.

Another step . . . another streak of fire shot at me from the dark air, more discernible than before. This time it sank directly into my head and my thoughts immediately turned to Tom. *He hit Rachel. He hit the woman I cared so much for. I want revenge!* Immediately, anger grew in me.

But at the same time, a rational understanding also occurred to me. I had seen the fire shoot from the wall . . . I knew I was being tempted from a new angle. The anger I was feeling, though justified, was just a wave of temptation. Clearly the plan to bury me in fear and depression had not worked, so the demons were trying to make me succumb to anger; but they would fail! I knew their game. I understood their plan.

The demons would try to get me to hate Tom, to be angry, but I could not allow it, because I was there for him, too. He and Katie were part of my purpose . . . part of my mission. The angels had sent me in there to save not only Rachel, but to reach Tom and Katie as well. Even more than the angels, God wanted to save them, too. And deep within me I knew that their souls were far more important than any earthly revenge I might want to exact.[357] They were the reason I was there, and that knowledge gave me perspective and focus, it protected me from deception.

Just like that, the anger abated as quickly as it had come. I saw more darts shoot at me, but I concentrated on what God wanted me to do and suddenly all of the darts began deflecting off me. Focusing on God's mission put everything into perspective for me. My anger with Tom was easy to move past because it simply wasn't important in the scheme of things. The sinister fiery arrows continued to pour in, increasing in rapidness and intensity, but they were ineffective; they could not get through. My mind was entirely my own because I sought after goodness; I pursued God.[358]

I pressed forward unseeing, but knowing I was almost to the end of the hallway, and for the first time, I felt guarded—almost safe. My fingers searched the wall ahead of me step after step, until finally I reached its corner.

I turned left, and at long last stepped into the doorway of the gym. My eyes flashed around quickly, but were unable to see even a hint of my old familiar gym through the veil of evil that covered the room. I hesitated at the doorway, reluctant to relinquish my grasp on the wall. Now, looking blindly into the gym, I knew once I took my first step I would have no wall to cling to. There would be nothing to guide my steps except hope and sheer nerve.

I took a deep breath and exhaled. This was the final moment. Like the silence before a storm, or peace before a vicious battle, I stood still, enjoying my moment of solitude. I did not know what was about to confront me, but I knew this was the moment that everything had been building toward. Finally, I could wait no longer. I stepped forward into the gym alone, with no guide and no friend, only able to stumble alone into whatever dangers were waiting for me.

My foot hit the gym floor with a thud that echoed through the room. I lifted my other foot to take a step, but just as I did, flames erupted on the court floor several feet away from me. I threw my arm in front of my face to shield myself and took a step back. This time there were two sets of the menacing wild fires running parallel to each other, toward the far corner of the gym. Just as before, these fires brought no warmth with them, and emanated only the dimmest of light.

I stood numb, stiff, and weak from prolonged exposure to the cold, watching the high roaring flames that once again moved as if being blown by a wind I could not see or feel. Yet, somehow, just like the fire on the ceiling that had guided me there, these flames stood locked into position. They were a path. I was supposed to walk between the two lines of fire. Nothing else was visible around me. Only the path between the flames was illuminated.

It felt foolish to walk down a path that was so obviously prepared for me by an evil spirit. I considered avoiding it and searching for Rachel somewhere else in the school, but there was nowhere else to go. Sinister and ferocious though it was, I was certain I was supposed to follow the path. Surely if the angels had sent me in there, then they would have expected me to follow whatever path I had to take to lead me to Rachel, Katie, and Tom.

My heart hammered against my chest in apprehension and fear as I stood for one moment knowing I was about to follow the path, but at the same time, fully believing that it was a trap. At last I started forward again, positive I was going the right way, yet just as positive I was moving closer and closer to danger.

I took several steps and I was almost to the entrance of the flames when something moved in the darkness behind me. I had no time to react.

CHAPTER TWELVE

– *CRACK* –

Something hit my head with a thud, sending me forward as stars scattered into my vision. I hit the ground hard, dazed with a splitting pain in the back of my head, and barely holding on to consciousness.

With my face to the ground and my brain feeling scrambled, I barely noticed the light from the flames had gone out. Doom set into the pit of my stomach. I had walked directly into a trap, just as I had feared. The path of flames had lured me into a perfect position to be blindsided by the attacker. I felt nauseated and my head swam in dizziness. I tried to gather strength to attempt to turn over, but as I moved, the air rang with another loud **CRACK** and pain seared through my leg as my ankle was crushed by a heavy blow.

I screamed and writhed in agony. My ankle was broken badly. I lay on the ground, completely helpless. I had been prepared for spiritual attacks, but nothing could have prepared me for being brutally beaten the very moment I arrived at the gym.

My sluggish mind raced to assess my situation. I had played enough sports to know I had a severe concussion and would have probably already blacked out had the situation not been so dire. The darkness made my eyes feel like they were already closed, making it that much more difficult to stay awake. With my awareness swiftly fading, my ankle crushed, and my attacker hiding in silent oblivion, there was no denying I was no longer there to rescue; now I needed saving.

Barely hanging on to consciousness, my ears perked as I

thought I heard feet shuffling around me, but there was nothing I could do to prevent another attack. Another fire sprang to life around me, but both my fear of being struck again and my own physical incapacitation prevented me from looking up to see it. Even in my barely coherent state, I was certain the flames had encircled me entirely, for I could hear their chaotic whipping all around me.

Then laughter and footsteps suddenly broke through the sound of the flames. Someone was approaching me from the gym entrance. I braced myself, waiting for another strike as the footsteps grew closer.

"Micah, no!" someone screamed.

The voice was familiar, but I was so close to passing out, it was impossible to tell who it was. It sharpened my senses though; just knowing that someone was there, someone who cared that I was hurt, gave me the slightest bit of hope.

"What did you do to him? Let go of me!" I heard the voice scream. With a **SMACK**, as if from a slap, the voice was silenced. This time I recognized the voice; it was Rachel. She was alive, she was still fighting . . . and she was still in danger.

Only that thought could have given me enough strength to turn over. I did not want to move, for fear of being attacked again, but I had to. Rachel was why I had come. With a quick half pushup movement, being careful to only use my good leg for support, I flipped myself over onto my side and spun my whole body around toward the gym entrance.

I lay on my side with my broken ankle flat against the floor. A great flaming wall had indeed encircled me completely, but I was once again grateful to this fiery foe as its light allowed my groggy eyes to penetrate the dense, black air just enough. There standing above me was Tom, with a baseball bat swinging menacingly in his hands. He had been there all along, waiting for me in the dark like a cold blooded killer, ready to strike.

"What are you doing here?" Tom asked.

I ignored his question and began searching for Rachel. She was nowhere to be seen. I pushed through the dizziness of my concussion and spun my head around, examining the entire wall of fire in haste, but Rachel was not there.

"Micah, are you okay?" I heard Rachel scream from beyond the fire.

"Rachel? Where are you?" I cried out.

"She's right here, you big baby," came a second female voice from out of sight. *"Rachel, where are you?"* she mimicked in a voice of mockery. "I guess that blow to the head has scrambled your brains, Micah."

The voice was growing closer, but was still beyond the flame. Then, to my complete surprise, Katie and Rachel appeared before me, walking directly through the fire as if it were not there. And for them, I was certain that it was not there; just like the darkness in the air was not.

My gaze rested on Rachel and Katie as they came into view near the center of the fiery circle. I gasped in shock as I watched Katie push a bound and battered Rachel into view. Katie, who had eaten warm meals cooked by Rachel's mom, who had stayed in the same room with Rachel and was dating her brother, now ushered Rachel in as her prisoner.

My vision was hazy, but I concentrated hard to make out Rachel's face, desperate to see if she was okay. She was bleeding from her mouth and nose, and looked battered and terrified, but alive and otherwise apparently unharmed. Resolution formed inside me; I had to get us out of there.

I returned my gaze to Tom, who seemed to pose the greatest threat. His face looked just as deranged as it had in the spiritual realm. His eyes were glazed over and he was thumping his bat in his hand while looking down at me with a sadistic grin. He appeared to be pleased with himself at having rendered me so ineffective. He knew I was no match for him now.

My sluggish mind resisted me as I tried to think of how I could get Rachel safely out of there. I was so weak. My eyes threatened to close at any moment. I had to stay awake; I had to think. *Could I distract them long enough to give Rachel a chance to run?* Even if I could, she probably would not leave me, and I was in no shape to run anywhere. Tom chuckled as if he had heard my thoughts.

"Thinking of running, Micah?" he questioned, noticing my eyes searching for a way out. "Gifted athlete though you are, I don't think you'd stand much chance against me right now," he said in an arrogant, knowing voice. He was right. He would be able to stop me, and he did not even know about the wall of fire that stood in my way. I had no idea what would happen if I tried to cross it, but I found that prospect nearly as terrifying as trying to run away from Tom with a concussion and a bum leg. Escaping was impossible.

"Are you here to *save* Rachel?" he asked mockingly. "It's her own fault that she's here, you know. Your girlfriend got a little too nosey and saw me talking to my supplier at the hospital when I went back to . . . restock," he said with a smirk.

CHAPTER TWELVE

Then Rachel spoke in a scared but determined voice, "Tom, those drugs are ruining your life. Please stop . . . "

– *SMACK* –

"NOOO!" I screamed. Words of light had issued from Rachel's mouth directed at Tom, but she had never finished her sentence. Tom had hit her in the head with his fist, rendering her unconscious immediately as her light glanced ineffectively off of his head and soared past the ring of fire. Katie stood there emotionless as she let Rachel sink to the gym floor just a few feet from me.

"Rachel!" I cried. I reached out toward her, but as I did, Tom turned to me with a swift swipe of his bat to my unguarded stomach, knocking all of the wind out of me. I gasped for breath, my eyes almost popping out of my head.

I had played rough sports before, and I had been in little scuffles growing up, but never had I received so thorough a beating. My mind began to sink as unconsciousness threatened to finally consume me; and as it did, my thoughts wandered to the angels. *What had they been thinking? Why had they sent me into the school alone?* I had been ambushed. Now I could not even get myself out, let alone try to escape with an unconscious Rachel.

"So, I guess you won't be saving Rachel after all," Tom said, interrupting my inner monologue and stirring me back into semi-consciousness. "You two have stuck your nose in where it doesn't belong, and now you're going to face the consequences." He lowered his bat and poked Rachel in the side with it, letting out a small satisfied laugh.

As he did so, a dart of fire leapt from the fiery circle and shot at me. It sank deeply into my head.

Instantly, my mind began to sharpen. I felt a jolt of adrenaline and rage began to swell in me. *How dare he touch her! How dare he harm Rachel!*

I wanted revenge. I wanted to hurt him. I wanted to sink my fist into his stupid face. He had never been so lucky that I was badly hurt. If I weren't, I would have beat him to within an inch of his life! . . . assuming I could have stopped.

But then, as if it were an echo in my mind, I heard the words of Joshua—*Have pity on Tom. He has been through things that have scarred him permanently. Be quick to mercy and grace; be slow to anger and wrath.*[359] *Tom is a life worth saving, too.*

My mind was beyond confused. I was so angry with Tom. He had caused so much trouble. He had hurt Rachel and presumably Brice, too. He had stolen Katie from Brice and was now messing up her life, but most of all, I was pretty sure he was contemplating murder at that very moment.

Without a doubt, Tom deserved to pay for his actions, but the reality was, I was defenseless. I was hurt too badly to be a match for him. I was fortunate to still be conscious, let alone take on a guy with a bat. However, even if I could have fought Tom, I knew the angels had sent me into the school to try to reach him, too. *Don't I at least have to try?*

Before I could think anything else, Tom raised his bat as if preparing to land another blow on me. I raised my hands instinctively to shield myself.

"Tom, stop!" I yelled.

He laughed, but paused his attack, if only to enjoy me

begging. "You can scream all you want . . . but no one will hear you in here. Katie was the one who thought to come to the school," he said, glancing at her with a twisted smile of appreciation. "Luckily, Coach forgot to ask for his keys back," he said with an evil grin as he tapped his jean pocket, causing the keys to jingle.

"It's a perfect place to go when you don't want to be . . . interrupted," he continued, clearly enjoying the power he had over me. I was unsure what to say or do, so I decided to just say what was on my mind.

"Tom, you don't want to do this," I pleaded.

"Go ahead and beg, but it won't make a difference," he continued coldly. "You've both seen too much." He then looked down at his shoes, and his bravado was momentarily gone. "You both know about my drugs; I can't let you tell on me," he said as if he were convincing himself. "I have to finish you!" he ended, with his eyes wide in hysterics.

"Tell on you about your drugs . . . is that all you're worried about?" I questioned him in surprise.

Tom paused again with a look of confusion. To him, his drugs were the obvious reason he felt threatened by me, the reason he had to get rid of us. But Tom had no idea what was really going on. He was not aware of the evil that was all around us. In his world, he was just a thug who had been caught with drugs and was about to tie up two loose ends.

It was almost amusing to me, given everything I could see, that Tom's main concern was being turned in to the police. He was about to make a choice that would take him from petty drug user to murderer; his life was being destroyed by the spiritual war at that very moment, and he did not have a clue. The fire and the darkness were as unreal to him as a fairy tale.

But at least I finally understood . . . Tom was not my enemy, he was just a pawn in a game who had been deceived by evil. Not that Tom was a victim in this instance, he was responsible for his decisions, but more than anything, he was a lost soul that mattered to God.[360] I had entered the school thinking I would have to fight Satan, but what I had really found was a human oblivious to the danger he was in. His situation was tragic. Anger, misfortune, deception, fear, and all of the wrong choices had led Tom to a point of decision. This would be a decision that changed his life forever, for good or for bad.

However, I knew no matter how dire the situation seemed, this did not have to be the end for Tom. In fact, I was certain that he could turn his life around because in that moment, the situation changed for me. Tom was quite obviously still dangerous. He was experiencing drug-induced paranoia and it was no laughing matter that he had the only weapon, while I was badly hurt and immobile. No, I was still afraid. However, the situation changed because a new sense of purpose coursed through my battered body.

Even though Tom had hit Rachel, even though he had seriously injured me and was quite possibly planning to end me completely, I could not hate him.[361] I felt sorry for him. He was lost, confused, and scared. He had believed the lie. He had been deceived; deceived into thinking that his terrible past and bad decisions had to perpetuate into making more wrong decisions until eventually his life would be completely and utterly ruined.[362]

I had to stop that cycle of destruction. I had known my mission was to help rescue all three humans, but for the first time, I really wanted to. For the first time, Rachel was not the only person I was worried about. Tom and Katie were souls, too. They needed help, and I was going to do everything I could to help them. Whatever happened to me, saving them from the consuming darkness was now my mission!

It was time to do the one thing the angels had sent me to do—influence others. With my mind made up, I spoke from my heart,[363] "Tom, I'm really sorry that life has been so awful for you, but you know what? God loves you."[364]

It happened immediately . . . as I spoke, white hot light shot from my mouth and hit Tom squarely between the eyes. But unlike Rachel's light, my light sank in, deeply. And then I felt something different. Somehow, I could sense Tom's emotions . . . I could sense his spirit. I felt his anger; his pain. I felt his confusion and fear. Encouraged by the change, I continued.

"You've made some choices Tom, and some of those will have consequences, but it's not too late for you to turn back. If you hurt Rachel and I further, like I know you have been planning to do, then that will have been your choice and your life will never be the same. But God does not want you to destroy yourself. He has plans for you, Tom. He has a purpose for you, and the evil you are thinking about doing—that's not it!"[365]

More white bolts of light shot into Tom's mind. He stood frozen in shock. It was working.

"You don't know what I've been through," Tom

suddenly said in a quiet voice.

"That's true, Tom, I don't know your story. I know you've had a rough life, but I don't know what all has happened to you. However, I do know that at some point you are responsible for your own life. If I've learned anything, it's that we always have a choice. And now, Tom, you are hurting other people the way you have been hurt. Look at Rachel—she would never wish you any harm. She would be one of the first to help you," I said as I glanced down at her in appreciation of who she was. Tom's eyes locked onto her too and suddenly I sensed a small amount of remorse in the air.

"And yet, you have hurt her," I said, turning back to Tom. "Is that who you really want to be in life? I ask you, Tom, stop while you still can. Stop before you make decisions that you will regret for the rest of your life." Each thought, each sentence shot from my mouth as if fired from a bow, bolting toward Tom's mind like the white lightning I had seen come from the angels. To my surprise, Tom didn't stop me from speaking. In fact, he was slowly lowering his bat.

"You don't know all the things that I've done, Micah," he said sadly.

"Whatever you have done, Tom, you can find forgiveness,"[366] I responded, still lying on the gym floor. White bolts continued to issue from my mouth with every word.

"Forgiveness?" he spat at me as a streak of fire shot out from the darkness and hit Tom squarely in the head. "No one would forgive me. No one even cares that I'm alive," he finished in a tone of deep hurt as the darkness began to steadily pelt him with fiery darts.

"No one cares for you?" I questioned. "Tom, do you know what God did for you?" He looked at me in silent confusion as my light sank into his head.

"You say that no one would forgive you, but that's exactly what God is prepared to do." Tom continued to stare at me. He seemed to be hungry for what I was saying. "Do you know the story of the Bible?" I asked.

"You know I don't care about that church stuff," he said, rolling his eyes and causing my bolt of light to glance off of his forehead.

"Well you should, Tom," I replied. "If you think no one cares for you and no one can forgive you, then that's only because you don't know about Jesus Christ." More bolts of light issued from me and sank into Tom's mind.

"I know about him," Tom said in a sarcastic tone. "He's the one all you uppity Christians think will get you to heaven."

"And do you know why, Tom?" I asked, ignoring his sarcasm.

He stood silent for a moment, thinking, and then finally shook his head.

"It's because of our sin. You see, your sin, and my sin both get us one thing . . . death.[367] Because of sin, we die physically, and one day sin would cause all sinners to die spiritually as well."[368]

"Yeah, that sure makes it sound like God loves us," Tom said sarcastically again.

"But don't you get it? We don't have to die. This is what Christianity is all about! Jesus paid the price for us![369] Jesus came down from heaven, lived a perfect life and died in our place.[370] If we give our life to Him, then God forgives us for everything we have ever done,"[371] I said as more of my light sunk into Tom's mind.

Tom remained silent. "You have a choice to make right now. You can choose to continue down the destructive path that your life is on. You can continue hurting others as you have been hurt, and live a life of misery and sadness, absent of love and healing, *or* you can stop now and you can give your life to Christ. If you turn to Christ, I can't promise life will get any easier, but I can promise that you will find love, and healing, and forgiveness. God is waiting for you to choose Him, Tom. If you just give yourself to Him, then He will take you in as His own son and give you a future beyond this world. The choice is in your hands, Tom. What do you want to do?" I finished.

Every last bolt of lightning from my mouth sank directly into Tom's head. The only thing left for him to do was decide, and I was beginning to feel optimistic for the first time since I had entered the school.

Tom's eyes seemed slightly less glazed over. There was a little more clarity and focus in his demeanor. He was close to making a decision. The bat slipped out of his hand and rolled behind him, bumping against Rachel, who still lay unconscious on the ground near where Katie stood. Tom's eyes welled in tears. He took a step backward and opened his mouth, but stumbled for the words to use.

"I . . . " he began.

– CRACK –

CHAPTER TWELVE

Tom crumpled to the ground from a vicious blow to the back of his head. To my shock and horror, Katie now stood over his unconscious body, clutching his bat and looking furious, insane, and dangerous. Tom lay still on the wooden gym floor, never having finished whatever he had begun to say.

"Katie, what have you done?" I asked in shock. I felt so drained. I did not have enough strength for another fight. My vision swam before me, threatening to pull me from the conscious world, but sheer will kept me glued to consciousness and my eyes locked onto the new threat: Katie.

Her chaotic face changed to a look of remorse so swiftly that my sluggish mind barely noticed. "I'm sorry, Micah. I know this looks bad, but I had to take the opening while his guard was down. I know what you were saying was good, but what if he didn't listen to you? I think you were getting through to him, but what if you weren't? What if he decided that he *did* want to hurt you and Rachel . . . and me? You're hurt and I'm no match for him; I had to take my chance while he wasn't looking," she said pleadingly as a barely perceivable streak of fire shot out of her mouth.

"What are you saying? Aren't you here with him?" I asked, dumbfounded, fighting to keep my eyes open and still completely immobilized on the ground. She kept silent as I searched her face for the truth. I was completely confused, and my battered brain was not helping matters. *What am I supposed to believe? What is really going on? Has Katie been Tom's captive? Has she only stayed with Tom out of fear?* Confusion continued to race through my weakening mind. Perhaps Katie had never really wanted to go down the dark path with Tom in the first place.

Maybe she was not as guilty as I had suspected. However, something in me would not let me accept Katie's innocence.

I wanted to believe her, but she had shown no signs of remorse when Tom had attacked Rachel in the field. She had freely chosen to take drugs with Tom and had also seemed all too willing to follow him out of the dark alley in search of more. She had let Rachel sink to the floor unconscious without even the slightest semblance of emotion. She had jeered as I suffered from being beaten with the bat. Yet there was no doubt that she no longer looked angry or deranged. Perhaps she had heard my words to Tom just moments before and had a change of heart. Her face was certainly sincere. So, why didn't I trust her?

"No, Micah," she said. "He made me take drugs. He grabbed me just like he grabbed Rachel," she said with the most genuine of looks on her face. However, as she spoke, a second streak of fire shot from her mouth and hit me directly in the head. My spirit seemed to act of its own accord, as I instinctively rejected it, sending it ricocheting off into the black unknown beyond the ever roaring circle of fire. And just like that, the evil within Katie was revealed. My spirit and my natural intuition both understood one very clear truth . . . Katie was lying.

I went on the offensive. "Why were you holding Rachel when you first came into the gym?" I asked, hoping to test her lie.

"Tom threatened me; he told me to hold onto Rachel or he would kill me." Another fiery dart shot at me, but I was not going to accept anything she had to say now. With my mind closed to her, the dart shot off beyond the flame and into the distance again.

"Katie, we need to call 911 for Tom and Rachel"—*and me,* I thought to myself—"they are seriously hurt," I said.

Katie did not hesitate in response. "We can't. You need to finish off Tom. He's evil. He'll come after me again," she said as another fiery dart swooped from her mouth toward me, but glanced off harmlessly once again.

"Katie, no! I couldn't do that!" I said aghast. My head was really throbbing now, but I was once again alert. Katie's betrayal had removed all threat of passing out because, for the first time, I felt like I was really staring into the face of the enemy. Not that Katie was my enemy, but I was more certain than ever that the enemy was controlling her to a much greater extent than Tom had been controlled.

Tom had just wanted to finish me off because he was worried I would tell on him, but Katie was more involved. *Why had she knocked out Tom for showing just a small moment of mercy? Why is she trying to tempt me to kill Tom now? What can she possibly gain?* No, there was far more to her than just a girl who had been caught getting high. She was Satan's real pawn. It was clear that the real danger had only just begun.

Katie interrupted my thoughts. "I can't believe how hard Tom hit her," she said in a shaky voice, pointing at Rachel, and continuing her masterful charade. Every word she spoke seemed undeniably sincere, and yet each and every word carried with it a fiery dart.

Katie sat down beside me on the gym floor where I lay sprawled out and in pain. "Micah, he'll kill her. He'll kill me. You have to end this. Please!" she begged, handing me the bat as another jet of fire shot toward me. Once again it ricocheted off into the darkness. Her eyes were glossed over just like Tom's had been.

"Please," she repeated in a whisper. Yet again, the fiery dart that accompanied her lie glanced off into the distance as the circle of fire continued to roar around us. Katie's eyes began to well up and a single tear dropped down her cheek as she inched closer to me.

Her performance was amazing, but futile. Not only were her words inconsistent with everything I had witnessed her do, but unbeknownst to her, the traitorous fiery darts continued to issue from her mouth with every word she spoke, secretly revealing her true evil intentions.

"Katie, I won't. Tom will be in trouble for what he's done, and so will you, but I'm not going to hurt him. Punishing him is not my job," I said as bolts of light shot out of my mouth, this time toward Katie. However, just as the fire had ricocheted off me, the bolts of light now instantly deflected off her.

Undeterred, I resumed, "Katie, what you're asking me to do is wrong. What Tom did is wrong. Taking those drugs, hurting Rachel, what you all did was wrong. You need to stop, now! Go! Go into the coach's office and call the cops. Let's end this," I encouraged as more of my words of light shot toward her, but continued to glance off her like a rubber ball off a stone surface. Her heart was impenetrable.[372]

She stared, considering me, her eyes emotionless once again. Then she smirked and nudged even closer. Too close!

"Micah," she said in her most innocent and sweet voice.

"You really are an amazing guy." She was so close that the fire from her words almost blurred her face from mine as they shot out from her and ricocheted off me.

"Most people would be so mad at what Tom has done," she continued. "They'd want revenge. You really are special," she said, leaning her head on my shoulder and almost lying on the ground beside me. More fiery darts erupted from her mouth and attempted to sink into my head. I was momentarily caught off guard by her beauty, temporarily mesmerized, but I quickly realized that her strategy had changed. She had given up on trying to provoke me to anger and was now hoping to seduce me again.

If my guard had not been up, I have little doubt that those fiery darts would have enchanted me at least as much as they had the first time we had almost kissed, but I would not let her get to me this time.

With me still lying on my side, and my broken ankle flat on the floor, Katie inched closer and closer to me. Finally, she lay all the way down on the floor in front of me, facing me, and reached for my hand. A flame of fire came with her hand. It was not a hand of peace; it was a hand of deception.

"Katie!" I said loudly, retracting my hand. "This is not going to work. I will not be tempted to hurt Tom and I will not be seduced by you. Go and call the police. Tom and Rachel need help *now!*" I said my words forcefully, implying a command, hoping beyond anything that she would feel obligated to obey. She pulled her hand back and stared at me. Her face was blank, but I thought I could see a little defeat in her eyes, a little disappointment.

Then, with great swiftness, more than she should have been capable of, she was back on her feet and looking down at me. She sighed and smiled a menacing smile. When she spoke, it was not her own voice, but a deep, sinister, and powerful voice.[373]

"We have tried, but he will not give in," she said, apparently to herself.

"Ah yes, I can see he is particularly stubborn," rang out a voice from the darkness, beyond the flaming circle. The voice was calm, but somehow deadly. It reeked of extreme arrogance and a malicious undertone that scared me more than anything else had up to that point. It was a man's voice, but perverted and twisted. It just seemed wrong, unnatural. The sound of it sent chills to my bones.

"I can see you are wise to my games, Micah," said the voice with a maniacal chuckle. "What a pity, I could have made real use of you. Your girlfriend has never cooperated either. What an annoying couple you two make. No matter, I suppose you cannot win them all," said the voice.

"Tie them up. . . . I want Micah to watch," he said with another small chuckle. Katie ran through the fire, unflinchingly and out of view. I strained my ears to hear her as she rummaged around in a room just beyond the gym floor, which I knew to be the coach's office. She returned seconds later carrying a rope.

At once, Katie grabbed me, Rachel, and Tom and pulled the three of us with unnatural strength toward the rim of the encircling flames and away from the entrance doors.[374] I winced as we approached, ready for the flames to burn, but right as they would have ignited us, they parted and allowed us to slide through unharmed. Now they formed parallel lines just like the initial fiery lines that had led me into the gym. Like slithering serpents, they crawled along the floor just ahead of us, as if once again acting as our guide.

Katie drug us toward a large opening in the gym wall that functioned as a sort of raised stage for school concerts and events. The stage was at least four feet high, but when we got to it, Katie lifted the three of us with ease—all at once. We landed with a *thud*, causing my head to spin and sharp pains to flare through my injured ankle.

Katie then grabbed Rachel and Tom and put our backs to each other, forcing me to sit up and swing my legs off the stage facing the dark evil that filled the gym. I knew that if I did not first black out, then I would have no choice but to look at whatever horrible deeds the evil voice had planned. Blood rushed to my ankle causing it to swell, while it dangled feebly over the gym floor.

I strained my eyes to see out into the gym, but nothing was visible besides the flames that had led us to the stage. Just as before, their dim light offered no illumination the way natural flames would have. I would not be able to see the owner of the sinister voice until he wanted me to see him. I was completely at his mercy . . . and I suspected he had none.

I felt my hands being bound to Rachel and Tom's behind my back. As little as I wanted my hands tied, I did not fight it; I could not have gotten away anyway. Even if I had the strength to move—which I didn't—I would have had to drag myself to safety. Katie would have been able to catch me easily and with her sudden increase in strength, she would have had no problem stopping me either. She finished tying our arms with the rope and reappeared in front of me.

"Katie, please stop. Whatever you're doing, you don't have to . . ."

She slapped me in the face, cutting my words off and sending my head swimming in dizziness again. Her deep and sinister voice spoke, "Now you will see. Now we will not be stopped. Now it will be *our* kingdom."

Her voice matched the chaos that radiated from her face. I was no longer speaking to Katie. I was speaking to the demon or demons who had taken her over completely.

The calm and dangerous voice then spoke again from the darkness, "Yes, Micah, now you will see. Now it will be *my* way, not *His* way any longer. I will be like *Him* in the end.[375] And you, Micah, you will have the great pleasure of witnessing the first step in my rise to power, since I know you are one of the few in the history of mankind who have even been capable of seeing into the spiritual realm. What a rare treat for you, then, to get to witness the beginning of the end of everything good," he said with a triumphant sound in his self-assured and poisonous voice.

"Let us begin," he commanded.

Suddenly the flames on the gym floor roared and expanded, extending from the stage toward the middle of the floor, where they rushed away from each other and then circled back, making a large fiery circle in the middle of the floor that opened toward me.

The evil black smoke in the air thinned and transformed into dark figures that began lining the flames. Demons! Dozens of them, all forming along the inner border of the fiery circle! The darkness in the air had cleared noticeably, but I suspected the smoke in the atmosphere still contained dozens if not hundreds more demons.

The feeling of evil continued to intensify as more and more demons joined the ring of fire. While I could still scarcely see anything else in the gym, the entire circle was now perfectly clear, giving me a horrifying view of the demons' faces as they solidified.

In terror I stared, unable to look away as I felt an odd and terrible familiarity with each demonic face. They did not bear unique facial features that distinguished one from another like humans . . . no, these demons seemed to have their appearances defined by certain sins. Just as a person might be described as having brown hair, or blue eyes, or a sharp chin, I could describe the faces of these creatures as something sinful. Their very essence seemed to be composed of their sin.

I recognized the hallucinogen demons I had seen in the alley, but they were apparently not the only two of their kind. Standing on the edge of the circle, facing toward the center, stood five hallucinogen demons that bore identical looks of derangement.

I searched the perimeter of fire for other sins. The demons closest to me bore the unmistakable expression of greed. Their hungry eyes stared toward the center of the circle in eager anticipation of something. Another demon stood alone. His was possibly the most terrifying appearance of all—hate. He glared at the center of the room, and I felt as if the intensity of his gaze might burn a hole in the very air.

One by one, I looked at dozens of these otherwise indiscernible figures, each with red eyes, each enormous, each one seemingly composed of thick dark smoke, yet each one completely identifiable because of the sin it represented.

All of the demons stood, waiting for something to happen. Then, all at once, they stiffened, standing more erect than before. There was complete silence. And then, in the silence I heard something moving closer. The farthest point of the fiery circle opposite me parted, and through the opening a dark serpent slithered in.

It was huge, deadly, and apparently revered by the other demons, for not one of them moved. When the serpent reached the center of the circle, it began to change. Dark smoke poured from it and rose into the air. In nothing more than a second, the snake had formed into a large, dark, misty creature, similar to, but far more terrifying than all of the other demons in the room.

I could feel this creature was powerful and evil; it was larger than all of the rest. Its eyes gleamed red and it stared directly at me. Rather than a face of one sin, this face bore all sin. In a fleeting look, my eye could catch a trace of greed, gluttony, hate, lust, and every other sin that could be named, but perhaps the most discernible sin marking its essence was pride.[376]

I could see that this creature was completely infatuated with itself. This was more than typical self-infatuation that any common teenager might go through. This was an all-consuming infatuation. If I could call it anything, I would call it self-worship. This pride stood out stronger than any other, but was still intertwined with a world of other sins. The creature was perversion to the highest degree.

Step by step, it walked toward the center of the circle in the middle of the gym. It stopped, looked at me, and smiled, causing chills once again to course through my body that had nothing to do with the freezing temperature. Nothing comforting or warm issued from the smile. It was a smile of malediction. With certainty, it contained murder and deceit, and I knew whatever upcoming event was causing the smile would surely be evil and destructive.

The creature stopped in the center of the circle. Katie then turned from me, faced the creature, bowed her head, and said with her demonic voice, "All hail, the Most High Lucifer."

"All hail, King Lucifer!" the chorus of demons echoed.

CHAPTER THIRTEEN

PROGENY OF THE DAMNED

The unthinkable has come to pass,
The heir is to be crowned.
The deceiver's goal within his grasp,
No help is to be found.
But why will you die, oh wicked?[377]
Can nothing be done to dissuade?
By assenting to evil desires,
The price of wrath must fully be paid.[378]
But you were designed for a purpose,
You were fearfully and wonderfully made.[379]
You're a marvelous and good new creation,
Don't let lies and deceit bid you stray.[380]
The choice is here at this moment,
No second chance at grace will He give.[381]
Do not choose the path of destruction,
But turn ye . . . turn ye . . . and live.[382]

*   *   *   *

FRIDAY, MAY 31 THRU SATURDAY, JUNE 1, 1985 (LATE NIGHT, EARLY MORNING)

"There were *Nephilim* in the earth in those days; and also after that, when the sons of God came in unto the daughters of men, and they bare children to them,"[383] the self-assured voice of Satan rang out to the large demonic assembly that surrounded him. Excitement pulsed through the air from everyone except me. Only I sat in petrified trepidation, watching as Satan paced around the center of the circle indulging in the moment he had clearly been anticipating a long time.

"We all know it has happened before with some of our

fallen brethren," Satan continued. "And now, this time, it will happen for me." His voice was now marked with the sound of victory. He raised his enormous, dark arms high into the air and the demons quivered as they joined in on his euphoria.

How could it be possible? I thought to myself. *How can any of it be real?* When Quentin had first explained to me Satan's plan to have an heir, it had seemed so surreal, so bizarre; but in reality, it was beyond bizarre. The situation was more horrific than anything I could have ever dreamed, anything I could have imagined. My worst nightmares seemed like a joke compared to what I now faced—surrounded by a horde of demons, beaten to a pulp, hobbled, and fearfully waiting for the great deceiver to produce an heir with Katie, my best friend's demon-possessed girlfriend—yeah, the word *nightmare* was not adequate.

"For too long have we been confined to this world," Satan resumed, allowing his massive arms to drop to his side.[384] "For too long *influence* has been our only ability, but never more than that! For too long have we been enslaved in the creation of *another*,"[385] he said, with his smoldering red eyes glaring around the circle and his face of darkness contorted into that of complete hatred. "But now it will be our time."

"*Our time,*" the demons echoed in their wide range of hideous, sycophantic voices. They were rapt with nearly palpable anticipation. Clearly, they had all been waiting a very long time for what was about to take place.

"We do not possess life like *HE* does,"[386] Lucifer said. This time his glaring red eyes stared into the sky in disgust.

"We cannot create life from nothing, but we can use *His*

creation against *Him*. The time of the *Nephilim* has returned, but this time there will be only one! *Mine!*" he finished with a satisfied hiss.

And then, as if commanded to do so, Katie walked away from the stage where I sat, still tied to an unconscious Rachel and Tom. I wanted to grab her, to stop her, but my hands were bound too tightly. I tried to speak, but in fear and apprehension, my throat had gone suddenly dry, feeling as if it had collapsed in on itself. It was as useless as the rest of me. But as Katie took a few more steps toward Satan, I forced my throat to work, choking out only one word. "Katie!" I cried, pleadingly.

A bolt of light charged after her, but deflected off the back of her head the moment it made contact. She turned back toward me, smiling, and spoke in the low sinister voice that she had used before, "Katie is no longer in control of this vessel."

Every hair on my body stood on end in horror. Katie was completely gone. There was no hope for her. There was no hope for any of us. *Why did Quentin send me in here alone?* Perhaps Rachel and I would be safe spiritually—and perhaps Tom *might* be as well—but I doubted very much that Satan would leave the three of us alone once the job with Katie was done. Despair set in. This would be the end of us, and Katie's spiritual battle would be lost for good.

But no! Something in me resisted. No matter how unreachable Katie seemed, she was still alive, and according to the angels, that meant I had to keep trying. The angel's advice had not steered me wrong up to that point. So, despite how unlikely my chances seemed, I had no other option than to keep trusting them. It was the only hope the four of us had to make it out of the gym alive.

"Katie, this is all wrong. Stop what you are doing!" Another light issued from my mouth toward her, but this time it was not deflected. Unlike before, it sank directly into her mind. Katie stopped and turned back toward me again, no longer smiling, but giving a blank look of confusion.

This is it! I thought. This was how I could save her; just as I had saved Tom; with my words, with a message about God. I was going to stop Satan's plans the same way the angels always tried to stop him, simply by influencing humans . . . and I knew exactly what I needed to say.

I yelled at her, "Katie, remember your dream." Immediately light sprang from me again, and bolted directly at Katie. Each word struck her like unstoppable lightning and sank in deeply. "Remember how you were being seduced, enticed to be pulled under water. You knew it was wrong, you knew it was dangerous, but you were also curious." She nodded with a vacant stare fixed firmly onto her face.

"But remember there was also a hand, Katie, a hand reaching out to save you. This is your choice, Katie. To be saved, or to be destroyed.[387] It's not too late. The voice, the pull, the longing, it's not what you want. You think you want it, but it wants to destroy you. It's not too late to do what's right; it's not too late to turn from darkness to light![388] It's not too late to turn from your sins and give your life to Jesus Christ."[389]

Jets of light erupted from my mouth with each word, each thought, and fired rapidly into Katie's face, illuminating her blank expression. It was working; my words were sinking in. She had to see clearly now, she just had to! I looked at Satan, expecting him to be staring at me, possibly even ready to attack me, but he had eyes only for Katie in that moment. He was not speaking, but he was sending his own messages silently. His fiery darts were shooting rapidly from his mind and sinking into Katie's. He was not giving her up without a fight.

I started to speak again, but Katie held up her hands, as if she were about to say something. I stopped speaking and I noticed that Satan stopped, too, but he had a smile on his face that scared me more than anything had up to that point.

"Micah," Katie spoke, finally in her own voice. She looked deeply into my eyes and then spoke slowly. "Micah . . . I know what you are trying to do . . . but I'm tired of being told not to take the cookie from the cookie jar. It's time to live life how I want."

"Katie, no!" I started to scream, sending a jet of light shooting from my mouth, but at the same moment the demons closed their dark circle in a swift *whoosh* like curtains closing quickly over a stage. They formed an impenetrable blockade of evil, deflecting my message of light beyond the fiery circle that still surrounded them, sending it off into the distance.

"Katie," I continued, hoping to speak through the dark wall of evil that now separated us. "Whatever he's telling you, it's a lie. He doesn't want to make you happy; he doesn't care about you. It's a trick. You will be destroyed!"[390]

The words of light from my mouth slammed into the dark barricade, but merely ricocheted off like tiny bullets hitting a large steel door they had no hope of penetrating. Thought after thought I yelled at Katie. I screamed truth after truth to her, but each message of light was rejected and discarded into the darkness without ever reaching its destination, without ever being heard.

After a while, I stopped yelling as defeat stole through me. I couldn't believe it. I just couldn't understand. I had been so certain that I would get to Katie, just as I had gotten to Tom; but I had failed.[391] Whatever Satan had enticed Katie with, it had worked . . . she had made her choice. She had willfully enclosed herself in the circle of evil, trapped of her own volition, her own decision to give in to Satan and his evil temptations—and there was nothing I could do about it. She couldn't hear me any longer. I couldn't influence her. She was beyond my reach. I had tried and I had failed.

As I stared at the dark mass at the center of the court, I was ready for it all to be over. I did not want to watch Katie destroy herself. I did not want to see Satan succeed in his plan. If only unconsciousness were still knocking at my door as persistently as it had been just moments before, then perhaps I would be able to just give in to sleep and never wake. Then I would not have to know the devastation Satan would soon cause, and I would not have to experience what Satan was bound to do with Rachel, Tom, and me.

I closed my eyes hoping for rest, but sorrow seemed to be holding me to consciousness. I stared in lament at the wicked circle of fire that licked the air with its terrible flames and surrounded the even more terrible demonic barricade. When Quentin told me that Katie would be chosen by Satan to give him an heir, never had it occurred to me that she would actually choose to let him. If only the angels were there to help me. If only God would put a stop to this evil . . .

And then, as the thought of God entered my mind, I realized what I should do. It was what I should have been doing all along: *prayer.* "God, stop this madness," I screamed into the darkness. "Please stop Katie from destroying herself. God, I want to trust You, I want Your will to be done, but I admit, I'm terrified of what Your will might be. I'm terrified about what might happen. Give me the faith to trust You, give me the strength to . . ."[392]

I had much more to say, but my prayer was cut short, for suddenly, a rumbling sound filled the gym. I looked around, expecting the cavalry. I hoped to see God, or angels, or something, but nothing new entered the gym. Neither angels, nor God had come to my rescue. In fact, my eyes were drawn to the center of the basketball court, as I realized the deep rumbling was emitting from the dark mass of demons huddled there. The rumbling continued to increase until finally it reached the magnitude of an earthquake, but to my surprise, the gym remained perfectly still. Only the spiritual realm shook. Everything in the physical world remained unmolested and unaware of the doom that was coming for it . . . except for me, of course. I sat alone, watching the cloud of evil that concealed what was certain to be Satan's heir being born to a girl who had given herself over completely to sin.

Then Satan spoke, his magnified voice overshadowing the mighty rumbling.

"Katie, I will make you great. Powerful! More beautiful than any other. All of your desires will come true. Do you accept?" he said in a voice of great anticipation.

"Yes," she said, her monotone voice easily as loud and

clear as Satan's.

"No!" I screamed in protest; but as I did, an explosion suddenly drowned out all noise, breaking apart the dark gathering at the center of the court with a mighty **BOOM!** The demons were blasted backward off their feet, and began to scramble away frantically.

The dark smoke started to clear, and light from the circle of fire now revealed the unobstructed center of the court. Satan was nowhere to be seen. Alone in the middle of the gym floor was Katie. Her eyes were closed, her expression was vacant as ever, and she stood perfectly still with her hands to her sides.

I had no idea what was wrong with her. I wanted to speak, to say something to her, to try to draw her back, but fear kept my throat locked again, and this time there was no opening it. Satan's absence terrified me even more than his presence. Whatever the reason for his sudden disappearance, it was surely terrible. I waited for whatever was going to happen next.

It began slowly. The tiniest streak of fiery black smoke began to empty out of Katie's head. Gradually it grew into a thick, terrible stream. For what seemed like an eternity, I watched as evil poured endlessly out of her mind, but rather than floating away into the air, it poured out onto the floor next to her, as if filling an invisible mold. *A mold of what?* I wondered.

The stream of smoke continued to build on the ground, forming a figure as it did; *but what was it?* It grew and grew until the last of the smoke left Katie's mind and a dense smoldering cloud stood beside her, nearly two times her height.

Then the cloud began to condense upon itself. It shrank and tightened until at last a large, dark, gruesome beast of smoke stood before me. It was Satan; his disappearance was now explained. Katie had experienced full possession by the most terrible creature ever created. Her vacant expression was in great contrast with Satan's, whose dark face now wore supreme satisfaction and victory. He had finished what he had intended to. It was too late. Satan had won.

He continued to stare at Katie expectantly. For a moment, nothing happened. Then Katie began convulsing violently. Instinctively, I tugged at my ropes trying to break free. I wanted to run to her and help, but I couldn't. I couldn't do anything for her. She had made sure of that.

I readied myself to speak to her again, to try to influence her, but at that moment, Katie's body gave one last hard jolt and then stiffened like a board. Her head tipped back and her face pointed toward the ceiling. Suddenly, crimson smoke erupted from her chest near her heart, and then from her eyes and mouth. Before long, her whole upper body began emitting huge amounts of blood-red smoke, making her appear as if she were being consumed by an unnatural fire.

The cloud of red poured from her and landed on the floor to her side, opposite of where Satan stood in barely contained glee. It was happening again. Just like the black cloud had flowed out of Katie and formed a large mass that eventually transformed into Satan, now the red smoke had begun piling on the floor and was forming a large red cloud. More and more smoke poured out, into a mold quite as large as Satan's had been. Finally, the smoke stopped, and Katie fell rigidly backward onto the floor with a loud and shattering thud.

Satan paid her no attention. He was too busy watching in

triumph as the red mass began to condense upon itself, just as his own black cloud had. When the process finally completed, there, next to Katie's still body, stood the *Nephilim*.

It was a terrifying creature, every bit as mighty as angels and demons. However, unlike the white of angels, or the black of demons, this creature was blood red, almost raw looking, as if its skin had been rubbed off—or rather, it looked as if its skin had never formed. Everything about it was red, even its eyes. It had the appearance of an immense human, larger than anyone I had ever seen or heard of. It was extremely muscular and powerful, but its power was not merely physical.

Just as I could sense the power of angels and demons, I could also sense the power of this creature. It was far more than human. In essence and might, it was akin to angels and demons. However, there was also something missing. Compared to angels and demons, there was a noticeable difference with the Nephilim. In my brief experience with angels, I could feel their presence as easily as I could see them. With the heightening of my spiritual awareness, I could tell an angel was good without them doing or saying anything. They radiated light, energy, and goodness.

With demons, it was the exact opposite. They propagated an aura of pure evil. It was the same feeling one gets when something terrible has happened, or when a person feels fatally threatened. A demon's very presence revealed its unbridled wickedness.

This new creature was different, though. It felt . . . *blank*. There was no other way to explain it. This creature looked and felt empty, almost as if it were simply a raw template of an angel or a demon. I could not tell if it was good or bad. It was like a blank slate, waiting to be written on. It emanated neither good intentions nor ill ones—simply power and potential. I was intrigued by the Nephilim almost as much as I feared it.

My eyes left the creature for a moment as I glanced at Katie, still collapsed to the floor unconscious, but I hoped still alive. Satan continued to pay her no attention. He had used her for what he needed her for and was now done with her. Her fate meant nothing to this selfish, evil being. He had no compassion for the girl he had just used and destroyed. He only had eyes for his creation, his Nephilim.

The demons returned to center court, forming dark lines on either side of the creature, just inside the ever-present walls of fire. The room pulsed with sadistic energy. The demons were clearly just as ecstatic as their brutal master, Satan.

"Welcome, my son," Satan said in jubilation. His open arms faced the Nephilim. "We have so much to do!" He clapped his hands together in excitement.

The Nephilim made no movement or acknowledgement that it had heard Satan, but stood still, facing me, standing beside Katie's fallen figure. Its eyes flickered to me, then to Katie, then to Satan. It was searching, learning; it seemed confused.

"You know how great we can be together. I have already shown you," Satan said, holding a finger to his mind. "So, if you wish to claim your rightful place at my right hand, then I need a demonstration of obedience." This time the creature nodded ever so slightly, its blood-red eyes fixed on the ground as if in deep thought.

CHAPTER THIRTEEN

"Good. Then you must destroy her," Satan said, his voice serious, issuing the command as he pointed to Katie. As he spoke, a streak of fire shot from his mouth into the side of the Nephilim's head. The Nephilim did not move. It did not respond in the slightest.

Satan continued. "After you finish with her, you must kill *them*," he said, pointing in my direction, as more fiery darts issued from his mouth and sank into the Nephilim's mind. "They have come to ruin our plans. *He* tried to stop you from being created," Satan continued, pointing at me and looking directly into my eyes with burning hatred. "He wishes you didn't exist," he went on, fiery darts issuing from his mouth with each word, sinking into the creature's head effectively.

The creature inched, turning ever so slightly toward Katie, but still seemed hesitant, undecided even.

"This is your job. Finish her now and we can rule all dimensions. We will rule Earth, Tartarus, and one day we will regain our rightful home in Heaven," Satan said excitedly. As he spoke, the dark flames continued to erupt from his mouth and hit his new creation, his son, sinking deeply into the Nephilim's mind.

"If you want power, if you want freedom, if you want to serve no one but yourself, then you will listen to me, and do as I command,"393 Satan said, shooting even more fiery darts at the Nephilim. The creature stood still.

"If you do this, you will have power no one else has had in a long time. The other Nephilim were destroyed long ago, but you, think of how much power you will have. Others will beg for your mercy. You and I can rule everything together. We can destroy this world if we wish. Whatever we want! You can have this power, but you must obey me *now!*" More fiery darts hit the creature, and its red tone darkened ever so slightly. Satan's influence was changing his son. He was turning him evil.

And then I realized Satan was influencing the Nephilim. With that realization, a thought hit me. *When God blesses a created being with intelligence, He also gives it choice.* The words erupted into my mind as clearly as if Quentin were speaking directly to me, and immediately I understood. This was it. I had hoped to influence Katie, but she had rejected God. But the Nephilim had not made a decision yet, and I had to help it choose God!

The Nephilim shifted his body once again, to face Katie more directly. It was on the verge of killing her and in so doing, it would seal its fate in darkness just as all the Nephilim had done before it, so many years ago. Certainty and purpose filled my weary body. This was my real mission. I had been sent there to save as many souls as possible, and that included this new creature.

The Nephilim's raw, blank appearance now made sense. It did not look bright like angels or dark like demons, and it emitted no sense of good or evil because it still had not decided whose side it was on. Satan was deceiving it, trying to force this creature to become evil. He was tempting its thirst for power, its pride, but the choice was not yet made.

"Wait!" I finally yelled. As my voice echoed through the gym, a bolt of light erupted from my mouth and hit the Nephilim directly in the head. It sank in completely. Surprisingly, the creature that had been eyeing Katie with a murderous look suddenly lifted its head and stared straight at me in startled confusion.

"He's lying!" I said, pointing directly at Satan. As I spoke, several white bolts of light surged from me and sank directly into the creature's mind. *This could work!* I thought in excitement.

"He isn't going to share power with you." More white bolts exchanged from me to the Nephilim. The creature did not move.

"And you might think you want power and authority, and anything else he's promised you, but at what cost? At the cost of your freedom? At the cost of murder? Are you willing to take her life just to elevate yours?" I asked, pointing at Katie as more bolts shot out and sank into the creature.[394]

"You can be powerful, yes, but do you want your power to be used for destruction? What about love? There is no greater action or emotion in the universe than love.[395] Wouldn't you rather have power to do good?"[396] I continued to question him, more bolts shooting from me to the Nephilim. Satan stood by, looking shocked. I continued since no one was trying to stop me.

"Now is the time to make your decision, but remember, you will have to live with your choice for eternity.[397] You can never go back from this moment. If you choose to listen to Satan, you will be condemned, just as he is. You will be miserable, forced to get your enjoyment from the destruction of others," I pleaded.

More bolts coursed into the creature as Satan finally turned to me and roared, "Enough!"

"No!" I yelled back. "I don't serve you!"[398]

PROGENY OF THE DAMNED

The demons sat quietly by. I hesitated, expecting them to try to block me out, but they just stood there, as shocked as their master. I wondered if they would not be able to interfere with this creature's freewill. Perhaps only the Nephilim could choose to shut me out. The demons had only blocked me from Katie once she had made her decision, and the Nephilim had not yet decided.

Unable to influence me, command me, or otherwise stop me, Satan reentered the spiritual battle in the only way he was allowed, through influence. He began to silently send his fiery darts toward his son, who had now returned to his original raw shade of red. Simultaneously, all of the demons followed Satan's lead. The Nephilim now stood in the middle of the gym, absorbing an endless volley of fiery arrows. Each arrow was sinking in and disappearing into his mind. The creature bowed his head again, staring at the floor and then at Katie, and began turning darker. I was losing.

What could I do when I was so greatly outnumbered and so greatly overpowered? I thought in panic. *How could I compete with a chorus of demons and the great deceiver himself?* I was just one voice. *But if this was why I had been sent there, I had to try.* Suddenly, I was thankful I was a preacher's kid because in that moment, a lifetime of my dad's sermons rushed through my mind.

I knew what I had to do. I had to speak words of truth, straight from my heart.[399] I was outnumbered, but my words would be much more powerful than anything Satan or his demons could deliver. For my words were truth; my words were life.[400] I was just one voice, but I would make a stand for God, no matter the odds, and no matter the foe.

CHAPTER THIRTEEN

"Whatever they are telling you, it is a lie," my lone voice rang out; only the soft swoosh of arrows and the crackle of fire competed with me audibly, but a world of evil competed with me for the influence of this creature's unclaimed heart. Yet, in the midst of a plethora of fiery darts, my sole bolt of white influence sank, unabated, directly into the creature's mind. With a jolt, it looked up at me again, its red eyes piercing me, as if pleading for more.

"Don't you see where sin leads?"[401] I asked. A bolt of lightning issued from me, causing the creature to cock its head to the side, not understanding my meaning.

"Look at Katie," I said calmly, nodding toward her collapsed figure on the floor. "Sin brought her here; she was promised pleasure, she was promised the desires of her heart by Satan and his demons, just like Satan has promised you.[402] But look where she is. She's unconscious on the floor because of *them*. How many of them have tried to help her since she collapsed? How many of them care if she survives?" White arrows coursed from me into the creature. At that moment, my first real sign of hope occurred as a few of the fiery darts were deflected away from the Nephilim's mind and shot harmlessly into the ceiling of the gym.

I hurried to continue. "Look at Tom," I said, gesturing toward Tom who remained unconscious and tied up behind me. "He has had a life of misery because of other people's sin, but his own sin brought him here. He believed the demons; he believed that drugs, and whatever else they promised him, were the way to happiness. At the first sign of remorse he showed, they attacked him. Now he's knocked out and tied up. Does it seem that Satan's promises lead to happiness?" I asked. "Does it seem like Satan cares about the people he uses? Do you really think you'll be any different to him?" All of my white arrows were sinking in, and now only some of the demons' darts were being absorbed; far more were being rejected.

"Rachel here has a heart that is extremely pure," I continued, now gesturing toward her, as my eyes filled with moisture. "The sins of Tom and Katie, the lies of Satan and his demons have brought her here, hurt her. Is that what you want your existence to be? Do you want to manipulate, ruin, destroy, and hurt? Is that the power you want? You are Satan's son, but Satan didn't make you. He said so himself; he doesn't have the power to give life. Only God can do that," I said, pausing to catch my breath.

Satan and his demons had not stopped trying to influence the Nephilim the entire time. Their darts poured endlessly toward him. Just due to sheer volume, many were still getting through. All the while, though, the Nephilim stared at me intently. He was listening eagerly, hungry for more. His red eyes cried out for me to continue, as if he were on the verge of drowning and my words were his only lifeline.

"And here's the thing," I hurried on. "This all comes down to whether you choose God, or whether you choose your own selfish desires. But here's the problem; all intelligent creatures will be judged by God in the end.[403] Satan cannot win. He can lie to you all he wants, but his fate is sealed. If you side with Satan, then your fate will be sealed, too. And here's the kicker: if you side with Satan, then you would be rebelling against a God who loves you, a God who gives life, and hope, and joy. God has created everything that is good in this universe, and He wants you to have an eternal life with Him. Why would you turn from a creator like this? Is it so you and Satan can destroy things? Is it so your life can be marked by sin, death, and judgment? Turn from those things, Nephilim! Give yourself to God!" The Nephilim continued to stare at me intently, but the demons were pouring in their messages as fervently as ever. I had no idea who was winning. All I could do was continue until the Nephilim finally decided.

"You can have a marvelous future," I resumed my plea. "You were made for a purpose and that purpose was not death and destruction.[404] God has chosen to give all intelligent created beings a choice, and now is the time for you to choose. But choose well, because what you decide to do now will define your entire existence. Your next choice will determine who you will be for all eternity. Satan's road might be tempting, but it will not lead to the happiness or the glory he has promised. It will lead to sin, and pain, and death.[405] If you choose him, then you will never experience love or mercy, faith or hope. So, here's my last question for you, Nephilim: do you want to destroy this young girl for your own gain, or do you want your existence to be something more? It is time for you to give yourself to God," I finished, the last of my arrows sinking in.

"Stop." The deep sound of the Nephilim's first word echoed throughout the gym. I was silent. Satan and his demons stopped issuing their arrows as well.

"I have decided," the creature went on.

The Nephilim was still red. I knew all of my words had sunk in, but so had hundreds, if not thousands, of the fiery darts of temptation from Satan and his demons. Both sides had presented our case. I had no doubt that everything Satan had said to the Nephilim would be tempting. Satan was, after all, the master of deceit. The Nephilim had no more reason to believe me than it did Satan. If anything, Satan was closer to him in nature. They were father and son. Who was I to this new creature?

Still, truth was so much more powerful than lies. I just hoped that I had said enough. Either way, there was nothing further I could do. I had said all I could; it was up to the creature now. It all came down to choice, just like it always does.

The creature knelt down; its hands were very close to Tom's bat. *Would the Nephilim even need a weapon to kill Katie?* He was more than powerful enough without it. He could probably rip any human apart. In fear, I also realized that if the Nephilim killed Katie, then Rachel, Tom, and I would be next.

Satan and his demons looked on, waiting for the creature to choose. The moment seemed to freeze. Even if I had not been bound tightly, I would have still been unable to move due to sheer anxiety. My heart beat heavily, my head swam from my concussion, my ankle throbbed, but I ignored it all. No one moved a muscle. It was the moment of decision.

The creature's hand trembled near the bat, as it continued to kneel by Katie, in deep thought. Its massive form towered over her. Then, with a movement more swift and yet gentler than any human would be capable of performing, the creature scooped Katie up and spoke directly to Satan . . .

"It seems . . . what you meant for evil, God meant for

good."[406]

In an explosion of light, the red creature transformed into a beautiful being, glorious, radiant, and white. Satan and the demons stumbled back in horror, screaming in agony as the light from the Nephilim shined upon them.[407] Regaining themselves, they gnashed their teeth, preparing to lunge forward to attack this new angel, the Nephilim that had chosen goodness over evil.

Then, as Satan and his demons were about to begin their assault, a rush filled the gym like the sound of a thousand waterfalls. I had the inclination to shield myself, in protection from whatever mighty force was approaching, but it came too fast; for at that same moment, a blinding white light filled the gym.

In swarmed Quentin, glowing hot white, with a look of determination, ferocity, and joy on his angelic face. He was ready for war! In stormed the angels Joshua, Erasmus, Roland, and even Brice's angel; but they were not alone. Following them, an army of angels poured in, more than I could count. A numberless swarm of angels, mighty warriors of goodness, raced into the gym, ready to fight; ready to rescue their new angel brother, the good Nephilim.

They flowed powerfully into the gym, forcing the demons and Satan to scatter before their light, like sand before a tidal wave. Every bit of darkness was forced out of the gym, through the walls as if they were not even there. The sinister fire in the center of the court was extinguished, and soon light completely filled the room. Not a drop of darkness remained.

Erasmus rushed over to the Nephilim to see Katie, relief

barely visible in his worried, saddened, and aged face. The Nephilim handed Katie over to Erasmus and nodded his head, indicating that she was alive. Then Joshua, Roland, and Quentin walked toward me, each one beaming.

"Micah! You amazing young man!" Quentin said, still a few feet away from me. "You steadfast and good man. You have done everything we could have asked from you and so much more." Then with one swift upward motion of his hand, somehow the ropes that had been binding me to Rachel and Tom magically loosened.

I turned to look at Rachel. She bore the marks of the abuse she had received. I desperately checked her for a pulse and let out a sigh as I felt her heart beating steady through her veins. She was okay. We were all alive. Relief spread over me. The nightmare was finally over. With the arrival of Quentin and the angels, we were saved. My job was done and I was ready to rest.

Instinctively, my body and mind relaxed, but with the relaxation came the pain I had been ignoring the entire time. My broken ankle was now extremely swollen and throbbing, and my head suddenly lost all of the sharpness that had carried me through the terrible encounter. With adrenaline no longer acting as my stimulant, my vision began to swim before me, and I felt myself losing the battle with consciousness I had been fighting for so long. Quentin reached out to grab me and caught my head just as my sight blackened and I finally gave way to oblivion.

CHAPTER FOURTEEN

PENITENCE, FORGIVENESS, AND PARTING

Other stories, other battles, other trials, other cares,
We might not think that they're around,
But they are always there.
They come to us and give us help, when we are most in need,
With goodness they protect us from the lure of evil deeds.
So, when the road is clearly marked,
But you know not what to do,
Remember, sin might have appeal, but doesn't offer truth.[408]
It's nothing but a tempter's snare. The pleasure doesn't last,
The temporary thrills will leave and pain is all you'll have.
So, recognize that all is vain,
There's no profit beneath the sun.[409]
For as vapor does our life go by;
Of your treasures—you'll keep none.
So, store your treasures where they'll last,
Which isn't on this earth,[410]
Heaven has eternal wealth, which carries far more worth.[411]
Fight the fight and run the race.[412] *Forgive and always love,*[413]
Turn from sin and serve the King. Obey our God above.[414]
Remember, we can freely choose, as long as life endures,
Evil tempts and goodness fights, but the choice is always yours.
So, turn from death and choose to live. Avoid the captor's sting,
The amazing thing about God's grace,
Is that it doesn't cost a thing.[415]

* * * *

SUNDAY, JUNE 2 THRU MONDAY, JUNE 3, 1985

I've had a lot to think about since the fateful night I gave
my life to Christ and was allowed to peer behind our world and
into the spiritual realm. I've thought about all the people I saw

and the many temptations they faced. I've wondered about the decisions we humans often make and the power that evil spirits regularly have over us. And as I've thought about these things, I've come to a few conclusions; Scripture says, "If the Son shall make you free, you shall be free indeed."[416]

For those who have never given their life to Christ, there is no such freedom; only misguided passion, disappointment, unquenchable temporary desires, the ensnaring power of sin, and a fruitless pursuit of the satisfaction that can only ever truly be found in God. This is all a life ruled by sin can ever really amount to.

But for those who have given their life to Christ, there is no reason to live under the yoke of sin any longer. While temptation can often be powerful and sin is certainly ensnaring, one thing is clear; if a person gives their life to Christ, they are no longer the victims of spiritual warfare.[417] I didn't say that they would never be affected by spiritual warfare, I said they were no longer its *victims*. No matter how tempting a situation is, Christians are *not* victims of sin. This is because there is victory in Jesus Christ.[418] Through Christ, Christians have freedom *from* sin, and victory *over* sin. But this reality often becomes forgotten or ignored. We succumb to sin, we get bogged down in guilt, and we forget to live our lives loving God, loving others, and walking in the purity of that love.[419]

However, I have realized that as a Christian, there is only one thing required for me to live the life of freedom and victory that God has graciously made possible for me—and that is my *obedience*.[420] For in my obedience, I am living in the freedom and victory that Christ has already attained *for* me.[421] And as I've obeyed throughout my life, I've discovered something else, as well; something remarkable, and unexpected. I've found that when we walk with God, no matter the foe, certain qualities begin to become prominent in us, qualities that we perhaps never knew we had. In the face of fear or failure, or even certain death, cowardice and selfishness would have us run and hide, and save ourselves. But if we walk with God, we can find the courage, selflessness, and love to do what is right, despite the consequences.[422] In the face of temptation, lust and greed would have us succumb to our desires, forgetting all those who we might hurt, and forgetting the price that will be paid. But if we walk with God, faithfulness and strength of character turn people away from their natural inclination toward fulfilling those sinful desires, and instead, turn us toward a better and more godly path.[423]

You see, as I have thought back on that terrifying and yet wonderful night, I have realized that there is something good and oh so immensely powerful when light stands up to darkness. When tested, the bonds of kindness, mercy, grace, and love can grow without end. When tried, bravery can be found in the last place anyone would have ever expected it to be. When tribulations come, patience, faith, and hope can be learned.[424] When goodness no longer plays the victim to evil, it is a great and glorious moment. For it is these moments that we long for in any story because these moments bring out the characteristics we hope would shine through in *us*, should they ever be called upon.

However, so often these characteristics never see the light of day. So often do people cower in fear, or succumb to sin, only to stand by and watch their lives crumble around them. So often do people give up on others, or write them off, while there is yet time, while they are still reachable. This is because of a lie that is almost universally believed. This lie has produced judgment, wrath, pain, and sorrow, instead of mercy, grace, hope, joy, and love.[425]

The lie is that darkness is more powerful than light. The lie is that darkness cannot be resisted or turned from, but nothing could be further from the truth. It is darkness that flees before light; it is darkness that is revealed by light. Light can be shut out, but it is always there, waiting to be let back in, waiting to shine on the darkness to reveal what has been hidden.[426]

Make no mistake, no matter how tempting evil might seem, goodness is greater than evil because light can overcome darkness, and most importantly, God is greater than all.[427] Wickedness expects the righteous to give up, to tremble and collapse. However, when the righteous do not fall, when they choose to hold on strong despite the odds and despite difficulty, it is then that wickedness can be overcome; and wickedness *should* be overcome. For followers of God have bonds that tie them together, which evil simply does not have: faith, hope, love, and purpose—these are things worth fighting for.[428]

Therefore, when evil comes your way—and it surely will come—when strife rips at your life, and when sin's shadow is on your doorstep, it is then that you should stand strong.[429] All that is needed is for people to turn to God, to hold fast to their faith, to have courage, and to turn from the things they know are wrong, even when it is difficult.[430]

So, I ask you to be strong, be courageous, be loving, be

patient, be righteous, be gracious, be merciful, be faithful, be temperate, be joyful, be wise, be gentle, and be kind to one another.[431] Do not *hope* to be these things, *choose* to be them— *choose* to be obedient to God. For in *hoping* to live well, we remain spectators and victims, destined to fail at our task. But in *choosing* to live our lives as God would have us live them, we become obedient to all that He means us to be. So turn from darkness, flee from sin, resist the flesh and do not walk in it.[432] Rather, choose instead to walk in the Spirit of your new birth.[433] Choose to walk with God. We *always* have a choice.

*　*　*　*

I awoke in a bed, opening my eyes slowly. *Surely it was all a dream*, I thought. I brought my hands to my stomach. "No!" I sighed, wincing slightly in pain. My ribs were sensitive to the touch, exactly where Tom's bat had struck me.

I opened my eyes all of the way and a bright light blinded me. *Am I dead? Is this heaven?* I waited as my eyes adjusted, squinting as I eagerly searched for angels; but I was not dead and there were no angels. It was just a bright day. The blinds to the window in the room were wide open, and the lights were turned on.

The light bothered me more than it should have. I tried to look around to see where I was and realized that my mind was still pretty sluggish. A dull pain in the back of my head cautioned me not to move too quickly and alerted me as to why I was having so much trouble adjusting to the light.

Finally, the room came fully into view. I was in the

hospital. I realized if my head and stomach injuries were real, then my leg injury would be, too. I looked at my left leg, which I noticed was elevated by pillows. Sure enough, it was in a cast that extended from my foot to about three fourths of the way up my shin. I could not believe it . . . it had all been real.

To my right was the window that was letting in so much sunlight. It was closed and the air conditioning unit beneath it was running full blast. It was cool in the room, but I could see that outside it was another hot summer day.

I turned my head over to my left and to my surprise, I saw my dad, fast asleep in a chair. I considered for a second whether or not I should wake him. Deciding that my injuries were serious enough that he would probably want to know that I had woken up, I called out to him.

"Dad," I said in a rough voice, not having used my vocal chords for as long as I had been out. He did not move, so I cleared my throat and tried again.

"Hey Dad, I'm up," I said, a little more clearly than before.

He began to stir. Gradually he came to and smiled wide as his eyes opened and met mine, "Oh good. You're up. How are you feeling?" he asked excitedly, reaching over to put his hand on my head as if checking for a fever.

"I can't really tell yet, but I think I'm fine. Still a little groggy and sore, but good," I said, trying to assess myself as I spoke.

"Good. I'm glad. Well, I better give your mom and Shelby a call. They've been worried sick," he said, immediately grabbing the phone on the hospital night stand.

CHAPTER FOURTEEN

He dialed our home number and in just a few seconds was reporting to my mom that I was awake. She spoke loudly in an excited and relieved voice, and I was sure I would be seeing her and Shelby before too long.

"They're on their way," my dad confirmed as he hung up.

"Dad, how long have I been out?"

"Well, what's the last thing you remember?" he asked inquisitively.

Suddenly, I felt anxious. I was uncertain what was public knowledge and what was not, so I was not sure what I was supposed to say. I did not want to betray Quentin, but I was sure he would not want me to lie, either. Deep down I also did not want to sound too crazy.

"Well, I remember I had the date with Rachel. Afterwards we went back to her house and found out that Brice was hurt and Katie was missing. Then I went to the hospital with the Jacobs, to visit Brice and . . . " I hesitated, making up my mind how to best edit the story. " . . . and then Rachel went missing and I went to the school to look for her and after that, it got all . . . weird," I finished knowing that this was vague, but definitely the truth. I hoped that a head injury might be a good enough excuse to get me out of providing too many details.

"So, how long have I been out?" I repeated, trying to get my dad to answer questions rather than the other way around.

"Ah yes . . . well, you've been out for a solid day. It's all very weird actually. You were found unconscious in the school with Rachel, Tom, and Katie early yesterday morning," he said. "Yesterday was Saturday," he added. "It's about midday on

Sunday, right now. One of the deacons filled in for me at church," he said, in case I was wondering if he was skipping church to be there. "It's weird because we aren't sure how all of you were knocked out," he said, staring at me inquisitively yet again.

"What about the others? Are Rachel, Tom, and Katie okay?" I asked, trying to distract him away from more questions. "Oh, and Brice; has he woken up yet?"

"Yes, Brice is awake now and on the mend," he said, finally giving me something to feel relieved about. "He's got a concussion, like you, but besides that and some flesh wounds on his head, he's been healing nicely. He's still at the hospital, but he'll probably want to swing by your room once he finds out you're awake."

"And the others? How is Rachel?" I asked, now excited to be hearing good news, and eager for more.

"Rachel was unconscious too, but she was not hurt nearly as badly as you. She was treated for some minor injuries and released early this morning. She could have been released sooner, but they wanted to let her rest.

"Katie and Tom are both okay, too," he continued, "but they are in some pretty big trouble. They admitted to abducting Rachel. They also admitted they had been taking drugs."

He hesitated. "They said they attacked you, too," he said with a frown. "Then, in their apparent drug high, they turned and attacked each other. At least that's what they think happened. They were pretty intoxicated, or whatever you want to call it. They don't really remember much of what happened," he said. Inwardly, I found it amusing that Tom and Katie's version of the story sounded a lot more believable than the truth.

"Sheriff Sentry will undoubtedly want to come by the house when you are released to take your statement," my dad continued. I looked up immediately at the mention of Quentin's name, but thankfully my dad did not notice and kept going. "He's also asked if Tom and Katie can come by . . . they want to apologize," he finished.

I nodded my head. With my brain still feeling a little scrambled, it was a lot to take in, but it seemed like everything had worked out. Tom and Katie would be in trouble, but they had not done anything that could not be repaired. Rachel was safe, and Brice and I would heal. It was as good of a conclusion as I could have hoped for.

The main thing I was curious about was Sheriff Sentry. I could not help but wonder how he would treat me now. Things would surely be different between us; they would for me at least.

A few minutes after my dad finished filling me in, my mom and Shelby arrived at the hospital. They fussed over me, despite my assurances I was going to be just fine.

Not long after that, the nurse came into my room and broke the news that I had to stay one more night for observation. The only consolation was that Rachel, Brice, and their parents, Mike and Diane, came to see me. Rachel was the only one who knew anything about what had really gone on. Though she had not seen everything that I had, she still knew there was far more to the story than just a "normal" abduction by two teenagers on drugs. She did not bring it up around the others, though.

The only subject Rachel brought up was the fact I had gone into the school to save her. I was happy she knew what I had done, but with her family there, the spotlight was making me pretty uncomfortable—like usual. Her parents gushed over me, telling me how thankful they were that I had saved their daughter.

Brice was glad we were both all right, but he was in a rough mood himself. Not only was he grumpy from his wounds, but he had taken the news about Katie pretty badly. She had confessed everything she could remember, so she and Brice were going their separate ways. The only plus side to Brice being in a bad mood was that he was not teasing me about his sister. I was thankful for that because Mike and Diane were carrying on quite enough to embarrass me sufficiently. By the time they were ready to leave, my face was as bright red as it had ever been.

In the end, it was all worth it, though, because Rachel had decided my gallantry had earned me a third date with her; and as a bonus, she did not even make me ask. She also said that since I would be hobbled, she would be coming over to my house to visit me a lot until I was better. That was all the reward I wanted, or needed. Brice and his parents left and allowed Rachel to stay behind to hang out with me, just the two of us.

Brice conveniently left behind an application to his university, and I was not surprised when Rachel decided it was time for me to fill it out, even offering to fill it out for me. However, I was surprised when she pulled out a second application and began to fill it out, too.

CHAPTER FOURTEEN

I reached forward and grabbed at the paper, a little too quickly actually, causing stars to pop into my sight. But I caught the paper and pulled it from her grasp. My eyes rested on something they didn't quite understand; Rachel was filling out her own application to the same school.

"What are you doing?" I asked. "You have a scholarship to your school. You can't give that up," I said, taken aback.

"Some things are more important than where you go to school," she said simply, though I noticed her cheeks blushed uncontrollably as she grabbed the paper back from me and continued to fill out the application. "Besides, I have already been working on a couple of scholarships to Brice's college, too," she said with a slight bragging smile.

"When have you had time to do that?" I asked, thoroughly impressed.

"Oh, I've been thinking about it for a while . . ." she answered sort of ambiguously. "Besides, this is a perfect time to make the switch. Now, you, Brice, and I will all be able to go there, together," she said.

It was music to my ears. Suddenly giving up my basketball aspirations did not seem to be that big of a deal.

Rachel and I chatted the evening away and decided, for right then at least, that we did not really want to talk about everything that had happened. We both knew we would get there eventually, but we had been through enough. We were ready for some happiness, ready to enjoy each other's company. I was able to spend the entire day with her, just talking—with the occasional nap squeezed in at the insistence of a rather motherly and persistent nurse. But every time I woke up, Rachel was there, waiting. When it got late, Mr. Jacobs came to take her home, but she assured me again that she would be taking care of me much of the week. I was perfectly fine with that.

They released me from the hospital around lunch time the next day and my whole family came to pick me up. My dad reminded me that Sheriff Sentry wanted to come by as soon as I got home. I did not really need reminding of that; I was eager to meet with Sheriff Sentry.

The only downside to seeing Sheriff Sentry was that I would also have to hear Tom and Katie's apologies, and I was not looking forward to that. Not that I held any grudge against them, but I just knew it would be awkward and uncomfortable, and it is well documented by now how much I hate awkward and uncomfortable moments.

Sure enough, on Monday when I was sent home, Sheriff Sentry came calling just after lunch, around 1:30. As I sat on the couch in the living room watching TV with my leg propped up, having just finished a healthy portion of my mom's spaghetti, I heard a knock at the door.

"Ah, Sheriff Sentry—and Tom and Katie, how good it is to see you," my dad greeted in his good natured and genuine voice. I knew that being a preacher, my dad had worked with kids who had made bad decisions before, but this was probably the first time those decisions had affected one of his kids so directly. It was refreshing, then, to hear the sincerity in his voice as he welcomed Tom and Katie in.

"Paul, might we have a few minutes alone with Micah?" Sheriff Sentry's low voice asked pleasantly.

"Of course," my dad obliged. I heard footsteps being led

down our hall toward the living room. I sat up a bit, feeling a little self-conscious, realizing I looked pretty ratty after having been in the hospital a few days, only to come home and just lie around on the couch. A bath would have been a smart thing, but my mom's spaghetti had been first priority. I was regretting that now.

"Micah, I trust you are feeling better," Quentin said, as he ducked into the room first, with a big smile on his face.

"Yeah, I feel fine," I said, sitting up even straighter on the couch, though unable to do anything with my broken leg, which was once again propped up on some pillows.

"Glad to hear it. Tom and Katie wanted to say some things to you," Quentin said graciously as they filed into the room behind him.

"Oh, no need . . ." I started to say, but Tom cut me off.

"Micah, that stuff you said to me, it really made me think," Tom said in a very sheepish tone.

"I really have been blaming my life on the things of my past. You were right; I need to start making my own decisions," he said sincerely. "I wanted to say two things to you. First, thank you for not hating me the other night. You could have wanted to fight me and hurt me back for what I had done. I know I would have. But you didn't. What you said to me . . . well," he started to choke up a little. ". . . well, just thanks. It meant more than you know. Second, I don't know if you'll ever be able to forgive me, but I want to tell you that I really am sorry. I'm very sorry I hurt you and Rachel, and . . ."

"Sure," I cut across him, waving my hand in an awkward way. "It's done. You're forgiven," I said as awkwardly as before, though very quickly, just wanting the conversation to be over with. I really did forgive Tom, and I really was glad he had decided to start changing his life around. I just did not want to make him have to say it anymore.

"Seriously, I'm not mad at you," I added, trying to ensure he knew I meant it. "We all make mistakes. You said you're sorry, and that's that."

He nodded at me appreciatively and then looked at Katie as if indicating it was her turn. She was already crying. This was going to be even worse than Tom's apology.

"Please Katie, I'm not . . ." I began, but just as Tom had done, Katie cut me off. She needed to say it.

"Micah, I realize you're going to be quick to forgive me. I also realize you probably just want this over with. Rachel has told me enough about you to let me know that you hate awkward situations. But I need to say something first," she said looking at me. I nodded in acquiescence.

She continued, "You were right about everything. You told me to turn back from those . . . temptations I had been having. You told me it was dangerous and it wouldn't be fulfilling like I thought it would. I was wrong. I was stupid. I believed the lie. My actions got you hurt, and Rachel, and Tom . . . and me . . . and . . . Brice," she said, starting to cry even harder.

"You were right about all of it," she continued through tears and heavy sobs. "Thank you for coming and trying to help us and for saying the right things. I'm so sorry we hurt you, but thank you for not giving up on us," she said as she cried more and more. Quentin put a caring hand on her shoulder.

That was all I could take. "Guys, okay! You're forgiven. It really is great you are deciding to change your paths. Seriously, I really am happy about that. Let's end this, though. I'm not mad, I'm not pressing charges . . . it's done. You are completely forgiven," I said quickly, just wanting the awkwardness to end. They both nodded, but with a pang of guilt, I noticed that they still looked a little dejected. Embarrassed or not, I had to finish the work I had been called to do.

"Wait," I said to them. They both looked up at me. "Look," I began, "if anything good is going to come of this, it has to start with us." They both remained looking at me, waiting for me to continue. "You guys can go clean up your life and go to church, like I did for years, but in the end, none of it will matter if you aren't saved. Sin will come back, and one day, when you die, your souls would be lost." I hesitated, feeling very uncomfortable, but also knowing that what I was saying was necessary and true. "I told you all about Jesus the other night, right?" They both nodded. "Well, He is the only cure for your sins, and the only hope you have beyond this life. Without Him, Satan still has you. Without Him, your only future is death and Hell."

They both looked at me as if they had been struck in the chest. They were silent. "So, is that something you all want to fix today? Do you want to have Christ forgive you of your sins so that you can have eternal life?" They both nodded their heads in unison. And with that, Sheriff Sentry and I led Tom and Katie to salvation through Jesus Christ.

After we all prayed together, Quentin spoke. His smile

looked as if it might never leave his face. "Okay, I need to talk to Micah alone now. The deputy is waiting for you all outside," he said as he nodded his head toward the door. With a final nod at me, they both turned and left. After a few seconds, I heard the front door shut behind them.

"Micah, Micah," he said, smiling at me. I had the funny feeling I was going to be embarrassed just a little bit more, but I had to endure it because Quentin was the one I really wanted to talk to.

"I know you don't like attention and I know you don't like people bragging about you, but I have to tell you how proud I am of you, for what you took part in today, and also for what you did the other night; for how strong and brave you were," he said with a continued smile.

"Er . . . thanks," I responded; heat filling my face as I blushed once more.

"Okay," he chuckled. "Enough of that. You know I could go on and on about what you did, so the last thing I'll say about it is this; as someone who has watched over people since the beginning of creation, I am as proud of you as I have ever been of any other human being . . . and that is saying something, because I have watched over some amazing people," he said, continuing to beam down at me.

"Thanks," I said sheepishly. "Did you want to say anything else . . . you know, more interesting stuff?" I asked, hopeful that Sheriff Sentry did not just want to talk about me. I knew all I needed to know about *me* and did not find the topic all too exciting.

"Actually, yes," he answered. "The real reason I wanted

to meet with you is I wanted to tell you that I've been reassigned," he finished in a less cheerful voice.

"What?!" I said, sitting upright too quickly for a person so recently concussed. I ignored the dizziness. "Why? We need you here! Where are you going?" I asked urgently.

"Easy, Micah . . . it is not customary for angels to stay in a location if they have been revealed. It creates too much difficulty for us and for the humans involved. It's best that we aren't known unless it's absolutely necessary. Anyway, I'm needed elsewhere now. There are other souls for me to fight for," he said.

"But what about our souls? This town?" I questioned in disbelief. "You can't leave us unguarded!" I accused.

"Micah, you know better than any other human on this earth that I'm not the only angel out there," he said smiling. "There are always other angels fighting, behind the scenes," he continued. "This town will be as well guarded as it has ever been. Besides, this town now has you," he said in a thoughtful voice.

"Me?" I asked. "But . . ." I was cut off for the third time, as Quentin finished my sentence perfectly.

". . . what can you do?" he said, grinning even broader still. "I would think your power is pretty obvious by now. You'll still be able to do the only thing that any of us can really do in the fight against evil; you'll be able to influence other people, to tell them the truth about the Gospel of Jesus Christ. Surely by now I don't have to tell you how powerful that can be," he said, raising an eyebrow for emphasis.

I resigned the argument, "So, will I still be able to see

stuff?" I asked, in curiosity.

"Ah, probably not. Unless I am mistaken, you probably are already seeing me back in my normal form now. Is that correct?" he asked.

I had not thought about it, but Sheriff Sentry *was* back in his normal form; albeit he was still big and impressive—but I could see nothing of his angelic essence.

I nodded that he was correct.

"One day you will see again," he said mysteriously. "Did you know that angels and humans are actually not that dissimilar?" he asked, with a happy look on his face. I did not know how to respond.

"It's true," he continued. "When angels were created, we were created as spirits that can turn physical, but when humans were created, God not only made them physical, but He also breathed a spirit, a soul, into them.[434] While you don't yet realize the full potential of your soul, you one day will. Humans have a glorious future of the full realization of both soul and body that awaits them."[435]

I sat and pondered what he was saying, but it was too much for me to understand at the time.

"Micah," he continued, realizing I was confused, "that is what your gift was. You have gotten a taste of things to come. You have seen with your soul in a way that only a handful of humans throughout history have been allowed to do.[436] One day you will see that way again. One day all Christians will," he said joyfully.

"But, while on Earth," he continued in a more instructive tone, "you are still an intelligent and good human being, and now you know the truth about Jesus, as well as the truth about the enemy. Now, when you see someone struggling against a temptation, you know that behind temptations are the fiery darts of Satan and his demons . . . you've seen it happen. You know it's real."[437]

"As such, Micah, my hope for you is that now you will be able to better recognize evil for what it truly is. There will be times when people need your help, and sometimes you will be able to help those people . . . if they want help, that is. As I have said all along, we all have a choice. Both good and evil are always at a heart's doorstep waiting to be let in. Angels will always be there fighting alongside the Holy Spirit to help humans choose goodness over evil, and God over sin, but the tragedy of humanity is that although they have eyes, they often do not see, and though they have ears, they often do not hear.[438] They close their heart to God and give in to evil instead.[439] But you are our ally now. You know the truth, so now, you are part of the fight," he finished proudly.

I paused, not really knowing what to say. Finally, I decided to bring the subject back to him. "So, where will you go?" I asked, not really expecting an answer.

"Ah, I'm afraid even I don't know that," he responded. "Unless we are directly assigned to someone, we don't usually stay in one place for too long."

I was sad. I felt like I was losing a best friend. He had been my guardian for longer than I had known and now he would be gone, just as I had come to see him for what he really was.

As usual, Quentin felt my thoughts. "Don't despair,

Micah; this is not the end of our friendship. Your life on Earth is like a vapor.[440] It's here today and gone tomorrow. I have seen the earthly lives of men come and go since the world was created, but this world is not the end of you.[441] This world is but temporary. You and I, though, we are on the same side . . . forever," he said with extreme happiness. I was speechless again.

"On a less serious topic," he resumed, "have you decided where you are going to attend college this fall?" he asked, clearly trying to get my mind on something other than his leaving.

"Oh," I said, surprised by the change of topic to something so normal. "Well, Brice's school doesn't sound so bad," I said, foolishly trying to hide my reasons.

"I bet it doesn't," he said laughing. Like usual, I was sure Sheriff Sentry already knew the answer to the question he had asked, and like usual, I was sure he knew my motives.

"You know that Rachel is transferring to Brice's school, don't you?" I asked in a half smile, unable to help myself.

"You know, I think I might have heard something about that," he said jokingly, as he stepped forward holding out his hand. I raised my hand, looking up from the couch in sadness at my long-time protector.

He shook my hand, and then patted my head like my dad would sometimes do.

"It has been a pleasure watching over you, my friend," he said with moisture in his eyes. "You were my best assignment to date and my happiest ending by far. Please take care of yourself and always remember, you were once in darkness, born of the flesh, but now you are light in the Lord, born of the Spirit unto God. As such, it is time to walk as a child of the light. It is time to walk as a child of God," he finished wisely.[442] Then he let go of my hand and turned to leave.

As he made it to the door, I thought of one more question I wanted to ask. "You knew what would happen all along, didn't you?"

He turned and looked at me. "Oh no, Micah, most of the time I'm not privy to knowledge of future events," he answered.

"But you knew it would work out?" I asked.

"Of course I knew it would work out," he said as his dark eyebrows contracted in surprise at the obvious answer to my question. "I don't know the future, but I work for the One who does. The only control I have is over my choices. As you well know by now, that's the only control any of us created beings have. We can all choose to obey God, to do the right things and trust that everything will all work out in the end; but I should also say, we need to do the right things, even if the end does not work out the way we want it to in this life, because it's the next life that matters.[443]

"So, no, I didn't know how it would all work out. However, like any situation, I was simply obedient and I waited patiently for it all to work out in the end," he finished with his typical good-natured smile. "Goodbye, my friend."

With that, he headed out of the living room, down the hall, and out of my parents' house. And that was the last time I ever saw my guardian angel and my messenger, Sheriff Quentin

PENITENCE, FORGIVENESS, AND PARTING

Sentry—in this lifetime at least.

APPENDIX

FINAL THOUGHTS

How do I get to heaven? Most people wonder if they will be found "good enough" to enter into heaven when they die. They wonder, perhaps, if they have done enough good to outweigh the bad in their lives. However, for a person to escape their sins and one day enter into heaven for eternity has nothing to do with how good or bad they are, and everything to do with being born again. There is *not* a heavenly weight scale that measures the amount of good or bad a person does in their life and then determines the person's fate based on the sum. Rather, Scripture teaches that even one sin disqualifies us from heaven (James 2:10). Just one sin separates us from our Holy Creator God. That means every single person who has ever lived is disqualified from heaven if left to their own merits.

However, this is precisely the reason God sent His Son, Jesus Christ. He lived a perfect life and died in our place. He paid the debt of death for us. So, if you truly wish to be forgiven of your sins and one day enter into heaven, or as the Bible calls it, "have eternal life," then I ask you to read the following verses from the Bible, and if you believe them, then pray to God and ask Him to forgive you of your sins, and accept Jesus as your Lord and Savior . . .

- **Romans 3:23** says, "For all have sinned, and come short of the glory of God."
    - o Because of this, no person is worthy to enter into heaven on his own. Therefore, the first step to inherit eternal life is to recognize that you are a

sinner. Then, a person must turn from these sins (repent).

- **Romans 6:23** says, "For the wages of sin is death; but the gift of God is eternal life through Jesus Christ our Lord."
    - o Because of sin, something has to die (Hebrews 9:22). Death is what sin caused when it entered into the world. Now, every human since Adam has died or will die—because of sin. The problem is, we are separated from God because of our sins, so if we die, we will also be eternally separated from God, in hell . . .
    - o . . . unless we place our faith in Jesus. We need to believe that Jesus came to Earth and lived a perfect life, and that He died in our place. He paid the penalty for our sins. To be saved, then, we must accept His sacrifice on our behalf by accepting Him as our Savior and Lord.
- **Romans 5:8** says, "But God commendeth his love toward us, in that, while we were yet sinners, Christ died for us."
    - o The message of Jesus Christ is a message of grace. God's grace is a gift that we did not deserve. He loved us, even though we sinned against Him. In fact, he loved us so much that He sent His Son, Jesus Christ, to die in our place.
- **Romans 10:9-10** says, "That if thou shalt confess with thy mouth the Lord Jesus, and shalt believe in thine heart that God hath raised him from the dead, thou shalt

be saved. For with the heart man believeth unto righteousness; and with the mouth confession is made unto salvation."

- o If you confess with your mouth that Jesus is your Lord (master), it means that you are turning away from your sins (once again, this is called repentance). None of us does this perfectly, but making Jesus Lord of our life means giving Him the authority in our life.

- o Believing in your heart that God raised Jesus from the dead is the final step. Jesus came and died for you and for me. However, He did not stop there. He also rose from the dead. Since Jesus was able to rise from the dead, we can know that He has power over death. Since He has power over death, we can know that He can also raise us from the dead and give us eternal life. You can have this hope, too, if you will accept Jesus as the Savior from your sins.

There is a real struggle for your soul. The spiritual battles are real, but so is your choice. If you are a Christian, then this story is more realistic for you because your choices really do demonstrate who you are letting have control of your heart: God or your sinful desires.

However, if you have never placed your faith in Christ, then no amount of good deeds will allow you to be forgiven. Only through placing your faith in Jesus Christ can your soul be saved. The Holy Spirit is knocking at your heart's door (John 16:7-11; Rev. 3:20). Don't ignore the call of the Spirit. Don't ignore your sinful state. Give yourself to Christ and be forgiven today. Fight the good fight, and hear the heart's voice, the good or the bad, it's always a choice; and that choice is Jesus Christ.

ABOUT THE AUTHOR

 Obadiah J. Dalrymple "Obie" is a former US Air Force communication technician. After serving four years in the Air Force, Obie continued to work for the Air Force as a civilian contractor while attending Liberty Baptist Theological Seminary online. Upon graduating with a Master's degree in Religious Education, Obie left the government contracting world and entered full time ministry. Visit Obie at www.obadiahjdalrymple.com.

ENDNOTES

1   Matthew 6:24; Luke 16:13; John 8:36.
2   1 Corinthians 6:18-20; 1 Corinthians 10:14; 1 Timothy 6:10-11; 2 Timothy 2:22.
3   John 3:18-21; 1 Corinthians 4:5; Hebrews 4:12; John 16:7-11.
4   Ephesians 4:17-19—the regressive, consuming, and ensnaring power of sin; see also Matthew 6:24 and James 1:14-15.
5   1 Timothy 6:10.
6   Ecclesiastes 2:10.
7   Matthew 6:19-21.
8   Matthew 6:19-21; 2 Corinthians 4:18; 1 John 2:15-17.
9   Matthew 16:26; Mark 8:36.
10 Matthew 6:19-21; Romans 8:1-18; 2 Corinthians 4:18; 1 John 2:15-17; Philippians 3:17-20; 1 Peter 1:23-25; Romans 9:8; John 3:1-7; 1 Corinthians 15:45-50; John 1:6-14; Galatians 5:16-25; Ephesians 1:13; Ephesians 4:30; Romans 7:13-25; Mark 14:38.
11 1 Corinthians 10:13; 16:13; Romans 7:13-25; James 4:7; Genesis 3:13-20; 1 John 2:15-17.
12 Matthew 28:1-6; Luke 1:13, 30; Luke 2:8-14; Judges 6:23; Daniel 10:19; Acts 18:9; Acts 9:1-8.
13 Matthew 6:19-21.
14 Matthew 6:19-21; Romans 8:1-18; 2 Corinthians 4:18; 1 John 2:15-17; Philippians 3:17-20; 1 Peter 1:23-25; Romans 9:8; John 3:1-7; 1 Corinthians 15:45-50; John 1:6-14; Galatians 5:16-25; Ephesians 1:13; Ephesians 4:30; Romans 7:13-25; Mark 14:38.
15 Genesis 19:24-26; Proverbs 26:11.
16 Matthew 6:24.
17 Romans 7:14-25.
18 Matthew 6:19-21; Romans 8:1-18; 2 Corinthians 4:18; 1 John 2:15-17; Philippians 3:17-20; 1 Peter 1:23-25; Romans 9:8; John 3:1-7; 1 Corinthians 15:45-50; John 1:6-14; Galatians 5:16-25; Ephesians 1:13; Ephesians 4:30; Romans 7:13-25; Mark 14:38.
19 John 16:7-11; 1 John 2:27.
20 Philippians 4:8.
21 Romans 12:21.
22 1 Corinthians 6:18-20; 1 Corinthians 10:14; 1 Timothy 6:10-11; 2 Timothy 2:22.

23 Ephesians 4:17-19—the regressive, consuming, and ensnaring power of sin; see also Matthew 6:24 and James 1:14-15.

24 1 Corinthians 10:1-13.

25 Ephesians 4:13-15; Isaiah 53:6; Matthew 18:11-14; Luke 15:3-7; 1 Peter 2:25; Proverbs 3:5-9.

26 Matthew 6:19-21; Romans 8:1-18; 2 Corinthians 4:18; 1 John 2:15-17; Philippians 3:17-20; 1 Peter 1:23-25; Romans 9:8; John 3:1-7; 1 Corinthians 15:45-50; John 1:6-14; Galatians 5:16-25; Ephesians 1:13; Ephesians 4:30; Romans 7:13-25; Mark 14:38.

27 Revelation 3:20.

28 The Christian life is right, but that does not mean it is easy—Matthew 7:13-14; Matthew 5:11; 1 Corinthians 4:11-13; 2 Corinthians 4:8-9; Romans 12:1; Matthew 16:24; Mark 8:34; Luke 9:23.

29 James 4:7; 1 Corinthians 6:18-20; 1 Corinthians 10:14; 1 Timothy 6:10-11; 2 Timothy 2:22.

30 1 Corinthians 10:12-13.

31 1 Corinthians 10:12-13.

32 1 Peter 5:8; Ephesians 6:12; John 10:10; Luke 22:31-32; Job 1-2.

33 Colossians 1:26-27.

34 John 14:6; Ephesians 6:19.

35 1 Corinthians 10:12.

36 1 Corinthians 11:28; Hebrews 4:12; John 16:7-11.

37 Ephesians 5:14; 2 Corinthians 4:6; Romans 5:5; John 1:4-14.

38 John 3:18-21; 1 Corinthians 4:5; Hebrews 4:12; John 16:7-11; John 12:35.

39 Matthew 7:13-14; John 1:5.

40 1 John 4:4; 1 John 5:4-5; Romans 8:36-39; 1 Corinthians 10:12-13; Galatians 6:7-8; Philippians 4:13.

41 1 John 4:4; 1 John 5:4-5; Romans 8:36-39; 1 Corinthians 10:12-13; Galatians 6:7-8; Philippians 4:13.

42 Romans 6:16-23; Matthew 6:24.

43 Matthew 13:24-30, 36-43; John 15:1-2.

44 John 1:4-14; John 3:18-21; John 12:35; Acts 26:12-18; Romans 13:12; 1 Corinthians 4:5; 2 Corinthians 4:6; Ephesians 5:7-8, 14; 1 Thessalonians 5:4-5; 1 Peter 2:9; 1 John 1:5-7.

45 Ephesians 5:16; Colossians 4:5.

46 Deuteronomy 31:6; Joshua 1:9, 18; 1 Chronicles 22:13; 1 Chronicles 28:20; 2 Chronicles 32:7; Psalm 23; Isaiah 35:4; Isaiah 41:10.

ENDNOTES

47 Matthew 6:19-21; Romans 8:1-18; 2 Corinthians 4:18; 1 John 2:15-17; Philippians 3:17-20; 1 Peter 1:23-25; Romans 9:8; John 3:1-7; 1 Corinthians 15:45-50; John 1:6-14; Galatians 5:16-25; Ephesians 1:13; Ephesians 4:30; Romans 7:13-25; Mark 14:38.

48 Matthew 6:19-21; Romans 8:1-18; 2 Corinthians 4:18; 1 John 2:15-17; Philippians 3:17-20; 1 Peter 1:23-25; Romans 9:8; John 3:1-7; 1 Corinthians 15:45-50; John 1:6-14; Galatians 5:16-25; Ephesians 1:13; Ephesians 4:30; Romans 7:13-25; Mark 14:38.

49 Matthew 6:19-21; Romans 8:1-18; 2 Corinthians 4:18; 1 John 2:15-17; Philippians 3:17-20; 1 Peter 1:23-25; Romans 9:8; John 3:1-7; 1 Corinthians 15:45-50; John 1:6-14; Galatians 5:16-25; Ephesians 1:13; Ephesians 4:30; Romans 7:13-25; Mark 14:38.

50 Matthew 6:19-21; Romans 8:1-18; 2 Corinthians 4:18; 1 John 2:15-17; Philippians 3:17-20; 1 Peter 1:23-25; Romans 9:8; John 3:1-7; 1 Corinthians 15:45-50; John 1:6-14; Galatians 5:16-25; Ephesians 1:13; Ephesians 4:30; Romans 7:13-25; Mark 14:38.

51 Acts 9:3-9; Acts 22:6-11; Acts 26:12-18.

52 Matthew 6:25-34; Philippians 4:6-7.

53 Matthew 6:19-21; Romans 8:1-18; 2 Corinthians 4:18; 1 John 2:15-17; Philippians 3:17-20; 1 Peter 1:23-25; Romans 9:8; John 3:1-7; 1 Corinthians 15:45-50; John 1:6-14; Galatians 5:16-25; Ephesians 1:13; Ephesians 4:30; Romans 7:13-25; Mark 14:38.

54 Psalm 34:7.

55 Matthew 6:19-21; Romans 8:1-18; 2 Corinthians 4:18; 1 John 2:15-17; Philippians 3:17-20; 1 Peter 1:23-25; Romans 9:8; John 3:1-7; 1 Corinthians 15:45-50; John 1:6-14; Galatians 5:16-25; Ephesians 1:13; Ephesians 4:30; Romans 7:13-25; Mark 14:38.

56 Matthew 6:19-21; Romans 8:1-18; 2 Corinthians 4:18; 1 John 2:15-17; Philippians 3:17-20; 1 Peter 1:23-25; Romans 9:8; John 3:1-7; 1 Corinthians 15:45-50; John 1:6-14; Galatians 5:16-25; Ephesians 1:13; Ephesians 4:30; Romans 7:13-25; Mark 14:38.

57 2 Corinthians 4:18.

58 John 10:10.

59 Philippians 3:18-21; Matthew 16:26; Mark 8:36; John 10:10.

60 1 John 2:15-17; 2 Corinthians 4:18.

61 1 John 2:16; Genesis 3:6.

62 1 Peter 1:23-25.

63 James 4:14; 2 Peter 3:12.

64 1 John 5:12; John 14:6; John 20:31.

65 Ezekiel 33:11; 2 Peter 3:9; 1 John 1:9; Galatians 5:16-25; Ephesians 6:10-18.

66 Revelation 3:20; Romans 10:9; Jeremiah 31:33; John 16:7-11.

67 Matthew 6:19-21; Romans 8:1-18; 2 Corinthians 4:18; 1 John 2:15-17; Philippians 3:17-20; 1 Peter 1:23-25; Romans 9:8; John 3:1-7; 1 Corinthians 15:45-50; John 1:6-14; Galatians 5:16-25; Ephesians 1:13; Ephesians 4:30; Romans 7:13-25; Mark 14:38.

68 1 Peter 5:8; Ephesians 6:12; John 10:10; Luke 22:31-32; Job 1-2.

69 Ephesians 4:17-19—the regressive, consuming, and ensnaring power of sin; see also Matthew 6:24 and James 1:14-15.

70 Matthew 6:19-21; Romans 8:1-18; 2 Corinthians 4:18; 1 John 2:15-17; Philippians 3:17-20; 1 Peter 1:23-25; Romans 9:8; John 3:1-7; 1 Corinthians 15:45-50; John 1:6-14; Galatians 5:16-25; Ephesians 1:13; Ephesians 4:30; Romans 7:13-25; Mark 14:38.

71 Revelation 12:9; Revelation 20:10.

72 Ephesians 4:17-19—the regressive, consuming, and ensnaring power of sin; see also Matthew 6:24 and James 1:14-15.

73 Psalm 139:14-16; Isaiah 43:7; Revelation 4:11; Psalm 8:4; Hebrews 2:6; 1 Corinthians 6:20.

74 Ephesians 4:17-19—the regressive, consuming, and ensnaring power of sin; see also Matthew 6:24 and James 1:14-15.

75 1 Timothy 6:10.

76 1 John 3:15; Exodus 20:13; Matthew 5:21.

77 Matthew 5:27-28; Romans 2:24-32; Ephesians 4:17-19—the regressive, consuming, and ensnaring power of sin; see also Matthew 6:24 and James 1:14-15.

78 James 1:13-15.

79 Proverbs 29:6; Romans 6:23; Romans 5:21; 1 Corinthians 15:20-22; Romans 6:16-23; Matthew 6:24.

80 Ephesians 4:17-19—the regressive, consuming, and ensnaring power of sin; see also Matthew 6:24 and James 1:14-15.

81 Matthew 6:19-21; Romans 8:1-18; 2 Corinthians 4:18; 1 John 2:15-17; Philippians 3:17-20; 1 Peter 1:23-25; Romans 9:8; John 3:1-7; 1 Corinthians 15:45-50; John 1:6-14; Galatians 5:16-25; Ephesians 1:13; Ephesians 4:30; Romans 7:13-25; Mark 14:38.

82 John 3:6.

83 Romans 9:8; John 3:1-7; 1 Corinthians 15:45-50; John 1:6-14.

84 1 Corinthians 15:45-50; Genesis 1:26-28; Genesis 2:5-7.
85 Genesis 5:5; 1 Corinthians 15:21-22; Romans 5:12.
86 Romans 5:12; Romans 9:8; John 3:1-7 (esp. verses 5-6); 1 Corinthians 15:45-50 (esp. verses 49-50).
87 1 Corinthians 15:45-50 (esp. verse 47).
88 Romans 5:12; Romans 9:8; John 3:1-7 (esp. verses 5-6); 1 Corinthians 15:45-50 (esp. verses 49-50).
89 Romans 3:23; Romans 6:23.
90 James 2:10; Romans 3:23.
91 Revelation 2:11; Revelation 20:6, 14.
92 Matthew 7:21-23.
93 Revelation 20:11-15; John 14:6; John 3:1-7 (esp. verses 5-6); 1 Corinthians 15:45-50 (esp. verses 49-50).
94 James 2:19.
95 Hebrews 11:6.
96 Genesis 15:1-6; Romans 5:1; Ephesians 2:8-9; Hebrews 11; Luke 18:42.
97 1 Corinthians 15:12-20; 1 Corinthians 1:23.
98 Romans 6:23; Romans 5:8.
99 Romans 3:23.
100 Leviticus 11:44-45; Leviticus 19:2; 1 Peter 1:15-16; 1 John 2:29; 1 John 3:1-3.
101 1 John 4:8; John 3:16; Romans 3:23-26; Leviticus 11:44-45; Leviticus 19:2; 1 Peter 1:15-16; 1 John 2:29; 1 John 3:1-3.
102 Romans 3:23-26; 1 John 4:8; John 3:16.
103 Matthew 15:8; Mark 7:6; Revelation 3:20; John 16:7-11.
104 John 3:16; Romans 3:23-26; Romans 5:8; Hebrews 9:22; Isaiah 53; Matthew 26:27-28; Mark 14:23-24; Luke 22:20; 1 Corinthians 11:25; Hebrews 10:9-18.
105 1 John 1:9; Romans 10:9; Ephesians 2:8-9; John 1:6-14; 2 Corinthians 7:9-11; Luke 5:32; Luke 24:46-48; 2 Peter 3:9; Acts 4:10-12; 1 Thessalonians 5:9-10.
106 Romans 10:9.
107 John 1:11-13; Romans 8:14-17.
108 Matthew 6:19-21; Romans 8:1-18; 2 Corinthians 4:18; 1 John 2:15-17; Philippians 3:17-20; 1 Peter 1:23-25; Romans 9:8; John 3:1-7; 1 Corinthians 15:45-50; John 1:6-14; Galatians 5:16-25; Ephesians 1:13; Ephesians 4:30; Romans 7:13-25; Mark 14:38.

[109] 1 John 4:4; 1 John 5:4-5; John 8:36; Romans 8:37-39; 1 Corinthians 10:13; 1 John 2:7-8; 1 John 2:12-14.

[110] Jude 1:9; 2 Peter 2:11; Psalm 8:4-5; Hebrews 2:6-7.

[111] 2 Corinthians 10:3-6.

[112] 1 Corinthians 4:7.

[113] 1 Corinthians 1:27; Also see the story of Gideon in the Book of Judges, Chapters 6-8.

[114] 2 Corinthians 12:9; 1 Corinthians 1:18-31.

[115] 1 Corinthians 6:18-20; 1 Corinthians 10:14; 1 Timothy 6:10-11; 2 Timothy 2:22.

[116] Psalm 9:9.

[117] Psalm 18:1-2.

[118] 2 Samuel 22:3.

[119] Psalm 62:6-9; Matthew 7:24-27; Luke 6:47-49; 1 Corinthians 3:11.

[120] Matthew 5:4; Matthew 11:28.

[121] 1 Corinthians 15:55-58; Romans 8:37-39; 1 John 5:4-5; 1 John 2:7-8; 1 John 2:12-14; 1 John 4:4; John 8:36; 1 Corinthians 10:13; 1 John 2:24; John 15:1-13.

[122] 1 John 2:7-8; 1 John 2:12-14; 1 John 4:4; 1 John 5:4-5; John 8:36; Romans 8:37-39; 1 Corinthians 10:13; 1 John 2:24; John 15:1-13.

[123] John 16:7-11; John 5:32; Ephesians 4:4; Hebrews 3:12; Revelation 3:20-22.

[124] 1 Corinthians 13:4-13.

[125] Revelation 1:8, 11; Revelation 21:6; Revelation 22:13.

[126] Matthew 11:28; Galatians 6:2.

[127] Matthew 6:19-21; Romans 8:1-18; 2 Corinthians 4:18; 1 John 2:15-17; Philippians 3:17-20; 1 Peter 1:23-25; Romans 9:8; John 3:1-7; 1 Corinthians 15:45-50; John 1:6-14; Galatians 5:16-25; Ephesians 1:13; Ephesians 4:30; Romans 7:13-25; Mark 14:38.

[128] 1 John 2:9.

[129] 1 Corinthians 13:12.

[130] It is God's strength, not ours that is important—2 Corinthians 12:9; 1 Corinthians 1:25-31; Ephesians 2:8-9.

[131] Matthew 5:4; Matthew 11:28; Romans 8:18; Psalm 31:24; Psalm 33:22; Psalm 130:5; Lamentations 3:24; 2 Thessalonians 2:15-17; 1 Timothy 1:1; 1 Peter 3:15.

[132] Job 1:21; Job 13:15.

[133] Matthew 5:45; Jeremiah 12:1.

[134] 1 Corinthians 13:13; Philippians 4:8, 2 Corinthians 10:3-5.

[135] Isaiah 22:13; Ecclesiastes 8:15-17; 1 Corinthians 15:32.

[136] Philippians 4:8.

[137] Romans 7:14-25; Galatians 5:16-26—the struggle between flesh and spirit

[138] See the book of Ecclesiastes for a lesson on the meaningless of "everything under the sun." Ecclesiastes 12:13-14 records Solomon's conclusion.

[139] 1 Peter 1:24; James 4:14; Luke 12:16-31; Ecclesiastes 8:15.

[140] Matthew 6:19-21; Romans 8:1-18; 2 Corinthians 4:18; 1 John 2:15-17; Philippians 3:17-20; 1 Peter 1:23-25; Romans 9:8; John 3:1-7; 1 Corinthians 15:45-50; John 1:6-14; Galatians 5:16-25; Ephesians 1:13; Ephesians 4:30; Romans 7:13-25; Mark 14:38.

[141] John 3:16; Romans 5:8.

[142] Hebrews 3:12.

[143] John 3:1-7.

[144] Romans 8:18-23; Romans 5:12; 1 Corinthians 15:20-28, 53-57.

[145] Genesis 1:31.

[146] Romans 2:11-16.

[147] Genesis 3.

[148] Ezekiel 33:11; Matthew 23:37; Luke 13:34; 2 Peter 3:9.

[149] Ephesians 5:14-17.

[150] Hebrews 9:27.

[151] John 11:25; Romans 6:4-11.

[152] Romans 3:23; Romans 6:23; Romans 5:8.

[153] John 9:1-41 (esp. verse 25 and 39); Acts 9:3-9; Acts 22:6-11; Acts 26:12-18; Isaiah 29:18; Matthew 15:31; Luke 7:22; John 12:40.

[154] Ecclesiastes 2:18; Matthew 6:19-21; Matthew 16:26; Mark 8:36.

[155] Matthew 6:19-21; Romans 8:1-18; 2 Corinthians 4:18; 1 John 2:15-17; Philippians 3:17-20; 1 Peter 1:23-25; Romans 9:8; John 3:1-7; 1 Corinthians 15:45-50; John 1:6-14; Galatians 5:16-25; Ephesians 1:13; Ephesians 4:30; Romans 7:13-25; Mark 14:38.

[156] 1 Corinthians 13:12.

[157] Genesis 2:7; Acts 17:24-25.

[158] John 8:32.

[159] Psalm 23:4.

[160] Deuteronomy 29:4; Job 13:1; 42:5; Isaiah 64:4; Jeremiah 5:21; Matthew 13:16; 1 Corinthians 2:9.

161 John 9:25; Hebrews 13:2.

162 Isaiah 14:12-15 (esp. verse 14); John 12:31; John 14:30; John 16:11; Ephesians 2:2.

163 1 Peter 5:8; Ephesians 6:12; John 10:10; Luke 22:31-32; Job 1-2.

164 Romans 5:12; Romans 6:23; Romans 8:2; 1 Corinthians 15:55-57; James 1:15; Revelation 20:10-15.

165 Galatians 5:13-25.

166 Ephesians 6:10-20; 2 Timothy 4:7.

167 Matthew 7:13-14.

168 Matthew 28:1-6; Luke 1:13, 30; Luke 2:8-14; Judges 6:23; Daniel 10:19; Acts 18:9; Acts 9:1-8.

169 The concept of guardian angels—Matthew 18:10; Acts 12:15.

170 Genesis 18:2, 22, 16-33, 19:1-24; Daniel 9:21-22; John 20:12; Hebrews 13:2 (appear as men); Isaiah 6:2-3; Ezekiel 1:4-28; Ezekiel 10; Revelation 4:6-8, etc. (appear as creatures).

171 Luke 15:10.

172 Psalm 148:5; Genesis 1:26-27; Genesis 2:7.

173 Psalm 103:20.

174 Psalm 34:7; Mark 1:13; Acts 8:26-40; Acts 12:7-11; Daniel 6:22; Psalm 91; Acts 27:23-24; Hebrews 1:14.

175 Revelation 12:3-4, 7-12; Isaiah 14:12-15 (esp. verse 14); Luke 10:18; Jude 1:6; Ezekiel 28:1-19 (esp. 13-17).

176 Revelation 12:3-4, 7-12; Isaiah 14:12-15 (esp. verse 14); Luke 10:18; Jude 1:6; Ezekiel 28:1-19 (esp. 13-17).

177 2 Peter 2:4; Jude 1:6; Matthew 25:41.

178 Revelation 20:10-15.

179 Revelation 20:1-15; 1 Thessalonians 4:16-17; 1 Thessalonians 5:1-9; Matthew 24:1-31; 1 Corinthians 15:51-58; Micah 4; Joel 2:31-32; Revelation 6:15-17; Isaiah 13:6-13.

180 1 John 2:15-17; 2 Corinthians 4:18.

181 The Fall—Revelation 12:3-4, 7-12; Isaiah 14:12-15 (esp. verse 14); Luke 10:18; Jude 1:6; Ezekiel 28:1-19 (esp. 13-17).

182 Creation of man—Genesis 1:26-27; Genesis 2:7; Temptation of man—Genesis 3:1-13; 1 Peter 5:8; Ephesians 6:12; John 10:10; Luke 22:31-32; Job 1-2.

183 Job chapters 1-2; Luke 22:31-32.

184 Ephesians 6:16; Revelation 12:9; Revelation 20:2-3.

185 Job Chapters 1-2; Luke 22:31-32; Ephesians 6:11-12.

186 Ephesians 6:12.

187 James 1:14-15.

188 Matthew 6:24.

189 Revelation 20:15.

190 Luke 15:10.

191 1 John 4:1; Philippians 1:9-11; Philippians 4:8; Romans 16:19b; 1 Corinthians 14:20; Proverbs 4:23; Psalm 24:3-5; Proverbs 23:12; Ephesians 5:15-17; Psalm 101:3; 1 Corinthians 2:14; Hebrews 5:14.

192 Christ and the Gospel are the light — John 1:4-14; John 3:18-21; John 12:35; Acts 26:12-18; Romans 13:12; 1 Corinthians 4:5; 2 Corinthians 4:6; Ephesians 5:7-8, 14; 1 Thessalonians 5:4-5; 1 Peter 2:9; 1 John 1:5-7; *Angels* are spirits, ministers of flaming fire—Hebrews 1:7, 14; Psalm 104:4; Matthew 4:11; Psalm 34:7.

193 Hebrews 1:7, 14; Psalm 104:4; Matthew 4:11.

194 Psalm 139:14-16; Isaiah 43:7; Revelation 4:11; Psalm 8:4; Hebrews 2:6; 1 Corinthians 6:20.

195 Genesis 12:1-3 (Abraham); Exodus 3:1-10 (Moses); Judges chapters 6-8 (Gideon); Acts 9:1-16; 26:1-18 (Saul/Paul).

196 1 Corinthians 1:27-31; Jeremiah 29:11; Romans 8:28; Proverbs 3:5-7.

197 Ephesians 4:17-19—the regressive, consuming, and ensnaring power of sin; see also Matthew 6:24 and James 1:14-15.

198 Revelation 12:3-4, 7-12; Isaiah 14:12-15 (esp. verse 14); Luke 10:18; Jude 1:6; Ezekiel 28:1-19 (esp. 13-17).

199 Ezekiel 28:1-19 (esp. 13-17); Isaiah 14:12-15 (esp. verse 14); 1 Timothy 3:6.

200 Genesis 18:2, 22, 16-33, 19:1-24; Daniel 9:21-22; John 20:12; Hebrews 13:2—angels in human form.

201 Psalm 104:4; Hebrews 1:7—angels as spirits.

202 1 Corinthians 15:40.

203 Matthew 22:30; Mark 12:25—speculative, not a direct reference.

204 Revelation 12:3-4, 7-12; Isaiah 14:12-15 (esp. verse 14); Luke 10:18; Jude 1:6; Ezekiel 28:1-19 (esp. 13-17).

205 2 Peter 2:4; Jude 1:6; Matthew 25:41.

206 Matthew 1:23; Matthew 3:17; Matthew 17:5; Mark 1:11; Luke 3:22; John 20:27-29; 2 Peter 1:17; 1 John 5:20; etc.

207 Genesis 6:1-2, 4—NOTE: The explanation of the *Nephilim* in this story is but one of several theories, and even then the explanation given here goes far beyond normal theory. It is, after all, a book of fiction

not a book intent upon outlining theology. Rather, this story seeks to have fun with theology.

208 Job 4:18; Job 15:15.

209 **Disclaimer**: The idea of angels lusting or sinning might bother some people. To this point, two things should be noted. *First*, this is a fictional story not a factual exposition. *Second*, while angels *may* be frozen in righteousness at the present time, it is certainly sustainable to argue from scripture that angels could at one point sin. After all, one third of them fell (cf. Revelation 12:3-4, 7-12; Isaiah 14:12-15 (esp. verse 14); Luke 10:18; Jude 1:6; Ezekiel 28:1-19 (esp. 13-17).

210 The only proper spiritual indwelling—Exodus 31:3; Exodus 35:31; John 14:17; John 16:13; Acts 2:4; Romans 8:9-11; 1 Corinthians 6:18-20; 2 Corinthians 1:22; Ephesians 1:13; Ephesians 4:30; Ephesians 5:18; 1 John 2:20, 27; 1 John 4:13.

211 Humans have a soul, but they are obviously still limited to the terrestrial realm (cf. 1 Corinthians 15:41-44; 1 John 3:1-3).

212 Have you ever wondered why demons possess humans (e.g. Matthew 8:28-34; Matthew 17:18; Mark 5:1-20; Acts 19:13-16)? Why do they not simply take physical form as angels do (Genesis 18:2, 22, 16-33, 19:1; Daniel 9:21-22; John 20:12; Hebrews 13:2)? Is it because they cannot?

213 2 Peter 2:4—The word "hell" is the Greek word *Tartaroo*. Compare to Jude 1:6—What are the chains if not figurative speech for being trapped? What is darkness if not imprisonment in their own sins, waiting for judgment?

214 Job cchapter 1-2; Luke 22:31-32.

215 Satan does come to the earth to tempt (e.g. Matthew 4:1-11; Genesis 3:1-13), though he is never seen in scripture as embodied. In fact, Genesis 3 has him in the form of a serpent. Why do that if he could be in the form of a man? Ephesians 2:2 calls him the prince of the power of the air, as well as a spirit, indicating he is unembodied. Finally, Ephesians 6:11-12 describes a spiritual struggle against the devil, not one of "flesh and blood."

216 Humans—Matthew 8:28-34; Matthew 17:18; Mark 5:1-20; Acts 19:13-16; Animals—Matthew 8:32, possibly also Genesis 3:1.

217 2 Peter 2:4; Jude 1:6.

218 1 Corinthians 6:18-20; 1 Corinthians 10:14; 1 Timothy 6:10-11; 2 Timothy 2:22; Psalm 9:9; Psalm 18:1-2; 2 Samuel 22:3; Psalm 62:6-9;

Matthew 7:24-27; Luke 6:47-49; 1 Corinthians 3:11; Matthew 5:4; Matthew 11:28.

219 Romans 8:37; 1 John 5:4-5; Zechariah 4:6.

220 Jeremiah 17:5-8; Ephesians 6:10-18 (note verse 10 explains the armor as how to be strong "in the Lord, and in the power of his might"); 1 Thessalonians 5:1-11; Psalms 61; Psalm 62.

221 Ephesians 4:17-19—the regressive, consuming, and ensnaring power of sin; see also Matthew 6:24 and James 1:14-15.

222 Enslavement to sin—Romans 6:1-23; Romans 7:15-25 (esp. verse 25); Romans 8:1-2; John 8:36; Fiery darts—Ephesians 6:11-12, 16.

223 Philippians 3:18-20; Matthew 6:19-21, 24; 1 John 2:15-17.

224 2 Corinthians 4:3-6 (the "god of this world" is Satan); Ephesians 5:14-17; Romans 13:12; 1 Corinthians 2:9-16; 1 Corinthians 16:13; 1 Corinthians 10:12; John 12:35-43.

225 The only proper spiritual indwelling—Exodus 31:3; Exodus 35:31; John 14:17; John 16:13; Acts 2:4; Romans 8:9-11; 1 Corinthians 6:18-20; 2 Corinthians 1:22; Ephesians 1:13; Ephesians 4:30; Ephesians 5:18; 1 John 2:20, 27; 1 John 4:13.

226 Romans 8:14-17; John 1:12-13; John 3:1-8; 1 Corinthians 6:19; John 1:33.

227 Ephesians 1:13-14; 2 Corinthians 1:22; 2 Corinthians 5:5.

228 James 4:7.

229 1 John 1:9; Luke 15 (entire chapter).

230 Genesis 5:24 (Enoch); 2 Kings 2:1-12 (Elijah); 2 Corinthians 12:2-9 (Paul); Also potentially John's Revelation (cf. Revelation 1:1, 10; 4:1-2).

231 Spirits, ministers of flaming fire—Hebrews 1:7; Psalm 104:4; Matthew 4:11.

232 1 Peter 5:8; Matthew 7:13-14; Ephesians 6:12; John 10:10; Luke 22:31-32; Job 1-2.

233 Ephesians 6:11-13.

234 1 Corinthians 10:12-13; James 4:7.

235 Matthew 7:13-14.

236 John 5:24; John 11:25-26; John 3:16, 36; Romans 6:23; John 8:32; John 14:6.

237 1 Corinthians 15:54-57; 1 John 5:4-5; Philippians 3:4-8.

238 Luke 14:27-30; 1 Corinthians 6:19-20.

239 The awesome appearance of angels generally evokes fear at first—

Matthew 28:1-6; Luke 1:13, 30; Luke 2:8-14; Judges 6:23; Daniel 10:19; Acts 18:9; Acts 9:1-8.

240 Angels with wings—Exodus 25:20, 37:9; Isaiah 6:2; 2 Chronicles 3:11, 13; Ezekiel 10:5, 19; Revelation 4:8; Ezekiel 1; 1 Kings 6:27, 8:6-72.

241 2 Corinthians 12:1-9; 2 Corinthians 5:1-8.

242 Genesis 5:24 (Enoch); 2 Kings 2:1-12 (Elijah); 2 Corinthians 12:2-9 (Paul); Also potentially John's Revelation (cf. Revelation 1:1, 10; 4:1-2).

243 2 Peter 2:4—The word "hell" is the Greek word *Tartaroo*. Compare to Jude 1:6—What are the chains if not figurative speech for being trapped? What is darkness if not imprisonment in their own sins, waiting for judgment?

244 Jude 1:9; Psalm 8:4-6; Hebrews 2:6-8.

245 1 Corinthians 13:1-13—Love is the greatest of all human responses, emotions, and actions.

246 The shield of faith fills the gaps and quenches the fiery darts—Ephesians 6:16.

247 Luke 15:10.

248 Ezekiel 1:14.

249 The tongues of angels—1 Corinthians 13:1.

250 Romans 7:14-25; Galatians 5:16-26—the struggle between flesh and spirit.

251 Matthew 6:24.

252 Spirits, ministers of flaming fire—Hebrews 1:7; Psalm 104:4; Matthew 4:11.

253 Galatians 5:16-25; Romans 8:1-17.

254 Psalm 8:4-6; Hebrews 2:6-8.

255 The shield of faith fills the gaps and quenches the fiery darts—Ephesians 6:16.

256 Psalm 8:4-6; Hebrews 2:6-8.

257 Since one-third of the angels fell, two-thirds must still remain in heaven—Revelation 12:3-4, 7-12; Isaiah 14:12-15; Luke 10:18; Jude 1:6; Ezekiel 28:1-19.

258 Romans 3:23.

259 Matthew 7:13-14; Romans 3:23; Romans 6:23; Romans 5:8; Romans 10:9-10.

260 Ezekiel 33:11; 2 Peter 3:9; John 3:16-17.

261 Ezekiel 33:11; Matthew 23:37; Luke 13:34; 2 Peter 3:9.

262 James 5:16; Job 42:10; 1 Timothy 2:1; Matthew 5:43-45.

263 Ephesians 6:18; Philippians 4:6; 1 Timothy 2:8; James 5:16; 2 Chronicles 7:14; 1 Thessalonians 5:17.

264 Exodus 2:23-24; 1 Samuel 7:8-9; 1 Chronicles 5:18-20; James 5:16.

265 To be fully prepared and to properly guard one's soul against the wiles of the Devil, put on the whole armor of God—Ephesians 6:10-18.

266 Matthew 5:14-16.

267 Matthew 5:13-16 (actions); Ephesians 4:29 (words).

268 Proverbs 27:17; Ecclesiastes 4:9-10; Galatians 6:2.

269 1 Corinthians 10:12-13.

270 Angelic ladders—Genesis 28:10-12.

271 Genesis 5:24 (Enoch); 2 Kings 2:1-12 (Elijah); 2 Corinthians 12:2-9 (Paul); Also potentially John's Revelation (cf. Revelation 1:1, 10; 4:1-2).

272 Matthew 5:14-16.

273 The concept of light and dark houses should not be seen as having any relation to a building structure. Certainly walls and ceilings don't protect families from sin. Rather, this fictitious depiction of houses of light and dark are instead intended to emphasize the importance and power of a godly and God-fearing home. Is your home a beacon of light or a place of darkness? "Choose this day whom you will serve . . . but as for me and my house, we will serve the Lord" (Joshua 24:15).

274 Fiery darts—Ephesians 6:11-12, 16.

275 1 John 1:9.

276 John 3:16; Romans 3:21-26.

277 The concept of guardian angels—Matthew 18:10; Acts 12:15.

278 James 5:16; Jeremiah 29:7; Psalm 122:6-7.

279 Psalm 34:1-8; Matthew 7:24-27; Luke 6:47-49.

280 Psalm 34:7; James 5:16; The decision—Romans 3:23; Romans 6:23; Romans 10:9-10; 1 John 5:11-12.

281 Matthew 6:33; Matthew 7:7-8; Luke 11:9-10; Romans 12:1-2; Revelation 3:20; The true teacher is the Holy Spirit—1 Corinthians 2:13; 1 John 2:27; John 16:7-11; John 14:16-17, 26.

282 Romans 5:8.

283 John 1:5; John 3:19-21; 1 Corinthians 4:5; 1 John 2:8.

284 John 16:7-11.

285 Romans 3:23.

286 Isaiah 43:7; Psalm 4:2; Romans 6:23.

287 Matthew 11:28-30; John 8:36; Romans 10:9-10; Galatians 5:1; 1 John 1:9.

288 1 John 4:4; 1 John 5:4-5; John 8:36; Romans 8:37-39; 1 Corinthians 10:13; 1 John 2:7-8; 1 John 2:12-14; 1 John 2:24; John 15:1-13.

289 Ephesians 5:8; 1 Thessalonians 5:4-5; Romans 8:18-23; Romans 5:12; 1 Corinthians 15:20-28, 53-57.

290 Much of this poem is based on different depictions of God's judgment on the wicked when the end comes—Mark 9:43-49; Matthew 13:24-30, 36-43, 47-50; Matthew 22:1-13; Matthew 24:45-51; Matthew 8:11-13; Revelation 20:6, 10-15; Psalm 112:10; Matthew 3:11-12.

291 Proverbs 4:14, 19; John 12:35; Acts 26:12-18; Romans 13:12; Ephesians 5:8, 14; 1 Peter 2:9.

292 Proverbs 12:26; 1 Timothy 6:9.

293 Romans 1:20; Romans 2:12-16; Romans 3:19-20.

294 Proverbs 11:5; Proverbs 13:6; Isaiah 55:7; Revelation 20:11-15.

295 Matthew 24:29-31; 1 Corinthians 15:52; 1 Thessalonians 4:16; Joel 2:31; Zephaniah 1:14; Malachi 4:5; Revelation 20:11-15.

296 Ezekiel 1:14.

297 Fiery darts—Ephesians 6:11-12, 16.

298 Multiple demon possession—Mark 5:1-19.

299 Psalm 139:14-16; Isaiah 43:7; Revelation 4:11; Psalm 8:4; Hebrews 2:6; 1 Corinthians 6:20.

300 1 Corinthians 16:13-14.

301 James 4:7-8, 10; James 1:14-15; 1 Corinthians 10:12-13.

302 The shield of faith fills the gaps in one's armor and quench the fiery darts—Ephesians 6:16.

303 Ephesians 4:17-19—the regressive, consuming, and ensnaring power of sin; see also Matthew 6:24 and James 1:14-15.

304 Jude 1:6; 2 Peter 2:4; Matthew 25:41.

305 James 4:7.

306 Once sealed with the Spirit, possession is not possible, but influence still is—2 Corinthians 1:22; Ephesians 1:13; Ephesians 4:30; 1 John 2:18-20; Romans 8:1, 14-17; Luke 22:31.

307 Fiery darts—Ephesians 6:11-12, 16.

308 The shield of faith fills the gaps in one's armor and quench the fiery darts—Ephesians 6:16.

309 Ephesians 4:29; Colossians 3:8-10; Matthew 12:35; Matthew 15:17-19; Luke 6:45.

310 Matthew 6:19-21, 24; Philippians 3:18-20; 1 John 2:15-17; 2 Corinthians 4:18.

311 1 Corinthians 6:18-20; 1 Corinthians 10:14; 1 Timothy 6:10-11; 2 Timothy 2:22; James 4:7.

312 Joshua 24:15; Matthew 7:24-27; Luke 6:47-49; 1 Corinthians 3:10-11; Colossians 3:15; Ephesians 6:10-18; Matthew 6:24.

313 Joshua 24:15; Matthew 7:24-27; Luke 6:47-49; 1 Corinthians 3:10-11; Colossians 3:15; 1 Corinthians 16:13; 1 Corinthians 15:58; 2 Thessalonians 2:15.

314 Once sealed with the Spirit, possession is not possible, but influence still is—2 Corinthians 1:22; Ephesians 1:13; Ephesians 4:30; 1 John 2:18-20; Romans 8:1, 14-17; Luke 22:31.

315 Romans 7:14-25; Galatians 5:16-26—the struggle between flesh and spirit.

316 Genesis 1:27; 1 John 4:19; John 3:16.

317 Matthew 6:19-21; 2 Corinthians 4:18; 1 John 2:15-17.

318 Psalm 139:14-16; Isaiah 43:7; Revelation 4:11; Psalm 8:4; Hebrews 2:6; 1 Corinthians 6:20.

319 Matthew 11:28-30; John 10:10.

320 Ephesians 6:10-18.

321 Psalm 23; Psalm 34:7; Psalm 91; James 5:16.

322 1 Corinthians 6:18; 1 Corinthians 10:14; 1 Timothy 6:6-12; 2 Timothy 2:22.

323 Matthew 6:19-21; 1 John 2:15-17; 2 Corinthians 4:18; Philippians 3:17-20; 1 Peter 1:23-25.

324 1 Corinthians 10:13.

325 Psalm 23:4.

326 This poem is largely a compilation of various verses from the book of Lamentations. It records the sorrow of the prophet Jeremiah over the fall of Jerusalem.

327 1 John 4:4.

328 1 John 2:12-13; 1 John 5:4-5.

329 1 John 2:6; 1 John 3:3; Galatians 5:13-25; Ephesians 5:8; Romans 6:1-13; 3 John 1:4; Romans 7:14-25.

330 1 Corinthians 10:13.

331 Multitudes of angels—Luke 2:13.

[332] The concept of guardian angels—Matthew 18:10; Acts 12:15.

[333] The concept of guardian angels—Matthew 18:10; Acts 12:15.

[334] Luke 15 (esp. verse 10); Matthew 18:12-14; 1 Peter 2:25.

[335] The concept of guardian angels—Matthew 18:10; Acts 12:15.

[336] John 14:15, 21; John 15:10-13; 1 John 2:3-6; 1 John 3:23-24; 1 John 5:2-3; Galatians 5:16-26; Ephesians 5:1-12; 1 Samuel 15:22; Exodus 20:5-7; Leviticus 26; Deuteronomy 4:39-40; Deuteronomy 5:29; Deuteronomy 6:1-3; Deuteronomy 10:12-13; Deuteronomy 7:9; Deuteronomy 11:1, 22-23, 27-28; Romans 6:15-18; 1 Peter 4:17.

[337] Deuteronomy 31:6; Joshua 1:9; 1 Chronicles 28:20; 2 Chronicles 32:7; Psalm 23; Isaiah 35:4; Isaiah 41:10.

[338] Ephesians 4:6; Hebrews 6:13; 1 John 4:4; 1 John 5:4-5.

[339] 1 Corinthians 10:13.

[340] Romans 12:9; Philippians 4:8.

[341] Proverbs 30:5; Psalm 115:11.

[342] Psalm 119:176; Isaiah 53:6; Jeremiah 50:6; Matthew 18:11-15.

[343] John 8:12; John 1:1-5, 14; 1 John 2:8.

[344] Proverbs 14:29; Proverbs 15:18; James 1:19; Psalm 103:8; Proverbs 21:21.

[345] Psalm 23:4.

[346] Isaiah 64:6; 2 Peter 3:14; Philippians 3:4-8.

[347] Acts 4:10-12; Acts 2:38; Romans 10:9-13.

[348] Psalm 51:7-10; Galatians 4:5; 1 Corinthians 15:20-22, 52-57; John 11:25; 1 John 1:9; Romans 3:19-26; Romans 8:1.

[349] Ephesians 6:10-18; John 16:7-11; Psalm 9:8; Psalm 98:9; John 12:31; Acts 17:31; Romans 5:12, 21; Romans 6:16, 23; 1 Corinthians 15:21, 56; James 1:15; Revelation 20:11-15.

[350] Deuteronomy 31:6; Joshua 1:9; 1 Chronicles 28:20; 2 Chronicles 32:7; Psalm 23; Isaiah 35:4; Isaiah 41:10.

[351] 1 John 4:4; 1 John 5:4-5.

[352] 2 Corinthians 4:8-9.

[353] Ephesians 6:12.

[354] James 4:7.

[355] Matthew 4:1-11; Psalm 119:105, 11.

[356] Psalm 9:9; Psalm 18:1-2; 2 Samuel 22:3; Psalm 62:6-9.

[357] Hebrews 12:1-2a; 2 Corinthians 4:18; 1 John 2:15-17.

[358] Romans 16:19-20; Philippians 4:8-9, 13; 1 Corinthians 14:20.

[359] Proverbs 14:29; Proverbs 15:18; James 1:19; Psalm 103:8; Proverbs

21:21.

360 Isaiah 53:6; Matthew 18:11-15; Luke 15 (entire chapter); 1 Peter 2:25; 2 Peter 3:9; John 3:16.

361 Matthew 5:43; Matthew 25:31-40; Luke 6:27-36; Romans 12:17-21; 1 John 2:9; 1 John 4:20; John 15:13.

362 John 8:36; Romans 8:37-39; 1 Corinthians 10:13; 1 John 5:4.

363 Ephesians 4:29; Colossians 3:8-10; Matthew 12:35; Matthew 15:17-19; Luke 6:45.

364 John 3:16; Romans 5:8; Galatians 2:20; 1 John 3:1; 1 John 3:16; 1 John 4:8, 10-11, 19.

365 Jeremiah 29:11; Isaiah 43:7; Romans 3:23; Romans 6:23; Romans 5:8; Romans 10:9.

366 1 John 1:9; Romans 6:23.

367 Romans 6:23.

368 Matthew 10:28; Revelation 20:6.

369 Romans 5:8.

370 Hebrews 4:15; 2 Corinthians 5:21.

371 1 John 1:9; Hebrews 8:12; Hebrews 10:10-17.

372 Hebrews 3:12-13.

373 The demon answered—Acts 19:13-16; Mark 5:1-20; Luke 8:27-37.

374 Unnatural strength of demon possessed individuals—Mark 5:1-20; Acts 19:13-16.

375 Ezekiel 28:1-19 (esp. 13-17); Isaiah 14:12-15 (esp. verse 14); 1 Timothy 3:6.

376 Ezekiel 28:1-19 (esp. 13-17); Isaiah 14:12-15 (esp. verse 14); 1 Timothy 3:6.

377 Ezekiel 33:11.

378 Matthew 26:28; Romans 3:23; Hebrews 9:22; 1 Corinthians 6:20.

379 Psalm 139:14-16; Isaiah 43:7; Revelation 4:11; Psalm 8:4; Hebrews 2:6.

380 Psalm 119:176; Isaiah 53:6; Matthew 18:12.

381 Hebrews 9:27.

382 Ezekiel 33:11.

383 Genesis 6:4.

384 2 Peter 2:4—The word "hell" is the Greek word *Tartaroo*. Compare to Jude 1:6—What are the chains if not figurative speech for being trapped? What is darkness if not imprisonment in their own sins, waiting for judgment?

---

[385] Creator God—Genesis 1-2; John 1:1-4, 1:14; Colossians 1:16-17; Psalm 148:1-5; Isaiah 42:5; Trapped—2 Peter 2:4; Jude 1:6; Romans 8:19-23.

[386] God, the only self-existent One—Exodus 3:14; John 1:4; John 5:26; John 8:58.

[387] Matthew 7:13-14; John 11:25.

[388] John 12:35; Acts 26:12-18; Romans 13:12; Ephesians 5:8, 14; 1 Peter 2:9.

[389] Romans 6:23; Romans 10:9-10; 1 Corinthians 15:3; Ephesians 2:1-9; 1 John 1:7-10.

[390] 1 Peter 5:8; Ephesians 6:12; John 10:10; Luke 22:31-32; Job 1-2.

[391] 1 Corinthians 3:5-7.

[392] Matthew 6:10; Mark 14:36; Philippians 4:6-7.

[393] Matthew 6:24; Luke 16:13.

[394] Matthew 16:26; Mark 8:36; Exodus 20:13; Deuteronomy 5:17; Matthew 5:21; Romans 13:9; John 15:13.

[395] 1 Corinthians 13.

[396] Proverbs 3:27; Amos 5:14; Romans 12:21.

[397] Revelation 20:10-15.

[398] Matthew 4:1-10 (Esp. 10); Luke 4:1-8 (Esp. 8); Exodus 20:3-5; Matthew 16:26; Mark 8:36.

[399] Ephesians 4:29; Colossians 3:8-10; Matthew 12:35; Matthew 15:17-19; Luke 6:45.

[400] John 14:6; John 8:32; John 20:31; 1 John 5:12.

[401] Romans 6:23; Romans 5:12; 1 Corinthians 15:20-22.

[402] Matthew 7:13-14; 1 Corinthians 6:9-11; Galatians 5:16-26; Ephesians 5:1-8; 1 John 2:15-17.

[403] 2 Peter 2:4; Jude 1:6; Matthew 25:41; 2 Corinthians 5:10; Hebrews 9:27; Revelation 20:9-15.

[404] John 10:10; Jeremiah 29:11-13; Romans 16:19-20; Philippians 4:8-9, 13; 1 Corinthians 14:20.

[405] Matthew 7:13-14; 1 Corinthians 6:9-11; Galatians 5:16-26; Ephesians 5:1-8; 1 John 2:15-17.

[406] Genesis 50:20.

[407] John 1:5; John 3:19-21; 1 Corinthians 4:5; 1 John 2:8; John 1:5; 2 Corinthians 4:6; 1 John 2:8.

[408] John 14:6; John 8:31-32; Romans 1:21-25 (esp. verse 25).

[409] Ecclesiastes 1:3; Ecclesiastes 2:11.

[410] Matthew 6:19-21.

[411] 1 John 2:15-17; 2 Corinthians 4:18.

[412] 2 Timothy 4:7.

[413] Mark 11:25-26; 1 Corinthians 13, 14:1; 1 John 3:23, 4:19; John 13:34-35.

[414] John 14:15, 21; John 15:10-13; 1 John 2:3-6; 1 John 3:23-24; 1 John 5:2-3; Galatians 5:16-26; Ephesians 5:1-12; 1 Samuel 15:22; Exodus 20:5-7; Leviticus 26; Deuteronomy 4:39-40; Deuteronomy 5:29; Deuteronomy 6:1-3; Deuteronomy 10:12-13; Deuteronomy 7:9; Deuteronomy 11:1, 22-23, 27-28; Romans 6:15-18; 1 Peter 4:17.

[415] Romans 3:23-28; Romans 6:23; Romans 5:12-15; Ephesians 2:8-9.

[416] John 8:36.

[417] 1 John 5:4-5; 1 John 4:4; Philippians 4:13; Romans 8:37-39; Deuteronomy 31:6; Joshua 1:9; 1 Corinthians 16:13-14; James 4:7; 1 Corinthians 10:12-13; 1 Peter 1:13-16; Hebrews 11:6; 2 Corinthians 11:2; 1 John 3:1-3; Isaiah 59:17; Ephesians 6:14; Galatians 5:16-26; Ephesians 5:1-8; 1 John 2:15-17; 1 Corinthians 6:9-11.

[418] 1 John 4:4; 1 John 5:4-5; Romans 8:37-39; 1 Corinthians 10:12-13; Philippians 4:13.

[419] Romans 13:8-10; 1 John 2:9-11; Deuteronomy 11:22-23; Ephesians 5:2; 2 John 1:6; John 14:15, 21; John 15:10-13; 1 John 2:3-6; 1 John 3:23-24; 1 John 5:2-3.

[420] John 14:15, 21; John 15:10-13; 1 John 2:3-6; 1 John 3:23-24; 1 John 5:2-3; Galatians 5:16-26; Ephesians 5:1-12; 1 Samuel 15:22; Exodus 20:5-7; Leviticus 26; Deuteronomy 4:39-40; Deuteronomy 5:29; Deuteronomy 6:1-3; Deuteronomy 10:12-13; Deuteronomy 7:9; Deuteronomy 11:1, 22-23, 27-28; Romans 6:15-18; 1 Peter 4:17.

[421] Romans 6:1-18; Galatians 5:13-25 (esp. 24-25); Galatians 6:14.

[422] Deuteronomy 31:6; 1 Chronicles 22:13; 1 Chronicles 28:20; 2 Chronicles 32:7; Psalm 23; Isaiah 35:4; Isaiah 41:10; 1 John 5:4-5; 1 John 4:4; Philippians 4:13; Romans 8:37-39; 1 Corinthians 16:13; John 15:13.

[423] 1 Peter 1:13-16; Hebrews 11:6; 2 Corinthians 11:2; 1 John 3:1-3; Isaiah 59:17; Ephesians 6:14; Galatians 5:16-26; Ephesians 5:1-8; 1 John 2:15-17; 1 Corinthians 6:9-11.

[424] Romans 5:2-8; James 1:2-4.

[425] This is not a message against the biblical discernment of sin. However, Christians can condemn sin without being harsh toward

individuals. We uphold God's standards with love, ever hoping and praying that God will change hearts—Proverbs 14:29; Proverbs 15:18; James 1:19; Psalm 103:8; Proverbs 21:21; Matthew 6:14-15; Matthew 7:1-5; Mark 11:25-26; 1 Corinthians 4:5; Ephesians 4:32; Romans 16:19; 1 Corinthians 14:20; Philippians 1:9-10.

426 John 3:19-21; Daniel 2:20-23 (esp. 22).

427 Ephesians 4:6; Hebrews 6:13; 1 John 4:4; Deuteronomy 31:6; Joshua 1:9; 1 John 5:4-5; Philippians 4:13; Romans 8:37-39; 1 Corinthians 16:13.

428 1 Corinthians 13:13.

429 1 Corinthians 16:13; 1 Corinthians 10:12-13.

430 1 Thessalonians 5:21-23; 2 Thessalonians 2:15; 1 Corinthians 16:13; 1 Corinthians 15:58; Deuteronomy 31:6; Joshua 1:9; 1 John 5:4-5; 1 John 4:4; Philippians 4:13; Romans 8:37-39; 1 Corinthians 16:13-14; James 4:7; 1 Corinthians 10:12-13; 1 Peter 1:13-16; Hebrews 11:6; 2 Corinthians 11:2; 1 John 3:1-3; Isaiah 59:17; Ephesians 6:14; Galatians 5:16-26; Ephesians 5:1-8; 1 John 2:15-17.

431 Deuteronomy 31:6; Joshua 1:9; 1 John 5:4-5; 1 John 4:4; Philippians 4:13; Romans 8:37-39; 1 Corinthians 16:13-14; James 4:7; 1 Corinthians 10:12-13; 1 Peter 1:13-16; Hebrews 11:6; 2 Corinthians 11:2; 1 John 3:1-3; Isaiah 59:17; Ephesians 6:14; Galatians 5:16-26; Ephesians 5:1-8; 1 John 2:15-17; 1 Corinthians 6:9-11; 1 Corinthians 13; Matthew 5:1-16.

432 1 Corinthians 6:18-20; 1 Corinthians 10:14; 1 Timothy 6:10-11; 2 Timothy 2:22.

433 How we walk is a choice. If it were not, God would not need to tell us to walk in the Spirit, not in the flesh, nor would he need to tell us to flee from sin—Galatians 5:16-26; Ephesians 5:1-12; *Spiritual birth*—2 Corinthians 5:17; Romans 8:14-17; John 1:12-13; John 3:1-8; 1 Corinthians 15:42-50; *Fleeing from sin*—1 Corinthians 6:18-20; 1 Corinthians 10:14; 1 Timothy 6:10-11; 2 Timothy 2:22.

434 Genesis 2:7; Ecclesiastes 12:7; Isaiah 42:5; Zechariah 12:1; Hebrews 12:9; Matthew 10:28; 1 Corinthians 6:18-20; 3 John 2; 1 Corinthians 15:35-58.

435 1 Corinthians 15:35-58; 1 John 3:1-2; 2 Corinthians 4:17-18; 2 Corinthians 5:1-11.

436 Genesis 5:24 (Enoch); 2 Kings 2:1-12 (Elijah); 2 Corinthians 12:2-9 (Paul); Also potentially John's Revelation (cf. Revelation 1:1, 10; 4:1-

2).

[437] Fiery darts—Ephesians 6:11-12, 16.

[438] Matthew 13:9-17; Mark 4:9-12; Acts 28:25-27.

[439] Hebrews 3:12-14; Proverbs 28:14; Daniel 5:18-20 (esp. 20); Romans 2:5.

[440] James 4:14; 1 Peter 1:24-25; 2 Corinthians 4:18; Romans 8:18; 1 John 2:15-17.

[441] John 3:16, 36; John 5:24; John 6:40; John 17:1-5; John 6:68; John 20:31; 1 John 5:11-12; Matthew 25:46; Romans 5:21; Romans 6:22-23; 1 John 2:24-25; Galatians 6:8.

[442] Galatians 5:16-25; Romans 8:1-17; John 3:1-7; 1 Corinthians 15:45-50; Matthew 6:19-21; Romans 8:18; 2 Corinthians 4:18; 1 John 2:15-17; Philippians 3:17-20; 1 Peter 1:23-25; Romans 9:8; John 1:6-14; Romans 7: 13-25; Mark 14:38.

[443] Romans 8:28; John 3:16, 36; John 5:24; John 6:40; John 17:1-5; John 6:68; John 20:31; 1 John 5:11-12; Matthew 25:46; Romans 5:21; Romans 6:22-23; 1 John 2:24-25; Galatians 6:8.